'Loved this book, so light-hearted and 2018

'A lovely read'

'Oh what a little treasure this is! A cast of great characters,
lovely Cotswold village and Beth trying to cope with the
disaster she has bought'

'Full of wit and charm'

'Great characters who have quickly become established and
rooted in my imagination. Very funny, but with deeper under-
currents woven in'

'Loved the story, couldn't put it down'

'Absolutely loved this book, hooked from the start'

'Three Words: Brilliant, Charming and Moving'

'This is a wonderful read'

Also by Bella Osborne

It Started at Sunset Cottage
A Family Holiday

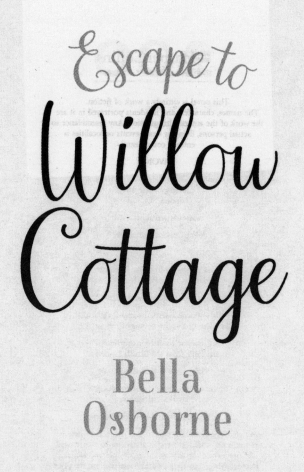

Escape to Willow Cottage

Bella Osborne

avon.

A division of HarperCollins*Publishers*
1 London Bridge Street,
London SE1 9GF

www.harpercollins.co.uk

A Paperback Original 2017

1

First published in Great Britain by
HarperCollins*Publishers* 2017

Copyright © Bella Osborne 2017

Bella Osborne asserts the moral right to
be identified as the author of this work

A catalogue record for this book is
available from the British Library

ISBN-13: 978-0-00-818102-4

Set in Minion by Palimpsest Book Production Limited,
Falkirk, Stirlingshire

Printed and bound in Great Britain

MIX
Paper from
responsible sources
FSC
www.fsc.org   FSC® C007454

This book is produced from independently certified FSC paper
to ensure responsible forest management.

For more information visit: www.harpercollins.co.uk/green

Acknowledgements

Huge THANK YOU to Charlotte Ledger and Caroline Kirkpatrick, who came up with the original bones of the idea for this book and have done an amazing job as joint editors. Thanks to my agent, Kate Nash, who is always on hand to steer me in the right direction and special thanks to Kim Leo and Alex Allden for my stunningly beautiful cover.

Special thank yous to my terrific technical experts: Sarah Butt and Helen Cottingham, and all at Rugby Deaf Club for sharing their experiences and making me feel welcome. Thanks to Charlotte Hancock for her Primary School Guidelines advice and Eamonn Finnerty from the Belgrade Theatre, Coventry, for information on signed performances. Thank yous to Helen Phifer for guiding me on police procedures, to Leo Fielding for emergency call and response information and to Dr David Boulton for answering all my medical questions. Thank you to Ruth Hooton for checking my Irish phrasing. Special thanks to my *Minecraft* guru, Grace.

Heartfelt thanks to those who shared their experiences of domestic violence – I admire your courage immensely.

Special thanks to my amazing grammar guru Chris Goodwin.

Without the support of my writing friends from the Romantic Novelists' Association (RNA), and in particular the Birmingham Chapter, I would have gone crackers long ago – so thank you for maintaining what is left of my sanity. Thank you to my other fabulously supportive group of writers at Gill Vickery's Writing Fiction class. More thank yous to everyone at Boozy Book Club for your support and, of course, the wine and nibbles.

A massive thank you to my writing fairy godmother, Katie

Fforde, for being on hand when I needed her.

Thank yous and hugs all round to the amazingly supportive blogging community, the unsung heroes of the book world – you are all amazing!

Mammoth-sized hugs of thanks to my wonderful family for always being there and for helping me to enjoy the real world as well as my make-believe one. Thank you to my husband and daughter who never complain and have managed to feed themselves when I am 'in the zone'.

Lastly thank you to all the lovely readers for taking the time to read my book.

In memory of a truly amazing woman, my grandma 1903–1993

Chapter One

Beth had spent the day surrounded by people who, she suspected, all looked exactly like their passport photos – not a smile between them. Beth yawned and stretched her arms above her head; it had been a long day.

'Bid from the lady on the right,' said the auctioneer as he carried on his high-speed number chant.

Beth spun round. *She* was on the right but it couldn't have been her, could it? Her eyes darted around the room. Nobody was moving, not even a twitch. Her heart was racing and she could feel the panic rising.

'Two ninety, at the back,' said the auctioneer and Beth let out a sigh of relief. That was a lucky escape.

'Any advance on two ninety?' The auctioneer was looking directly at Beth.

What the hell had she bid on? She snatched up the catalogue and quickly thumbed through the pages, past her first choice of apartments she had come to buy and that had shot high above her budget.

'Selling for two ninety,' said the auctioneer, looking at someone at the back. 'Lot 37, Willow Cottage, selling for two hundred and ninety thousand pounds.'

Beth found Willow Cottage in the catalogue and speed-read the blurb. It sounded like a slice of paradise – a cottage overlooking a traditional village green in the heart of the Cotswolds. She bit her lip. It was like that moment on eBay when you quite like something; it's not exactly what you were after but the urge to grab a bargain and be termed a winner suddenly surpasses everything.

'All done at two hundred and ninety thousand pounds? Going once, going twice …'

Beth waved her bidding card in the air. 'Three hundred thousand,' she croaked, wondering what on earth she was doing. She was meant to be waiting for her second choice of flats to be auctioned.

'Three hundred thousand on my right, thank you,' said the auctioneer. After checking with the other bidders he finally concluded. 'Sold to the lady on the right brandishing the upside-down bidding card.' And the gavel gave a satisfying thud as it hit the wood.

'You have reached your destination,' announced the Sat Nav with ultimate confidence. Beth pulled the hire car into the kerb, switched off the engine and looked around. She was parked by a large area of greensward, which was dotted with trees and encircled by impressive old properties of differing sizes.

Beth picked up the auction catalogue and peered at the small grainy photograph, then reread the description underneath – *'Willow Cottage stands in a secluded position overlooking the village green within the picturesque Cotswold village of Dumbleford. Rare opportunity to purchase this freehold detached dwelling. Plot circa 0.6 acres with stream running through the property. Renovation opportunity.'*

Somewhere in the back of Beth's mind she recalled a certain person saying that he wouldn't live in the countryside if his life depended on it and right now that felt like an added bonus. She checked the back seat. Leo was stirring from his journey-induced slumber and he instantly smiled when he saw his mother. The six-year-old was too tall for his car seat and would soon need to upgrade to a booster, but for now Beth just wanted to keep him safe.

'I wish you'd brung my iPad,' said Leo as he stretched.

'I'm sorry. I couldn't find it. And brought is the past tense of bring. Okay?' What did they teach them at these private schools? 'Shall we go and explore our new home?' Beth waved the auction details excitedly.

Leo yawned and stretched. 'I'm hungry, Mum.'

Having anticipated this, Beth went to rummage in the boot and handed Leo a small bag of dried mango pieces as he got out of the car. Beth crouched down and showed Leo the small photograph of Willow Cottage on the auction sheet.

'Now all we have to do is find our cottage. Which one is it, do you think?'

They both studied the small photograph. It was taken at an angle and part of the cottage appeared to have a climbing plant growing prettily up one side. There was a biggish garden in the foreground and very obviously a willow tree. It was quite a dark picture so it was hard to make out much else.

'It can't be hard to find a cottage with a tree like that in the garden, now can it?'

Leo shook his head as he shoved another mango piece into his already full mouth. He thrust the empty packet at his mother and hand in hand they started to walk around the green, checking out each house.

'There's no swings in the park,' observed Leo.

Beth chuckled. 'It's not a park, it's the village green. It's more like a garden.'

'Whose garden is it?' asked Leo.

'No one's and everyone's, it's for everybody to use.'

'Huh,' said Leo, looking a little perplexed at the concept and possibly at the pointlessness of a space such as this without any swings.

It really was a divinely pretty village, thought Beth as she looked about her. The village green itself was the biggest she'd ever come across with well-worn paths crisscrossing it and a mixture of mature trees that she would need to consult Leo's *Book of the Countryside* to identify correctly. Well cared for benches, with no signs of graffiti, were dotted at strategic points and the whole area was surrounded by the prettiest white chain-link fence that scalloped its way from post to post around the perimeter. A very grand mock-Tudor building had a prized position overlooking the centre of the green and two very symmetrical red-brick buildings either side stood slightly back, as if knowing their place. A couple of the smaller ones were thatched and Leo shouted excitedly as he spotted a thatched figure on the roof.

'Pigeon!' he squealed.

Another sign her son was London born and bred. 'No, I think it's meant to be a peacock,' said Beth, squinting a little at the odd-shaped creature with the long tail. A small pond was home to a handful of fat ducks and what looked like a few of this year's ducklings. There was a tearoom that had the look of a converted cottage, the only thing giving it away was the swinging sign in the shape of a large teapot. Each window had pristine white shutters making it stand out against the other not so well dressed properties. At the other end of the green was the village store cum Post Office, which appeared to be semi-detached to a very sweet looking cottage with a white picket-fenced front garden. Beth studied the small photo again. No, Willow Cottage was meant to be detached and there was no sign of the tree. Next to the store was the pub – the Bleeding Bear. It had a pub sign that could easily give a six-year-old nightmares so Beth hurried them past. As they drew near to the hire car Beth realized they had done a whole circuit. She spun round to

4

see an ornate sign that clearly stated 'DUMBLEFORD' so they were definitely in the right place, but where was Willow Cottage?

A clanging bell announced that the door of the village store was opening and Beth and Leo watched as a figure dressed head to toe in beige came out, pulling a tartan wheelie trolley.

'Let's ask someone,' said Beth, and she and Leo approached the hunched-up person. 'Excuse me. Please could you direct me to Willow Cottage?'

The beige-clad old lady jumped and clutched at her heart. She was barely bigger than the trolley. 'Oh my life, you gave me a turn!' she said as she started to rummage in her trolley. She pulled out a bottle of sherry, unscrewed the top and took a large slug of the contents. Beth knew her eyes were as wide as an owl right now and she was very unsure what to do. Leo was mesmerized. The lady went to return the bottle to the trolley but stopped and suddenly thrust it under Beth's nose.

'Mind my manners, dear. Would you like some?'

'Uh, no, thanks.'

The lady shrugged and returned the bottle to the safety of the trolley, giving the lid an affectionate pat as she did so. She then stood up as straight and tall as nature would allow and grinned a perfect false-teeth smile at Beth. Neither of them spoke. Beth sort of half grimaced back. The lady raised an eyebrow and tilted forward on her toes as if about to speak and Beth and Leo waited expectantly.

'Willow Cottage?' said Beth when she could stand the suspense no longer.

The old lady started to laugh; it was a giggly laugh that befitted her size. She stepped forward and gently shoved Beth in the middle. 'Huh, silly me. Of course.' She stopped laughing and frowned. 'Who wants to know?'

Beth shook her head slightly. She had no idea what was going on but she had an uncomfortable feeling rising inside and she didn't like it. She'd asked what she thought was a very simple question and a very simple yes or no really would have worked a treat.

'I'm Beth ...' she thought for a second and decided on a whim to amend her name slightly. 'Beth Browne. I've bought Willow Cottage.' Just saying it out loud made Beth smile. It sounded so perfect. It was the last place she had intended to buy when she went to the auction but, when the sensible-looking flats had been snapped up for more than she wanted to pay, she made a snap decision and went with her heart and Willow Cottage was the result.

'Huh?' said the old lady screwing up her wrinkled face and making it look like a discarded piece of parchment.

Beth handed her the estate agent's details, tapped the photo with a perfectly manicured fingernail and repeated slowly, 'Willow Cot-tage.'

The little old lady scrutinized the page and started to laugh again. This time it was hysterical giggles that were coming in waves. As she laughed her head bobbed about making her mop of unruly white hair swirl about her head like smoke.

'Mum, can we go now?' whispered Leo, clutching his mother's hand tightly.

But the lady was already moving off across the green giggling and shaking her head as she went. Great start, thought Beth. Round one to the local bag lady.

'It's okay, Leo. Let's ask in the shop.'

The clanging bell sounded their entry to the small dark store, which was crammed full of stock. Beth thought she saw movement at the back so she led Leo in that direction down the narrow aisles. A cheery round-faced woman beamed into view. 'Hello there, what can I get you? We've got lots of offers on.'

'Thanks but I'm hoping you can help me.' The woman's face looked decidedly less cheery. 'I'm looking for Willow Cottage.'

The woman's eyebrows shot up and she tilted her head like

an alert spaniel, her wavy brown hair adding to the comparison. 'Willow Cottage?'

Beth nodded. She was starting to get that uncomfortable feeling again.

'Willow Cottage,' repeated the woman. 'Oh, you mean Wilf's place?'

Leo looked at his mother and she looked at the woman behind the counter. 'I don't know who lived there before but it's ours now.'

The woman's eyebrows went a fraction higher and something akin to sympathy passed across her face. 'Down the side of the pub next door.'

'Right. Thanks.' Beth was pleased that they were definitely in the right place but how they had missed the cottage she wasn't sure. She didn't remember seeing anything next to the pub other than a driveway to what she'd assumed was the pub car park.

'Sure I can't interest you in …' the woman searched the shelves frantically with her eyes. 'Some discounted noodles? They're only recently out of date.'

'No, we're fine, thanks. But I'm sure we'll become regulars in here very soon.'

'Lovely,' said the woman instantly cheering up. 'Oh and good luck.' There was that sympathetic spaniel look again. Beth and Leo left the shop to the clang of the bell and walked purposefully past the pub next door. Leo stared open-mouthed at the pub sign – a frightening looking chained bear that was bleeding from a number of wounds. At the other side of the pub was the gravel track. Looking up the driveway she could see a rickety picket fence behind which was a sea of tall straw-like grass and a willow tree.

'We've found it,' said Beth, almost dragging Leo up the track. The closer they got the more of the willow they could see. But that was all they could see. It was a willow tree of mammoth proportions. Beth and Leo stood in front of it and gazed at the mass of gently swaying greenery as the summer breeze lightly fanned it.

'Wow, that's the biggest tree I've ever seen!' said Leo, his eyes darting over it as if taking in every pale green leaf. It was impressive but Beth was rather keen to see the cottage. She opened the gate that was held on by string and the rest of the rotting structure fell into the grass.

They stared at the remains. 'Oh well, never mind,' said Beth, her hopes still high as she and Leo stepped over the broken gate and skirted around the willow tree. And there was Willow Cottage, their new home. They both stood and gaped at the sight before them. Beth swallowed hard; this wasn't exactly what she had been expecting.

Carly stood in the kitchen of her small flat and read the text again. It was spread over three messages because her ancient mobile phone couldn't cope with long texts and she had an unnatural hatred of technology, which was why she had only now switched it on.

> Hi Carly I bought a cottage at the auction – yay! It's a bit further away than I'd planned – it's in The Cotswolds. Please don't say anything to anyone in case it gets back to Nick. Completion should be in a few days as I'm paying cash and using same solicitor as seller but I can't wait so we're going to take a look at it in the morning. I'll call once we've found somewhere to stay. Missing you already. Beth & Leo xx

A bit further away? The Cotswolds was up north somewhere, wasn't it?! Carly wasn't sure but she did know it was a very long way from Kentish Town, London. She blew out a sigh and it made her lips flap together like a child blowing a raspberry. She missed Leo already and she'd only seen him three days ago. Carly loved her godson and, with little to give her hope that she would be having any of her own anytime soon, he was her kiddy fix. But however she was feeling about not seeing Leo, she could multiply it a thousand times for Beth. She understood why Beth had had to leave but it didn't make it any easier to face.

'The Cotswolds?' she muttered to herself. It wasn't even a city. What was it? A giant chunk of countryside in the middle of nowhere? She'd get the map out later and look it up.

Carly poured herself a large glass of Chablis and another for Fergus. She had a quick look at the veggie pasta bake turning golden and bubbling happily in the oven.

She pushed open the door to the spare room. 'Dinner.'

A harassed Fergus stuck his bristly face round the door. 'Give me ten minutes. Okay?' He blew her a kiss and disappeared.

'The pasta bake won't give you ten minutes. Eejit,' she muttered and she took a large mouthful of wine. She was fed up. She loved Fergus but they had been bobbing along together for nearly three years now and there was still no flicker of likelihood that he was going to propose. She'd tried dropping hints and staring longingly in jeweller's shop windows but he had the hide of a pickled armadillo and nothing was getting through. Carly wished she could forget about weddings and marriage and enjoy being a couple because they were happy together, but having been brought up by her grandmother, she was a traditional soul at heart. She wanted to have children and knew Fergus did too, but she wanted to be married before they considered it. And more than anything she wanted to be a bride. Well, who didn't fantasize about having their perfect wedding?

An unpleasant aroma wafted in Carly's direction and she puzzled for a second as to what it was. Then, remembering the pasta bake, she grabbed the oven gloves and dived towards the oven. 'Sod it!'

Chapter Two

Willow Cottage stood on the other side of a sizeable sun-scorched wilderness that may once have been a front garden but was long since abandoned to the forces of nature. Beth inched forward, blinking; she really wanted this to be a trick of her eyes or at least to look a little better close up. It didn't. Ivy and traveller's joy had covered most of the cottage's boarded-up front door and continued to rampage down one side of the property and across the roof. The front of the property was symmetrical and that appealed to Beth's sense of order but where there should have been four windows there were large sheets of board nailed in place. One of the boards displayed the auctioneer's sign with the date of the auction and another flaunted a particularly good graffitied picture of a pink chicken.

Beth dragged her eyes away from the boarded-up shack to look closely at the photo on the auctioneer's details and then back again. It was a masterpiece in artifice or perhaps plain old dishonesty. Whichever way she looked at it, she'd been had.

She felt a small hand clasp her own and she looked down at Leo. He was taking it all in and she suddenly felt that yet again she'd let him down.

He grinned at her. 'It's crap,' he said. And although he was right she was still shocked by his turn of phrase.

'Leo! Where did you hear that word?'

'School. I learnt it in Reception … and you said it when you were arguing with Nick and …'

'Sorry, darling.'

'Can we go now, Mum?' asked Leo, swivelling round and tugging at her arm.

'Not yet.'

'Can we go inside then?'

'No, not at the moment,' said Beth. Not now, not ever, it's most likely unsafe, she thought.

But that wasn't going to stop Leo exploring. He let go of his mother's hand and marched with his knees high through the long grass until he reached where the boarded-up front door was barely visible through the overgrown greenery. Beth followed but, as she got closer, Leo disappeared down the jungle side of the property.

'Hang on, Leo. Careful!' she called, wishing she hadn't worn a skirt and heels. Leo squeezed himself between the ancient wall and the plant and disappeared. 'Leo! Ouch!' she said as her bare legs found some hidden nettles. When she eventually managed to wriggle through the gap, destroying her Ted Baker blouse in the process, her eyes searched quickly for Leo. He was leaning over a low wire fence into a field looking at three horses that were eyeing him speculatively.

'Look, Mum, horses!' said Leo as he jumped up and down with delight. When he stopped bouncing Beth stood behind him and hugged him. It was a view to behold. The field the horses were in was part of a magnificent patchwork thrown over the undulating hillside that surged away from the cottage. They could see for miles. A small stream trickled its way down the side of the cottage, the gentle natural sound of flowing water instantly calming Beth's senses. She breathed in the light warm air that held a hint of lavender. Somewhere in this forest of a back garden there must be a lavender bush, she thought. The back garden was considerably smaller than the front, as if they had built the cottage as far from the willow tree as they could and without considering the best layout for the occupants. Or perhaps it was to angle the cottage so it had these amazing countryside views from the rear windows?

She hugged Leo as he excitedly pointed at his surroundings. Beth suddenly felt very out of her depth. What had she been thinking to move this far away from London? She'd never lived in the countryside before, she'd only ever lived in the city. It all looked very picturesque but already she could feel her nose tickling, perhaps it was hay fever. She knew nothing about the countryside and, if it were possible, she knew even less about restoring a dilapidated property.

Willow Cottage from the back was no prettier than the front. More boarded-up windows and more galloping greenery. Beth left Leo, who was frantically waving grass at the horses who were observing him mildly as they chewed their own plentiful grass supply. She stood by the back door; it was a stable door, split in two and sturdy. It was unusual and she liked that. Beth stepped back and took in the old tired building. It was in a state but perhaps it was better inside. She decided she wasn't going to give up just yet as she felt a sprig of optimism take root.

'Come on, Leo, let's find somewhere to have a drink. That tearoom looked good and I bet they do a good scone.'

'Yay, cake,' said Leo, throwing the grass over the fence and wriggling his way back through the gap at the side of the cottage. Beth followed and was taking Leo's hand as they reached the willow when the bush-like branches of the tree parted and an old man stumbled out towards them. His face was red, he was waving his arms and looked rather cross, a little like a baby who had been woken from a nap.

'Argh!' shouted Beth as Leo screamed and ran towards the gap in the fence where the gate had once been. Beth ran after Leo and didn't look back until she had hold of his hand and they were safely on the village green. Leo started to laugh. Fear and adrenalin mixed inside her and, whilst Beth was now frantically looking back towards the willow tree, she was laughing too.

'Does he live in our garden?' giggled Leo.

'I really hope not,' said Beth with feeling.

They were still chuckling as they entered the tearoom. Having not seen many people about the village, the tearoom held the answer – it was packed. There was one small table left near the door that appeared to be where the other customers had deposited used cups and plates. Leo sat down and Beth automatically handed him her mobile phone to play games on. Beth piled up the empties as best she could, creating a bit of a teacup tower and turned with the laden tray to return them to the counter.

As she turned, the door swung open and caught her elbow. As the heavy tray started to tip its load towards her son she countered the effect and promptly deposited the entire cargo over the person entering. The crash was quite spectacular as everything smashed on the floor.

'Oh, for Christ's sake!' yelled the man who had failed to dodge the impact.

'I am *so* sorry,' said Beth, feeling the prickle of sweat on her chest as a violent flush engulfed her. Leo giggled behind her.

'Look at the state of me!' declared the teacup tower victim as dregs of tea and coffee dripped off his otherwise pristine white shirt. Beth surveyed the man who was now trying to kick cake crumbs off his shoes. He was in his mid to late twenties, clean-shaven, his dark hair had a hint of auburn and under neat dark brows were the palest grey-blue eyes she'd ever seen. Right now they were glinting like ice crystals as he grumbled to the fully tuned-in audience who all sat in silence staring at the floorshow.

A big-haired woman came bustling from behind the counter wearing a floral waist apron. 'Oh, Jack, whatever happened?' she said, attempting to dab at his suit trousers with a sponge.

'Your new waitress threw a tray at me.'

'Excuse me, I don't work here,' said Beth, feeling her temperature go up a notch with indignation.

'Then why did you have a tray of crockery?' asked Jack with a frown.

'Yes, why?' added the aproned woman.

'I was helping, well trying to …' said Beth, her voice now a lot smaller than it had been.

Jack huffed, 'Yeah, great help.' He shook his head and then watched the aproned woman as she continued to dab at his lower half.

'Er, Rhonda, that's not helping.'

Rhonda appeared to be in her own little world for a moment. 'Oh, um, sorry. Here,' she offered him the sponge.

'Could you get me a double espresso to go, please, and I'll be back in five minutes when I've changed.' He aimed the last words in Beth's direction and turned and left.

'I'll pay for that and the broken crockery,' offered Beth.

'It's okay, accidents happen,' said Rhonda. Beth crouched down as best she could in the fitted skirt and started to pick up the worst of the broken porcelain.

She was thankful for the sympathetic smile Rhonda gave her. 'Don't worry. Maureen will do that.' A large lady who would be a prime candidate for over-60's cage fighting, if there were such a thing, appeared from behind the counter brandishing a dustpan and brush.

Beth retreated to the small table and sat down. As Maureen cleared up, the tearoom clients went back to their drinks now that the entertainment was over. Beth waited patiently and Leo swung his legs and huffed a lot. The tearoom was equally quaint inside with mismatched crockery and simple wooden tables and chairs with gingham seat cushions in an array of colours.

Out of the window they had a good view of the village; a car trundled past and stopped to let the ducks waddle across the road before it drove through the ford and out of the village. Beth checked her watch. She needed to book them in somewhere for the night and she hadn't seen any hotels since they left the motorway.

'What do you want?' asked Maureen, gripping a small notepad, her stubby pencil poised, her tone disgruntled.

'A cranberry juice and a caffeine-free Coke, please,' asked Beth with her best 'I'm sorry' smile.

Maureen stared at her and a muscle near her eye twitched. She tapped the laminated card on the table. 'Teas, coffees, hot chocolate, lemonade or squash.'

'Oh,' said Beth hurriedly, familiarising herself with the items on the card. 'Is it sugar-free lemonade?'

'No.'

'What flavours of cordial do you have?'

'Orange and it's squash,' said Maureen. There was more twitching.

'Hot chocolate, hot chocolate …' Leo chanted.

'Um,' Beth frantically reread the list again. 'Just two iced waters then, please.'

Maureen didn't bother to write it down. She shoved her note-pad in the front pocket of her apron and marched off behind the counter. Beth let out a sigh. This wasn't going well. A couple went to pay and, although she couldn't quite hear the conversation, Beth was pretty sure they were discussing her. A series of furtive looks over their shoulders accompanied by huffing from Maureen confirmed her suspicions.

The door opened and in came Jack. He was wearing a similar well-fitted dark suit and despite his deep frown he was quite good looking. He strode purposefully across the tearoom to collect his espresso. When Beth saw him get out his wallet she dashed over to intervene.

'I'll get that,' she said, opening her purse. As she looked up she saw she was moments away from bashing into Jack once again. 'Oh, sorry.'

Jack shook his head. 'Bloody tourists,' he murmured as he sidestepped her and exited the tearoom. Beth felt decidedly awkward as she handed over a ten-pound note and silently Rhonda gave her the change and passed the two glasses of tap water to her.

'Could you tell me where the nearest hotel is, please?'

'There's the B&B on the south side of the green and there's the Bleeding Bear,' said Rhonda. 'The Bear does a great breakfast.'

'Right. Thanks. And where would be the nearest Hilton or Marriott?'

Rhonda thought for a second. 'That'd be Tewkesbury but Cheltenham's nearer and there are hotels there.'

'Thanks,' said Beth and she slunk back to Leo with the glasses of water.

'What about the scone, Mum?' asked Leo looking totally unimpressed with the glass of water and its solitary ice cube.

'Not now, Leo. Let's drink this and go.'

A few short phone calls later she discovered that, thanks to a Medieval Festival, there was no room at the big hotels in Tewkesbury or Cheltenham or anywhere nearby. Staying in a bed and breakfast was never going to be the first choice for Elizabeth Thurlow-Browne. However, it appeared the village of Dumbleford was pretty short on options and she didn't like the sound of the Bleeding Bear pub despite its recommended breakfast.

Thankfully, the landlady at the B&B was very friendly and keen to have residents for the night. She welcomed them by bustling around and thrusting leaflets at Leo that detailed all the local attractions.

'And there's the Morris competition tomorrow on the green. You'll love that!' she insisted. Leo let out a giant yawn.

'Morris? Are they those funny little cars?' asked Beth.

The landlady laughed, 'No, dancing. Morris dancing, it's a big thing round here. You might get to join in if you're lucky!'

Beth could think of nothing worse.

She settled Leo in front of the small television and dashed out to the hire car to grab their case and Leo's rucksack of toys. Seeing as it was dark she also grabbed her pink unicorn onesie from the overstuffed small car and shoved it under her arm. The hire car was parked further away than she'd thought and Beth was concentrating on where she was walking as she struggled with the case.

It was the dog she spotted first. A huge muscle-bound beast with flailing jowls that intermittently showed large white teeth as it hurtled towards her. Beth tried to get out of the way as the huge dog ran past her but at the last second she saw a large hooded figure running behind the dog and they barrelled into her, sending her sprawling across the pavement. If she hadn't been winded, she would have had a lot to say.

'Where the hell did you spring from?' came a gruff and accusatory male voice that was worryingly familiar.

'Could you get off me, please,' was all Beth could manage, her response muffled by the onesie over her face. The large hooded figure was heavy and she was pinned to the case. He rolled onto his haunches, sprang up and dusted himself down. Beth pulled the onesie off her face and tried to hide the mass of pink furry material. She looked up and despite the hoody she recognized her assailant – it was Jack.

'I think that makes us quits,' she suggested as she sat up and started to get her breath back.

The dog must have kept going at first but now, realizing it was running alone, it was racing back towards them. Jack made a lunge for the beast's collar and missed, and Beth found herself lying on the pavement again, this time with a huge dog slobbering all over her.

'Argh! It's trying to bite me!' she yelled.

'Don't be ridiculous, Doris wouldn't hurt a soul.' He got hold of the collar and winched the large dog off. He held out his other hand to help Beth to her feet.

'I'll manage, thanks,' huffed Beth. 'That thing should be on a lead.'

'You should look where you're going. Come on, Doris.' Jack turned and jogged away.

Chapter Three

Carly had finished work for the day and stopped off at a small café on her way home. She sipped her black chai tea and jotted down her latest contract into her diary. As a British Sign Language interpreter she was in demand and received many different requests. Hospital work was her bread and butter but she took on other projects when they interested her. She popped the lid back on her half-finished drink, slipped the papers into her over-sized handbag and left the café. She loved her job but sometimes it did feel like she was the grown up with the proper job and Fergus was ... well he definitely wasn't a grown-up with a proper job.

Carly loved Fergus, there was no question about it, but some of the things she loved about him were also the things that drove her slightly crackers. As she opened the front door she could hear him chattering excitedly in his playroom. That was what she called their spare room; he grandly referred to their converted second bedroom as his office but, seeing as all he did was play computer games all day, she thought her label was far more appropriate. She pushed on the door so it opened a fraction. It went quiet inside and he popped his head round the door in greeting.

'Hiya, C. Good day?' he asked, his game controller clutched between his thighs and his uncombed dark hair falling across his face.

'You've not got dressed.' Carly puffed out her cheeks.

Fergus looked down at his *Minecraft* lounge trousers and grinned. 'I have, I was wearing Batman ones this morning.' The door shut behind him. Every day was a pyjama day to Fergus – how he managed to pay his share of the bills into the joint account each month Carly had no idea. He had tried to explain how it worked a couple of times but, whilst she did use the Internet occasionally, she didn't really get it and it still baffled her how he got paid for playing children's games.

She pouted at the shut door and listened to him gabbling on to himself like a total loon. His own grandmother's phrase popped into her head, recited in her broad Irish accent, 'Thick as manure but only half as useful.'

Carly started chopping vegetables for a stir-fry and found the action quite therapeutic, although the more she chopped and sliced the more disgruntled she became. It was Wednesday night and she always saw Beth on a Wednesday night; it was takeaway and natter night, a chance to have a night off from signing and give her aching wrists a rest. That had all changed now that Beth had gone.

The flat's door entry buzzer interrupted her thoughts. She put down the knife and went to see who it was. There was a hunched figure on the screen.

Carly pressed the button to speak. 'Yeah?'

'Carly, it's Nick. Can I come up?'

Carly felt her heart start to race. 'No, you bloody well can't. Sod off.' She leaned across the hallway and opened the playroom door. Fergus looked irritated at first until she pointed at the screen to show Nick's face peering at them in black and white.

'Come on, Carly. Elizabeth has blown this all out of proportion. I want to fix things but I can't if she won't take my calls.'

Carly felt the need to shout, 'Out of proportion! You shit, you hit her!'

'Carly, this is between me and Elizabeth. Tell me where she is. I just want to know she's all right.'

'I don't know where she is,' she lied, 'but she is fine now she's away from you.'

'What's he saying?' asked Fergus and Carly relayed the conversation. 'Tell him to feck off,' said Fergus.

'I've tried that. You go down and see him.'

'Dressed like this?'

Carly shrugged; perhaps he would now see the benefits of getting dressed on a daily basis. She turned her attention back to Nick.

'Nick, you can stand there till Christmas for all I care. You're not coming in and I'll never tell you where she is … even if I knew.' She put down the entryphone. Nick stood and stared at the screen for a bit. She watched as he tried the door a couple of times and pressed the button again. Carly ignored it. Nick leaned on the button.

Carly swore and then answered. 'I'll call the police.'

'I need to speak to her.' Nick's voice had a harsh tone to it now.

'Never going to happen.'

'I will find her. I guarantee it,' warned Nick as he stared into the monitor. Carly watched him, her heart racing. He gave the door one last try and then walked away.

Fergus hugged Carly. 'You okay?'

'No, not really. Beth said he'd come looking for her. I think I'm starting to understand why she's run so far away.'

Beth woke early in the small twin room of the B&B and pulled the pink candlewick bedspread up to her chin. It was many years since she'd slept under sheets and although she'd heard stories of bedspreads this was her first. She plucked at it as she listened to Leo snoring lightly. She hadn't slept much, her mind full of buyer's remorse. What had seemed a wonderfully romantic and spontaneous act at the auction now seemed like the epitome of stupid. Despite the state of the cottage, she had had a good feeling when she stood in the back garden with Leo. But her plan of buying something, doing superficial restoration, some painting and decorating and then a flourish of interior design before moving on to the next property was not likely to work with Willow Cottage. It needed major renovations, shoring up most likely or possibly knocking down, and she didn't know where to start.

What *was* she doing? She was a Business Operations Manager. She knew about planning and executing efficiency strategies and adhering to compliance as well as how to cope in a male dominated world. She knew nothing about renovation and she feared the money she had would soon be gobbled up by this project. Most of her money was tied up in the London flat and discussing its sale with Nick was something she couldn't face anytime soon. He had successfully blocked her access to their joint account so that didn't leave her with much. Just thinking about him made her feel anxious.

Leo stirred and Beth turned onto her side to look at him – her gorgeous boy. He had slept well. He seemed okay even though he was miles away from London but at least he was safe. Maybe everything wasn't such a disaster after all.

Beth was rethinking that statement later that day as yet another Morris dancer whooped towards her with a handkerchief and an exaggerated wink. Leo was dancing and laughing as if he was high on sugar, which he definitely wasn't as Beth was fairly strict with both his sugar and fat intake. There had been lots of skipping about, banging of sticks and plenty of very repetitive music but it was quite jolly and Leo loved it. It was all a bit bonkers and quintessentially English, especially when it was performed on a village green.

After a jacket potato for lunch in the hectically busy tearoom, where the unsmiling Maureen served them, Beth decided they should have another look at Willow Cottage. She was really hoping that her brain had exaggerated what she had seen yesterday and now in the full sunshine it wouldn't be quite so bad. Beth was also keen to see if she could get a look inside because that might actually be better than the exterior would have her believe. With the lure of an apple, Beth persuaded Leo to come and have another look at the cottage. She liked the fact that she didn't have to answer to Nick, she could do what she wanted here and even if Willow Cottage had been a stupidly impulsive decision, at least it was her own decision. The village was a hive of activity today and there were cars parked everywhere and slow-moving jolly people clogging up every inch. They mingled their way through and, as they reached the pub, someone called to them.

'Yoo hoo! Hello!' It was the small elderly lady with the wheelie trolley. Beth looked around but nobody else was acknowledging the woman so she assumed she must have been talking to her.

'Hello again,' said Beth, stopping and waiting for the woman to get to her.

'Now, lovey, tell me again,' she said, slightly puffed by the effort of the last few steps.

'Sorry?' said Beth totally confused.

'I want to make sure I heard right. What was it you told me yesterday?'

Beth raised an eyebrow, the bag lady was clearly quite potty, poor old soul. 'I asked you where Willow Cottage was because I've recently bought it.'

The old lady burst into hysterics and all Beth and Leo could do was watch her in puzzled bewilderment.

Eventually, after lots of hand waving, she caught her breath and slowed to a chuckle. 'Oh, my, I haven't laughed that much since Maureen shat herself at the harvest festival.' The memory of this event seemed to set her off again. 'Mittens,' she said as if remembering something.

'Right. Well, it was nice to see you again,' said Beth as she tentatively inched Leo away.

'She's funny, Mum,' observed Leo. 'She said "shat"! Is that the past tense of …?'

'Leo!' warned his mother.

There was no breeze today and the willow tree stood resplendent, a magnificent cascade in shades of summer green. Beth felt herself smile as she stepped over the broken gate, a new one of those couldn't be that expensive. She made Leo wait there as she peeked into the willow to see if their lodger was in residence. Thankfully he wasn't.

'Come on,' said Beth, her spirits starting to lift as she tried to take Leo's hand. Leo pulled it away and munched on his apple as they stood and examined the cottage again. She didn't know what she was looking for. She moved forward to look at the brickwork. On closer inspection it was obviously very old but there were no major cracks that she could spot. Goodness only knows what is under the climbing plants, she thought but for now she couldn't worry about what she couldn't see. They squeezed round to the back of the property and Leo immediately went to see the horses, who were soon attracted by his apple and came walking over with interest.

Beth had a closer look at the stable-style back door. It was quite beautiful. She gave it a rattle. It didn't seem to fit too well in its frame so she gave it a shove. Surely it couldn't be breaking and entering if it was practically your own house?

From right behind her there came shouting and Beth jumped away from the door as if it were alarmed. Fear punched her in the gut. The old man that had scared them half to death yesterday had come back to finish the job, only this time there was nowhere for Beth and Leo to run. He was blocking their exit down the side of the house. Beth backed away and clutched Leo to her. The horse that had so very nearly made it to the apple made a bolt back across its field.

'Arghhhhhhh!' shouted the man. Beth had no idea what to do. Was this village full of mad people? Her heart was racing and she wanted to run but there was nowhere to run to.

She decided to try to be the voice of reason. 'Look, it's okay, we're not burglars. This is our house.' There was a flicker of recognition although he was still shouting. Leo had his hands pressed tightly over his ears and looked frightened. 'We've bought the cottage,' said Beth, her voice raised just enough to be heard. 'It's ours.' She pointed to the cottage. The man stopped shouting.

'No. It's Wilf's,' he said, his words muffled as if he had a speech impediment. Beth remembered the lady in the shop saying something about Wilf yesterday.

'Yes, it was Wilf's but he's sold it to me,' she explained in what she hoped was a calm and soothing tone. However, this had the opposite effect as the man started to shout again.

'Arghhhhhhh!'

There was a rustle in the climbing plant and Jack suddenly appeared, his face full of concern. Beth felt the stiffness in her shoulders ebb away as she was so thankful to see someone come to her rescue.

'Ernie, what's wrong?' said Jack to the shouting man, his voice smooth and gentle and far less gruff than the tone he had used towards her when they'd bumped into each other.

Ernie pointed at Beth. 'Breaking in!'

'What do you think you're doing exactly?' The gruffness instantly returned to Jack's voice as he turned his attention to Beth.

'I wasn't breaking in.' Well, maybe she had been trying to a little bit but now was not the time to confess all. 'I was only looking at the cottage, seeing what work would need doing.'

'This is private property. I suggest you leave.'

Beth felt her eyebrows shoot up involuntarily at the resolve in Jack's voice.

'Did you notice what was on the board on the front of the property?' she asked, starting to feel more in control of the situation as she knew she was about to wrong-foot him.

Jack pulled a face that made one of his eyes squint up and he looked quite comical. 'It's a picture of a chicken.'

Beth was starting to get frustrated. 'No, not that one. The one that shows when the auction was. Well, it was last week and I bought it. So technically *you* are on *my* private property and *you* should leave.'

Jack rubbed his chin. 'You can't have completed on this place that quickly,' he said, as Ernie looked on, his face etched with concern.

'No, not exactly but everything is going through and we complete next week.'

'So, technically none of us should be here.' He was being pedantic now and that was quite irritating.

'Then we should all leave. Come on, Leo,' and she ushered Leo through the gap in the plant and squished herself through after him with as much dignity as she could muster with the leaves tangling in her hair.

As they all stumbled into the overgrown front garden Beth tugged bits of greenery and small white flowers out of her hair and walked off with Leo. A glance over her shoulder saw Ernie disappear under the canopy of the willow tree and Beth stopped in her tracks, nearly making Leo trip over.

'Come on, Mum,' he said, his voice a borderline whine.

'Hang on,' Beth had her hands on her hips now as Jack approached. 'Who is that dangerous man exactly?' she pointed to the tree.

'That's Ernie. He's not in the slightest bit dangerous. He's part of the village; lived here all his life.'

Beth felt the dig, Jack wasn't one that was going to accept outsiders easily.

'He shouldn't be living under a tree.'

'He doesn't,' said Jack with almost a smile forming on his lips. 'He has a bungalow near the school.' Jack pointed past the B&B.

'Then why is he sat in my garden like a hostile garden gnome?'

Jack shook his head slowly as if he couldn't be bothered to speak any more and wandered off towards the pub leaving Beth more confused than ever.

'Mad. They're all stark staring bonkers in this village.'

Beth's phone rang. 'The voice of sanity! Hello, Carls.'

'At last it's not your wretched voicemail. How are you and where the hell are you?'

'I'm feeling surprisingly normal in the village of the totally insane. How about you and Fergus?'

'Nick came round here last night. We didn't tell him anything but he says he's going to find you.'

Beth couldn't help the feeling of ice fear that trickled through her body. Her mind flashed back to the night she left. Beth looked around her: another troop of Morris dancers was in the middle of the green hopping up and down as another group practised nearby. People were chatting and laughing and the sound filled the air. This was a world away from her London life; there was absolutely nothing here that could connect her to what she'd left behind. Despite the state of Willow Cottage it made sense to stay here for the time being.

'He'll never find me here.'

'Where is here exactly?'

'Dumbleford. It's west of Stow-on-the-Wold.'

'Sounds like place names from Narnia to me. What's it like?'

'The cottage I bought is practically a ruin, there's a man living in my willow tree, the only person under fifty thinks I'm an idiot, everyone else is barking mad and today they are having a Morris dancing competition on the village green.'

'Actually, I like the sound of that. The Morris dancing, not the rest of it.'

27

Beth lowered her voice and took a step back from Leo so he wouldn't hear what she said. 'Between you and me I think I may have made a huge mistake with the cottage. I'm speaking to the solicitor tomorrow to see what options I have. I'll keep you posted.'

The rest of the day was spent watching the Morris dancing and reading books in bed at the B&B. Beth tidied the small room for the second time that day. The stupid things I've brought from London and the important ones I haven't, thought Beth as she picked up her glue gun and wished it was her hairdryer.

She pondered the day and hated the fact that Carly's statement about Nick had dominated it. Everything was Nick's fault. If Nick hadn't refused point blank to leave the apartment they would still be in London. She missed London. She had choices in London; she could have any type of food she wanted, stay in a variety of hotels, shop for virtually anything. Here food was limited to the tearoom or the pub, there were no hotels and the handful of shops sold knick-knacks, souvenirs, and out-of-date noodles. If Nick hadn't sounded so menacing when he said he would find her wherever she went then maybe she wouldn't have ended up here.

Chapter Four

The solicitor confirmed what Beth had feared – that she was committed to the purchase of Willow Cottage, there were no get-out clauses not even with the dilapidated state of the property. All responsibility for investigating the property before purchase rested with the buyer and, as she hadn't done any of that, it was entirely her own fault. The solicitor did impart what he felt was good news: that they were completing even sooner than they'd hoped and she could pick the keys up from their offices near Stow the next morning.

'How would I go about putting it back up for auction?' she asked, as a sigh escaped.

'Oh, well, I could do that for you.'

'You see, I think I may have made a mistake and I need to sell it quickly and get the money back.'

There was a long pause at the other end of the phone. 'I think I should probably inform you that this was the third time this property has been presented at auction. It's been looking for a buyer for seven months.'

'Seven months?' Beth flopped back onto the B&B single bed. It was bouncier than she'd noticed before as her body jiggled about involuntarily.

'I'm afraid so.'

She closed her eyes and processed the information. Beth felt her plans had been thwarted, she was stuck here with no obvious escape or quick fix. She felt a sense of resignation. 'Do you know any good local builders?'

The B&B landlady, Jean, was not doing a bad job of keeping Leo entertained, as it turned out her own grandchildren lived in Canada so having a child in the house was a novelty. It was a shame that Leo wasn't able to see his own grandparents but, as they had been Nick's first port of call when she left, they wouldn't be seeing them for a while. At least it gave Beth precious time to ring a local building firm and set up a quote. She decided that if she could get away with doing the minimum required to make the cottage habitable maybe she could get it back on the market and then make good her escape. The plan had always been to buy somewhere, do it up and then move on and repeat the exercise until she felt that Nick had given up looking for her. It probably wasn't the finest plan but it was what she had dreamed up when she had found herself staring at another mini-bar in another random London hotel.

Beth picked up the keys to the cottage from the solicitor as planned and with Jean showing Leo how to make fairy cakes she headed off to meet her first tradesman at Willow Cottage. As she walked down the side of the pub she could see the back of a white van that was parked in front of the cottage, which was a good start. However, seeing Ernie peering into the driver's window was not. Beth's mobile rang; she didn't recognize the number so answered it but didn't speak.

'Hello? Hello, Ms Browne? This is Kyle from Glancey Construction. I'm at the property now but …'

Beth walked round to the passenger window. The young man inside was leaning away from the driver's door as Ernie's gnarled face loomed large. She tapped on the glass making the young man jump. 'Hello,' she said with a wave.

Kyle didn't answer, he just pointed at Ernie.

'Oh, that's Ernie. It's okay, he won't hurt you, he's not dangerous,' said Beth into her mobile. She wasn't entirely sure that was true but she needed Kyle to get out of the van. Kyle switched off the phone and scooted along the seats until he could climb out of the passenger door.

'This way,' said Beth, keen to ignore the Ernie situation.

'Is he a bit …' Kyle tapped his head to finish the sentence.

'I'm not sure really, but he seems to fit in well here.'

Beth took Kyle round the back of the cottage and he was already sucking his teeth before he'd even seen the inside. Beth tried each key on the plastic cable tie that was keeping them together. Every key was old, some were rusty but none of them fitted. Kyle was busy poking at brickwork and shaking his head at the roof so she systematically tried each key again – no luck. As she stepped back she noticed another lock further down on the bottom half of the stable door.

'I wonder,' she muttered to herself as she crouched down. The third key she tried turned grudgingly in the lock and she was able to push open the bottom half of the reluctant door and it creaked in protest. 'I'm in!' she called to Kyle as, adopting an unattractive walking crouch position, she waddled inside.

It was dark and musty. Beth squinted and still she couldn't see anything. Suddenly a beam of light blinded her and Kyle appeared carrying a large torch and doing the same odd crouching walk that she'd done. They stood up and dusted themselves down as Kyle shone the torch around to reveal that they were in a kitchen. That was if a ceramic butler-style sink and an elderly stove was enough to qualify it as such. A brief glance at the floor revealed chunky-looking floorboards, a much darker shade than they should be thanks to the dirt. Beth was aware of something where the window was despite it being boarded up so she pointed for Kyle to shine the torch in that direction.

It appeared that the plant that dominated the outside of the house was also doing a comprehensive job on the inside too. 'Oh my God!' said Beth, as she took in the expanse of the creeping vegetation and the maze of spider's webs clinging to it.

Kyle strode out of the kitchen leaving Beth with only two choices – stay in the dark with the spiders or scuttle after him. In the dark she tripped up a small step that led out of the kitchen but thankfully the dark hid her blushes as she scooted after Kyle. There were two more rooms downstairs; one was completely empty and the other had an open fireplace with a large beam above it. From the glimpse she saw, it looked promising and definitely the sort of feature she could emphasize as a focal point. As Kyle headed upstairs the torch glinted off something on the grimy wall. Beth reached out to touch it before the light disappeared and the contact of her fingers sent it crashing to the ground.

'Hang on, Kyle. Shine that torch this way would you, please.'

Kyle reappeared and shone the light in her face. With her eyes tight shut she pointed at the floor and the torch beam followed her finger. She opened her eyes to see a dusty photo frame in pieces at her feet. Beth bent down and, carefully sifting through the broken glass, she picked out the photograph.

Holding it in the light she could study the black and white picture. Its edges were tatty implying it hadn't spent its life in the frame. There was a middle-aged woman, her hair pinned back in a style reminiscent of the war years. She was laughing and in front of her she was hugging a small boy who was beaming a smile at the camera. Beth felt herself smile. She turned it over and read the swirly writing on the back: *'Dearest Frank/Daddy With all our love at Christmas time Elsie & Wilf (Christmas 1944)'.*

Kyle coughed and the torchlight wobbled. 'Do you want to stay down here while I take a look upstairs?'

'No, I'll come up, thanks.' Beth put the photograph safely inside her T-shirt so that it didn't get damaged. The smiling faces gave a little hope that once upon a time a family had been happy here. So perhaps she could restore it to somewhere liveable for another family in the future.

'Best be careful. It may not be stable,' said Kyle, pointing at the stairs. He proceeded to demonstrate his caution as he took each stair one at a time and tested it first with a stomp of his boot before putting his weight on it. Halfway up Beth huffed her frustration at the slow progress.

When they eventually reached the top, Beth could see they were on a small landing and a beautifully carved balustrade, with the odd missing spindle, which was protecting them from the stairwell. Kyle opened a door to reveal the grimmest-looking bathroom Beth had ever seen – even the spiders hadn't settled in here. Its avocado bath and toilet mismatched with the pink sink and the curly-edged linoleum floor finished off the ghastly ensemble, which was all covered in a layer of grime. The last two rooms were the bedrooms; both were a good size but one was particularly attractive as it had a sloped ceiling on one side, even if it did have a large brown patch in the centre, and there was also a step down making it into two levels. She was pleased with the quirky nature of its layout and could see what a lovely room it would make for a child but the thought of the work required took her breath away. She gave herself a small shake; she had to think of this as a business venture, as a project to be managed. This wasn't going to be their long-term home, she couldn't afford to invest heavily in it right now and she didn't need to lavish it with the same love and attention she would her own home. She just needed to do it up and get it sold.

Beth was deep in thought when a bang made her jump. Kyle swung round and aimed the torch beam at the stairs to reveal Ernie. He was clutching the handrail tightly and frowning deeply, only an arm's reach away from Beth.

'Out!' he shouted, his voice deep and raspy.

Beth stood her ground although her pulse was racing. 'Ernie, please don't shout. Let's go outside and I'll explain.'

'Out,' he repeated, but with less ferocity as Beth gently guided him back down the stairs with Kyle erratically waving the torch above her head. When they reached the back door, Ernie stood back so that Beth could go first. She resumed her crouching position and shuffled out under the stable door.

She heard Ernie expertly wriggling a bolt on the top half of the door, it opened and he and Kyle walked out. Thanks a bunch, thought Beth as she dusted herself down.

'Ernie. This is my house now.'

Ernie didn't seem to understand as he was shaking his head. 'No. Wilf's house.'

Beth remembered the photograph. She retrieved it from under her T-shirt, at which Ernie looked a little alarmed.

'Here,' she offered him the photo, 'Wilf.'

Ernie leaned forward to take a proper look and a grin spread quickly across his haggard face.

'Wilf,' he repeated.

Beth tried to pass him the photograph but he refused with a wave of his hand.

'I'm going to live here with my son.' Ernie looked confused again. 'Like Elsie and Wilf did.'

'Elsie?' Ernie's voice was soft and his eyes instantly welled with tears. Beth's heart went out to him and she willed him to understand.

'Yes. Leo and me. We'll live here like Wilf and Elsie. Oh and,' she checked the back of the photo. 'Frank.'

Ernie wiped away a tear with his sweatshirt sleeve. 'Not Frank.'

'Oh, um.' Beth didn't know what to say and she could see that Kyle had finished jotting notes down with an exceptionally small pencil and was keen to get her attention.

'Frank died,' Ernie's voice was shaky.

'I'm sorry. Shall we …' but she didn't get to finish the sentence as Ernie was already scrambling back down the side of the house and he was gone.

'What sort of budget are we looking at for this, then?' asked Kyle, sucking his teeth again.

'As cheap as possible. Could you send me the quote? I'm sorry, I need to go after him and make sure he's all right.' Ernie hadn't gone far; a swift peek into the willow tree revealed his hunched form sitting on the ground.

'Come on, Ernie. Let's get a cup of tea and you can tell me all about Elsie and Wilf, okay?'

Ernie rubbed at his eyes with his sleeve like a child and gazed at her. Eventually he spoke. 'Tea and cake?'

Beth laughed. 'Yes, if you like.' She held out a hand to help him up and he took it and held on to it with his thin bony fingers.

The tearoom was quiet so when Rhonda brought over their order she sat down too and Ernie smiled his greeting. Beth wasn't sure if the smile was for the cake or Rhonda.

'Hello again, I'm Rhonda.'

'I'm Beth.'

'I know. So you've bought Wilf's old place, then?' asked Rhonda, folding her arms and leaning forward. Beth was instantly uncomfortable with Rhonda's over-friendly approach.

'Like Elsie and Wilf,' said Ernie through a mouthful of coffee and walnut cake.

'Willow Cottage,' said Beth, feeling that she needed to have her wits on high alert in order to not be tricked into giving away too much information.

'Never heard it called that before. Must be the spin the estate agent put on it,' said Rhonda, pulling a face to match her statement.

I've been had again, thought Beth.

'Partner not with you?' ventured Rhonda, eyeing Beth's ringless fingers.

'Er, no, I'm single.'

'Holiday let or permanent?'

Beth was thinking. 'Renovation project.'

'Project to live in or sell?'

The quick-fire question round was making Beth exceedingly uncomfortable. 'Sell.'

Rhonda looked disappointed. 'What we need is new blood in the village. Young blood.'

Beth tried very hard not to think of vampire films as she looked at Rhonda's pale face. Maureen snorted her derision from behind the counter, so she was clearly listening in.

'The village school is struggling, I think it's down to twenty-two children now.'

'Per class?' asked Beth. That was well below national average and would be a good place to ease Leo into the routine of a new school, even if he might only be there for one term.

'No,' chuckled Rhonda. 'In total! They have to put them all together to make enough for one class. And that's after trying to encourage them in from surrounding villages too.'

Ernie wiped his mouth with the serviette and got up to leave.

'Oh, Ernie, are you going? You were going to tell me about Elsie and Wilf,' said Beth.

Ernie looked teary again and he shook his head. He pointed at the now spotlessly clean plate that had once delivered his cake. 'Thank you,' he said and he left.

'Poor old Ernie,' said Rhonda. 'Lived here all his life, never left the village.'

'He seems quite attached to Willow Cottage.'

'Ah, well, that was Wilf's old place you see and he and Wilf were like brothers. Ernie's mother was pregnant when they evacuated her from London during the bombing. Elsie took her in. She was on her own too, both waiting for men to come back from the war you see.' Beth nodded her understanding, she was engrossed in the nostalgic story and was waiting for the happy ending. 'Thing was, it was a difficult birth. Baby got stuck, which is why Ernie is the way he is. His mother died in labour so Elsie brought him up.'

Beth swallowed hard, she was still looking for the happy ending. 'Was her husband okay with that when he came back from the war?'

'Oh, Frank, he never came back; he was shot down. It was just Elsie and the boys. Ernie moved out some years ago and he lives in one of the new bungalows up the way,' she pointed in a random direction. 'But the cottage was always his home. He and Wilf were inseparable. You see, Wilf used to sort things out for Ernie. With Wilf dead, Ernie is pretty much alone in the world. I'd better get back to work.' Rhonda smiled briefly, collected up the empty teacups and plate, and went behind the counter.

Beth felt near to tears. There was no happy ending to this story. She placed the photograph on the table and took in the faces again. They looked so cheerful.

Chapter Five

Carly was gabbling on the phone and it was difficult to interrupt.

'Slow down, Carls, I'm only picking up every third word, it's like trying to decipher a coded message,' said Beth.

Carly took a deep breath and tried to quell the excitement that was bubbling up inside. 'So, in summary – I think Fergus is going to propose! Eek!'

Beth pulled the phone away from her ear. 'Now hang on, we've been here before. Do you remember the large Christmas present that sat under the tree for weeks and you convinced yourself that it was like a Russian doll full of smaller and smaller boxes until you got to a ring box?'

Carly made a non-committal noise as she bit her lip at the memory and winced. 'But it could have been …'

'And what was in the large box?' Beth's voice had gone all school teachery.

'A new sleeping bag.'

'Precisely. I'm just saying be careful. Don't go getting your hopes up.'

Carly paused before the excitement grabbed her again. 'But this time it's different. He's asked me to meet him under the statue of Eros in Piccadilly Circus! I mean how romantic is that?'

'It's on a busy traffic junction.'

'Stop being a killjoy. Anyway, think about it. Piccadilly Circus is very close to the Ritz. Perhaps he's taking me there for afternoon tea to propose.' She emitted another more stifled eek. 'Oh my God, I need to change!'

'No, you don't. You always dress pretty smart for work.'

Carly was staring down at her outfit and it all looked very different when she surveyed herself this way compared to how it did when she checked herself in the full-length mirror before leaving the flat each morning. 'I'm wearing a dress but with flats!' She didn't give Beth a chance to respond. 'And Tiffany's is not far from the Ritz. Oh my God, Beth, I've got to go …' The line went dead.

Beth groaned. She truly hoped that this time Carly had got the right end of the stick and that she wasn't winding herself up into a frenzy of happiness only to have it peed all over.

Beth sat at the table in the B&B and studied the various quotes she'd received. It was not looking good. Number one priority was the electrics so she had no choice but to confirm the work for that, which was a sizeable chunk of money. Basically, everything needed something doing to it and it was going to cost more money than she had. Having walked out on a well-paid city job she only had a small amount of savings to rely on until she sold Willow Cottage and hopefully turned a profit. Beth was feeling at a loose end as Leo was watching some cartoons on the small television and Jean was dusting around them both.

'Why don't you go to the pub tonight? It's quiz night,' she suggested. Beth struggled to think of anything worse. Bingo, actually, bingo would have been worse.

'They do bingo first, so if you go early you'll catch that too.'

Beth openly sighed. 'I think I'll give it a miss, thanks.'

'They are friendly, you know, folk round here. If you're going to be here for a while it would do you well to make some friends.

Just a bit of motherly advice,' she chuckled as she whisked the plates into the kitchen. Beth didn't want to make friends. This was a temporary thing; she didn't need new friends. She had Carly and … she realized nobody else from her old life had been in touch but that was because nobody else had her new mobile number. She'd been too worried about it making its way into Nick's hands.

Something else she could lay firmly at Nick's door, not only had she left behind the life she'd built for herself in London, her job, her parents and pretty much everything she knew, she had also had to cut herself off from her friends. But if she thought about it she knew this hadn't happened overnight. Hindsight was a wonderful thing. When she looked back she realized things with Nick were changing long before that fateful day. Nick's apparent easy-going manner had been replaced over time by a persuasive argumentative one that manipulated Beth into doing what Nick wanted. The seemingly throwaway comments about the people Beth socialized with were all intended to drip-feed his messages of control and it had worked. Slowly Beth saw less and less of her friends until it was just Carly on a Wednesday night. Carly and Fergus were pretty much her only friends now but if she had them then that was all she needed.

It was the middle of the afternoon and, despite her mercy dash home to swap her shoes and redo her make-up and hair, Carly had been fifteen minutes early arriving at Eros's statue. She hadn't enough time to do a proper job but a quick go with the straighteners had spruced it up a treat. She got out her clear lip-gloss and applied another coat to make sure. She wanted to look and feel perfect when he proposed. Carly checked her watch again – only five minutes to go. Her stomach was doing all sorts of things; it felt like it was full of hungry caterpillars instead of butterflies.

Carly searched the busy streets for Fergus. He was tall, quite lanky really, so often was easy to spot in a crowd but there was no sign of him yet. The minutes ticked by as she watched the busy hum of London life around her: the Big Issue seller on one side and the young person with a large sign directing people to a new shoe shop on the other; it interested her that the Big Issue seller was a lot more enthusiastic than the sign holder.

Carly checked her watch again. Now Fergus was late. She had to keep moving out of the way for tourists to take photos of Eros, and photos of them pulling silly faces and kissing each other in front of the statue. It was starting to get annoying. She watched couples hand in hand heading into the Criterion restaurant looking all loved up and happy. People kissing each other good-bye as they piled out of taxis. Others sat on the steps of the statue watching the world go by.

Fergus was fifteen minutes late. Carly's feet were starting to hurt. These heels looked fabulous but they weren't designed for standing about in or walking any distance. She thought about texting him but he rarely felt the vibration of the phone so that was probably pointless, and right now she didn't trust herself to text something that may spoil the mood of the ever-so-romantic proposal she was sure was about to materialize.

Carly spotted a mop of unruly black hair bobbing her way and instantly relaxed. It was Fergus, he was late but he was here. As the crowd parted she saw his grinning face. He looked partic-ularly pleased with himself, which was a good sign. He was dressed which was definitely another plus but he was wearing jeans and a Star Wars T-shirt – not her first choice for the beautiful memory of his proposal but now was not the time to get picky, she thought.

Fergus kissed her. 'Sorry I'm late.'

'It's okay.'

'The blog chat ran over,' he explained but Carly wasn't really paying attention – that didn't matter now.

'Where are we going?' she asked, her eyes sparkling with anticipation.

'Wait and see.' He took her hand and led her into the tube station. Immediately her spirits plummeted. She was wrong about the Ritz and Tiffany's and she tried hard to erase the pictures of the stunning rings she'd seen in magazines. Her feet didn't take kindly to the tube station steps but she was trying to stay positive.

A few sweaty minutes later they emerged at St Paul's and Carly tried to think of nearby places that were ideal for a proposal. She was struggling to think of any; all that was nearby was the London Stock Exchange and St Paul's Cathedral, its dramatic white dome visible above the grey office buildings. Fergus gave her a reassuring smile. Perhaps he could sense her anticipation, but did he realize how important this moment was to her?

Carly had been dreaming of the perfect proposal and perfect wedding ever since she was a girl and watched Monica and Chandler on *Friends*. He led her through the streets, past the front of St Paul's and then into the magnificent cathedral by the sightseeing entrance. Carly had been here as a child but remembered little of its vastness and awe-inspiring interior; it did take your breath away.

Fergus pulled her close and hugged her. She held her breath. 'This way.'

The steps at the Underground were nothing to the ones she was facing now. The sign told her it was 528 steps to the Golden Gallery. She gulped hard, pointed at the sign and then at her shoes.

'It's okay, we're not going all the way to the top,' Fergus told her with a cheeky smile.

At about the 150-step mark it got better because the burning feeling in her toes was replaced by a numb sensation, which was still painful but didn't make her wince with every step. Fergus gave her reassuring glances every so often as he almost jogged up the steps in his well-worn trainers. Carly forced a grimace onto her face. Dear God, this had better be worth it, she thought.

She was about to admit defeat and resign herself to a life of spinsterhood when Fergus beckoned her up the last few steps and into the first gallery. They stood by the balustrade. The views in all directions were breath-taking and the ornate dome above them was resplendent in symmetrical perfection. Carly did her best to ignore the smug-looking faces peering down on her of those that had climbed all the way to the upper gallery. She was certain they would not have done it in heels like hers. She tried hard to ignore the throbbing in her feet and blanked out the thought of the descent that was yet to come.

Fergus guided her to the wooden seating that ran around the gallery walls.

'This is the Whispering Gallery,' he told her and she nodded. She had forgotten all about it until he said but now she could hear the echoes of a foreign language as another couple shared their messages into the architectural phenomenon. Fergus kissed her gently and then walked around to the other side of the gallery.

Some children appeared and proceeded to share obscenities around the walls until their parents emerged at the top of the steps and intervened. The walls echoed with the sound of their stifled giggles. Carly was glad of the sit-down and so were her feet. She so wanted to take off her shoes but she dare not remove them in case she couldn't get them back on.

Eventually the gallery was silent. Fergus sat on the far side of the dome. Carly felt her heart rate quicken and she took a deep breath. Fergus gave her a little wave and she saw him put his face to the wall. This was it. She closed her eyes and listened to his melodic Irish accent magically emanating from the wall behind her.

'I love you, Carly Wilson,' he said and she felt a tear form. 'And to prove it to you … I'm taking you away for a magical weekend in a treehouse.'

There was a very long pause. Carly didn't want to open her eyes. She played the words around her head again but it didn't matter – whatever she did, that was definitely not a proposal of marriage. She opened her eyes to see Fergus giving her a thumbs-up from the other side.

'You utter tosser,' she said with feeling into the wall and, for the first time, she was grateful that Fergus was deaf.

It was early evening and Leo was gently purring in his sleep. Beth looked around the small room with its ancient wardrobe, candle-wick bedspreads and plastic framed scenic pictures on the wall. Jean was lovely but staying here was slowly draining the life from her. She needed a plan and she needed to take action. Perhaps a trip to the pub was exactly what she needed.

Jean was more than happy to babysit Leo and seemed thrilled that Beth was taking her advice, so Beth slung her bag on her shoulder and headed out. There was a breeze but it wasn't cold. The sun was setting and Beth stopped for a moment to take it in. The colours were majestic; the soft orange hues melding with a deep yellow glow as the sun slowly melted into the silhouetted countryside. The only sounds were the light wind rippling through the trees and a few birds squabbling over where to roost for the night.

The scary pub sign was creaking gently and Beth pulled her eyes away. As she reached the pub, she could hear the welcoming chatter inside. She truly hoped it wouldn't stop as soon as she entered like it did in all good horror films. The heavy old door took a bit of shoving and unbeknownst to her a large man inside the pub had seen her approaching and had got up to give it a pull just as she gave one more hard push. The door opened swiftly and as it disappeared from beneath her touch Beth stumbled inside with a clatter of heels on wooden floor but thankfully she managed to stay upright and avoided falling to her knees. The large man was awfully apologetic, as was Beth who had almost landed in his lap. Beth recovered quickly and realized that nobody was really watching, they were all thankfully engrossed in chatter.

'You okay?' asked the smiling barmaid nodding at the door.

'I feel a bit of an idiot. Otherwise, I'm fine, thanks.'

'I'm Petra, landlady,' she said in a soft, but indistinguishable, Eastern European accent as she offered a hand across the bar. 'What can I get you?'

'I'm Beth. Gin and tonic, please. What gin do you have?'

'Ah, just the standard, I'm afraid. Nothing fancy here.' She pointed to the optic.

'That's fine,' said Beth, trying to look like she meant it.

'You're in time to join a team, quiz is about to start.' She pointed to a bald man with a rather large belly who was blowing into a microphone.

'No, really, I'm fine, thanks. I'll observe.'

Petra shook her head. 'Jack, here's your fifth team member,' she called and Jack turned round from his position on a nearby stool. Beth was sure there had been a smile on his face a split second before he'd realized who his fifth member was going to be. He stood up and beckoned her over, his expression resigned.

Three rather more friendly faces greeted her and budged up to make room on the bench seat as they machine-gunned their names at her – Melvyn and Audrey, who were clearly a couple, and Simon who was very smiley and whose ginger hair had receded back to his ears. As she glanced around she could see this was by far the youngest group in the pub and, apart from her and Jack, none of the others were under forty.

'I'm Beth,' she said, with a self-deprecating smile.

'Eyes down, look in,' bellowed the tubby man who clearly didn't need a microphone. Beth felt her blood run cold. Not bloody bingo, she thought. 'Noooo, only joking!' There was the equivalent of human canned laughter before it went silent and he carried on. 'Welcome to the Bleeding Bear Pub Quiz. Round one: the nineteen sixties. Are you ready? Question one ...'

Oh, terrific, thought Beth, I wasn't even born in the sixties or the seventies and didn't spend very long in the eighties for that matter!

She was as much help with the answers as she expected she would be, which was no help at all, and it made her feel quite the simpleton. Thankfully it was Melvyn and Audrey's era so, as a team, they had something written down for each answer. Not for the first time, Beth was missing her job. It had been pressured and demanding but she was good at it and valued by her boss. Here, she was a dunce, who, when the question was *Who was famously assassinated in Dallas?* she said – J.R. Ewing. At least it got Jack laughing. There was a brief pause at the end of round one and everyone started to chatter again.

'What's this I hear about you bribing the locals with cake?' asked Jack, avoiding eye contact and taking a sip from a near full pint of Guinness which gave him a milky moustache.

Beth frowned for a second. 'Oh, you mean Ernie. I thought I should at least try to get to know the man who is virtually living in my willow tree.'

'How's the cottage coming along?'

'Well, it's not. The quote I had was sky high. I mean I'm sure it was accurate it's just that so much needs doing to it.'

'It can't be that bad,' said Jack.

'It is.' She resisted the urge to sulk.

'But Wilf was living there up until he had the heart attack, so I don't see why you can't live in it while you do it up yourself a bit at a time.' Jack was blunt.

'Maybe Wilf and I have different views on what constitutes liveable.' Beth could feel she was starting to get grumpy. She finished her drink. She decided now might be a good time to leave but as if to thwart her plans Petra appeared at the table and replaced her empty glass with a full one.

'On the house. You deserve it if you're putting up with this lot,' said Petra. 'Welcome to Dumbleford.' She couldn't leave now.

Round two was no better as it was naming the national anthems of various countries, and round three was sport, but thankfully Simon on their team knew everything there was to know about

46

football and cricket so they were covered. As round four approached Beth was losing the will to live.

'Round four is countries' internet name extensions.' There was grumbling from the teams. 'You know like dot co dot UK for United Kingdom. Which countries do these letters represent …?'

Beth sprung forward, this was something she knew. Working in London she'd dealt with people from all over the world so this was her opportunity to add some value to the evening's proceedings. Jack noted her sudden alertness and moved the answer sheet square in front of him. Beth noted the gesture and the battle lines were drawn. As each question was read out they both whispered the answer at the same time. As they reached question seven she could sense Jack's annoyance.

'C-h,' said the tubby compere.

'China,' whispered Jack at the same time as Beth whispered, 'Switzerland.' Jack turned to look at her, his face full of superior smugness. 'I think you'll find it's China,' he said, as he wrote it on the sheet.

'You're wrong, I know it's Switzerland,' Beth was emphatic.

Jack gestured to the rest of the team for an opinion and they all pulled puzzled faces and shrugged.

'So what's China then if it's not c-h?' asked Jack.

Beth pondered the question. She did know someone in China but their email finished in dot com as many did. She bit her lip and pondered some more. She saw Jack smirk. 'Look, I may not know what it is, but I know what it isn't. And it isn't c-h!'

'Um, could it be Chile?' offered Simon and he was instantly shot down by Jack.

'No, it's China!'

Questions eight and nine were uncontentious as they both spat out the same country names at the same time but number ten set them against each other again.

'M-c is Monaco,' said Jack for the second time.

'I think it's Morocco,' repeated Beth, and Jack sighed his frustration. 'Okay, like you said to me, if m-c isn't the Internet initials for Morocco then what is?' She folded her arms.

It was Jack's turn to have a hard think. 'I think it's m-a,' he said at last.

'M-a?' snorted Beth. 'How does that fit with Morocco? There's no "a" in Morocco.' Jack studiously ignored her and started checking that their answer sheet was all filled in.

Beth bought the team a round of drinks, which was well appreciated especially as it appeared that Melvyn and Audrey were planning on making their single drinks last the whole evening. Beth's competitive side had been reawakened and there was no way she was going back to the B&B until she had been proved right. Her and Jack were still sniping about it when the answers were read out.

'Number seven is Switzerland ...'

'Ha!' said Beth with feeling in Jack's right ear, making the compere turn his attention to Jack's table.

'Did you get that one, Jack?' asked the compere, his ruddy face in a beaming smile. 'Seeing as you're the school IT specialist.'

Beth sat with her arms folded and her eyebrows high, radiating smugness – she was enjoying this. Jack looked from Beth to the compere.

'Uh, no. We got that one wrong, I'm afraid.'

'I didn't,' grumbled Beth, as she took a swig of her drink.

'Sorry,' mumbled Jack but before Beth could ask him to repeat what he'd said the answers for nine and ten were being read out.

'Nine, South Africa and ten, Monaco.'

A huge grin spread across Jack's face. 'Monaco, not Morocco. Do you have something you'd like to say?'

'Sorry,' mumbled Beth. Jack looked complacent.

'Another drink? To show there's no hard feelings.' Jack was already on his feet. 'You need to stay for the results – we might have won sausages!'

Beth shook her head. Had she misheard him with all the babble in the pub?

Jack returned with the drinks. 'Petra says I need to play nice,' he said, tilting his head towards the bar where Petra was wagging a finger in his direction as well as giving him a sultry wink.

'She's right,' said Beth, taking her drink.

'Look, it's the school holidays so I have a few days to myself. Would you like a hand with the cottage?'

'I don't think I'm ready for my IT to be installed just yet but thanks.'

'I meant taking the boards down and stuff. I renovated my place but, mind you, it wasn't as neglected as Wilf's.'

'What makes you think I need your help?' Beth's tone was waspish.

Jack looked taken aback. 'I've seen Wilf's place and from the car you arrived in I'm guessing you've not got a ladder stashed in there?'

Smartarse, thought Beth. She was tussling with her defences, which were on high alert following Nick but at the same time her common sense told her this was a genuine offer, not an attempt to patronize her.

'Will everyone please stop calling it Wilf's.' She knew she sounded prickly. 'Sorry, but it's really annoying.'

Jack sipped his Guinness. 'I think you'll find it'll be Wilf's for a while yet. People round here take time to adjust to change. The bungalows where Ernie lives are always referred to as the "new" bungalows. They were built in 1975!'

'Blimey,' said Beth, feeling more than a little silly for her outburst.

'The offer of help is there if you want it. Do you usually get people in?'

Beth sipped her drink again and shook her head. What was Jack talking about? She'd never done this before.

'I assumed you renovated places for a living?' he added.

Duh! thought Beth. The alcohol was letting her guard down. The last thing she wanted to do was start giving away information about her previous life. She shook her head theatrically. 'I do get people in for anything structural but this is my first project like this. Usually it's more of a general spruce up; painting and decorating, interior design. That sort of thing.' She took a deep breath, she found lying was quite uncomfortable.

'Right,' said Jack, looking satisfied with the explanation. 'So, do you want a hand then? I'm free tomorrow.'

Beth was taken aback by the offer. She could say no but that wouldn't be making a stand for independent womankind; it would be cutting off her nose to spite her face.

'I know that's probably the Guinness talking but I'm going to say yes, please.'

Simon, Melvyn and Audrey already had their cardigans on ready to leave as the compere started up again. 'Third place are the Village Idiots.' Beth leaned forward to get a look at that team because, quite frankly, that could be half the village. 'Second place tonight and only three points behind the winners was the Quizzly Bears. Sorry, Maureen.' Everyone looked over to where Maureen was downing her pint with a face like a thundercloud.

'And the winners are … The Spanish Inquisition.'

Jack jumped up, narrowly missed knocking over the glasses as the other team members started shaking hands. Melvyn and Audrey got up to leave.

'I'm guessing that's us then,' said Beth, as Jack gave her a huge bear hug and then instantly looked rather awkward and pulled away. 'First time we've won since Easter.' He looked genuinely thrilled and Beth had to admit that she too was feeling quite pleased with herself. The compere came over to hand out the prizes.

'Um, thanks,' said Beth, as she really didn't know what else to say when someone hands you a dozen pork sausages.

Chapter Six

Fergus had lost his hearing due to contracting a severe case of mumps as an adult. He had spent the first year after it happened confined to his old flat. A lot of it was shock at the sudden loss of a primary sense but with that comes fear and erosion of self-confidence. Losing his ability to communicate had made him feel cut off and frustrated. Even simple tasks were suddenly much harder and took more effort, for example trying to find out information was no longer just a phone call away. Fergus was shocked too by the number of people who treated him like he was mentally slow just because he couldn't hear.

He had made a positive move when he had joined a British Sign Language course and the added bonus had been falling for one of the tutors, Carly. She had introduced him to the deaf community and all the support that brings from people that actually know what it's like to be in the same situation. Although his experiences were different from those who'd encountered discrimination all their lives he had found learning sign language immediately expanded his social group and set him on the road to recovery. Sadly, some people never do manage to adjust to such a trauma but, with support and all the latest gadgets, Fergus had slowly progressed and was now living again.

This meant engaging in all aspects of normal life including arguing with your partner. Carly found it was exceedingly difficult to have a row with a deaf person. No matter how competent you were at sign language you couldn't get the words out quickly enough and if they chose to look away the argument was over. Fergus was looking perplexed and kept signing 'sorry', which was probably because he felt she was overreacting a little to the fact that he'd used the last tea bag but, after a sleepless night, Carly was desperate for a cuppa. All of her frustration at the non-proposal was flooding out into tea-gate. She added a couple of digs about him playing games all day and not getting dressed, then grabbed her bag and stormed out. She slammed the door behind her. He wouldn't hear it but it was likely the vibration would convey her level of annoyance.

She stood outside the flat door and screamed. It was a primal scream that went on long enough to make a front door open to check what the matter was, which for London, where everyone kept themselves to themselves unless something disastrous had happened, was quite exceptional.

'Sorry, I needed to let that out,' said Carly, as the door quickly shut again. It had worked, she felt a fraction less frustrated, although her desire for a cup of tea was still raging. Fergus was so laid-back about everything and most of the time that was a good thing but sometimes it drove her potty. She felt it wasn't unreasonable for her to be thinking about getting married after three years together but she was beginning to wonder if Fergus would ever get around to proposing. She sent Beth a text but when she didn't respond immediately she called her.

'I'm guessing it didn't go well as I didn't get an excited phone call from you last night,' said Beth.

'Didn't go well! That's a bloody understatement. He took me up 257 steps in heels to ask me if I wanted to spend a weekend in a bloody treehouse.' Carly was indignant.

'Ooh, a treehouse sounds nice, when's he taking you?'

'Did you not hear what I said? 257 steps up to the sodding Whispering sodding Gallery at sodding St Paul's.'

'What a lovely thing to do. I think you're being a bit mean. He's booked a nice mini-break and he took you to a wonderful place to tell you about it.'

Carly pouted as she stood on the pavement outside the flat. 'It would have been a perfect place to propose.'

'Maybe, but there are other perfect places for a proposal.'

'I'd like it to feel like the world has stopped for one moment, just for me. That's all,' said Carly with more than a hint of despondency evident in her voice as she moved to one side to avoid being bumped by frowning pedestrians.

'I dare say you would and I'm sure that will happen but, in the meantime, you should enjoy the lovely thoughtful man you have and look forward to your weekend in a treehouse.'

'Thoughtful? 257 steps. In heels!' was all Carly had to say. She shoved the phone into her bag and crossed the road. She didn't see Fergus who was watching her closely from the window.

Leo was finishing his sausages and beans when the theatrical musical doorbell of the B&B hummed the tune to 'Twinkle, Twinkle, Little Star'. Jean opened the door and preened herself as she greeted Jack. What was it with the women in this village and Jack? He seemed to send them all aquiver.

'Are you ready?' he called brusquely, after exchanging pleasantries with Jean.

'Yep,' said Beth, grabbing the rusty keys and gently steering Leo away from the table.

'You're wearing that?' asked Jack, blunt as ever, as he gave Beth's outfit the once-over.

She looked at her fitted white T-shirt, designer skinny jeans and smart low-heeled leather boots. 'Yes, what's wrong with it?' It wasn't like she was wearing a skirt and heels as she had the first time she'd investigated the property.

'Nothing wrong at all but you're about to get absolutely filthy working on the cottage and that outfit will be trashed.'

'These are the least precious clothes I've got and if they get trashed then so be it. But I'll be careful.'

'What do you usually wear for this sort of work?' asked Jack, his expression curious.

It was too early to make stuff up and Leo was listening. 'This,' she said and walked out of the door with her head held high. Jack shook his head behind her.

Jean displayed a fixed smile as she witnessed the exchange. 'Well, have a nice time anyway,' she said, as she waved them off.

'Here,' said Jack, handing Beth and Leo small white face masks. 'It'll help to stop the dust.'

'Thanks but I'm going to play in the garden,' said Leo brandishing a tennis ball.

'He's not had a garden before,' explained Beth and Jack patted Leo on the back sympathetically.

'You can do me a favour, keep an eye on Doris here,' he said as the huge dog skidded up the path to greet them. Doris had a dark face but the rest of her short coat was a golden blonde and she was very nearly the same height as Leo. Beth protectively stepped in front of Leo and Doris seized the opportunity to sniff Beth's crotch. Jack expertly pulled her away as Beth rolled her eyes; sniffing crotches and licking their own private parts was probably the two main reasons why she wasn't a dog lover. The third thing that Beth disliked about dogs was when they lifted up both their back legs and dragged their bums along the carpet although she had to admit that was always funny as long as it wasn't your carpet.

'I don't think that's a good idea,' said Beth.

'But, Muuuum,' moaned Leo from behind her.

Jack was eyeing her as if awaiting an explanation for her actions.

'It's a very big dog, and dogs …' she knew they were all waiting for her to say the word 'bite'. '… dogs can be unpredictable. So, no, I'm sorry but I don't think so.'

'Shame. That means she'll have to spend the day in her cage,' said Jack, looking forlornly at Doris who was happily bashing her tail against his leg.

'A cage?' Leo looked outraged. Beth looked a little shocked too.

'It's okay, it's to stop her wrecking the house.' The expressions of alarm didn't change. 'Seriously, she's an English mastiff, she'll eat her way through a wall if I leave her on her own!'

'But still. Putting her in a cage?' said Beth, eyeing the behemoth of a dog.

'It's a proper extra-large dog cage but she'd rather be with me, obviously.' Jack pulled a sad clown face.

'Fine, bring her along,' relented Beth, and Leo whooped his delight.

'You'll grow to love her,' said Jack, as he patted Doris's flank and the dog promptly wiped her slobbery jowl down the side of Beth's jeans as she passed. Beth recoiled in disgust.

'I doubt it,' she muttered.

A large estate car was parked outside with a ladder strapped to the roof bars. Doris leaped into the boot and Jack jumped in the driver's seat.

'See you there,' he shouted as he pulled away.

'Fine,' said Beth. She didn't need a lift – she could almost see the willow tree from the B&B, but it would have been nice to be offered one. She put on her sunglasses and took Leo's reluctant hand.

When they got to the cottage, Leo checked to see if Ernie was under the willow tree but he wasn't. Jack already had his toolbox out and was studying the boards that covered the windows and the door.

'Galvanized bolts,' he said, nodding. 'That's good. It means they won't have rusted. I've got just the thing for those.' He pulled a large spanner from the toolbox and set to work.

'Let's get these off and see what we're dealing with,' said Jack.

Beth wasn't comfortable with Jack dishing out the instructions but she agreed as she didn't have a better idea.

As he undid the last bolt Beth stood and took the weight of the large sheet of ply board. At the last second the board slipped in her grasp but Jack stopped it from falling.

'Ow,' complained Beth, checking her hands – splinters and a broken nail. She breathed out hard; this was starting to look less and less like her kind of thing. Lifting down the board revealed the window. There had once been white paint on the wooden frame but now most of it had peeled off. However, the sight of the series of perfect little square panes in the windows brought a smile to both their faces.

'Georgian windows,' said Jack, helping Beth to put down the board and lean it against the wall.

'They're lovely,' said Beth leaning closer, 'but not exactly good for keeping the cold out. I expect they'll need swapping for double-glazed ones.'

'No!' said Jack crossly. 'These are a thing of beauty. I'll put some linseed oil on to protect them until you can get around to painting them but trust me they'll keep the cold out. It's the gaps round the edges that you'll need to sort.' He indicated where someone's attempt at filling the gaps was already crumbling away.

'Right,' said Beth, feeling further out of her depth.

'Flemish bond,' he said, nodding at the brickwork.

'Is he? I'm not really into films,' said Beth, distractedly.

Leo and Doris played fetch with the ball until Doris put a large hole in it. Beth and Jack removed the other three boards and thankfully all but two of the small panes of glass were intact. Jack expertly taped some plastic over the broken ones so that they didn't let in any rain. They both stared at the largest piece of board covering the front door, which itself was also covered by the sprawling ivy and white flowering plant.

Jack disappeared to the car boot. 'Shall we?' he said as he produced two large pairs of loppers.

'Can I help?' asked Leo.

'Sorry, mate, these are a bit deadly but you can pull down as much of that traveller's joy as you can.' He pointed at the greenery covered in pretty white flowers and threw him some gloves.

Leo shoved his hands into the gloves. 'They fit!'

Beth looked surprised. 'They're only those very stretchy ones; I thought they might come in handy,' Jack said, setting to work with the loppers. Beth stood and watched. She wondered what she was doing. She couldn't help – she'd never used loppers before and had no idea where to start, they were quite heavy and unwieldy. Every time she lifted them up they seemed to sway off to the right like some kind of giant magnet was pulling them. She put them down. The whole project was looking more and more ridiculous. Doris came up behind her and rested her heavy head against Beth's hand, her droopy eyes making her look as forlorn as Beth felt. Beth sidestepped away from the drooling creature hoping Jack hadn't noticed. She picked up the loppers again and tried in vain to control them as she snipped wildly at the air around the plants.

Thanks to Jack and Leo's concerted efforts a little while later they were ready for the big front door reveal. The first thing Beth saw was more peeling paint but this time in a shade of bright pink.

'Wow!' exclaimed Leo.

'I'm glad I'm wearing my sunglasses,' said Beth.

'It's not all bad. It's a pleasant style and the glass is a nice touch.' Jack pointed to the four small panes that made a bigger square at head height. It was going to take a bit more to convince Beth.

Jack soon had the boards off the windows at the back of the house and loaded them into the boot of his car.

They grabbed two takeaway coffees and a squash from Rhonda and then set about the inside. Beth wasn't sure if it looked better or worse now that the windows were letting in light. They both stood sipping their coffees while Leo sat on the bottom step of the stairs playing games on Beth's iPhone.

'Okay, boss. What are you thinking?' asked Jack. Beth was sure she could sense derision in his voice. She was actually thinking 'Oh shit, I've well and truly cocked up here' but instead she said,

'Number one priority is to make sure it's watertight.' She was pleased with the conviction in her words, she almost sounded like she knew what she was doing.

'Lovely summer we're having, hasn't been any rain for weeks. How about you check upstairs for any obvious signs of leaks and damp patches and I'll be back shortly.'

Beth didn't have time to query what he was planning to do as he had already left, so she carefully went upstairs and started looking around. It was very difficult to identify damp patches under the general grubbiness. She exhaled loudly; how were you meant to get a house that was this dirty clean again? Would it ever be clean again? Actually, had it ever been clean? Then she thought of the photograph of the lovely smiling Elsie who was so selfless as to have taken in and raised Ernie. Beth was sure Elsie would have kept the house clean; it must have been in Wilf's later years that things had got out of hand.

Every room upstairs was wallpapered and she had vague recollections of helping her dad as a child with removing wallpaper with warm wet sponges and a scraper. It had taken most of a half-term holiday for them to do one room, it would take for ever to do the whole cottage on her own. She heard voices outside and then an odd whooshing noise, and then she felt the sensation of ice-cold water trickling over her. She looked up to have her face washed by a steady stream of water coming through the ceiling above.

'Shit!' She stomped to the nearest window and tried hard to ignore the sight of the dingy bathroom that surrounded her. She struggled to open the window to shout at Jack who was merrily hosing down the roof but the window wouldn't budge. By the time she had made it downstairs and pointed out the dripping to Leo who was lost in a game, the noise and water had stopped.

Jack sauntered into the cottage. 'Did you find any leaks?' he asked with a smirk.

'You bloody idiot! I'm soaked. What if that gets in the electrics?' Beth shook her hands and droplets of water flew off her.

'Electrics are switched off. I assumed you'd be getting a professional to check those over before trying them.'

Beth wanted to scream. She hated pretending she knew what she was doing and she hated Jack's smugness. He was obviously playing games.

'Yes, the electrician is already booked but dousing everything, including me, in water is not the way to find out where the leaks are!' She made a show of pulling her hair into a ponytail and wringing it out.

'Okay, so how would you have done it?' Jack looked intrigued.

'Well, I … I would have looked for damp patches, like you said before and … gone up on the roof to check the pointing.' She wasn't entirely sure she'd used the right term but she had heard her dad talk about pointing before so it was worth a punt.

She noticed that Jack momentarily raised an eyebrow, perhaps she was on the right track.

'Don't let me stop you,' he said. 'The ladder is outside.'

Beth swallowed hard. She was okay with heights when she was inside and safe like in a lift or looking out on a spectacular view; then she was fine. Climbing up ladders, on the other hand, she was not good at but she wasn't going to back out of this obvious challenge. 'Fine, could you hold the bottom for me?'

Jack failed to suppress a schoolboy smirk. 'Sure thing.'

The first few steps were fine. She kept telling herself it was like going up stairs, only it wasn't. Her foot slipped a fraction. She squealed and tried to hide it with a cough. She didn't want to fall. Beth was trying hard to control her breathing but the fear was making it speed up. She clutched the cold metal tightly and slowly moved her hands up as she took another step.

'You okay?' said Jack.

'Wonderful,' lied Beth, as she muttered a string of inaudible obscenities to herself.

Each step was a fear conquered as she went higher and higher. She was suddenly very grateful that she hadn't bought anything taller than a cottage. As she neared the roof a thought struck her. What the hell was she going to do when she got there? She had no idea how to check the pointing. She didn't even know what pointing meant. When her feet were at last level with what remained of the cottage's ancient guttering, she slowly moved her head so that she could scan a section of the roof.

'Are you getting on the roof?' called Jack, followed by something that could have been a cough or a laugh or a bit of both.

'Um, no, I can see perfectly well from here,' she replied, her voice shaky.

'What's the pointing like?'

Beth stared at the tiles, row upon row of them. They all looked the same, all shimmering wet as the summer sunshine glinted off them. 'I think they're okay.'

'Really?'

'Well … they're definitely all pointing in the same direction.'

Chapter Seven

Carly loved going to the hairdresser's. Danny had been keeping her style on trend for the last few years and he was full of gossip, so it was an indulgent couple of hours that she always looked forward to. As she expected, Danny was on form and he got completely carried away when she told him about the treehouse getaway and the imminent proposal.

'OMG. That is the epitome of romantic. This boy's a keeper,' said Danny as he snipped confidently. 'You know, there was an amazing article in one of the mags only the other day about treehouses and one of them was like this microcosm of luxury. I bet that's where he's taking you. Lucky bitch.'

Carly giggled.

'You should look it up on the internet,' he said with a wave of his scissors. Carly wrinkled her nose. 'Dear God, have you still not joined the twenty-first century. Carly darling, you need to catch up with the human race. Here,' he handed her his phone – the latest from Apple.

'It's okay, thanks. It's just not my thing.' She gave the phone back.

'You sound like one of those people that said a hundred years ago "planes will never take off!"'

Carly wasn't sure if the pun was intended but it made her laugh anyway. She was feeling good about things. She was over the whole non-proposal upset and it was only a couple of weeks to the weekend away and she was now convinced that the idea of a proposal in a treehouse was so much more romantic than the Whispering Gallery.

While Carly was paying at the reception desk, Danny hunted for the magazine. 'I can't find it, darling, but I will if I have to turn this place into Primark. I will leave no surface unturned. I'll drop it round to the flat when I uncover it.'

'Are you sure? That's really kind, thanks.'

'Ooh, looks like someone is getting another surprise.' Danny pointed to the door. As it opened a large bouquet of yellow and white roses came in and a smidge of dark hair was barely visible above them. Carly's stomach did a little flip although at the same time her brain was telling her that the roses' deliverer wasn't tall enough to be Fergus. The roses came towards her, obscuring her view of the holder as Danny vigorously nodded his approval at her side. As she took the flowers she saw who was holding them.

'Nick?'

She immediately pushed away the flowers. 'I don't know where she is.'

'These are not for Elizabeth. They're for you to say I'm sorry for being a jerk the other night. It's all getting on top of me. I love her, Carly. I need her back.' He handed her the flowers.

Carly shooed Nick out of the salon and away from the open mouths of clients and stylists alike. 'Here,' she thrust the flowers back at him crushing them slightly. 'I don't want your flowers.' She turned and started to walk purposefully away. Unfortunately, it was in the opposite direction of the flat and at some point she was either going to have to turn round and look like the numpty she felt or walk miles out of her way.

Nick caught up with her. 'Can I walk with you?'

Carly stopped. 'How did you know I'd be here? Are you stalking me? Because there are laws against that.'

Nick looked contrite. 'I came here earlier in the week to see if Elizabeth had booked herself in.' He cast his eyes downward at the same time as Carly's jumped up. This was proper resourceful stalker territory. 'And I saw your name on the screen. I figured there weren't two of you in the area. I'm sorry if I've overstepped a line.' He looked sorry. He looked lovely. Carly had always liked Nick; he was funny and easy on the eye – everybody liked Nick. On some level she felt he had hurt her too by doing what he had done to Beth.

'You overstepped the line when you hit my friend.' Carly's jaw tightened.

'Can we talk somewhere? Can I get you a coffee? Can I at least explain? Please.' His eyes looked full of remorse and, against her better judgement, Carly said yes.

Carly sipped her black chai tea and eyed Nick wearily. It was difficult to reconcile what she had heard from Beth with the calm and worried-looking man who sat opposite her. Nick was looking his usual immaculate self. Black hair in a neat but trendy short style. He was wearing a fitted white shirt, his suit jacket neatly placed on the back of his chair. He didn't look the type to hit anyone but there was rarely a typical look for someone that dished out domestic violence. That was the problem, you just didn't know. Carly glanced around at the other hotchpotch of London life catching a few minutes respite from the busy world outside. They all looked pretty ordinary but who was to know what any of them were capable of when under pressure.

'How have you and Fergus been?'

'We're fine, Nick.' Carly felt she had to ask the responding question. 'And how about you?'

'Awful. Devastated. I think I was in shock at first when she left. Now I'm just sick with worry.' Carly didn't speak but she hoped her expression conveyed her lack of sympathy. 'I love her, Carly. I can't believe this has happened and I need to get her back.'

'I don't think that's going to happen, Nick.'

Nick briefly put his head in his hands. 'I keep going over and over it.' He looked up slowly and held Carly's gaze. 'Leo was being so testing …'

'He's six, that's kind of his job,' pointed out Carly.

'Yes, I know, but he was pushing all the boundaries and with Elizabeth not there he seemed to think he could do what he liked. All I did was tell him off and he went crazy.' Nick emphasized his point with his palms spread wide. 'I had to restrain him or he would have hurt himself. That was all I was doing. I swear to you.'

Carly sipped her tea as Nick awaited her response. 'Beth saw you hurting Leo.'

'No, no, she didn't. She thought she did but I was grappling with him and trying to catch hold of his hands so he would stop lashing out.'

Carly was quiet while she mulled over Nick's new version of events. 'Even if she did misunderstand what she saw, I'm not saying that she did but *if* she did, then how do you explain you hitting Beth?' Carly stared at him unblinking, watching his face, studying his response, trying very hard like all the TV detectives she'd ever watched to spot a sign that he was lying.

Nick blew the air out of his cheeks and shook his head, then stared at his hands for a bit as if they held the answer. Finally he looked up and made eye contact. 'I don't know.'

Carly's eyes widened. 'You don't know how you hit her?'

'No. I've no idea how it happened but the important thing is that it wasn't intentional.'

Carly snorted and wished she hadn't as it irritated her throat and now she was coughing uncontrollably.

'You okay?' He looked concerned.

'Fine, carry on,' she croaked.

'One minute it was just me and Leo and he was screaming and, God, can that kid scream.' He gave a half-laugh. Carly sipped her tea carefully which soothed her throat as she waited for him to explain further. 'I think Elizabeth came up behind me as I stood up and somehow she got knocked into the wall. But, honestly, I don't know exactly how it happened.' He shook his head. 'Carly, what do I do?'

Carly didn't like this. Nick's version of events did sound plausible but then so had Beth's, and Beth had the bruises to prove her account. However much she hated herself for it, Carly couldn't help but feel a little sorry for Nick. It all seemed so out of character. She studied his face – was that a tear in his eye?

Carly wasn't sure what to say. She would always be steadfastly loyal to Beth but was there even the smallest possibility that Beth had misread the situation?

'I don't know what you should do, Nick. But I guess if you really love her you try to put things right.'

'That's exactly what I intend to do. Whatever it takes. But first I need to know where she is.'

By the time Beth was safely at the bottom of the ladder Jack had finally stopped laughing. Beth was breathing heavily through her nostrils and was aware that she sounded a little like a cranky horse.

'What is so funny?' Her stern face seemed to set Jack off again.

He took a deep breath to quell the laughter. 'Come on, I'll buy you one of Rhonda's famous bacon butties.'

Beth didn't like being laughed at. At school she had never quite fitted in and had frequently been the butt of jokes she never quite understood and, right now, she felt exactly the same – self-conscious and awkward. Having made a concerted effort after Leo was born to carve out a successful career for herself, she was filled with dread at the thought of shrinking back into the uncomfortable and unsure person she had once been. It appeared all the old doubts had never actually gone away; they were just dormant awaiting a situation like this to reawaken them and bring them flooding back at full force.

'Thanks, but I don't think so,' said Beth as she looked around for something to busy herself with. Jack had stopped laughing and was watching her closely and Beth found she was grinding her teeth so she stopped.

'I didn't mean to upset you.'

'You've not.' Beth took hold of the ladder and, finding the catch that released the upper sections, she pushed it into place with her thumbs. The ladder slid down at speed.

'Noooo!' Jack lunged at the ladder and managed to grab the first rung, only just stopping the rest of it from sliding into Beth's face.

She looked startled and stumbled backwards.

'Bloody hell, Beth, what did you do that for?' He was still clutching the rung of the ladder and he looked cross.

'Well, not for fun! It was an accident!' She felt foolish enough without him pointing it out.

'Are you okay?' he asked, as he finished the job and laid the ladder on the grass. Beth nodded. She daren't speak because for some ridiculous reason she felt like crying and if she opened her mouth she feared it may be a great blubbing sob that escaped rather than something coherent. 'Come on, I need a bacon butty. Okay?'

Beth nodded.

'I'll take Doris home, and you and Leo can meet me at the tearoom.' His voice was still gruff. She knew he was still cross with her but his eyes seemed to convey concern.

The tearoom was teeming with the Dumbleford lunchtime rush but Rhonda quickly cleared them a table by the window and Beth was soon staring at the biggest pile of bacon slapped between two halves of a white roll that she had ever seen. She couldn't remember the last time she'd eaten white bread; living in London there were always lots of options and Nick had had wheat intolerance so they'd mainly eaten rye. Beth and Jack reached for the ketchup at the same time and when their fingers touched they both recoiled in a flood of apologies. Beth didn't like how her body had reacted to the contact.

Jack quickly turned his attention to his butty. 'Dive in,' he said, his bouncing eyebrows giving away his enthusiasm.

Leo didn't need telling twice. He grabbed his and stuffed as much as he could into his mouth, making his mother wince at his lack of table manners.

Beth gave her plate a sideways look. 'There's like half a pig in there.'

'I know, it's fabulous!' Jack took a huge bite out of his.

Beth wanted to ask for a knife and fork but even then she wasn't sure how exactly to tackle the teetering tower, the smell of which was making her senses tingle. Sod it, she thought as she picked it up, opened her mouth as wide as it would go and bit into it. Leo grinned at her.

Beth closed her eyes as she chewed. It was crispy bacon heaven. Without speaking Beth and Leo communicated their mutual enjoyment with a series of exaggerated facial expressions and eye rolls. Beth popped the last morsel into her mouth and almost felt sad – she didn't want the bacon butty to end.

'I told you they were the best.' Jack's expression conveyed that he was pleased with himself.

'Amazing,' said Leo. 'I'm bored now. Can I play outside?' He looked to Beth for her approval.

'Well, okay,' she said reluctantly, 'but stay on this side of the village green where I can see you.' Leo didn't respond – he was already running for the door and artfully dodging Maureen and a laden tray.

'I'm sorry about laughing earlier,' said Jack.

'It's okay. I'm not used to this sort of renovation so it's ...'

'I don't think you're used to renovation at all,' stated Jack over the top of Beth's explanation. She was about to protest but he continued. 'Pointing is the cement-like filler between tiles or bricks and over time it crumbles and therefore lets in moisture.'

'Right,' said Beth, feeling embarrassment flush in her cheeks.

'And when I said I liked the Flemish bond I meant the wall, it's a style of brickwork.'

'Right, not James Bond then?'

'Nope.'

Beth looked at Jack and into his pale grey-blue eyes. He looked sympathetic rather than mocking but she felt stupid all the same. She sighed. 'Look, I might not have been entirely truthful, but the thing is …'

A wheelie trolley suddenly appeared at the side of their table interrupting Beth's flow.

'Hello, Jack. Hello again, crazy lady,' said the old woman, with a chuckle.

'Shirley, this is Beth. Beth this is Shirley, one of Dumbleford's oldest residents.'

'Aye, cheeky!' said Shirley, giving him a pretend clip round the head.

'I mean you've lived here the longest.'

'Oh, okay, I'll give you that.' She eyed their mugs of tea and winked at them dramatically. Shirley bent over and rummaged in her trolley before producing a hip flask. 'Just the thing to liven up tea,' she said unscrewing the top.

'We're okay, thanks, Shirley,' said Jack, and Beth looked relieved at not having to refuse whatever was in the flask. The woman was a mobile off-licence although it could be poison for all Beth knew – she was clearly potty. Shirley looked disappointed but returned the flask to the trolley and patted the lid affectionately. She then shuffled next to Beth. 'Budge up,' she said, as she lowered herself onto Beth's chair. Beth only had a moment's notice to move over to Leo's vacated seat. Beth recoiled and tried very hard not to breathe in through her nose but when she did she wasn't expecting the gust of lily of the valley thrust up her nasal passages. She was surprised; not pleasantly surprised as she loathed the smell, but it was better than she had been expecting from the bag lady.

'So you've heard about Wilf's place?' Shirley said to Jack.

'Yes, I'm giving Beth here a hand,' said Jack, trying to pull Beth into the conversation.

'Huh, she'll need more than that! More like a miracle!' Shirley started to giggle.

'I think the property is sound, Shirley. Did the survey throw up much?' asked Jack, turning to Beth.

Beth blinked hard and failed to hide her annoyance, which was mainly with herself at the rash bidding decision that had landed her here, but also at being interrogated.

'I didn't actually have a survey done but there was one I received when I got the keys and …' Beth tailed off as Shirley had slowly swivelled round and was staring at her from an altogether far too close proximity.

'And?' prompted Jack.

'And I started to read it but it was all a bit overwhelming.' Beth shuddered at the memory of how many times the report mentioned the words 'significant defects', 'overhauling', 'upgrading' and 'inadequate'.

'I could look at it for you?' offered Jack.

Beth felt a stab of humiliation as Jack gave her a pitying look. How had she gone from being a totally in control sought-after individual in the business world to this? Nick, that was how and she hated him even more for it.

Chapter Eight

Beth had the survey report clutched in her hand and she put it on the B&B kitchen table before answering her mobile.

'Before I forget, Danny says you're due a cut and colour,' said Carly as soon as Beth picked up.

'Hiya, I don't know where I'll go for that.' There was no hairdresser in the village and nobody she had come across had a haircut that would prompt her to ask where they got theirs done.

'Anyway, Danny had seen this article on treehouses in a magazine in the salon and, love him, he dropped it round to the flat and they are simply stunning. Beth, you want to see them, they're amazing. They're like the best hotel suites up in a tree and some are catered, so they deliver this gourmet meal for you to have by candlelight. One of them was full of flowers; flower garlands, arrangements and even flowers threaded around the bed headboard.'

'They sound lovely.'

'Eek, I can't wait,' said Carly, her excitement obvious. 'They are the perfect place for a proposal. He is such a sweetheart. We both love the outdoors and we like a touch of luxury, so this combines the two perfectly.'

Beth loved her friend and the last thing she wanted to do was burst her bubble of happy expectation but she did feel that, although it all sounded very plausible, she was setting herself up for another possible disappointment.

'That does all sound fabulous. Are they expensive, these tree-house breaks?'

'Yeah, hundreds, but when you are looking at something so unique then that's what you have to pay.'

Beth hesitated before she spoke. 'And do you think this is the sort of thing that Fergus could afford on his income?'

There was silence and Beth felt awful for having brought Carly crashing back to reality. Eventually Carly spoke but a lot of her previous gusto had dissipated. 'Perhaps he's been saving up.'

'Yeah,' said Beth, trying to sound enthusiastic, 'you're right, he could have been building up to this for ages. I'm sure it will be totally brilliant.' There was a silence that went on a fraction too long.

'Nick has been in touch again.'

Beth could tell by Carly's voice that there was more she wanted to impart. 'And?'

'He looks really sorry about everything that happened and he says he wants to put things straight between you. He's really worried about you, Beth. He's looking for a second chance.'

'No way! Why would I risk me or Leo being in the firing line the next time he loses his temper?'

'Oh, I know,' said Carly, 'I was just passing on the message.' There was an uncomfortable pause in the conversation. 'He nearly cried,' added Carly.

'He could be bawling his eyes out for all I care. I'll never go back. Carly, please don't get suckered in by him. He's a tricky bastard.'

'No, of course not. You are completely right. He's a bastard. A very charming and handsome one, but a bastard all the same.'

Beth hadn't shared everything with Carly, so the fact that Beth and Nick's relationship ended so abruptly had been a shock to her. She'd talk to Carly about it when she had eventually sorted it all out in her own mind but for now Beth was still trying to make sense of it all herself.

When the call was over Beth started to think about the treehouse. It sounded like a lovely place, but then so had Willow Cottage but now it was a disaster she was stuck with. Perhaps she could knock down bloody Willow Cottage and build a treehouse in the willow. She was pretty sure it would cost less and it would definitely be easier than sorting out the mess she currently had to deal with.

Beth was drowning her sorrows in a particularly large glass of Chardonnay as she sat in the B&B kitchen mulling over the full structural survey report. It didn't make for an entertaining read. She felt sorry for herself. She knew it was a bit pathetic but she couldn't help it. It was like she'd been dropped into someone else's life and it was alien. Everything here was almost the opposite of what she was used to: before she had a clean, sleek and modern home and now she had a tumbledown filthy wreck. She used to have a good job, now she was playing at being a property renovator – and doing it very badly, she thought, as she ran a thumb over her reddened palms that were sore from the splinters. And love it or hate it she was used to the noise, bustle and vibrancy of London and now she was in a village that was so sleepy and inactive if it were a person it would be lying on a slab with a tag on its toe. She was the proverbial fish out of water or in her case she was the middle-class mum out of Waitrose.

She was also trying very hard not to think about Nick. It was bugging her that he'd been in touch with Carly but it niggled her more that Carly had obviously listened to him. Nick was charming and that was a wonderfully effective mask to hide behind.

This was all Nick's fault. If he had only been all the things he had promised to be, and not the hateful manipulator with a swift backhand, then right now she and her little boy could be sitting in the apartment she loved, and had worked so hard for, with the man of her dreams. Because, before Nick had shown his true colours, that was exactly what he had been. At first when Nick had done things for her she was flattered, pleased that someone was thinking of her and it had made her feel special. The few thoughtful gestures had become more and more frequent until virtually everything outside of her work was sorted out for her by him, making her feel cosseted. It was a while before she noticed that her independence was evaporating, almost unnoticed, like a puddle in the sun. Perhaps on some level she was missing Nick too. She started to feel anxious as the memories forced their way into her conscious mind and she washed them away with a large slug of wine. There was no point going over the past. Beth realized she was grinding her teeth and stopped herself; it was a nervous thing she seemed to have developed, thanks to Nick, and she needed to break the habit.

She looked around the B&B kitchen – it was painfully twee. Frilly floral curtains hung at the small window and were tied back with ribbons, the units were all pine which overpowered the small room, on top of the wall cabinets was a collection of pottery jugs in various gaudy colours, most of which clashed spectacularly with the migraine-inducing magenta walls. Beth knew she was being uncharitable but she was used to clean lines, minimalism and good design, none of which was evident here.

She looked round the kitchen again. It was all superficial. The kitchen wasn't a bad size; but was overcrowded by cupboards and overwhelmed by colour and chintz. She could easily change it given the chance, it was only one room. That was it. She could easily change one room. Willow Cottage was the same; she needed to look at it as a series of single rooms, one thing at a time, rather than one massive insurmountable disaster. The cottage might have a lot that needed changing but, with the exception of the roof, there didn't appear to be anything structurally wrong. Yes, it needed repointing – thanks to Jack she now knew what that meant – it needed rewiring and a damp course but that was all doable. She took another swig of wine. That was the last time she was going to feel sorry for herself; from now on, she was going to change things bit by bit and she was going to start with moving out of the B&B.

Jean failed to hide her obvious disappointment at losing her guests and she seemed rather concerned about Beth's plans.

'Honest, Jean, we'll be fine. We've loved it here but it makes sense to move out now.' Beth needed to have a much tighter hold on her money than she had done up until now. The B&B had been ideal but in a prime Cotswolds location it wasn't cheap. Beth had no regular income so for the first time in a long while she had to get used to living on a budget.

Leo shook his head as he followed his mother to the car and they drove away. Beth swung the car past the pub car park, pulled up outside the cottage, jumped out and flung open the boot. An earlier trip into town had allowed her to stock up on a cleaning product for every known surface type, as well as two long-handled brushes of differing brush coarseness, and a mop and bucket with spare heads. She also had industrial quantities of bleach, most of which was destined for the toilet and bathroom.

'Right, we are only cleaning one room. That's all. We've got all day. Ready?' Beth was bubbling with enthusiasm. Leo was not.

'But it's just the two of us and it'll be soooooooooo boring!' Leo's shoulders slumped dramatically forward.

Beth's plan was that since the living room appeared to be water-tight even if the upstairs landing wasn't, they could get that one room liveable and then work on the rest bit by bit. The electrician was due to start rewiring in a few days and she had already called Kyle the builder to fix the pointing. She had felt so proud when she had explained what pointing was, though Kyle hadn't seemed that impressed. Beth gathered up armfuls of cleaning products and headed towards the cottage with a spring in her step. Leo huffed and harrumphed behind her. She nearly dropped the whole lot when Ernie jumped out of the willow tree.

'Hello,' he said, his voice brittle. She hoped he hadn't been there all night.

'Good morning, Ernie. We're going to give the cottage a spruce up. Well, the living room at least.' Ernie grinned and, without asking, he followed Beth and Leo inside. Beth ignored the feeling of *Great Expectations* as she bobbed under a large cobweb in the hallway and went through to the musty-smelling living room. There was a wide windowsill that, like the rest of the room, had a layer of dust on it. After a lot of shoving and grunting on Beth's part she finally managed to open the window. She put on the mask that Jack had given her and handed the other to Leo, which he put on and briefly found entertaining before quickly returning to being bored.

Beth wiped down the windowsill and laid out the cleaning products.

'Let's start at the top and work our way down,' she said, her voice bright.

Leo pointed at the bulb hanging from the light fitting. 'I can't reach up there. Can I go and explore somewhere?'

'No, Leo, I need you to help. You can sweep the floor.'

'What?' Leo looked alarmed but reluctantly took the brush from his mother and despite it being taller than him he started to slowly push it around the floor.

The next couple of hours were a slow torture as Beth dusted, brushed and scrubbed to the background white noise that was Leo's whining. Ernie had given up and gone to sit under the willow tree. Beth flung another bucket of black grime-saturated water over the big plant in the back garden and filled the bucket up again from the outside tap. She straightened her back and watched a couple of cabbage white butterflies dance around the out-of-control purple buddleia before disappearing. It was a lovely sunny day and it did seem to make the countryside come alive, even the horses in the field looked a bit more frisky today. She would have liked to have been sat outside in the garden – even in its overgrown state, it was more welcoming than the inside of the cottage – but she had work to do, so lounging in the garden would have to wait. She picked up her half-full bucket and went back inside. She stopped in the living-room doorway and surveyed the room. It looked a little better than it had done. It certainly smelled better. The floor had sturdy-looking floorboards that now looked a dark oak colour and Beth could already start to visualize what they would look like offset against white walls and with a cosy rug placed on top of them. Leo was sitting on the window ledge looking thoroughly bored.

'One more mop over and we'll get some lunch. Okay?'

They decided to try out the delights of the pub for a change and see if they had a less heart-disease-inducing menu than the tearoom. As it turned out, it wasn't too bad; not a gastro pub but good honest home-cooked food, and there were two salads on the menu. It was the right weather for salad, with the gentle breeze and persistent sunshine, and what better way to eat it than in the pub garden. There was a lonely swing there that Leo made a run for and he only got off it when his food arrived.

Petra, the landlady, came out with a third plate and a knife and fork and set it down next to Beth.

'You don't mind, do you?' asked Petra. As Beth was about to protest, Ernie joined her on the bench seat and started to tuck into his pie and mash dinner.

'No, it's fine,' said Beth, with a smile.

While they were eating, a small boy with a mop of black hair came outside and stood hugging a football. As Petra ferried past another round of meals he asked her something.

'No, Denis, you can ask him yourself.'

The boy sidled over towards the table where Beth, Leo and Ernie were eating and stood a few feet away, hugging his football tighter still. Leo looked up and the boy smiled.

'I'm Denis, you wanna play football on the green?'

'Yeah,' said Leo, shovelling the last piece of chicken into his mouth and clattering his cutlery down onto his plate and the remaining salad. 'Can I go, Mum, pleeeeeeease?' said Leo, as he stood up.

'I'm not sure,' said Beth, craning her neck to see if she could see enough of the green from where she was sitting.

'He'll be fine,' came Petra's gentle voice behind her. 'Denis is my son. Everyone knows him and he plays there all the time. People round here keep a look out for each other.' Beth didn't like to say that it was the people round here that bothered her the most.

Beth wasn't sure but Leo was already pushing back his chair and his face was a contortion of pleading expressions.

'Okay, just for a few minutes.' But Leo was gone before she had finished the sentence. Ernie finished his food, laid his knife and fork dead centre on his clean plate, and left without a word.

Beth sat alone and looked around her. Everyone else was chatting, lots of groups of people and couples. She had no idea who was local and who was a tourist. She wasn't sure what category she was in. She didn't feel like she belonged here but she had nowhere else to go.

Petra's voice broke into her thoughts. 'I'll watch the boys if you want to get on. I've seen you working at the cottage.'

'Cleaning mainly but it's okay. I'll get Leo to give me a hand.'

Petra raised an eyebrow. 'A boy that cleans?'

Beth laughed. 'Well, no, not exactly.'

'Then let him play. Look, he's having fun with Denis.' Beth watched as the boys raced after the ball and wherever they kicked it they seemed to be celebrating a goal. It was good to see Leo smiling and Beth realized she hadn't seen him do that much since they'd been in Dumbleford.

'Okay, if you're sure.' Beth headed back to the cottage for round two of cleaning the living room, her first step at conquering the cottage and, if she felt very brave, she might blitz the bathroom too.

Beth switched her phone to music and with some of her favourite teenage tunes belting out she got to work. She found it was a lot easier to clean when you were singing and also doing the odd dance move with the duster. She was giving a particularly energetic rendition of 'Is This The Way To Amarillo', including overenthusiastic waving of thumbs over her shoulder, when she thought she saw something out of the window. She didn't hear anything because it wasn't possible over her screeching.

Beth turned the music down and crept to the window: she couldn't see anyone but she suddenly felt self-conscious and smoothed down her hair. She went to the front door, just to check, and there on the doorstep was a black kettle barbecue. Beth looked around but there was nobody about, not even Ernie. The barbecue was a little battered and whilst she was pondering what it was doing there she lifted up the big dome-shaped lid. On the very clean grill inside was a sticky note, which read:

'I was chucking stuff out and thought of you – Jack'

Blunt as ever, she thought. She picked up the note and saw that under the grill was a bag of charcoal and she smiled. The barbecue looked quite old but it would definitely do the job and there was nothing quite like eating outdoors to pick up your spirits. It was a nice gesture. Perhaps the villagers weren't so bad after all, even Jack.

Chapter Nine

After they'd eaten as many barbecued sausages as they could manage, Beth and Leo had settled down for their first night in Willow Cottage. Camping stuff wasn't exactly ideal to be sleeping on but it was better than the bare floorboards and, despite all of Leo's complaining, he was now actually enjoying the indoor camping experience. The day she had left London Beth had loaded the car at high speed and once again she acknowledged she had grabbed an odd assortment of things, including the camping stuff that had been waiting to go back in the loft, her mother's cuckoo clock, her glue gun, and a large canvas photo of Leo as a baby as well as a few items that would actually be useful to them. The thin camping mattresses weren't the height of comfort but they would do until Beth had managed to order some beds.

The room was cool, but not cold, so they snuggled into their sleeping bags and chatted for a while as the upturned torch lit up the cracked ceiling and gave a mystical glow to the room.

'Good day?' asked Beth.

'Okay.'

'Are you and Denis friends?'

'Kinda, I guess. It's cool that he lives in a pub; he gets fizzy drinks and crisps whenever he likes!'

'Mmm, does he go to the local school?'

'Yeah, he's a year older than me but he says we'll be in the same class ... and I can sit next to him if I want.'

'That's kind. So are you liking it here now?' asked Beth, shifting a little in her sleeping bag like a fat maggot so that she could see Leo's face better.

He pouted as he thought for a bit. 'I like Denis and Doris and I like the food at the tearoom but,' he paused and took a deep breath. 'I miss my friends back home and the computer and my tablet and my Lego and my other toys and climbing club and ...'

Beth could feel her heart squeezing with every new item added to the list. 'Once we're a bit more settled we can get some new things and I'm sure there are some local clubs we could find out about.'

Leo didn't answer. He was chewing his thumbnail and looked like he was pondering his mother's response. Outside it started to rain, the droplets making a soothing pattering sound against the old, but now very clean glass.

'Could we get a big computer? Like the one Nick had and wouldn't let me use? And a massive telly that does everything?' Leo was staring at his mother, without blinking.

'Not right away but we'll see,' said Beth, ruffling his hair. 'I think it's time us indoor campers got some sleep, don't you?'

Leo started to settle and then he sat bolt upright. 'Did you bring a telly?'

Beth shook her head, 'No, sorry. They were all screwed to the wall, remember?'

'No telly?' Leo's eyes were wide with horror.

'Only until we get things sorted out. Okay?'

Leo was already shaking his head and muttering to himself. 'No telly ...' He looked around the room at the shadows he was making as he moved. 'There aren't any ghosts living here, are there?' Leo looked pensive. 'You know, like Wilf or Elsie?'

'No, don't be silly. They were lovely people, why would they haunt this place?'

'Dunno, it's really old and old places always have ghosts.'

'Only if you're really lucky,' said Beth, zipping up his sleeping bag.

'Ok-ay,' intoned Leo doubtfully and he burrowed down further into his sleeping bag until only the very top of his head was visible. Beth leaned over and kissed him and then set about trying to get herself comfortable. She had worked hard on cleaning the living room and felt better for it. The builder and the electrician were scheduled to get started on the essentials list in a few days' time. Things were starting to head in the right direction. Beth closed her eyes and began to drift off to sleep as the rain outside started to pelt out a soothing rhythm on the window.

Beth wasn't sure how much later it was when she stirred and brushed something off her face as another splosh landed on her forehead. She opened her eyes to see a steady stream of drips coming through the ceiling above her. She shuffled quickly out of the way and out of her sleeping bag. She turned to look at Leo. He looked like he was dry and still sound asleep. Beth clenched her teeth; this was irritating but it wasn't the end of the world. She grabbed the bucket and stuck it under the drip. Then she found a bin bag, made three holes in it and shoved it over her head; the last thing she wanted was soggy pyjamas. She tied another one around her head like a turban, popped her sockless feet into her boots, picked up her keys and the torch and crept out of the cottage.

Her mission to the car was successful. She was coming back with the pop-up tent as a rain-hood clad Shirley was shuffling past. Shirley stopped and so did Beth and they eyed each other suspiciously.

Shirley shook her head slowly, 'Ahh. Mittens …' she said.

'Crazy!' they both said simultaneously and then scuttled off in opposite directions.

Beth was relieved to see that Leo was exactly where she'd left him and was still asleep. She tiptoed round the living room trying to find a dry patch. She wasn't sure why she was tiptoeing because probably even a volcano wouldn't wake Leo right now. Behind the door seemed like a good bet as the floorboards were dry and the ceiling looked free of cracks.

Beth released the pop-up tent from the confines of its bag and a bright orange three-man tent instantly appeared. It didn't take long to drag over her bedroll and sleeping bag. That approach seemed to work so she grabbed hold of Leo's bedroll and dragged it, with him in residence, all the way inside the tent.

She felt a huge sense of satisfaction at not being beaten by Willow Cottage as she settled down to sleep for the second time.

Carly was tired and grumpy when the taxi finally deposited them in a farmyard a few miles from Newport, Gwent. A middle-aged man introduced himself, took one of the bags from Fergus and produced a rather large torch that emitted an impressive beam of light for them to follow. The man was wearing wellies. Carly was wearing her sparkly sandals, which had been very comfy on the train but were spectacularly inappropriate for trudging across an uneven grassed field that was liberally scattered with sheep poo. The torch didn't reveal many sheep – only the odd small group here and there. Surely there was no way those few animals could have made all this? There was poo everywhere. Carly looked like she was undertaking some elaborate dance as she tried to keep up and find a poo-free spot for every step.

In her mind, Carly was holding on tight to the treehouse pictures she'd seen in the magazine. Every bounce of the torch beam only revealed yet more undulations and poo. They followed a line of trees until a rough path appeared and at last a wooden structure was just visible through the trees. Carly was grinning as she felt her right sandal slide quickly through something moist. It didn't matter, she wasn't going to let a silly thing like sheep poo spoil this weekend of luxury. The man handed them a much smaller version of his torch, with a beam that was pathetic in comparison, and bid them a good night.

Fergus kissed Carly seductively and all thoughts of poo were forgotten. They giggled their way up the rustic spiral staircase and onto a platform where they could get a good look at the treehouse. It was rather shed-like with moss on the roof and French windows. Carly kicked off her dirty shoes, Fergus opened the door and she stepped inside. She looked around as Fergus joined her and shut the door.

It was small inside, but she had expected that; it was up a tree after all. It smelled of wood but everything in it was made of natural wood so, again, no surprises there. However, what she hadn't expected was what looked like a bench seat from a caravan circa 1985 and bunk beds. She'd been looking forward to spending the weekend with Fergus on top of her but bunk beds was not what she'd pictured. She turned round to gauge Fergus's expression but he was already merrily lighting an array of used candles that lined the narrow shelves and the lanterns that hung from the ceiling. She waited until he'd finished lighting his current lantern and blew out the match.

'So, what do you think?' she signed, trying very hard to smile.

'Fantastic,' said Fergus, his smile almost as bright as the farmer's torch beam had been. Oh, great, thought Carly, as she attempted to contain her disappointment.

Fergus produced a bottle of champagne from his bag and Carly's mood lifted a fraction. A couple of glasses later she was starting to relax and there was something terribly romantic about signing by candlelight. Fergus's classic features were enhanced by the flattering glow. 'Big day tomorrow,' he told her. 'Let's get some sleep.'

Carly fished her wash bag out and then looked around, slightly stumped as to where the washroom was. Fergus steered her towards a makeshift sink in the corner replete with plastic washing-up bowl. They washed and cleaned their teeth together and Carly searched deep to find something special in this but she failed. All she could think about, now, was where was the toilet? Was it all the way back at the farmhouse? In which case she really wished the farmer had mentioned it.

As if anticipating her next question Fergus pointed outside. 'I'm going to check out the loo. You coming?' Of all the offers she'd hoped to hear this weekend, this was definitely not near the top of her list.

'Yeah, great.'

On the other side of the decked platform were three little steps down to what looked like a wooden cupboard. Fergus opened the door and shone the torch inside. Carly's first thought had been pretty accurate as it was barely bigger than a cupboard. Notices lined the walls, explaining how the toilet system worked and the dos and don'ts of using the facility. But the main thing that drew her attention was the toilet seat that Fergus had now lifted, and the unpleasant smell that was emanating from an oval hole it had revealed in a long piece of wood. Carly's eyes searched frantically for a button, a lever or something that would indicate a flushing mechanism of some sort.

'Where's the flush?' she asked. There was a bucket on the seat next to the hole. It was a rather lovely handmade bucket with rope handles. Inside was sawdust and a wooden scoop. Fergus grinned and picked up the scoop.

Oh shit, thought Carly.

The sun was up early and lit up the treehouse like a Christmas lantern, which might have been lovely if she hadn't been awake half the night thanks to the noise of sheep. Who knew sheep could be so loud? They had baa'd their way throughout the night as Carly had tossed and turned as much as she could in her narrow bunk bed whilst Fergus slept like a baby. One of the benefits of being deaf was peaceful sleep, thought Carly. She took in some deep breaths. She was dying for a cup of tea but any liquid would mean, at some point, she would have to use the toilet and she was planning to avoid that unless completely necessary, i.e. her life depended on it. Right now having a catheter fitted felt like a good idea.

Carly had to remain positive. This may not have been the luxury break she had hoped for but she could see why Fergus had booked it. It was a world away from the hustle and bustle of London and they were both outdoor people so she could understand the appeal. Although maybe Fergus was more of an outdoor person than she was. And, she thought, if we've got a big wedding to save up for, then the budget option was the sensible choice. She was still convinced that today he was going to ask her to be his wife. The question was exactly when and where would that happen?

Beth woke as the loudest and oddest noise filled the room.

'What the f—' She came to in an instant and was momentarily freaked out by the strange orange glow the world had suddenly taken on but, remembering she was in the tent, she concentrated her senses on what the hellish noise was. It soon all became apparent as she thrust her head out of the tent to see a torrent of water heading her way and a very large hole in the living-room ceiling where dust-like debris was still billowing out.

'Shit!'

'Mum!' admonished a sleepy Leo with a giggle.

There was no way of saving themselves from the water as it meticulously seeped into everything. Beth and Leo scrambled out of the tent and splashed through the huge puddle. Beth went to open the window to let out some of the dust and sent Leo into the hallway, which seemed a safer place for him to survey the devastation while she ventured over to study the large hole in the ceiling. She skirted round the big pile of soggy bits of ceiling and boards. Beth peered up through the jagged hole and was amazed to see a glint of sunlight. She blinked hard. She could see all the way up to the roof. Beth looked at the fat sodden pile of wreckage at her feet: this was from two ceilings and a floor. So much for yesterday's cleaning efforts, she thought.

'There's a hole all the way through the cottage,' she said slowly, pointing a disbelieving finger above her head.

'Cool,' said Leo. 'Like a giant doughnut!'

The leaky roof had let in water, which must have gathered at a weak spot in the loft that then brought down the bedroom ceiling, which in turn brought down the one in the living room. Whichever way she looked at it, this did not look good.

A very soggy Beth and Leo shuffled out of the cottage. Each wrapped in a black bin bag, they looked like rejects from a penny-pinching marathon. Outside they could hear jolly voices; the sun was up and had already set to work on drying out the village with the exception of their front room but it still felt early, especially for a Saturday. Beth checked her watch: it was 6:40. Without speaking they headed towards the voices that were coming from the village green. In the morning sun it seemed somehow richer in colour, the neat grass sparkling from the moisture left by the overnight rain. In the middle was a large marquee, resplendent in off-white, and stalls were being put up all around it.

Although it wasn't cold, a damp Leo started to shiver. They shuffled closer to watch as another stall was erected in lightning-quick time as Jack put together the frame and another couple of older men pulled the canopy over the top. Jack must have sensed he was being watched as he turned to look directly at Beth. She felt like she'd awoken from a daze as she realized what she must look like, so she started to herd Leo back towards the pub car park and the safety of the car.

'Beth! Wait up!' called Jack, as he jogged towards them. This was the last thing she needed. She found herself studying his flexing biceps as he ran and mentally gave herself a shake. What was she thinking?

Jack joined them and his eyes scanned the wet pyjama-clad pair. 'What the hell happened to you?'

'The ceiling came crashing down!' said Leo, who appeared to have forgotten about the shivering and was now bouncing up and down.

'Christ, were you in there? Are you okay?' Jack asked, concerned.

'Yeah, we were sleeping underneath it ...' said Beth and Jack looked alarmed. 'But then we moved because of the drips so it didn't fall on us.'

'That was lucky, you could have been killed if a beam had come down. What were you doing sleeping in there?' Jack's voice was harsh.

'Don't get cross with me,' said Beth. 'It's my cottage, I can sleep in it if I want to.' Who the hell was Jack Selby to tell her what she could and couldn't do? She'd had enough of that from Nick. She didn't need a virtual stranger doing it too. Doris bounded over but after a few sniffs of Leo's pyjama leg she dashed off back towards the marquee, probably one of the few structures that made her feel small.

Jack huffed and ran his fingers through his hair. 'What are you going to do now?'

Beth shrugged. 'Go back to the B&B, I expect.' And she started to head off again with Leo in tow.

'The B&B is full. So is the pub and so are most places. It's August bank holiday weekend,' said Jack, the frustration evident in the tone of his voice.

Bugger, thought Beth.

'Here,' said Jack, tossing her a set of keys, which she instinctively caught. 'Go round to mine, get yourselves showered and changed and something to eat. I've got at least another hour here setting up the Summer Fete.' He waved a thumb at the green behind him and the small group of men of varying ages that had formed a small crowd and were gawping in their direction.

Beth hated being told what to do, she'd had enough of it and now it made her hackles rise. 'No, we're fine, thanks.' She threw back the keys.

'Don't be daft. Look at the two of you. Otherwise, what are you going to do?'

Beth didn't have an answer. Her brain sped up but nothing plausible sprang to mind. 'We could dry out in the car with the car heater on.'

'Then what?' Jack put a hand on his hip and frowned.

Beth shook her head. 'Oh, give me the sodding keys then,' she mumbled, snatching them back.

'Have you got a telly?' asked Leo, raising his head hopefully.

'Yep,' said Jack, looking a little puzzled by the question. 'It's the cream cottage, just up there,' he pointed to the road that led out of the village. 'Next to the Old Police House. You can't miss it.'

'Thanks,' said Beth gratefully, but Jack was already jogging back to join the ogling group on the green.

'Morning,' waved Beth. She might as well brazen it out. There were mumbled responses and the group dispersed.

Jack gave a fleeting smile as she and Leo scuttled past.

'Can we go to the fete, Mum? Please?'

'Yes, I think that will be just the thing to cheer us up.' She'd had enough of Willow Cottage for the time being, that was for certain.

Chapter Ten

Carly breathed in the damp air as she stood outside the treehouse and tried to stay calm. 'What do you mean we're going on a hike?' asked Carly. 'Everything is soaked after last night's colossal rainfall.'

'Yes, but it'll be fun.'

'No, it won't.' Carly needed the toilet but there was no way she was using the khazi, as it had now been termed much to Fergus's amusement.

'Come on, Carls. It's sunny and once you get in the fresh air …'

'Fresh air? It smells of sheep poo! Where exactly are we going?' Perhaps there was a purpose to the hike, thought Carly, and her interest improved slightly.

'Dunno,' shrugged Fergus. 'Thought we could have a wander …'

'And what about tonight?'

'Tonight?'

'Yes, what's happening tonight?' asked Carly, tilting her head in expectation.

'Dunno. Find a pub? What do you want to do?'

'So you've got nothing planned, then?' Carly leaned forward slightly as she spoke, keen to catch every nuance in Fergus's response.

'Nope. It's a free and easy weekend.' Fergus gave a toothy boyish grin.

'Grrr!' said Carly, there wasn't a sign for that but her expression said it all. 'Well, I'm not staying here. It's not luxury, there's no gourmet food, and you're … you're not doing anything!' She ran out of steam.

Fergus signed his reply very slowly. 'It's a treehouse.'

'I know it's a sodding treehouse, and I've had enough of it and its stinking khazi!'

Carly stomped back inside, threw the few things she'd unpacked into her bag and stormed out with Fergus close behind. She was muttering to herself as she reached the bottom step and diligently stomped across the field trying to avoid the sheep poo.

'Please don't walk off, Carls. I hate it when I can't see what you're saying.'

She turned briefly. 'I'm going home!' she shouted, and felt her foot skid as she stepped on a fresh sheep poo. She heard Fergus start to laugh behind her and that sent her annoyance sky-high and drove her on across the fields and back to the farm. He was such a child and she was losing all hope of him ever growing up.

Carly was pleased to find that the farmer was very accommodating and happily called her a taxi for the station. She spent the twenty minutes she had to wait obsessively wiping her sandals on the grass nearby in a vain attempt to rid them of the poo. There was no sign of Fergus. He had given up the chase after the first field.

Thankfully, when the taxi arrived it was driven by a rare breed of taxi driver – an unchatty one that delivered her to the station in virtual silence where she stared in disbelief at the travel chaos. Apparently flash floods had caused all sorts of problems and there were loads of cancellations. She joined a long queue and eventually got her turn in front of a very stressed-looking woman.

'I want to get to London.'

'Not from here, not for a while. Sorry. The rain and floods

have taken down trees and there's been a passenger incident on the London line.' The woman pulled a sympathetic face, probably in the hope that this piece of information would stop Carly from ranting at her. 'Bank holiday weekend,' she added, as if that explained the suicide. At least my weekend isn't as bad as that poor soul's, thought Carly.

'So where can I get to?' asked Carly, realising as soon as she'd said it what a stupid question it was.

'Um, trains to Gloucester are running okay …'

'Gloucester? I've a friend near there. Thank you!' Carly hurried back to the departures board.

Beth and Leo were fresh from the shower and sitting at Jack's kitchen table munching on muesli when he walked in. Leo had a towel wrapped round him and Beth was wearing a Jedi dressing gown that was far too big for her but had been conveniently hanging on the back of the bathroom door.

'Sorry, I didn't think to go back for dry clothes,' she said by way of explanation.

Jack was suddenly frowning at Beth, making her look down, which was when she realized the dressing gown was gaping open. She quickly wrapped it around herself with a firm motion and tied the belt securely. 'Whoops,' Beth said as she felt her cheeks colour and she had to look away. They stayed in uncomfortable silence for a few moments, both wondering what to say next.

'The stalls are up, so I slipped away. How are you two feeling?' Jack gabbled as he got himself a glass of filtered water from a jug in the fridge.

'Better, thanks,' said Beth. 'Oh, and thanks for giving us the barbecue, that was kind of you.'

'No problem.' Beth noticed Jack almost smiled before looking away.

'You've got a huge TV!' said Leo, shovelling in another spoonful of muesli.

'Not that we've had a nose around,' said Beth, her voice quickening up. Obviously they had had a good nose around. 'It's a lovely cottage, Jack. Bigger inside than it looks from the front.'

'It wasn't a lot better than Wil—' he stopped himself. 'Than your place, well, before the ceilings fell in anyway.' Beth rolled her eyes. 'I had to rip everything out, refit the kitchen and bathroom and replaster everywhere.'

'You need a strong wrist action for that, don't you?' asked Beth innocently.

'Mmm, yeah.' Jack blinked hard, cleared his throat and carried on. 'The only thing I got someone in for was the electrics.'

Beth looked around the sleek and compact fitted kitchen. 'You did this?'

'Yeah, Simon gave me a hand. He's a carpenter by trade but earns more working at the supermarket, if you can work that one out.'

'Nick was rubbish at DIY,' said Leo, without looking up from his bowl.

'Nick is my ex,' explained Beth. 'He was rubbish at a lot of things.'

'Right.' Jack looked uncomfortable. 'The toughest bit was getting up the flooring in here.' Jack was rummaging in a drawer as he spoke and he pulled out some photographs. 'They'd used some sort of super-strong adhesive and every tile shattered and every bit of adhesive had to be chipped off the floor. It took me days.'

Beth wasn't listening, she was thinking. She didn't like asking for help but this was an opportunity she couldn't pass up. 'Do you fancy getting a bit more involved?'

Jack looked startled at the proposition. Beth held his gaze. He rubbed his chin and looked from a smiling Beth to Leo, who was helping himself to another bowl of muesli. Jack fiddled with the photographs in his hands.

'Thanks … and everything but I'm not …'

'Oh, I'd pay you,' said Beth, 'I wouldn't expect you to do it for free. It's not a favour I'm asking; it would be a business arrangement.'

Jack's frown deepened. 'You're a lovely, um, woman, but you know I'm not ready for a relationship … or business arrangement … of any kind right now or anytime soon.'

Beth looked momentarily confused until she realized how what she'd said may have sounded. 'Oh, God, no!' She got a fit of nervous giggles. 'I meant more involved in Willow Cottage. Not with me!'

'Oh, I see.' Jack looked thankful.

'Sorry. That sounded okay in my head.' Beth giggled as her nerves took over. Leo rolled his eyes and carried on eating.

'No. My mistake,' said Jack, trying to look anywhere but at Beth.

'To be clear. I'd pay you to help at Willow Cottage. Nothing else.' Her cheeks were burning and she hated to think what colour they had turned. At least the heat might help to dry off her hair, which was hanging loosely around her shoulders.

'Right, of course. Sure, I'd be happy to help.' Jack gulped down the rest of his water.

Beth wasn't sure if Jack meant it but, if it was embarrassment at his mistake that had made him agree, she was okay with that as Jack clearly knew what he was doing when it came to renovation.

'What are they?' asked Beth, pointing at the photos, desperate to change the subject. Jack looked down too and jolted his head as if he was just noticing them for the first time.

'They're before and after pictures of this place.' He stepped closer and leaning over Beth's shoulder he placed the photographs on the table in pairs. Beth could smell his aftershave and the closeness of him made her pulse quicken. What on earth was going on? Perhaps being naked under the bathrobe was setting off some sort of primal alarm. She tried to concentrate on the pictures in front of her. She reached out a hand to pick up the after photo of the living room as Jack reached across and her hand connected with his forearm. Some sort of zing made them both spring apart. Beth looked up and then realized how close her face was to Jack's. There was a moment where they both froze.

'I like your wood …' started Beth, realizing her mouth had gone dry. She pointed to the driftwood shelf in the picture. 'It's really lovely.'

'I can give you one if you'd like?'

Beth's eyebrows shot up and Jack's face registered the overtone of the otherwise innocent conversation. Their eyes widened at the same time.

'Anyway, I had better get back …' Jack was looking awkward as he moved quickly towards the front door.

'Oh, and us too.' Beth stood up, clutching the robe around her, and beckoned Leo to his feet. He stood up, holding his towel with one hand and still spooning food into his mouth with the other as he inched round the table. 'We need to get the tent dried out.'

Jack opened his mouth to speak but nothing came out.

'It's a long story,' said Beth, as she squeezed passed him. 'Thanks for the use of the shower and for breakfast. We really appreciate it.' She took the spoon from Leo and dropped it in the sink as they passed. 'We'll wash these and drop them back sometime,' she said, indicating the bathrobe and towel as she slipped out of the front door and let out a sigh of relief. It was still early so hopefully not too many people would see them make the dash back to the cottage but anything was better than being trapped in an innuendo nightmare with Jack.

A couple of hours later Denis called for Leo and the two disappeared to play in the pub garden as the green was fully occupied with lots of people rushing about with boxes, cakes, plants and large vegetables. Thankfully, Kyle the builder had heeded her plea and arrived early and imparted the glorious news that he thought the ceilings might be covered by her insurance. A few lengthy calls later and it was agreed that she could get quotes for the water damage and an assessor would visit the following week.

Beth felt surprisingly good walking Kyle through her priorities and from his previous visit he was able to confirm what he could and couldn't do for the money she was prepared to pay. Kyle did some makeshift repairs to the roof so it was temporarily watertight, and promised to drop the quote round for the insurance work in the next couple of days.

Beth went out into the back garden to check on the progress of the tent, sleeping bags and bedrolls that were drying out nicely on the improvised washing line which was one of the bushes. She thought she heard a noise like someone knocking on a door and, suspecting that Leo was back, went back into the house and opened the front door.

'Surprise!' said an overenthusiastic Carly as she threw her arms round Beth and squeezed her.

Beth stood rooted to the spot. Her mind went a complete blank for a moment, perhaps she was in shock. Eventually Beth hugged her back. 'Wow, um, this is a surprise. Where's Fergus?' she asked, looking behind Carly.

'Huge disaster. Treehouse was exactly that. It was a hut in a tree in a field and there was no proposal so … bloody hell, this is a shithole!' she said, suddenly noticing the hallway she'd walked into. She glanced into the living room. 'What the hell happened?' Carly swung round and it was as if she went into slow motion giving Beth time to observe every detail; she was immaculate from her sleek dark glossy hair, to her perfectly pedicured toes. She was wearing a petite summery dress and casual jacket and looked like an advert for summer. Beth on the other hand had dried-by-itself hair with roots that were well past the 'need touching up stage', was wearing a now rather tatty Ted Baker blouse, thanks to its encounter with the cottage's overgrown shrubbery, and a pair of cheap flip flops. She wiggled her unpainted toes self-consciously.

Beth didn't like the feeling that came over her. It was a mixture of embarrassment and jealousy and it wasn't pleasant to admit to. The contrast between her and Carly was now a chasm whereas only a few weeks ago they had been like two perfectly fashioned peas in an organic designer pod. Beth found she was grinding her teeth again, so she stopped.

'Let's go to the pub and I'll explain,' said Beth, putting an arm around Carly and steering her out of the front door. Carly put on her sunglasses and didn't argue. As they walked towards the pub, Beth sniffed the air. 'Can you smell poo?'

Two large glasses of wine later, both women were feeling a whole lot better having offloaded all of their woes to the other. Beth was feeling more settled in Carly's company and now felt bad for having had her earlier pang of jealousy. It was lovely to see Carly even if it was unexpected. And at least now Carly had seen Willow Cottage in all its awfulness she would appreciate its transformation when it was eventually renovated.

'I've missed this so much, Beth. I've missed *you*.' Carly looked teary as she reached out a hand.

'I've missed you too.' Beth gave Carly another hug. She'd missed having someone to talk to that knew her inside and out. 'Right, you get yourself another glass of wine and I'll take Leo and Denis to investigate this Summer Fete. That should buy us some more chatting time.'

The boys were like pinballs at the fingertips of the legendary pinball wizard as they charged around the village green from stall to stall. A lot more children seemed to have appeared, some of whom Denis knew, and before long there was a small gang of children dominating one stall at a time. All the old favourites were there; Hook A Duck, Coconut Shy, and Splat the Rat as well as newer ones like face painting, temporary tattoos and Football Penalty Shootout. The latter was a big hit with the boys and, while they were rejoining the lengthy queue for yet another go, Beth went to investigate the marquee. She walked across the spongy grass taking in the pale azure sky and the sound of people laughing and generally having a good time. Beth was enjoying the village green fete, you didn't get anything quite like it in London. The marquee was huge inside and had been sectioned off for different competition items; the results of the best cake were being announced as Beth made her way nearer the front and tried to ignore how uncomfortably warm it was.

A woman in a floaty top and leather trousers was tapping a microphone. 'So, in third place … Mr Pleasance with his giant pineapple cake. One to rival Mr Plumley's marrow,' snorted the woman at her own joke. Mr Pleasance happily accepted his third-place rosette and returned to the crowd amidst lots of backslapping. 'Second place goes to the wonderful gooey chocolate cake by Mrs Oldham.' A lengthy round of applause followed as a miffed Mrs Oldham, putting on her best valiant-loser face, accepted her rosette and prize. 'And the worthy winner of Dumbleford's Summer Fete Best Cake Competition is …' The woman left too much of a pause and the crowd started heckling. 'Mrs Pritchard and her 1960s cherry and almond cake!' Beth was wondering what qualified it as 1960s when a violently coloured swirly patterned cake was lifted up high to whoops of applause.

To Beth's surprise, the person that collected the red rosette and glinting glass trophy was none other than Shirley the bag lady. Beth joined in the enthusiastic clapping as Shirley took the microphone. 'It's also a proper 1960s cake inside, if you know what I mean! Pound a slice, come and get it!' Before she could hand back the microphone there was a surge of people towards her.

Beth was laughing as she left the marquee and on checking her watch realized that the time had sped by and she had left

Carly on her own for a lot longer than she'd intended. She found the now-penniless boys who were sitting under a vast gnarled oak tree swapping sweets they had won, and the three of them made their way back into the pub.

Leo and Denis disappeared out into the garden and Beth strode towards where she had left Carly. She could hear Carly's raucous laughter before she saw her and it made her smile. The small table now had two empty wine bottles on it and someone else was sitting there with Carly draped over them. For a moment Beth thought that Fergus had turned up until she took a proper look. Jack had his arm around Carly and she was going in for a kiss.

Chapter Eleven

'Carly!' said Beth, her voice sharp.

Carly spun in Beth's direction with an exaggerated movement. With slow blinks she looked at Beth until something registered.

'Beth! This is … um … what was your name again?' She swung precariously back towards Jack who stopped her falling on him with one hand whilst holding the pub table steady with the other.

'I know who it is.' Beth was trying to suppress the annoyance that was rapidly developing within her.

'He's lov-erly,' cooed Carly whilst she stroked his arm in a deliberate action.

'I'd like to know what he's planning on doing with my drunk friend?' Beth retorted. Jack let go of Carly as if she were a lit firework.

As the accusation slowly registered, Carly looked hurt. 'I'm not dunk!' she protested as she slowly slid towards the floor.

Jack was looking blindly from one woman to the other as if he'd just been teleported there. 'I was just …'

'For someone that wasn't looking for a relationship a few hours ago you've sure as hell come round to the idea quick!' Beth stepped forward and grabbed Carly by one arm and hauled her into a standing position. 'Come on! We're leaving now.'

Carly wobbled on unsteady legs, grinned inanely at Jack and was towed away.

They stumbled into the sunshine and the mêlée of the Summer Fete quickly surrounded them.

'Ooooh, coconuts!' squealed Carly, veering off.

Now that the flash of temper had subsided Beth wasn't entirely sure where she was heading. Having separated Carly and Jack she wasn't certain why she'd interfered but in that moment it had seemed like the only thing to do.

'Beth, hang on!' called out Jack, jogging up to them and catching Carly mid-sway.

Beth raised her eyebrows. 'Shall I leave you to it?' she asked, her question aimed pointedly at Jack.

'I'm fine, really fine. Oh, hello, it's *you* again!' Carly grinned broadly, full of surprise at the sight of Jack keeping her upright.

'She needs to sober up. Help me take her back to my place, will you?' asked Jack.

'And how safe will she be there?'

'Bloody hell, Beth, I'm trying to help here.'

Beth didn't really have another option. She couldn't see Carly being able to crawl into her tent even though it purported to be a three-man version; she and Leo hadn't had enough space.

'You always have the answer, don't you, Jack Selby?' Beth was indignant.

'You got a better one?' He was frowning at her.

'That's not the point.' People were slowing down and stopping to listen. 'Right, fine. Come on, then.' She stood on the other side of Carly, put an arm round her and began to frogmarch her towards Jack's.

'Carly, walk straight!' Beth ordered.

'She can't, she's drunk!' said Jack. Then he leaned across to try to catch Beth's eye. 'Does she have a problem?' he asked, his voice softer.

Beth halted and Carly swung forward precariously. 'Are you calling my friend an alcoholic?'

'No, I'm asking if she …'

'Ooooh, shops,' said Carly as they were waiting to cross the road at the far end of the village.

'A butcher's, a gift shop and a dress shop for anyone that wants to look like a pantomime dame. *Come on*,' said Beth, surging ahead.

'A bit harsh,' said Jack, evidently trying to lighten the somewhat frosty mood.

'Ooooh, I like panto,' slurred Carly swaying unsteadily.

'Oh no you don't,' Jack replied, which set Carly off into a fit of giggles. Was he still flirting with her?

Beth stopped in the middle of the road and leaned round a wobbling Carly to speak to Jack. 'Look, in case you hadn't realized, this is my best friend Carly Wilson. She is almost engaged to a wonderful man called Fergus. I do not want you sticking your oar in or anything else come to that!' Beth held Jack's glare.

'Traffic!' he said, forcing Carly and Beth onto the pavement as a stream of cars trundled towards them. It was difficult to have a conversation with someone swaying in the middle so Beth focused on moving Carly along as quickly as possible.

'It's like a three-legged race,' said Carly, 'but with, one, two, four … *lots* of legs!'

Once inside Jack's cottage, an overexcited Doris greeted them with slobbery kisses so Jack left Beth to cope with Carly while he escorted Doris into the garden.

'Have a lie-down and see if you can sleep it off,' said Beth, guiding Carly onto the sofa.

'Ooooh, look, pretty shelf,' said Carly, reaching out a hand towards the driftwood and sideswiping a small wooden box that was nestled there, sending it clattering onto the floor. 'Whoopsie,' she said with a giggle, as Beth dashed to rescue the item.

Beth crouched down and retrieved the box, which had an intricate inlaid design on its lid, and as she picked it up a metal disc fell out. 'Bugger,' said Beth, picking that up too and trying to work out how to fit it back into the recess in the lid.

'Why doesn't this stereo work?' complained Carly from the other side of the room, where she was pressing all the buttons on a black box.

'Because it's a printer,' announced Jack as he came in from the garden, leaving a disgruntled Doris barking behind him.

'But we need moooosic!' whined Carly, swaying precariously as Jack expertly steered her onto the sofa.

'Great idea. You lie down there and I'll sort out some music.'

Beth was frantically shaking her head at Jack. The last thing they needed was an uncoordinated Carly pogoing around the living room; nothing would be safe.

'I think I've got "Is This The Way To Amarillo" somewhere,' he said, raising an eyebrow in Beth's direction. Beth felt her cheeks instantly colour up – so he had seen her the day he left the barbecue. He joined Beth and took the small box from her.

'I'm sorry, is it broken?' she asked, screwing up her face and hoping the box wasn't as expensive as it looked.

Jack shook his head. 'Completely ruined.'

'Oh dear, is it?' Beth bit her lip as she took a closer look.

'No, the humidifier has popped out, that's all,' he said flatly, expertly replacing the disc and returning the box to the shelf. 'It's a cigar box.' Beth looked suitably surprised. 'It was my grandfather's.' They stood and looked at the box for a moment until they were interrupted by a large snore from Carly.

'Come on, let's leave Sleeping Beauty and get a coffee,' said Jack, leaving the room.

Beth sent a quick text to Fergus to let him know where Carly was and that she was okay, which was stretching the truth slightly. He replied immediately.

Thanks B. You're a ★. Was worried.

Jack was busying himself with his coffee maker when Beth came into the kitchen. 'I only have decaff. Is that okay?' he asked, holding up a pod.

'Yeah, fine. I'm sorry if I was a bit overprotective before but I meant what I said about Carly and her boyfriend,' said Beth.

'About them being almost engaged? What is that exactly?' asked Jack.

Beth was finding Jack particularly irritating today. 'Her long-term boyfriend is about to propose.'

'Right. Is this the same guy who she's been waiting to ask her for three years?'

'She told you?'

Jack turned round and rested against the worktop, a hint of a smile on his lips. 'She told me a lot of things.'

Beth tilted her head in interest but she was not going to ask, even if the curiosity proved fatal. She hoped Carly hadn't revealed anything about her. For some reason it mattered to her what Jack thought.

'Then you'll know that she loves him and she's not looking for a one-night stand with … with someone like *you*.'

Jack chuckled. 'Hell, who made you her mother?'

'So, that was your plan then. Get her drunk and …'

'Hey, not so fast. She was at the bottom of wine bottle number two when I found her. She asked me if I knew you and we started chatting. I was only being friendly.'

They shared looks of mutual contempt.

'Where's Leo?' asked Jack.

Beth was instantly irritated by his combative tone and she glanced at her watch. 'He's with Denis but I'd better go. Don't touch Carly while I'm gone!' Beth strode out of the door and sprinted across the road and the village green towards the pub. Engrossed in the kerfuffle with Carly, she had lost track of time. She knew Leo was safe with Denis, but she still felt awful for being so distracted.

Beth escorted a moaning Leo out of the pub. On the green the same gang of people were taking down the stalls as the last few revellers milled about. Shirley was sitting on a bench conducting an imaginary orchestra while two couples waltzed around in circles. Beth couldn't be sure if it was the usual level of bonkers for Dumbleford or if Shirley's 1960s cake had something to do with it.

Beth spotted Jack. As soon as she approached him he held up his hand as if to stop her. Leo got distracted by a butterfly and started to follow it from buttercup to buttercup nearby.

'I'm done with the accusations, Beth. Your friend is at my house. The door is unlocked so you can get her whenever you want. I'll be a couple of hours and I'd like to think she'd be gone by the time I get back.'

'The door's unlocked?'

'Yes, Dumbleford is a quiet little village. Not London. Get used to it!'

Beth was taken aback by how vehement Jack was but now, having calmed down a bit, she wasn't sure herself why she'd made such a thing about him and Carly. She guessed it was because she was being protective of her friend. Yes, that must be why she reacted like that.

'Right, thanks. Will do. Sorry if I was a bit …'

Jack paused mid-walk, waiting for her to finish her sentence.

She shrugged. 'Sorry,' she repeated and walked away, collecting Leo as she went.

Three fully leaded takeaway coffees later, Carly and a sick bag were on their way back to the train station. Leo was zoned out playing a game on Beth's phone, so Carly and Beth were able to have a hushed conversation in the front of the hire car.

'I can't believe you were going to kiss Jack,' said Beth.

'I wasn't!' protested Carly, although she was scowling as she spoke. 'Well, it was only going to be a little kiss on the cheek not a full-on snog fest!'

'You were not heading for his cheek!'

'That was probably the wine doing the steering,' said Carly glumly rearranging her sick bag.

'Why were you going to kiss him at all? You don't know him, he's a stranger and you have Fergus.'

'He said something lovely … but I can't remember what,' said Carly pulling the same face she pulled when she accidentally switched on *University Challenge* and tried to join in. She sighed. 'I'm sorry I was drunk.'

'And what did you talk about anyway?'

'I'm so sorry, but I can't remember,' said Carly, hugging the sick bag as Beth went a little too fast over another village speed bump.

'Nothing at all?'

'Nope.' Carly shook her head. 'Ouch. Wishing I hadn't done that,' she said, putting a hand to her forehead.

'Me too,' muttered Beth.

'Are you and he … you know?' asked Carly.

'No! Seriously, do you think I would get involved with someone else so quickly after Nick? Or even get involved with anyone at all after Nick?' Beth's voice was rising.

'I don't know.' Carly's expression was pained. 'No. Of course not. Again, very sorry.'

'Good,' said Beth, relaxing her tight grip on the steering wheel.

They bumped along the hedgerow-lined lane in silence for a while before Carly spoke. 'You can't pledge not to have any more relationships because of Nick.'

'I can,' said Beth with a snort.

'You shouldn't,' said Carly, as Beth opened her mouth to contest. 'I don't want to argue. I'm your friend and I'm just saying, you never know. And while I'm at it from what I can remember

Jack was really nice to me, so don't judge him the same as Nick. If he wants to help you, give him a chance.'

'I'm thinking he might not want to do that after today,' said Beth and she started to grind her teeth.

Beth was pleased to be waving Carly off on the train back to London but she was a little sad too. Carly was her best friend and despite the chaos she had managed to cause it had still been good to spend some time with her. Sometimes, all you needed was a friend you could be yourself with. They had both been cheered up by the revelation that there were direct trains from Moreton-in-Marsh to Paddington so they could be together in approximately an hour and forty minutes, assuming there were no delays.

Now that Beth had taken back her phone, Leo was chatty in the car on the way back to Dumbleford. He was reliving all the fun he'd had with Denis at the fete.

'Am I definitely going to go to Denis's school?' he asked. It was hard to tell his true feelings on the subject from his neutral tone.

'I think so,' said Beth. 'I'll need to speak to the head teacher once the new term starts.'

He needed to go to *a* school and the village one was the logical answer. She no longer had the income to fund a private education and she couldn't imagine home-schooling. There was a pause before he answered and Beth held her breath whilst glancing at him in her rear-view mirror. This could go either way, she thought.

'Okay,' he said eventually, breaking out into a smile, and Beth started to breathe properly again.

By Monday, Carly was once more feeling like a human being as opposed to a small furry-tongued creature that had been trampled by marauding Vikings. Her weekend had been an utter disaster and it was all her own doing. She knew it wasn't Fergus's fault that she had built up the image of the treehouse, although he could have warned her that there wouldn't be any flushing toilets. Equally he wouldn't have been aware of the large amount of sheep poo, though the fact that the treehouse was on a working sheep farm might have been a clue. However, the lack of a proposal was definitely down to Fergus. She didn't know what to do about that.

Going to Dumbleford had not salvaged the weekend as she'd hoped. Beth had abandoned her in a pub when she was feeling glum, so that bit was Beth's fault. She probably should not have finished the second bottle of wine but it was a long while since she'd been that drunk and she was pretty sure that she hadn't offended anyone, so no real harm done.

She shrugged off any residual guilt, sipped her black chai tea and perused the paperwork in front of her with interest. She'd been asked to sign at pantomimes before but usually refused as, despite having some experience, there was a lot of preparation required for only a handful of signed performances. But this one was different. This one was at a new theatre in Gloucester and Carly was now familiar with its proximity to Beth and the fact that it was an easy train journey from London. It would mean being away from Fergus for a few nights but perhaps that would do them good? There had only been the briefest of text messages exchanged between them and Carly was apprehensive about his return.

Hopefully, by the time the panto season arrived Beth would have made the cottage liveable and she could stay there and spend some quality time with her friend. She was missing Beth, and an opportunity to stay with her was something to look forward to as long as she could convince Fergus that it was a good idea. *Oh yes I can*, she thought and chuckled out loud as she folded up the proposition. She'd speak to Fergus about it tonight when he got back from the treehouse. She sighed to herself. She really hoped things were fixable between them.

Chapter Twelve

The following week was a blur of activity for Beth, with workmen to liaise with and sorting out Leo's new school. The head teacher was thrilled to have another pupil joining them and confirmed that Leo would be in the same class as Denis. His uniform was easily purchased direct from the school too, so a day after term started Leo was walking to the local primary, chatting at high speed to Denis. Petra and Beth followed behind. Beth was grinding her teeth – something she seemed to do whenever she was stressed.

'Look at him, he'll be fine,' Petra said, giving Beth a reassuring look. 'It's a nice school. I like that there aren't many children, it means they get more attention. Boys need a watching eye.'

'I guess so,' Beth replied. Seeing him in a new uniform brought home the fact that she had wrenched him away from everything he knew and forced him into this situation, although she had to admit that right now he seemed fine about the change. Beth knew that as soon as the cottage was finished she would be looking to move, so this new school situation, and the feelings that accompanied it, would be a recurring state of affairs and another wave of guilt engulfed her.

The builder, Kyle, was on site with two colleagues and they got to work alongside a small weasel-like man who was the electrician. Beth was impressed by the amount the four of them could get accomplished as she battled on her own with the triffid-like plant that had been hell-bent on taking over the kitchen.

Kyle had explained that they were going to do their best to reproduce the original lath and plaster ceilings with modern materials. But they were leaving out the horsehair; Beth had wholeheartedly agreed with that as it just seemed a very bad idea to put any part of a horse in anything. She was also quite keen to get a smooth finish and she hated it when a hair from a paint-brush became immortalized in a painted surface, let alone lots of them.

There had been a steady stream of boards carried into the living room and upstairs, and repeated banging whilst they were nailed into place before it went eerily quiet and the plastering commenced. Beth had poked her head around the living-room door a couple of times and each time she could see a vast improvement from before. She was so pleased to see that they had protected the large beam over the fireplace with sheeting. She loved the look of the old beam – it was a real feature in the room. For a moment, she could imagine her own knick-knacks and photographs on it above a roaring log fire but she dispelled the image quickly as Willow Cottage was meant to be a project. Getting sentimentally attached to it was a very bad idea.

When Beth checked her watch, it was time for school pick-up and she wondered how all the hours had dissolved so quickly. She washed her hands and looked at the stubborn plant stump that was still poking its way through the window frame. She wouldn't be beaten by it; she'd hack at it from the other side when she got back.

Beth met Leo with more than a little trepidation but she needn't have worried. Apart from handing her his rucksack with a muffled 'Hiya,' he barely acknowledged his mother as he was far too busy discussing football with Denis and two other boys.

Petra gave her a knowing nod. 'What is it you say in this country? I told you so.'

September proved to be a beautiful month as the daytime hours got noticeably shorter and the colours changed around the village. The village green's trees put on a vivid display as they took on their autumn hues, with the rich bronze of the large beech trees and the deep red shades of the ash and rowan being Beth's favourites. The last of the ducklings were just distinguishable from their parents and were now glad of a feed midweek, as the tourists only seemed to appear at weekends. The morning skies were almost lavender, and although there was more cloud about, it was still comfortingly warm.

The school did a brilliant job of putting on the harvest festival, which was very well attended by the villagers and which Leo loved taking part in. He had one line to remember which he delivered perfectly, much to his delight and Beth's relief. She noticed that Jack gave him a big thumbs-up when he came offstage too.

Beth was working on the cottage every day. She was up before Leo and could easily get an hour in before he stirred. Thanks to the electrician, the entire cottage was rewired and totally safe, so despite still sleeping in the tent, the introduction of a fridge/freezer, microwave, kettle and toaster had improved things greatly. All the new appliances were residing in the hallway whilst Beth tackled the kitchen, making a little progress each day.

By the end of the month, Kyle had finished all the essentials, so Beth now had two new ceilings, a new bedroom floor, a leak-free roof, and a damp course. She had been making progress herself – the whole house had been scrubbed and bleached to within a dust speck of its very existence and she was now making inroads on the kitchen, having banished the creeping plant. In fact she was down to the stage she'd been looking forward to most: designing a fitted kitchen.

The reality of handing over a large chunk of her savings to

pay for the work and the lack of anything coming into her account worried her, and she knew it was time to economize further. Within hours, she was literally waving goodbye to the hire car, much to the embarrassment of Leo and the hire-car collector. She hadn't used it much since they'd got there and trips to the supermarket and launderette could be accomplished on the bus, but she would build up to that adventure; there was only so much she could cope with at once.

The next milestone came in the form of two large flat-pack boxes and heralded the end of sleeping in the tent. Leo was seriously excited at the prospect of having a real bed again, which made Beth choke up. After an exciting day of screwing together the beds, Beth found herself in the pub on carnivorous quiz night, so called because it was sponsored by the local butcher, and all the prizes were meat- or poultry-related. Only in the Cotswolds, thought Beth and, more accurately, only in Dumbleford. Leo and Denis were in the flat above the pub watching *Dr Who* on DVD, giving Beth a little time to herself. It felt good to be away from the cottage. She sat at the bar sipping a small glass of wine and engaging in stilted conversation with Petra, who flitted from one customer to the next as they got their rounds in before the quiz started.

Jack suddenly appeared at Beth's side. She felt his presence before he spoke. 'Beth,' was all he said, with a curt nod of his head.

'Jack.' She mimicked the nod before returning to her drink. This was their level of interaction since the whole bank holiday debacle with Carly.

'Oh good, you two are friends again,' gushed Petra, as she pulled a pint of Guinness for Jack. Both Jack and Beth went to speak but it seemed neither had the heart to contradict her. 'You doing the quiz tonight, Beth?' asked Petra. Beth shook her head as Jack shuffled coins around in his hand whilst waiting for his drink. Petra leaned over the bar conspiratorially, 'You should.'

She winked slowly. Beth glanced at Jack in an attempt to gauge his reaction. She'd hardly spoken to anyone all day and, if she were honest with herself, she wouldn't have minded joining in.

'Petra, you're being all mysterious. What do you know?' asked Jack, paying for his pint.

'I couldn't possibly say but, trust me, you need Beth in the team tonight. Unless of course you want another crushing humiliation like last week?'

'Come on, then,' said Jack, walking away from the bar. It was very similar to the way he spoke to Doris. Oh to be held in that high regard by Jack, thought Beth, as she smirked to herself. She joined the usual team members at their table and they all asked her the same questions that everyone did: *How are you settling into the village? How is the cottage coming along?* Beth had fairly set answers for both which she repeated, and then picked up her glass to indicate the interrogation was over.

Jack let out a slow steady breath and Beth stiffened. 'I'm surprised you haven't got on with weatherproofing the window frames before the weather changes.' Jack was talking into his pint. She had expected some sort of criticism from him but she wasn't going to rise to it. She knew she wasn't going to be friends with Jack but she didn't have the energy to be enemies either.

'Hmm.' She pondered his statement. 'I don't know why I haven't either.' Jack looked briefly in her direction and raised one eyebrow in a look of disbelief. 'It's probably because there's only me doing it all and I thought getting the place hygienic so that Leo and I don't come down with some fatal dirt-related disease was more important. Oh, and focusing on getting the kitchen fitted so that we can actually eat something different to barbecued meat and microwaved jacket potato.'

All eyes at the table studied their drinks intensely as silence reigned.

'You need a hand?' asked Jack at last, a slow smile playing on his lips.

'No, thanks,' she answered almost before he'd finished the sentence.

Simon bent forward. 'Did you say you were fitting your own kitchen? Because I'm a chippy by trade and I'd happily give you a hand. Only if you wanted me to, obviously.' He appeared keen to avoid the same rebuff as Jack.

'Thank you, Simon, that's really kind of you, but even with your expert help I'd be hopeless at fitting a kitchen so I'll pay the store to fit it.'

'No,' said Jack, loud enough for Audrey to almost spill her Martini and lemonade. 'Sorry, I mean, don't do that, they'll charge the earth and they rush things. If you don't mind it taking a bit longer, me and Simon could do it evenings and weekends for you.' He was signalling to Simon as he spoke, and Simon was nodding so hard Beth feared he might injure his neck.

'I don't know,' said Beth, looking at them both. Simon looked quite excited at the prospect. Jack was now giving off his usual hard-to-read aloofness. 'What would it cost me?'

Simon spoke first. 'I only take payment in strong tea and custard creams.' He gave her a warm friendly smile, which she returned. They both looked at Jack for his response.

He rubbed his chin. 'Dog-sitting.'

Beth's brow furrowed. 'Dog-sitting? Looking after Doris?'

'Yep. I'm at home less and less and she's unhappy being left on her own. If you're in all day you could have her at yours and keep each other company.'

'I don't know,' said Beth. The thought of the giant hound in the small cottage didn't sound like anyone's idea of a smart combination. 'Do I have to pick up poo?'

Jack chuckled. 'No, she goes first thing, so you should be all right. But, in case of emergency, put a bucket over it and I'll sort it when I pick her up, okay?'

Beth was still assessing the proposition as the fat man with the shiny head took to the mike. 'Welcome to the Bleeding Bear

Pub Quiz. Round one: the London Underground. Are you ready? Question one …'

Beth looked over her shoulder to see Petra giving them the thumbs-up and another unsubtle wink.

Fergus was sulking. Things hadn't been great since the treehouse fiasco, mainly because Fergus didn't know what he had done wrong and Carly wasn't able to explain it to him. When she'd asked Beth for advice, she had suggested that they needed to speak to each other more. Her choice of words may have been ill thought through but her sentiment was spot on. They had been interacting less and less recently and Carly needed to do something before things became irretrievable.

The fact was that they were drifting apart and Carly felt it acutely. So now she was going to do her best to engage with Fergus and to show an interest in the things he was interested in. The last thing she wanted was for the relationship to break down; she loved him and she knew that was all that really mattered.

Carly made Fergus his favourite vegetable curry with naan bread, poppadoms and mango chutney, which they ate in silence. She opened him a chilled beer and passed it across the table.

'Thanks,' he said.

'Fergus, I want to know about …' Carly stopped signing as Fergus wasn't watching her, he was drinking his beer with his eyes closed. She waited until he put it down. She waved to make sure she had his attention. 'Fergus, I want to know about your work,' she signed.

'Why?' He didn't look pleased at the prospect.

'I'm interested and I don't know anything about it.'

He pursed his lips. He had full lips, eminently kissable lips. Carly was distracted and missed what he'd signed. She signed to him to repeat it and he looked frustrated with her.

'Why don't you play a few games on the computer with me and then you'll get it.'

This was what Carly had feared most. She didn't get computer games. In her view they were just for children and she didn't see the point of them. To her it was all a big waste of time but she knew she had to overcome her prejudice for the sake of their relationship. 'Okay, I'll clear away the dinner things. You set something easy up and I'll give it a go.'

Fergus was grinning broadly. He looked thrilled that Carly was going to play his game with him. Bless him, she thought.

An hour later she wasn't thinking *bless him*. She was thinking that she could have merrily battered him to death with the computer mouse. He had explained to her at length about *Minecraft* and the myriad creatures that occupied its strange world. She had then been let loose on the game herself, with Fergus giving instructions over her shoulder, and now she'd had enough of being chased by ghasts, creepers and endermen, or whatever the stupid creatures were. It was so stressful and watching the screen lurch about was making her feel nauseous too.

'What do you mean I'm now a flowerpot?' shouted Carly.

Part of the confusion seemed to have come with Fergus explaining verbally to Carly what he felt were very clear instructions but, as they were both looking at the screen and Carly's hands were busy using the controls, any questions she asked went unheard and unanswered.

'No, you need to act like a flowerpot or someone will spot you and kill you. Ahh, there you go, you're dead.' Fergus stretched over, tapped on the keyboard and the screen changed. 'Here, forget the mini-games, let's try building something again.'

Carly dropped the controller as if it were molten lava. She would rather have her eyeballs tattooed than play for another minute. As the earlier lesson on building had also turned into a one-sided shouting match, Carly knew she had to walk away before she did or said something she would regret.

'Beer?' she signed and he signed 'Please,' which allowed her to escape to the kitchen where she could have a good rant without being heard.

Chapter Thirteen

Beth was juggling a PE kit and a lunch box as she tried to leave the house. 'Hang on,' said Beth as she locked the front door. She didn't want Leo charging off without her. 'Have you had Jack, I mean Mr Selby, teach your class yet?'

'Nope,' said Leo, fidgeting as he saw Denis come out of the side door of the pub.

Beth couldn't work out why Jack was so busy if he wasn't teaching. The school only had one class and, from what she'd gleaned, he was their IT teacher. Things weren't adding up. On the walk to school, Petra was having a rant about brewery deliveries so Beth just listened and nodded in the right places.

Leo was swallowed up by the ancient school entrance without giving his mother a backward glance. It jabbed at Beth's heart but she was pleased that he had settled in so well. As she walked back with Petra, the subject changed to being a single parent.

'I don't know how you run the pub as well,' said Beth, who was truly in awe of Petra. There was no question that Beth was better off without Nick but it was no picnic managing everything alone.

Petra shrugged off the compliment. 'How long have you been on your own with Leo?'

'Since he was a baby. There was a boyfriend until recently but that didn't work out. How about you?'

'The same,' she said, with a sad smile.

'Leo's father died. What happened to Denis's?'

'Disappeared,' said Petra, wiggling her fingers into the air. Beth was smiling at the gesture but Petra wasn't.

'Like magic?'

'Like the Devil,' said Petra, with a frown. Beth wanted to ask her more but they were level with the pub and, with a forced smile and a wave, Petra was gone.

Beth started to think about what she had on her 'to-do' list for the day and decided that, although it pained her, Jack was right and she needed to get on with the outside paintwork. The trees on the green were turning all the colours of a fanned flame; some were starting to drop their leaves and, though the weather was fair and dry today, there was no telling how long that would last.

As she rounded the willow tree, she saw Jack. He was suited up and checking his watch. Beth slowed her pace for a second to give herself a moment longer to admire him. There was no getting away from the fact that Jack Selby was rather good-looking. His hair was neater than usual and his suit showed off his broad shoulders and slim hips. He really did suit a suit, she thought, and it made her giggle. Doris sat at his side looking around and probably wondering what was going on.

'Good morning and welcome to doggy daycare,' said Beth, striding past them to unlock the door. Doris padded in and started sniffing everything.

'Here's her bowl and blanket. She's been fed, she just needs water. She's been for a run so she'll most likely sleep all day. Any problems, give me a call.' This was going to be easy, thought Beth.

'Have you got a busy day ahead?' she asked but as soon as the words had left her lips she wanted to curl into a ball. She sounded like her mother; if she wasn't careful she'd be asking if he'd got clean underwear on next. She shook her head to dispel any thoughts of Jack's underwear.

Jack gave a half-smile. 'Just the usual.' He handed her a business card. She was still reading the card and holding the dog's bowl and blanket when she realized that Jack had gone and Shirley was walking past, taking in the scene and shaking her head.

'Morning, Shirley,' she said, with a wave.

'Morning, crazy lady,' said Shirley, as she and her trolley shuffled by. Beth felt a thump in her thigh as Doris charged past her. Doris's gruff bark made Beth jump and cost her valuable moments as she lunged unsuccessfully for her collar. Doris bounded up to Shirley, making Shirley look even smaller than usual.

'Doris! Come here! Heel! Stop! Halt!' Beth tried a series of commands as she ran over to the barking dog, but Doris wasn't paying attention. Doris was fixated on barking at Shirley and her wheelie trolley.

'Stupid animal!' said Shirley, waving her arms about wildly, which put the dog on her guard and she stepped back and wagged her tail whilst continuing to bark.

This gave Beth a chance to grab hold of her collar and she marched a reluctant Doris back inside. 'Sorry!' Beth called over her shoulder. Shirley shook her head, muttered something, patted her wheelie trolley and moved off again.

Beth guided Doris inside, shut the door firmly, and the dog recommenced her exploration of the cottage whilst Beth reread the business card.

Jack Selby
IT Consultant
Selby Systems

She was intrigued. Was he moonlighting? Or just bigging up a very small part? She turned the card over in her hand, looking for more clues, but that would have to wait until later as there was a noise coming from upstairs. Beth started up the stairs but, before she got halfway, her tent appeared in the bedroom doorway. Doris had somehow managed to get inside the tent but now was unable to get out of it and looked as if she was wearing it as a fancy dress costume. She tried and failed repeatedly to get through the doorway but the springy tent frame bounced her back each time as she whimpered her frustration. Beth blinked hard; maybe this wasn't going to be that easy after all.

Carly was waiting on the cobbles in Covent Garden. She and Fergus were having a date night. She froze when she saw the bouquet of pale roses coming towards her but relaxed as soon as she saw it was Fergus carrying them.

'You okay?' he asked, planting a kiss on her lips.

'Yes. I wasn't because, for a second there, I thought you were Nick.'

'Whoops. I got the roses because you really liked the ones he bought you.'

She had to admit it was a lovely thought, even if it was borrowed from Nick. 'Your bunch is bigger than his.'

'I know,' grinned Fergus, before handing them over and giving her another kiss.

Date night was another of Beth's ideas and Carly hoped it would end better than the *Minecraft* tutorial. Carly and Beth had slipped into having long conversations on the phone on a Wednesday evening and it was definitely helping Carly's state of mind. There were few people that Carly would listen to but Beth was one of them. She had suggested that the proposal was becoming a destructive obsession and that Carly needed to recognize this. It wasn't what Carly had wanted to hear but she knew her friend was right. And now she was trying very hard to shove it firmly to the back of her mind.

Fergus had booked the restaurant so Carly was a little apprehensive, although she had said that they could pay for it from the bills account in the hope that it would steer Fergus away from fast food. Fergus was wearing trousers and a jumper. No jogging bottoms or lounge trousers in sight – it was a very good start.

They strolled around Covent Garden for a while, popping in and out of the stalls and shops. Covent Garden was always full of life but especially in the early evening when the theatre crowd descended. People were sitting outside making the most of the lack of rain and mild September weather. Music was coming from somewhere but, before they could investigate, Fergus took her arm and guided her away. They ambled along Garrick Street until Fergus stopped and opened the door to a small restaurant.

'It's new,' he whispered, 'but I've heard good things about it online.'

It looked as if a lot of other people had heard good things – the restaurant was heaving. Every inch of available space had a table in it and every table had as many chairs around it as possible but the jolly waiting staff seemed to squeeze through the awkward set-up with ease.

The menus arrived and, on realizing Fergus was deaf, their young waitress proceeded to shout at Fergus, 'Can you hear me now?'

'No, I'm still deaf,' said Fergus, to the puzzled young woman. 'I can lip-read but it's easier if you don't shout.' She blushed and proceeded to go through the specials at a normal volume. Fergus had long since stopped getting cross with people who thought shouting at him would solve the problem; their lack of awareness wasn't meant as a personal attack.

The food was incredible and, for the first time in too long, they signed to each other and had proper conversations in between courses. At first, Carly felt the intrigued eyes of other customers on them but they soon lost interest.

Fergus talked about them getting away to Ireland. There were places he wanted to show her, parts of his history he wanted her to see for herself. He brought to life the smell of the peat fires and the noise of the bars as well as the madness of his family.

She had met his parents a few times when they'd visited London and she'd been to Ireland once but it had been a flying visit where she was wheeled round elderly relative after elderly relative before they attended his cousin's wedding. On that trip she had got to know quite a lot of his relatives, the fun and overwhelming volume of an Irish wedding reception, and the effects of too much Guinness, but sadly nothing of County Westmeath.

At the end of the meal, they sat and sipped tea until one of the waitresses coughed and they noticed they were the only ones left in the restaurant.

Fergus took Carly's hand across the small table. 'Are you happy, Carls?'

She didn't have to think. 'Yes, I am.' Things were looking better and, more importantly, things *felt* better. She wasn't foolish enough to think everything was completely fixed but they were definitely heading in the right direction.

'That's good, 'cause I'm happy too. Just the way things are.' Carly wasn't sure what that meant. She tried to keep smiling but her brain was working overtime now. Was he trying to tell her something? She wanted to ask him but he was smiling at her and she didn't want to turn the happy moment into a deep discussion or, worse still, a row.

The bill arrived, Fergus paid with his sole account card and they walked to the tube hand in hand and in silence. Carly tumbled his words over in her mind but the only way she could interpret them was that Fergus didn't want anything to change and she assumed that included marriage because that would definitely change things.

'So why didn't you say something right then, at that moment?' asked Beth, the irritation obvious in her tone as she tried to balance the phone between her ear and shoulder. 'That was the perfect opportunity to raise the whole marriage question.'

Carly was pulling faces on the other end of the line. 'I know, but then the bill arrived and the moment was gone and you can't go back to a conversation later on, it doesn't work.' She'd been worrying about it all night and, thanks to fitful sleep, she felt wretched.

'Yes, you can. How about saying, "I've been thinking about what you said in the restaurant and … " then you start talking about it again.'

'Oh, that is rather clever,' said Carly, 'but still it was yesterday, he might not remember what he said.'

'Then remind him. Jeez, you do make things hard sometimes, Carls.' Beth was simultaneously unpacking what she'd bought from the DIY store.

Carly pondered her mixed emotions. 'The thing is, I'm kippered either way because if I say I want to get married and he says he doesn't, then …'

'Then at least you'll know … drop it, drop it now!'

'What?' Carly was shocked by Beth's scolding.

'Not you, sorry, Doris. Drop the mop, Doris. Good dog. Sorry, I'm dog-sitting.'

'Dog-sitting? I didn't know you even liked dogs,' said Carly.

'I'm not sure I do. It's a long story. Anyway, carry on.'

'Well, it's even worse if Fergus says he does want to get married because he might just be saying it because I've said it and then he'll only be asking me because I prompted him to and, worse still, he might opt for the "shall we get married then?" type of proposal which isn't a proposal at all.' Carly puffed out her cheeks. It was a conundrum and it weighed heavy on her.

'Then I think you have to explain to him about your dream proposal.'

'How do I do that without looking slightly mad and obsessive?' She knew she wouldn't be able to discuss it with Fergus without gushing or getting overexcited; in fact, it was very likely she might even cry. And she couldn't show him her scrapbook of all the articles she'd collected over the years, he'd think she was proper crackers then. She was even starting to wonder it herself.

'I'm afraid I don't know,' admitted Beth after a short pause. 'Sorry, got to go. Doris has found the laundry bin. Bye, Carls … Drop my pants! Doris, pants! Drop them now!'

The phone went click before Carly could say bye. She cradled the phone in her hands. She was back in that uncertain space where she wasn't sure where their relationship was going next and she had no idea what to do. So she'd just take a deep breath, carry on and keep hoping that everything would be okay.

Beth finally wrestled her now slobber-covered pants from Doris and dropped them disdainfully into the laundry bin. 'Bad dog.' Doris seemed to know what this meant because she grumbled and lay down flat on the floor, looking up at Beth with her big dark eyes.

'Don't give me that,' said Beth, and Doris started to swish her tail from side to side. Beth had an idea. She put Doris's lead on and led her outside. Doris had a sniff around the front garden then went into the willow tree for a snuffle under there. Eventually she lay down.

'Great,' said Beth, and she knocked a tent peg into the ground nearby and hooked the end of the lead around it, before knocking it flush to the earth. 'Good girl. Stay.'

Beth set to work on sanding down the outside window frames. Her plan seemed to be doing the trick as, every time Beth peeped through the now yellowing and sparse willow branches, she could see that Doris was asleep. After a couple of hours, Beth could barely lift her head up from the aching in her shoulders. Her hands, and especially her thumbs, were sore and all she had to show for it was one and a half sanded window frames. This was hard labour. This wasn't what she had signed up for and certainly not what she was used to. She yearned for an air-conditioned office as she pushed her hair off her sweaty forehead. Oh, the glamour, she thought.

Despite a quick break for a sandwich and a coffee, Beth worked non-stop until school pick-up time. She decided taking Doris with her was the lesser of two evils and Doris, to her credit, walked very obediently on the lead. For the first time, Leo left his new friends and came running straight to his mother or, more accurately, straight to Doris. The two were very pleased to see each other.

'Can I hold the lead, Mum?' asked Leo, and he visibly puffed up with pride when Beth handed it to him. It was an odd sight; the small boy walking next to the huge dog, her head level with his chest. As Leo neared the edge of the pavement, Doris sat down, which made Leo stop and carefully check the road was clear before starting to cross. Perhaps Doris was teaching Leo a thing or two about road safety, mused Beth as she followed close behind.

When Jack arrived to collect Doris, she greeted him excitedly and Beth thought that sometimes it would be nice to receive half as much reaction from Leo. 'How did it go?' he asked.

Beth pursed her lips. 'Well, she went bonkers when she saw Shirley and I thought she was going to eat her.' Jack pulled an unimpressed face at Beth's overdramatic description.

'It's the trolley, she hates that thing.'

'She mauled my mop and she trashed my tent and some … clothes but it's okay.'

'Sorry,' said Jack. 'So, no more dog-sitting then.' He took the lead from Beth and clipped it onto Doris's collar as she sat looking adoringly at her master.

'No,' said Beth, surprising herself. 'It's okay really, she can come again. We just needed to suss each other out.'

Jack looked astonished but pleased. 'If you're sure?'

'Yep, no problem.' Beth held up Jack's business card. 'Branching out from teaching IT, are we?' She had to ask.

Jack gave a sly smile. 'No, the other way round. Business first, helping out the school with IT in my spare time.'

'All-round saint then, really.'

'Yep, that's me. See you tomorrow. Come on, Doris.'

As Jack left, he eyed the roughly sanded-down window frames and smiled.

Chapter Fourteen

Beth was woken by a terrifying noise near her head. Like a scene from a horror movie, she expected to see a masked murderer leaning over her, brandishing a chainsaw, but, when she opened her eyes, there was nobody there although the awful racket continued.

Leo ran into the room, jumped onto the bed and pointed at the window. 'It's Jack. Hello!' He waved at the window. Beth rubbed her eyes and twisted in her bed to see Jack's grinning face at the glass behind her. She came to very quickly and pulled the covers up protectively. Jack was wearing goggles and he waved a power sander for her to see before setting it back to work on the window frame.

Beth had an instant headache and seeing as all she was wearing was a pair of pants, since she'd never got around to buying new pyjamas, she didn't want to give Jack an eyeful by getting out of bed. After a surprisingly short amount of time, Jack waved and disappeared down the ladder then moved on to the next window, giving Beth the chance to speed-dress and get some painkillers.

By the time Beth and Leo had finished breakfast, Jack was working on the back of the house and when they emerged for the school run he was packing up.

'All done,' he said. He was covered in white dust, giving Beth a glimpse of what an older version of Jack might look like. A silver fox perhaps. Not bad at all, she thought.

'Thanks, this was kind of you. I mean the sanding, not the waking us up bit.' She smiled warmly.

'You're welcome. It's the least I could do after the mop and the tent ...'

'And Mum's pants!' added Leo loudly.

Beth blushed and ushered Leo away as Jack laughed behind them.

'I'll bring Doris over in about twenty minutes, okay?'

'Perfect,' called back a red-faced Beth. Kids and animals, she'd heard the warnings and it seemed they were all warranted.

Beth managed to get the window frames and front door painted, in a subtle shade of sage green, before the typical October weather took hold and put her back on inside jobs. After some final checking and measuring from Simon she had ordered her flat-packed kitchen which was now scattered throughout the downstairs rooms in more boxes than she could be bothered to count. Her task now was to tackle the living room. At the moment, evenings were spent either in the pub, curled up in bed or sat on one of the two hard wooden chairs that Rhonda had donated because they'd got too tatty for the tearoom.

Beth set up in the living room, which interested Doris; she was especially taken with the bucket of warm water, which she had a few laps at, but eventually she settled in the opposite corner of the room where she could keep one eye on Beth in between snoozes.

With a large sponge Beth doused the wallpaper with the warm water. She concentrated on soaking one wall first and, when she was happy, went back to where she had started with a wallpaper scraper and set to work. Things seemed to go well for a bit as layer after layer of wallpaper came off in small pieces. Eventually the area Beth was clearing had grown to the size of a pillowcase but she appeared to have uncovered a large patch of pattern in beige, green and pink. She touched it with her fingers. It was vinyl wallpaper and this was as far as the warm water had been able to penetrate. She took a deep breath and soldiered on.

After a few hours of relentless scraping, Beth stood back to survey the wall. Apart from a few scratches from the scraper, she had a whole wall of what appeared to be 1940s vintage vinyl wallpaper. It wasn't the prettiest thing she'd seen; dominated by leaves with the odd recurring flower, but it was probably the height of sophistication for the time.

'Sorry, Elsie, it's got to go,' said Beth out loud, making Doris lift her head momentarily.

Beth found the wallpaper scraping oddly therapeutic. It gave her a chance to pick through her relationship with Nick. As she worked she mentally sorted his actions into categories. The 'control' section was overflowing whereas the 'because he loved me' section was rather sparse, although there was an odd overlap between the two. When he'd said there were things in his past he wasn't proud of she wished she had pushed him on it. Perhaps if she'd understood more about his past then their future might have been different. But then the old adage 'a leopard never changes its spots' came to mind. The more she scraped at the wall the more her picture of Nick changed in her mind. How had she missed so many signs?

Beth attacked a particularly stubborn piece of wallpaper with vigour. She was getting good exercise working on the cottage and it was probably on a par with the workouts at the expensive gym she used to go to occasionally when she lived in London.

Hours passed until a knock on her newly painted front door dragged her away from her work.

As Beth opened the door, a rather disgruntled-looking Leo marched in. Petra and Denis stood on the doorstep.

'Oh my God, I forgot!' gasped Beth in horror.

'It's okay,' said Petra as Denis rolled his eyes. 'I thought that's what had happened. The teacher knows me and I'm down as one of your contacts so I brought him home.'

'I'm so sorry.' Beth was mortified. 'I was stripping wallpaper and lost track of the time.' She couldn't explain that she'd been trying to analyse her last failed relationship.

'Really, it's all right. I wondered if you fancied doing a tag team with the boys anyway. You do drop-off and I'll do pick-up?' said Petra, with a relaxed shrug.

'Yes, that would be great.'

'Okay. See you tomorrow,' she said, before leaning past Beth to shout goodbye to Leo.

Beth was horrified that she had forgotten to collect Leo from school and so grateful to Petra for bringing him home. In London, she had paid for a childminder to do school drop-off and pick-up so hadn't had to think about it before, but that was no excuse and she felt wretched. Leo was in the living room cuddling Doris. Beth went over and put her arms round both of them – well, as much of Doris's large frame as she could.

'I'm truly sorry, Leo. No excuses. I got caught up here. Forgive me?'

Leo's bottom lip was stuck out and his eyebrows were knitted into a deep frown. He returned his mother's hug but said nothing. Beth got the message loud and clear.

It took days to get to all the wallpaper off and the wall underneath was a disappointing treasure to unearth. The plaster was old and cracked and a lifetime of bumps had made its surface worse than a crumbling cliff face. Beth made a cup of tea, brought in one of the kitchen chairs and sat and stared at the wall for a while. Doris sat next to her and looked too. From time to time the dog tilted her head as if admiring a great work of art. 'I know, it's bumpier than a teenager's face,' said Beth, and Doris groaned appropriately before settling down for a nap. Beth couldn't afford to get a plasterer in but if she painted over it now it would look such a mess and nothing like the smooth sleek white walls she had dreamed about.

Beth decided to leave it for now, mull over her limited options and, in the meantime, she would tackle Leo's bedroom, or what would briefly be Leo's room. She was thrilled to discover there were only three layers of wallpaper on those walls so it was relatively easy, and she was just finishing as Petra dropped Leo off.

Leo followed his mother upstairs. 'We've been learning about rockets and fireworks at school,' said Leo, fidgeting from one foot to the other as Doris circled him. 'And about firework safety too.'

'Great,' said Beth, scraping at a tricky bit next to the skirting board.

'They have this massive bonfire on the village green and there's a competition to make the best guy and, if it wins, it goes on top and gets burned! Can we make a guy, Mum, pleeeeease?'

'Yeah, sure.' Beth was pleased to see him excited about something.

'Can I use your trousers?' he said as he ran to her bedroom with Doris close at his heels.

'No!'

Beth was regretting letting the hire car go. It was true she hadn't used it much but, in a village where the arrival of a bus was seen on the same scale as water into wine, she was fast realizing the benefits. A quick trip into Stow-on-the-Wold and a rummage round the couple of charity shops there would most likely turn up an outfit for a guy, but there wouldn't be a bus until tomorrow and then it would be when Leo was at school.

Leo and Doris were in the back garden and Beth was meant to be drinking a cup of tea that had long since gone cold. She found she was grinding her teeth as she watched Ernie sitting huddled under the willow tree. She was mulling over whether to ask someone for a lift. It didn't sit comfortably, as she wasn't the sort of person that liked to rely on others, but she had a small boy who she would do anything in the world for. She listed the options in her mind: Petra had a pale pink moped but she wouldn't be insured to ride it and wouldn't fancy having Leo on the back either, so that was out of the question. Simon had a car but she had no idea when he was at work and when he wasn't and didn't want to disturb him. It was looking increasingly like she was going to have to call Jack if she wanted a lift.

She boiled up the kettle and invited Ernie in for a cuppa. He came into the kitchen, sat on the tearoom reject chair opposite Beth, and hugged his mug.

'Do you go to the shops in Stow, Ernie?' she asked. Ernie shook his head. 'I need to go to Stow but I don't have a car any more.'

Ernie's eyes were fixed on his tea so she assumed he wasn't really listening.

'I need to get a lift from someone with a car. Someone that isn't Jack,' she said as she mimicked Ernie and stared into her mug.

'Shirley got a car,' said Ernie, without looking up.

'Shirley?' said Beth. Ernie nodded. 'Has got a car?' Ernie looked up and nodded again. 'Shirley with the wheelie trolley has a car?' Ernie was looking worried as he nodded for a third time, this time much slower. 'Thanks, Ernie, that's good to know.'

Ernie finished his tea, thanked Beth, let himself out and went back to sit under the willow.

When there was a knock at the door, Beth was still chuckling to herself about Ernie's revelation, although she doubted he had got his facts right. If Beth was smiling as she opened the door it soon disappeared as she took in the sight of Shirley, minus her wheelie trolley, wringing together gloved hands.

'Ernie says you need a lift urgently,' said Shirley, as she nodded her head to the driveway. Beth looked over to see a very shiny old car.

'It's not exactly urgent,' said Beth, feeling her palms start to sweat.

'Do you want a lift somewhere or not?' asked Shirley, as Doris came to investigate though she soon wandered off again without a sound when there was no trolley. Leo took Doris's place and Beth felt his small warm hand grip hers.

She took a deep breath. 'Okay, yes, please, a lift to Stow would be terrific. If you're sure?' Shirley was already walking back to the ancient car. Perhaps she lives in the car, thought Beth.

Beth put the lead on Doris and a coat on Leo and they joined Shirley at the shiny car. Shirley pointed at the dog without saying anything. 'I didn't like to leave her because Jack says she eats walls if she gets left,' said Beth, making what she hoped came across as an apologetic face.

'In the back,' said Shirley, pointing at Doris and then at Leo who was wrestling with his car seat.

It was a strange little car. It had a domed bonnet, a lot like an old Beetle, and wooden edges at its van-like rear. Beth got in the passenger seat and was relieved to see seat belts, which she hurriedly did up. She checked on Leo and he was strapped in too. Doris was next to him taking up the rest of the back seat, sniffing wildly. The car smelled heavily of vinegar. Beth looked around for any evidence of it being a mobile chip van or of Shirley living in it, but there was nothing to suggest either. As Beth was looking around she spotted that right in the very back was Shirley's wheelie trolley, and she prayed that Doris didn't spot it too.

Shirley fiddled around the steering column and, at last, the vehicle chugged into life. Shirley took hold of the very large three-pronged steering wheel and gripped it tightly as she revved the engine. 'Ready?' she said, her eyes glinting like a racing driver's.

'Er, well …' but it was too late for second thoughts as the little car took off down the gravel track leaving Willow Cottage and a happily waving Ernie behind.

Beth found she was clinging onto the seat and bravely let go.

Shirley was so small she was actually looking through the steering wheel rather than over it. Due to the recent rain, the ford was flowing nicely through the village and across the road. Beth looked at Shirley and then back at the ford. She wasn't going fast but she certainly needed to slow down. Some tourists were crouched down innocently feeding the ducks as Shirley's little car hit the water at about twenty miles per hour and sent a beautifully arced shield of water over the top of them. The ducks took flight, quacking in alarm as they did so. Shirley and Leo started to cackle with laughter as Beth looked on in horror.

'What sort of car is this?' Beth asked, the question more to take her mind off imminent death than anything else.

'Nineteen sixty-four Morris Minor Traveller,' replied Shirley, turning to give Beth her beaming false-teeth grin. 'Marvellous, isn't she?'

Beth could think of quite a few words to describe the death trap she was destined to spend her final moments in but marvellous wasn't top of her list. 'Oh, she's something else,' said Beth, nodding her encouragement in the hope that Shirley would turn her eyes back to the road. Shirley seemed happy with the response and returned to facing forward. Beth exhaled and looked in the back; Leo looked quite relaxed and smiled at his mother, Doris on the other hand appeared to have a strong sense of foreboding as she was hunkered down on the seat. Beth and Doris exchanged worried glances.

The same short and straightforward journey in the hire car was like a rally event in the Morris Minor, as Shirley appeared to know a short cut that took them down various back roads, each one getting narrower and narrower. When they met the inevitable tractor coming the other way, Beth actually breathed in, which was going to make no difference to the size of the vehicle. She heard the hedgerow clatter against the paintwork on her side but somehow they made it past without crashing. Eventually they popped out onto a normal-sized road, which thankfully led them quickly to the A429, and Beth at least knew they were nearly there.

As they drove into Stow-on-the-Wold, Shirley took her eyes off the road again and turned to Beth. 'So, where are we going exactly?'

'Charity shops, please.'

'Charity shops?' repeated Shirley, with more than a hint of a question in her voice. Shirley continued to look at Beth, who was amazed that they were still going in a straight line and hadn't hit anything.

Mercifully, Leo stepped in to provide an answer. 'I want to make a guy to go on the top of the huge bonfire they have on the village green.'

'Oh, now you're talking!' said Shirley, and she swerved the car across the road and headed towards a neat line of parked cars. Shirley appeared to be braking but very little was happening to slow the car down. Beth closed her eyes as she imagined the cars all concertinaing as they hit the first one. The car halted without a crash and Beth opened one eye.

'Here we are then,' said Shirley, her tone relaxed. 'See you back here in thirty minutes.' Shirley got out of the car as if everything was completely as it should be. Beth gave herself a mental shake and hoped her heart rate would eventually return to normal. She got out and collected Leo and a sullen-looking Doris from the back seat as Shirley opened up the back doors and retrieved the wheelie trolley. Just in time, Beth managed to steer Doris away before she saw her nemesis.

A short walk brought them to a jam-packed charity shop. Doris sat outside and looked forlornly through the glass door. The charity shop was a whole new experience for Leo and he was amazed at the eclectic mix of clothes available. The first pair of trousers he chose were orange and in a size that reminded Beth of their tent. She was trying to dissuade Leo on the basis of the huge amount of stuffing that would be required when he found some average-sized bright red cords that he loved even more. A white shirt, with long pointy ends to its collar, and a black suit jacket completed the ensemble. Leo was disappointed that they didn't have the right style of Guy Fawkes hat but Beth was able to persuade him that they would make one along with a papier-mâché head. She wasn't totally sure how, but that was a problem for another day.

Whilst browsing Beth also found some denim dungarees in her size that would be a much better option for decorating than her skinny jeans. She discovered the hat section, and like a child in a sweet shop, she marvelled at the variety that was there. Beth had always had a thing for hats; she loved them and found herself smiling as she picked some out. She put on a navy beret and looked in the mirror – it really suited her but her smile faded as she remembered why she had stopped wearing hats. It was one of many things Nick had encouraged her to change about her appearance. She held on to the beret as she rummaged through the others.

Armed with their purchases, they returned to the Morris Minor at the same time as Shirley and the wheelie trolley. Doris went apoplectic and Beth struggled to restrain her as she barked frantically and lurched at it.

Shirley calmly rolled her eyes, put the trolley in the boot of the car and went round to the driver's door. 'Well, get in then.'

Being in the car with a large dog barking at full volume was no fun. Leo had his hands tightly over his ears as Beth hung on to Doris's lead from the passenger seat whilst Doris was hanging over the top of the back seat only inches away from the trolley. Shirley seemed oblivious as she manoeuvred the car into the path of a bus and they started the treacherous journey back to Dumbleford.

'Doris! Be quiet!' shouted Beth, but she was barely audible. Doris briefly glanced over her shoulder, her expression one of a plea for support. 'Come on, Doris, be a good dog.' Beth tried to mollify the animal to no avail. After an ear-splitting fifteen minutes they arrived back in Dumbleford, sailing through the ford again at speed and creating a mini tsunami that made the ducks take flight once more.

Shirley drove the car around the green and up to the large Tudor house that dominated it, and then confidently down the side of the property, directly into a large open garage at the back. As the darkness of the garage enveloped them, Doris paused for a moment, giving Beth a chance to hook the lead onto the handbrake as she scooted out of the car. She leaned back in through the rear door, released the lead and was then able to drag Doris out. She was keen to get her as far away from the trolley as quickly as she could.

'Thanks for the lift, Shirley.'

'You're welcome,' said Shirley, heading for the back of the vehicle. Beth pulled Doris away and turned round to see Leo picking up conkers from under a giant horse chestnut tree.

'Come on, Leo,' she called, as she took in the large garden and equally impressive rear view of the house. Beth had lots of questions she wanted to ask Shirley but now was not the time. Beth vowed not to make assumptions about people after this, although she knew she probably would.

Chapter Fifteen

Carly shut the kitchen window as the flat was starting to feel chilly. 'It sounds like Beth and Leo are going to have fun on Bonfire Night,' signed Carly. 'Shall we go out somewhere?'

'No, thanks,' replied Fergus.

'But there are some really good displays in London. They had a funfair at Wimbledon Park last year and the fireworks at Alexandra Palace are meant to be spectacular.'

'Too many people. Too much noise,' said Fergus, with an apologetic shrug. Whilst his confidence was good at small social gatherings he was still not great in a crowd. The indistinguishable noise was often overpowering and always seemed to outweigh any enjoyment. He had become much more confident over the last couple of years as his sign language and lip-reading skills had improved but there were still some things he shied away from.

Carly was a little downhearted; she liked fireworks night. It had always been a big thing when she was a child and there was something about fireworks that she found mesmerizing.

Fergus was fiddling with his phone. 'Nick texted me today.'

'What did you do?' asked Carly.

'Deleted it. Did you get one?'

Carly nodded slowly. 'Yes.'

'What did you do?' asked Fergus, tilting his head slightly and making his dark hair flop to one side.

'I said I'd meet him for a coffee.'

Fergus's eyes widened. 'Why? He's a shit who hit your friend.'

'I know, but I feel sorry for him.'

'You shouldn't. There's no excuse. I'm not happy about you seeing him on your own, Carls.'

Carly wasn't used to the laid-back Fergus making statements like that and she chuckled. 'Why? Because he's a good-looking charmer?'

'No, because he hits women. I'll come with you, if that's okay?'

Carly felt a little glow of something inside. Despite all her values of being an independent woman, there was still something powerful about a man who wanted to protect you.

Carly pondered what he'd said and Fergus waited. 'Okay. Fine. Anyway, I've been thinking about what we talked about in the restaurant.'

Fergus pulled a face. 'Going to Ireland?'

Exactly as she thought, he had forgotten. 'No, about us being happy.'

'I'm still happy.' He pulled her into a hug and squeezed her tight. He relaxed his grip a little and kissed her tenderly on the end of her nose, making her smile. 'I love you, Carly Wilson,' he said.

Her hands were trapped in the hug so she spoke instead. 'I love you, too.' He smiled broadly. 'I know you said you were happy just as things were but I've been thinking. Do you want to take the next step?' She knew she was talking fast.

He was squinting at her lips, which probably meant he hadn't understood her or it meant he had understood and that was his reaction. The silence stretched between them. Sod it, thought Carly, time to change the subject.

She pulled her hands free. 'Shall we watch a film?'

'No, football is on.' He was still looking puzzled and still focusing on her lips as if they held the answer. Carly subconsciously licked her lips and the spell was broken. Fergus let her go and settled himself on the sofa and Carly's shoulders sagged. Where did she go from here?

Jack and Simon were now regulars at Beth's house most evenings as they worked on the kitchen. The units appeared to have been the easy part and they were all put together in a couple of nights. Fitting them to the exacting standards of Jack and Simon was another challenge. They had both approved of her choice of cabinets, doors and worktop which she liked to think didn't bother her but if they had not been impressed she knew she would have taken it personally. Having left behind a state-of-the-art stainless steel and black gloss kitchen in London, she knew she had to choose something that fitted with the cottage's history as well as feeling up to date. What she had chosen was simple grooved oak doors painted in an off-white shade with worktops in natural oak stave – it was the best she could afford.

She had managed to salvage the sink and the men were measuring and remeasuring before they committed to cutting a sink-sized hole in the longest length of worktop. Jack's lean muscles tightened under his T-shirt as he moved the worktop to a better angle. Beth found herself mesmerized and, realizing, she hastily looked away. 'Anyway, I have a guy that needs stuffing,' she said quickly and left them smirking over their fresh cups of tea and custard creams as she retreated to the living room.

Leo had given the finishing touches to the papier-mâché head and hat before he had gone to bed and they were drying on the windowsill in the living room. Leo had worked hard on the project and seemed to have absorbed a great amount of detail about Guy Fawkes in the process. This was especially true of Guy Fawkes's death. It didn't seem to worry Leo, unlike the thought of ghosts, but she'd caught Leo giving a particularly graphic description of hanging, drawing and quartering that seemed to distress Ernie more than a little.

The ladies of the Women's Institute had provided oodles of straw for anyone making a guy so, having stitched up the leg holes on the red cords, Beth was now ramming straw into them which was strangely satisfying. She'd found that the physical work on the cottage made her tired but it was a very different sort of tired to the mentally drained feeling she had experienced in London. Like most roles at that level, her job had been high-pressured and stressful but she now acknowledged the level of stress she had been experiencing at home. The creeping invasion of Nick's control over all aspects of her life had been gradual but tenacious. She didn't like dwelling on it and even less admitting to herself that she had been totally duped by his charisma and doting nature. He had loved her, she didn't doubt that, but she could never have predicted how that would manifest itself. She forcefully rammed some more straw into the trousers.

By the time she had finished stuffing and sewing the guy, she was beyond tired.

'Do you want to have a look?' Jack's face peered round the door.

'Do I?' said Beth, leaving the guy's headless body propped up on the chair by the window as she went to inspect the kitchen.

'Wow! It looks like a kitchen!' She had been aware of them moving things from the hall but she was still surprised to see the white goods in their allotted places and the worktop fitted. 'This is amazing. It is such a professional job. Thank you, both.' Simon was still checking the fit of the worktop to the wall but he visibly puffed with pride at Beth's praise.

'We'll fit the washing machine tomorrow night, okay?' said Jack.

'No, it's Bonfire Night. You *guys* need a night off!' She laughed at her own pun and then felt a little foolish when they didn't join in.

'It's okay,' said Jack. 'Leave the cottage unlocked and I'll pop in.'

Beth's face gave her answer. It wasn't so much about the people of the village, she was getting used to them and their quirky ways; it was her general fears and there was nothing that would convince her to leave it unlocked.

'Why not do the washing machine then come to the fireworks with me and Leo. I'll buy you a hot dog,' she said with a tilt of her head. Jack was pulling faces. 'And you, Simon. Petra tells me they have a beer tent too.'

'If you insist,' said Simon. 'I'll see you tomorrow.' He shut his neatly packed toolbox and left.

Jack was rubbing his chin. 'Yeah, go on then. I'll need to take Doris home before the fireworks because they freak her out.'

'Great. Do you fancy a coffee?' she asked, flicking the switch on the kettle.

Jack checked his watch. 'Yeah, milk no sugar, please.' He sat down at the small table and they looked awkwardly at each other until the kettle started to boil and Beth busied herself with making the drinks.

She ferried the drinks to the table and sat down.

'Thanks,' he said, taking the mug. 'Are you going to paint the walls in here?'

'I think I'll try my hand at tiling above the worktop and paint the rest.'

He nodded his approval. 'The walls are fairly even so tiling should be okay.'

They looked at each other across the table. The silence fizzed between them and Beth felt her temperature start to rise. Perhaps a cold glass of Chardonnay would have been a better idea?

'How's your friend? Carly, was it?' he asked, then took a sip of coffee.

'Oh, she's fine. Still a bit embarrassed about getting drunk but otherwise fine.' Beth tried to think of something to ask him but her mind was a blank.

Thankfully, he broke the torturous silence. 'You and Petra seem to get on well.'

Beth nodded enthusiastically; here was a subject she could gabble on about. 'Yes, she's lovely. And it's nice to have another single mum around. She gets what it's like to be on your own. Don't get me wrong, I'm quite happy on my own. I like being single. It's just that you can't have a day off and hand over to someone else because there isn't anyone. But there also isn't any chance of someone letting you down because there's just you and if you don't do it then it doesn't get done.' She realized gabbling on probably wasn't a good idea as she watched Jack's eyes slowly widening as she speeded up. She hugged her mug and had a drink to stop herself talking.

'Yeah, I guess,' he said, looking like he was still trying to process all that she'd said.

'Petra seems to have settled well into life here.'

'She has, so there's hope for you yet,' said Jack, with a warm smile. Beth found she was smiling back at him. Their eyes locked and Beth found it hard to look away.

Feeling the colour rising in her cheeks, Beth quickly finished her coffee. 'Now, can you give me a hand with something, please?'

'Sure.' He stood up and followed her into the sparse living room. 'I know you're not a charity case but do you want some furniture for in here?' he said, looking about.

Beth looked at the virtually empty room. It wasn't huge but it was made to look so much bigger by the empty open fireplace and the single chair currently occupied by the guy.

'No, I'm okay, thanks. It's the walls that have got me stumped. They need to be plastered or dry-walled? Is that right?' She was still learning the terminology.

Jack walked to the nearest wall and ran his hands over it and then studied his hand. 'These are sound walls. I can't see any damp.'

'But look at this crack,' she said, walking to the opposite wall and pointing at a meandering fracture in the old plaster. Jack came over and stood close; he ran his finger ever so slowly along the line the crack took. Beth found herself transfixed as her eyes followed his finger inching its way slowly down the wall.

'I can patch that. You then put on a primer and finish off with a good quality latex paint. It won't be a perfect finish but it will look fine.' Jack took his hand away. The spell was broken. 'It's a character property, Beth. Let its character shine through.'

'Mmm, I'll think about it. Now, hold on to this,' said Beth, handing him the guy's head, 'while I try to sew it onto its body.'

After a few minutes Beth was getting neck ache and she hurried the last few stitches. 'Right, give it a tug.' She wanted to check that the head was going to stay on.

Jack had a good hold of the head and pulled hard as she pulled at the same time, wrenching the head from the body. Beth was about to complain but a face that had appeared at the window was screaming hysterically. 'Ernie!' said Jack as he threw the head to Beth and ran out of the cottage after the old man.

'Terrific,' said Beth as she watched through the window and hugged the head under her arm.

More screaming started behind her, making her jump. It was Leo and he looked suitably terrified by the ghostlike image standing with its head under its arm. It never rains but it pours, she thought, as she dropped the head and went to comfort her son.

All next day, the village green was a hive of activity as people delivered all manner of burnable items for the bonfire and the ladies of the WI, and associated husbands, supervised the building of it. Apparently there were too many risks associated with building it before the day of the bonfire, which Rhonda was only too happy to reel off to Beth as she collected her coffee.

'Number one, the weather. Two, hibernating hedgehogs. And three, the idiots that light it early. All of which have let us down in the past.' Maureen made what Beth thought was a noise of agreement but it could have been wind; it was difficult to tell.

'Have you got a stall tonight?'

'Oh, yes. Sausage rolls and hot dogs, we always do very well. So does Shirley and her mulled wine,' said Rhonda with glee.

'I bet she does,' said Beth, thinking about how much it must cost to run the biggest house in the village.

'Now, I wanted to talk to you about cottaging,' said Rhonda, her tone suddenly serious.

Beth's eyebrows arched and stayed there. 'Cottaging?'

'Yes,' said Rhonda emphatically.

Beth opened her mouth but her brain was unable to supply a coherent sentence so instead she simply asked, 'Why?'

Rhonda frowned. 'I thought you'd know about all about cottaging? Should I Google it?'

'No!' said Beth forcefully, the thought of what might appear made her blink rapidly. Her mind started to whir and she hit on a possible explanation. 'Do you mean renovating a cottage?'

'Yes,' said Rhonda.

'That's not cottaging,' said Beth, slowly in hushed tones, as if addressing a child.

'Isn't it? What's cottaging, then?' said Rhonda, looking incredulous.

Beth made some poor excuse about having to get back to the cottage in a hurry and almost fell over her own feet in her haste to escape having to answer Rhonda's question. She was grateful to return to her latest masterclass, which today was tiling the kitchen walls between the worktop and the wall cupboards. She'd picked up an array of 'How to' leaflets when she'd last visited the DIY store and they were proving quite useful. The only problem was that she didn't have the tools required to do the tricky bits

145

where you had to cut the tiles to slot them into gaps. Nothing was ever straightforward with Willow Cottage.

A very excited Leo hurtled into the cottage after school and wanted to go straight to the village green as he'd seen what he had termed a 'ginormous bonfire' and wanted to investigate further.

'Sorry. Spellings first. Then you need to get changed and then Jack is coming over so we can all go together.'

Leo's expression changed. He watched his mother closely. 'Is he your new boyfriend?'

Beth felt the colour instantly spread up her neck. 'No. Goodness me. Of course not. Why would you think that? No. Definitely not … No.' She may have overdone her response. Leo's expression was fixed. She wondered what he was thinking. She pursed her lips and waited.

'Okay,' he said and he disappeared into the living room and returned with the guy. 'His head isn't on straight.' Leo held the guy at arm's length. It was bigger than him.

'Yeah, I know. It's the best I could do. And I figured if he'd been hanged then his head might be a bit cockeyed.'

'Cool!' said Leo, his enthusiasm instantly restored.

Chapter Sixteen

Jack turned up, as agreed, and set to work patching up the crack in the living-room wall.

'Was Ernie all right last night?' Beth asked.

'No, he took a bit of calming down to be honest. I got away at about midnight.'

'You took him home?'

'Yeah, but he was still restless so I got him a cocoa and did a couple of bits that needed doing there.' Beth must have been frowning. 'You know, bank statements and bills that sort of thing. Wilf used to do it for him but …'

'That's kind,' said Beth, feeling that 'kind' didn't really cover it.

'Like you said, I'm an all-round saint really.' He gave her a cheeky lopsided grin and returned his attention to fixing the crack. Beth went to get showered and changed and when she emerged the washing machine was humming gently in its spot in the kitchen.

'That was quick.'

'It's easy when you've done a few. You've done a good job with the tiling. I'd give it forty-eight hours before you grout.'

'I've still got the fiddly bits to do. I don't suppose you have a

147

tile cutter do you?' Beth winced as she asked. She hated asking but she didn't really want the extra expense of hiring one and she definitely didn't want to buy one. She wasn't planning on a career in renovation after this experience.

'No, but I know a man who does.' Jack was turning out to be a useful person to know.

'Do you know about Guy Fawkes?' asked Leo but before Jack could reply Leo was already into full gory storytelling mode.

As soon as it got dark, Leo started to panic. If he knelt on his mum's bedroom windowsill he could catch a glimpse of the village green, depending on which way the wind was blowing the willow. This was where he stayed on watch in case they lit the bonfire early.

In the last couple of days the weather had turned decidedly chillier, so Beth wrapped Leo up in scarf, gloves and coat, but he refused to wear his woolly hat, even though she made a thing of putting on her own. It was a floppy wool beanie and she was quite pleased with it. She'd found it in a shop in Stow-on-the-Wold; it had been cheap but the style seemed to suit her. She remembered the last time she'd worn a much-loved hat and Nick had laughed and shaken his head. After a full-scale row about it, he had cut it up into tiny pieces with the kitchen scissors. They were excellent scissors, she thought, and she wished she hadn't left them behind.

Despite Leo's worries, they arrived in time to register their guy for the judging. Leo was incredulous when they asked him the name of the guy. 'It's Guy Fawkes, of course!' They later understood the question when they saw more guys arrive purporting to be various politicians as well as a very good Cruella De Vil, complete with two-tone wig, and a Frankenstein that apparently was a recycled Halloween costume. Beth's hopes for Leo winning were fading fast.

They went for a wander around, met up with Jack, Doris, and

Simon, and Beth bought them all hot dogs as promised. Beth wasn't sure how many people she had expected to be there but she hadn't anticipated quite such a crowd. The pub car park had a 'car park full' sign up and cars were parked by every available piece of kerb.

Shirley and the wheelie trolley were on duty at the mulled wine stand and it seemed possible that Shirley had been testing the product for some time because she was swaying steadily. Beth left Leo with Jack and Doris while she went to get the mulled wine; they didn't dare let Doris get too close to Shirley and the trolley.

'Mittens,' said Shirley, a fraction before she slowly and quite gracefully turned to face Beth.

'They're gloves, actually, but they do the job. Three mulled wines, please.'

'Crazy lady,' muttered Shirley with an exaggerated smile as she filled three cups. Beth handed her the money and weaved her way back through the crowd. The others were admiring the towering bonfire, and a full-blown discussion was under way as to whether or not it was as big as the previous year's. The chatter was interrupted by the arrival of the mulled wine and the adults all warmed their hands on the cups and sipped it appreciatively.

A gathering of WI ladies signalled the imminent announcement of the results of the guy competition and the crowd moved in closer. Leo dashed to the front where he found Denis. Beth excused herself and snuck through after him.

'That one there is from the pub darts team. I helped make that,' said Denis, pointing to the most overstuffed of the politicians. Leo pointed his out. The lady who had announced the winners of the cake competition back in the summer stepped forward, wearing the same leather trousers she'd worn for that event though now they were teamed with an extra-long cardigan and a bobble hat.

'The results of the Dumbleford Guy Competition are … In

third place Cruella De Vil by Dumbleford and Henbourne-on-the-Hill Bridge Club.' A ripple of approval went through the crowd as they applauded and a tall gentleman went forward to collect the rosette.

'In second place Mr Asquith by Dumbleford WI ...'

'Fix!' yelled Jack and then looked behind him when the leather-trouser-clad woman glared in his direction. A lady nearby quickly collected the rosette and disappeared into the crowd.

'And, drumroll, please. The winner is ... Guy Fawkes by Leo Browne!' A beaming Leo, grinning from ear to ear, stepped forward to collect his first-place rosette and box of chocolates while the crowd clapped and Jack whistled loudly. He stepped back under the safety barrier, and Beth pulled him to her in a tight hug.

'Well done, Leo. I'm so proud of you.' She had to bite the inside of her mouth to stop herself blubbing proud mum tears.

'Thanks, Mum. You won it too,' he said, giving her a brief glimpse of the rosette before he and Denis studied it closely.

'Well done, mate!' Jack gave Leo a high five. He looked at Beth and she smiled. Beth glanced over to where Shirley was sitting and she gave Beth a double thumbs-up before swaying and then disappearing behind her stall. The leather-trousered WI lady rushed to her aid and Shirley was soon upright again and still holding her thumbs up. Beth chuckled and returned the gesture. Leo's was the biggest of the guys; perhaps not the best but it looked as if he had some strong supporters in the village.

They watched as the three chosen guys were all strapped to chairs at the top of the bonfire in a similar style to that of Olympic medallists, with Leo's first place on the very top and the others each a fraction further down. The remaining guys were dotted around the base. The ladders were removed and the large bald compere from the Bleeding Bear weekly quiz came forward with a long lit baton, and a countdown from ten started as the excitement built up.

Leo and Denis were shouting each number and the crowd all

whooped when they reached zero and the bonfire, thankfully, ignited. The crowd was at a safe distance behind a barrier but when the fire took hold, the heat was intense and those near the front, including Beth and Leo, moved further back.

'Wow, that is some bonfire!' said Beth, admiring the roaring pile from a more comfortable distance.

'He's alight, he's alight!' shouted Leo. Beth watched all her hard work become engulfed in flames and quickly blend into the rest of the bonfire. She breathed in the bonfire-scented air. It took her back to her childhood – a childhood that had been far simpler than Leo's and she felt a pang of guilt for the poor decisions that had led to her and Leo constantly looking over their shoulders in a village miles from home.

Petra appeared and handed Simon and Jack something in a plastic pint tumbler. 'Dark Winter, it's a real ale we've put on for tonight,' she explained, and they took them gratefully. She soon returned with drinks and crisps for the boys and two smaller tumblers of wine for her and Beth.

'Thanks,' said Beth, taking the drink, 'How's it gone tonight?'

'Really well. I'm leaving the bar staff to it. I'm, how do you say it? Cream crackers?'

'Nearly. Cream-crackered,' corrected Beth with a chuckle and they squished their tumblers together in a cheers motion that was decidedly lacking in clink.

'I'm losing a barmaid tonight. It's her last night working for me. She started university a few weeks ago and the two don't mix well together. So it'll be just me and Chloe and, at busy times, that's not enough.'

'Oh,' said Beth, enjoying the feel of the wine as it chilled and warmed her insides at the same time. She wasn't sure if that was Petra's way of making a job offer and, if it was, she was unsure how she felt about it. 'Are you replacing her?'

'Definitely. Christmas isn't far away and we're fully booked for most of December.'

Beth nodded and bit her lip. 'Would you consider taking *me* on?' she asked. 'I don't have any experience but I'm willing to learn.'

Jack stepped forward and butted in. 'There was that time you worked at the tearoom,' he said, behind a huge grin. Petra was looking puzzled so Beth nudged him playfully out of the way.

'Ignore him.'

'I usually do,' said Petra. 'The job's yours, if you want it.' They raised their plastic cups in another toast. Beth wasn't sure what she had let herself in for but she needed the money and a small income was much better than none at all.

Beth and Jack stood together watching the bonfire light up the village green. The light breeze was enough to make the flames swirl up in elaborate patterns before disappearing into the night sky.

'It's mesmerizing, isn't it?' said Jack, turning to look at Beth for a moment.

'It is. There's something magical about fire. I love Bonfire Night.'

'Me too. Always preferred it to Halloween. My mum used to do jacket potatoes smothered in butter and cheese and wrapped in foil, which we'd eat outside. We'd have them another time on a plate but they never tasted as good as they did outside, watching the bonfire.'

Beth's eyebrows danced at Jack sharing something personal; this was a first. She felt she should reciprocate. 'We'd have sausages and my dad would always run outside with the plate shouting, "Look out! Bangers!" and it always made me laugh,' said Beth.

They both chuckled and then relaxed into an amiable silence. Perhaps it was easier when everyone around you was chatting and providing a background noise? Another person ambled through the packed crowd and Beth and Jack got pushed closer together but neither made a move to step away. In such close proximity to Jack, Beth felt surprisingly at ease and safe.

When the fireworks were announced, Jack made his apologies and took Doris home moments before the first ones went up. Doris hoovered up as many pieces of dropped sausage she could as she was escorted off the green. Beth watched them leave until she was aware that Petra was eyeing her and she looked away, self-consciously adjusting her wool beanie. It was silly really but she felt she wanted to chat more to Jack and a part of her was a little downcast that he'd had to leave early.

It was a classic firework display that produced oohs and ahs from the well-trained crowd who were all huddled together, staring into the cold clear sky. Leo was happy for Beth to hug him while they watched the rockets whizz and bang and the pretty sparkles light up the deep blackberry sky. Things were starting to look up, thought Beth.

Carly and Fergus sat in silence in the pub. Fergus was scrolling through the music on his phone and every so often he'd show a particular album or artist to Carly. She knew how much he missed music and it was hard for her to imagine what it was like to lose something so important to you. The door opened and Nick arrived looking as if he'd stepped out of a magazine; his hair was perfect and his clothes were on trend. He gave a warm confident smile when he spotted them and strode over. Fergus stood up and shook Nick's hand firmly but was reluctantly pulled into a brief man hug.

'It's so good to see you, Fergus.' Nick spoke at a deliberately steady pace, facing Fergus so that it was easier for him to lip-read. Fergus nodded, his stony face easy to read. Nick bent to kiss Carly lightly on each cheek and gently whispered, 'I'm so grateful that you came.'

They agreed a drinks order and were soon sitting at a table for four with one empty chair. Carly eyed the empty chair rather than make direct eye contact with Nick as she sipped her drink and waited for the inevitable awkward conversation to start.

'Thanks for coming. I really appreciate your support,' said Nick. Carly was about to relay it to Fergus but he was already answering.

'You don't have our support, Nick.' Fergus's tone was cold. 'I am here because Carly felt sorry for you.' His eyes were locked on Nick's.

Nick's eye twitched but he hid his reactions well. 'Fergus, I know how this looks …'

'And I know how this is.' Fergus turned to Carly and silently signed. 'We shouldn't have come.'

Carly spoke to Nick but signed so that Fergus could stay involved. 'Nick, Fergus is right, we can't help you.'

'It's okay, really. I do understand, you're supporting your friend. I would be exactly the same.' Nick's voice was downcast and he lowered his gaze until it was on his Diet Coke.

Fergus was still staring at Nick. 'She should have reported you to the police,' he said. Carly was feeling more uncomfortable by the second. Fergus was right, they shouldn't have come. She hadn't appreciated quite how strongly Fergus felt about the situation but, watching him now, she could see the loathing he had for Nick.

Nick looked up and his expression had changed; he no longer looked dejected. 'She could still report me if she felt she had something to report. But she hasn't.' There was an imperceptible shrug of his shoulders. Carly could feel the tension between the two men. The last thing she wanted was for this to turn into a full-blown row in a public place.

'If you had any decency, you would leave her alone …' started Fergus.

Nick began to object on the grounds that he didn't know where she was but Fergus chose to carry on talking over him. 'You would stop searching for her, and you would seek help for your condition.'

Nick laughed and shook his head as colour rose in Fergus's

face and Carly leaned forward in case she had to intervene. 'Okay, mate …' started Nick.

'I'm no mate of yours,' said Fergus, standing up. Nick automatically rose with him. Shit, thought Carly, and she too stood up but felt scarily small next to the two men. There was just the table between them. Fergus had the height advantage but Nick was more muscular and, whilst Carly adored Fergus, she could easily see who would win any physical fight.

'This was a bad idea. We should leave,' said Carly. Nick waved them away, shaking his head, his face now stern. They walked to the door and Fergus opened it for Carly to walk through. As she went out into the street she realized he was no longer behind her. She raced back to see Fergus stooping over a now-seated Nick, speaking into his ear whilst a firm hand on his shoulder kept him in his chair. He then turned and walked back to her at the door.

'What did you say to him?' asked Carly, but Fergus shook his head and quickened his pace.

It was Sunday so Beth and Leo got the bus to the DIY store and purchased the paint, brushes and trays to decorate the living room. It was almost too heavy to bring back on the bus but somehow, with a little help from some friendly fellow travellers, they managed it. Beth had decided against the stark white she had originally wanted and instead went for a warmer hue, still very much the blank canvas she wanted to create for whoever ended up buying and living in Willow Cottage but more in keeping with its age. Leo helped to cover the floor with newspaper and they set to work.

Sunday went by in a decorating blur that even Leo enjoyed. Just at the point where he was getting bored, Denis arrived and the two went off clutching plastic boxes to explore for blackberries behind the pub garden. Beth took a look around and decided she would pack it in for the day and finish the living room on Monday. It was Sunday and she fancied a proper lunch.

Despite it being late in the season, Leo returned from the blackberry hunt with enough for Beth to incorporate into an apple and blackberry pie. It felt so good to be cooking again. She couldn't help feeling a little smug when they sat in their new kitchen and tucked into a proper home-cooked meal.

Monday arrived and after the school run it was back to the decorating. Doris was very interested in the changes and in particular the smell in the living room but, once she had settled down, Beth got on with finishing the painting.

Beth had her music on loud while she stood on Simon's borrowed stepladder and gave the ceiling its second coat. She had her head tilted to the ceiling as she rollered merrily and wasn't aware that Doris had moved and that she'd come up close to investigate. The stepladder wobbled precariously when Doris landed her great paws on the steps on the opposite side to Beth. Beth immediately brought down her hands to steady herself but in so doing the hand gripping the paint-clad roller accidentally whacked Doris on the head.

'Sorry, Doris!' said Beth instinctively as the paint-splattered dog retreated quickly. Beth then spent the next twenty minutes trying to coax Doris to come to her and stay long enough so that she could wash the paint off her head. She couldn't send her home looking like a punk badger.

The last of the dog treats and two slices of leftover beef later, Doris had a wet but paint-free head and a more cautious look in her eye.

'Now don't go and rat on me to Jack,' Beth whispered to Doris, who grumbled and settled down for a nap in the hallway, keeping one eye trained on Beth.

The rest of the day's decorating went without incident and Beth proudly surveyed the results. She was pleased with herself and had to admit that she had enjoyed it. Perhaps doing the rest of the cottage wouldn't be such a chore after all?

Jack had been correct about the painting. She doubted very

much that she would expressly tell him that but, looking over the finished walls, she knew he had been right. They were never intended to be perfectly smooth; plastering would have erased a little of the cottage's history. The walls were smooth to the touch but when the light bounced off the surface the imperfections and undulations could be seen, and Beth liked it. Now it was time to make it look like it was lived in.

Chapter Seventeen

Beth's first night of working at the Bleeding Bear loomed large and she felt first-night nerves. She was going over to the pub only a few minutes early for Petra to show her the ropes, even though Beth had suggested that perhaps a day's training might be more appropriate for a novice like her. Petra had insisted that, once you had the knack, pulling a good pint was the easiest thing in the world and the till was child's play. Beth remained sceptical on both counts.

She showered, changed, checked she didn't have paint in her hair, did a delicate job on her make-up, and surveyed the result as best she could in her pocket mirror. It was difficult to tell. She knew her hair badly needed cutting because it hadn't seen a stylist since she'd left London, so she tied it back in a rough pleat. Leo was very happy to be spending the evening somewhere that had a television and free-flowing crisps and fizzy drinks.

In theory, the job was ideal. Granted, it was a world away from her city job but it was a new challenge and a chance to get to know a few more people. She was fretting a bit but she was quite excited too. Her life was different now; *she* was different. I'm enjoying being Beth again. I'm not Elizabeth any more, I never really was, she thought. Beth definitely wasn't the gullible woman who had fallen for Nick's charms, or the pliable individual he had subsequently moulded. She was back to being her old independent self and this was where she took the next step.

The pub was a little eerie without any customers as her heels reverberated on the wooden floors. The echo was repeating itself somewhere in the pit of Beth's stomach. How daft to be nervous, she thought, but sometimes nerves and fears weren't rational and rarely were they controllable. She realized that she wanted to be good at something again, which had added a little more pressure to the situation. Beth took off her coat and looked around the empty pub. It was exactly how you would expect a country pub to be: lots of beams, nooks and crannies and a big fireplace that was blackened with the memories of the past. Petra appeared and her smile dissolved any nerves Beth was harbouring.

'You came! Let me start with a simple pint,' said Petra, and so her training began. As she had expected, she didn't do well the first time she pulled a pint, nor the second nor the third, but after that she had a feel for it as well as the feel of beer on her jeans. But it was okay. She was smiling and to her surprise she was enjoying it.

Her first evening was a quiet one, which helped, and Petra was on hand like a mother bird hovering nearby to keep a watchful eye on her fledgling. Beth had a slack few minutes and was wondering why they didn't have a bar stool on her side of the bar when Petra returned from checking on the kitchen, and handed her a lemon.

'In between the customers you do everything else: chop lemon for drinks, check crisp stocks, collect glasses from tables and bar, load dishwasher, unload glasses from dishwasher and wipe down and tidy up.'

'Right,' said Beth, as she set about slicing the lemon. Petra was right, there was always something to do and as soon as there was a gap between customers Petra was using it to explain something else to Beth. The real ales were a bit of a worry to Beth and she felt she ought to try to learn them as homework.

When there was a brief pause, Beth seized the chance to chat to Petra. 'I hadn't appreciated how intense it is running the bar and the kitchen.'

Petra grinned. 'I love it. My kitchen staff are excellent so they don't really need me. A young keen chef is a godsend. And this', she waved her hand over the bar top, 'is all I've known since I came to England.'

'But you didn't come to work in a bar. Did you?'

'No. I came to study.' Petra looked uncharacteristically serious.

'What happened?'

Petra was staring at Beth, her expression grave. Beth wanted to reach out and reassure her but she didn't know why. Petra shook her head and the solemn moment was gone. 'I'm not as clever as I thought I was,' she said, with a forced laugh.

'You're very good at running a bar though,' said Beth and she meant it. 'You're wasted here. You could be earning serious money as an office manager in London,' she added with feeling.

Petra chuckled and shook her head. 'I would hate an office. Here I have my regulars and I meet new people all the time. It may not pay the big bucks but it pays enough and the pub is mine ... apart from the huge mortgage of course!' She laughed again and went towards the other end of the bar even before the next punter had fully walked inside, and greeted them warmly.

Beth pondered their conversation for a moment. She'd not seen Petra look as tense as she did when she spoke about giving up her studies. Another customer approached the bar and Beth went into efficient barmaid mode and the thought was lost.

When they were down to five customers, Petra sent her home.

'You did well tonight. Very well,' said Petra.

'Thanks,' said Beth, feeling ridiculously pleased with herself. A tired Leo staggered into view and the weary duo wended their way the few short steps back to Willow Cottage and their beds.

* * *

On a bleak frosty morning, Jack walked past the carpet delivery van that was parked outside Willow Cottage. The front door was already open. He unclipped Doris's lead and handed it to Beth and Doris trotted happily into the cottage.

'You might have wanted to get the chimney checked and cleaned before you had the carpet fitted,' called Jack as he sauntered away.

Beth faltered in the doorway; she couldn't look at him but she knew he was radiating smugness. He had walked too far before Beth had a chance to reply. She stuck her tongue out at his back. It was childish but it made her feel better. She watched as the almost white carpet was pulled from the van.

'Hang on!' yelled Beth at the two startled carpet fitters while she jogged over to them. 'I'm really very sorry but you can't fit the carpet today.'

After a lot of huffing, two mugs of sweet tea and half a packet of custard creams, the carpet fitters took the carpet away so that she could arrange a fitting at a later date. A few frantic phone calls later and Beth had found an actual chimney sweep who was able to come round later that day. She didn't like having the confrontation with the carpet fitters but getting the chimney cleaned first was the smart thing to do and she was pleased that a potential crisis had been averted. But why did Jack have to know best?

Beth found herself humming the 'Chim Chim Cher-ee' song from *Mary Poppins* on and off throughout the day so when the chimney sweep finally arrived, and disappointingly looked nothing like Dick Van Dyke, she had to make a concerted effort to suppress the urges to continue humming. He was an older gentleman and knew everything there was to know about chimneys and fireplaces. He soon got to work, starting first with a chimney inspection inside and out.

When he carried in the brushes Beth decided to leave him to it. After a while, she brought him a cup of tea and was shocked to see the large boxful of twigs, ash and unidentifiable charred remains that had been removed from the chimney.

'Birds', he said with a firm nod, 'like to nest in chimneys. I've put a bird cowl on the top of it to stop 'em.'

'Great,' said Beth. She had no idea what that was but if it stopped the twig mess she was pleased.

'Found this an' all,' he said, handing Beth a crispy piece of scorched paper. 'Bit of history.' He smiled, and started to pack away.

Beth carefully unfolded the brown tinged paper and her heart clenched as she read the clumsy writing of a small child.

Dear Father Christmas
Ernie and I have tried all year to be good for Mummy.
For Christmas I would like the new Rupert Bear book, a pencil box, soldiers and a pair of gloves.
Love Wilfred
P.S. Ernie would like an orange scarf and any little toys you have spare.

Beth looked back at the fireplace. It was amazing that the letter had survived.

'Caught on a ledge,' said the chimney sweep as if anticipating her next question. 'Sweet, isn't it?'

'It's pure magic,' said Beth, swallowing down her emotions. She went to the kitchen, opened her favourite cookbook and stowed the letter safely inside. She didn't know what she was going to do with it but she knew she had to keep it safe.

Beth paid the bill and the chimney sweep gave her a certificate to say her chimney was checked and safe to use.

Right, thought Beth, now to rearrange the huffing carpet fitters.

Fergus had not been quite himself since they'd met Nick at the pub and Carly was running out of opportunities to tell him about the contract for her to interpret at the pantomime. The contract was actually a signed and posted one because Carly had decided she definitely wanted to do it and now she was worrying about how Fergus would react. They had been together three years and had rarely had a night apart, the exception being the recent treehouse debacle, which she knew had caused issues for Fergus. He didn't like having to explain to people that he was deaf and, as soon as he did, half would then instantly start talking to him like he was an idiot. Carly was quite proud of him for getting home on his own without any issues but she knew it wouldn't have been easy. So, with more than a little trepidation, she decided now was the time to tackle the pantomime.

Fergus was looking morose as he scrolled through his catalogue of music he could no longer hear on his mobile.

'I've had an exciting job offer,' signed Carly. Fergus twitched but didn't show a lot of interest. Undeterred she continued. 'It's to do a pantomime.'

Fergus gave a sly smile. 'Oh no it's not.'

'Very funny, I expect there'll be a lot of that. So you don't mind?'

'Why would I mind?'

Carly realized that the key piece of information had been omitted. 'It's in Gloucester. There will be a rehearsal and a couple of shows. I thought I could stay with Beth.'

Fergus had stopped smiling. 'Why can't you come home afterwards?'

'I can but they usually finish late and I thought it would be nice to stay with Beth.'

'You said the cottage is a shithole.'

Carly chuckled. 'It was, but she's doing it up a bit at a time and it's liveable now.'

'Can I come?'

Carly felt like she was about to kick a puppy. 'What would you do while I was working?' Fergus shrugged his shoulders. 'To be honest, I thought it would be nice to have some time with Beth.'

'Okay.' Fergus looked doleful.

'Okay, I can go?'

Fergus was frowning. 'I'd never stop you doing anything you wanted to do. I don't ever want to be the one that holds you back.' Things were feeling serious.

'I know. I've sent off the contract anyway.'

'Then why ask?' Fergus's signing actions were getting jerky. It was a sign he was getting cross; when they started getting really big that was when to worry.

'I was being polite,' signed Carly. Fergus's eyebrows twitched and it irritated Carly. 'I'm not a comfort blanket.'

'You're my carer now, are you?' said Fergus but before Carly could respond he was already leaving the room. He picked up his coat and headed for the front door. There was no point calling after him, so she just watched him leave. When you were deaf you got the last word or at least the last one to be heard.

The willow tree now offered no protection from the elements, having lost most of its leaves. However, Ernie still liked to sit under it. Beth looked out of the bare window and took in the sight of the willow covered in frost. It sparkled in the morning sun and had a distinctly magical feel to it. It was too early for Ernie. It was too early for most people but today Jack was dropping off Doris sooner than usual and she watched him stop for a moment and take in the beauty of the tree before he knocked on the door.

Doris barged past the moment the door was opened; she was now very comfortable in her adopted home and nicely settled in the routine.

'It's stunning, isn't it?' said Beth, as Jack was glancing over his shoulder for another look at the willow's crystal-encrusted fronds.

'It's the hoar frost that gives it that look,' Jack explained and Beth nodded politely although she had no idea what hoar frost was. 'Anyway, I was actually thinking that now's the time to cut it back,' he said, with a smile. His smile grew into a beaming grin as he looked at Beth. She wondered for a moment what it was then she remembered she was still wearing her pink unicorn onesie.

'It's cold. This is warm.' Embarrassed, she tugged on the unicorn horn protruding from the hood.

'I didn't say a word,' said Jack, stifling a laugh. 'I think it … suits you.' He could no longer hold back the laughter. Beth laughed too and took a pretend swipe at him.

'I'll take that as a compliment,' she said. His eyebrows danced and he handed her the sander.

'Fully charged,' he said. 'But it still might not make it to the end of the kitchen floor.'

'Thanks, this unicorn has a busy day ahead,' she said playfully. 'See you later – and thank you, Jack.' Beth had investigated the costs for hiring proper floor sanders and it had put her off. Jack's hand sander wasn't designed for the job, but the kitchen floor surface was quite small, especially with all the cabinets in place, and Beth was very much embracing the rustic look so if it wasn't perfect that was okay with her.

She was methodical in her approach and spent the next few hours inching her way across the kitchen, sanding down very old floorboards that had been hidden for years under dirt and grime. Viewed from her kneeling position, it looked damn near perfect and she was particularly pleased with herself for her hard graft and for the money she'd saved. Being in one position for a few hours had taken its toll on Beth's back. It was no longer flexible, it had gone rigid and every sinew of her neck and shoulders ached. She eventually straightened up her fatigued body.

Despite the top section of the stable door and window being open all day, there was still so much dust in the air it was like she'd stuck her head in a cloud. The mask Jack had given her, back in the summer, was now past its best and she let it hang round her neck on the elastic. Beth twisted and turned in an attempt to loosen up her stiff muscles when a keen wind blew in and swirled the dust around, making her cough.

She held her aching back as each cough jarred it a little more.

'You look well,' said Petra from the other side of the stable door.

Beth opened the bottom half and Petra stood back when the wind swirled the dust in her direction.

'Sorry!' coughed Beth, trying to usher a reluctant Leo inside. Petra covered her mouth and nose with her hand, peered into the kitchen and looked over the floor.

'Wow, that is beautiful, Beth.' She was right, it *was* beautiful. The years of use had given it an original patina and oodles of character. All that was left to do to the floor was to finish it with a hard-wax oil but that would have to wait until the weekend when there was no Doris, and Leo was playing at the pub.

'You look like a ghost,' said Leo with a grin as he traipsed past his mother. 'Denis is practising penalties on the green. Can I go too?'

'Yes, if you change out of your school uniform,' she said over her shoulder and Leo ran upstairs.

'You do look like a ghost,' chuckled Petra.

'Thanks, friend,' said Beth as she ruffled her own hair with her fingers and sent yet more dust in Petra's direction.

'I remember my father doing this back home,' said Petra, waving away the dust cloud. 'It is tough work.'

'Do you see much of your parents?' asked Beth, brushing herself down.

Petra seemed to freeze. She shook her head, then relaxed a fraction. 'No. We don't speak.'

'Oh, that's a shame, especially for Denis.'

'It is.' Petra was staring at the floor.

'I can't imagine not speaking to my folks. I haven't seen them for a while and I hate that, but we talk on the phone.' Beth waited but Petra didn't speak. She was still staring at the floor, her expression one of solemn thought. 'Can't whatever it is be fixed?' asked Beth tentatively, although she was very aware that she was intruding into Petra's thoughts.

Petra seemed to come back to the present. She shook her head. 'No. They do not approve of Denis. It cannot be resolved.'

Beth tried to hide her shock. How could grandparents not approve of their own grandchild? Beth wasn't sure what to say, so she gave Petra a tentative hug, which was reciprocated.

Petra broke free. 'Right, I had better go,' she said with a brief frown, and she left.

Beth looked about her. The cottage was starting to look better and she'd made a friend in Petra. She was even getting on well with Jack. Very gradually, things were starting to come together.

Chapter Eighteen

It was just before midnight and Beth was drifting into a well-earned deep sleep when suddenly banging echoed through the hallway and around the small dwelling. Who would be banging on the door at this time of night? thought Beth. She scrambled up onto her pillow and looked out of the window and into the dark. Nope, it was no good, she'd have to go downstairs. When she reached the bottom of the stairs, she saw someone was trying the door handle and it made her freeze. Who would do that? The banging started again. She could think of only one person – Nick.

Leo stirred upstairs. 'What's up, Mum?'

'Shh. Nothing. Go back to bed.' Her voice was tight and her breathing was panicky. Her mind was awash with scenarios and none of them ended well. Beth inched towards the door while fear tried to pull her back. She wondered if she should call the police but banging on a front door wasn't an offence. She wished she'd thought through this possible scenario before now. Perhaps she and Leo could escape out of the back of the cottage without being seen. If Nick had found her, she didn't want to think about what he might do. Despite the dark, she could see a figure through the glass. She edged closer to get a better look and a face loomed up at the pane, distorting it somewhat and making her jump.

Someone spoke. 'Beth, it's Jack. I need a big favour. Beth?'

Beth's whole body relaxed instantly as a wave of relief washed over her, followed by a tinge of annoyance. She opened the door and Doris trotted in.

'Who bangs on a door and then tries the door handle?' she said sharply.

Jack looked momentarily confused. 'It was on the off chance that you'd left it open. Look, I'm really sorry but there's an emergency and I need to go to work now.'

Beth smirked. 'An emergency in IT?' Her annoyance was forgotten, a grin was spreading across her face and her heart rate was returning to normal.

'Yes.' Jack was frowning hard. 'I can't explain, official secrets and everything, but trust me it's serious. Can you have Doris?' he asked, as he handed her his house keys.

Beth's smile disappeared. 'Of course. Are you a spy?' The question was out before she could regulate it.

Jack gave her a stern look. 'I don't know when I'll be back. Get what you need for Doris from my place. I'll call you.' He put up his hood and jogged into the darkness.

'Bloody hell,' said Beth to Doris. She heard sniggers from Leo. 'Back to bed!' she called up the stairs.

It wasn't the best night's sleep she'd ever had. Doris was happy to lie on a blanket in the hall during the day but apparently that wasn't comfortable enough for night-time. She had paced outside the bedroom door, her claws scraping on the floor, until Beth had reluctantly let her in, and she had now made herself rather comfortable on Beth's double bed.

What Beth had thought was a generous-sized bed was now reduced considerably by Doris's sprawled bulk. Although it was obvious that Doris was a very big dog, she appeared to be even bigger when she was stretched out and she was completely impossible to move despite lots of shoving on Beth's part. Doris seemed to be in a very deep sleep and she vibrated with her dreams, making her judder all over the place, which was quite comical to witness, though it was more than a bit disconcerting to keep being woken by a dog snoring in your ear. However, she had to admit that it was a chilly night and she was secretly grateful for the warmth that Doris was sharing, but that was the only positive thing about it.

Even without all that Doris's presence brought, Beth's sleep was sporadic thanks to the spectre that was Nick. She had so quickly assumed it was him at the door, and the feelings that had gripped her maddened her. She thought she had left the fear behind but she had only been fooling herself. He still had a hold on her and somehow she had to break that control.

When Beth had finally slipped into a profound slumber, the alarm started to beep and Doris started to bark. Apparently she didn't like being woken by the alarm, either. Three tired figures all padded down to the kitchen. Doris looked hopeful when the toast was served.

'We'll get you something on the way back from the school run,' Beth told Doris, whose nose was inching ever closer to Leo's plate. Beth gently guided her away and scratched her head to distract her. Doris drifted into a trancelike state, her eyes closed and her tongue lolling out of her wide jaws at an angle. She was a soppy creature really.

'Is Jack really a spy?' asked Leo a little while later while he wrestled with the inside-out sleeves of his school coat. His mother pulled them through and helped him put the coat on.

'Nooo! Don't be silly. We were joking.'

Leo's nose wrinkled. He was thinking. 'Shame,' he said eventually, 'that would've been SO cool.'

Beth gave what she hoped was a neutral smile and they all left the cottage.

Having dropped the boys at school, Beth was now at Jack's place. The kitchen was an odd sight. It looked perfect as usual, all clean and tidy with the exception of a meal at the table and a single glass of white wine but no bottle. Beth had a sniff. She'd only ever seen Jack drink Guinness at the pub – perhaps this double life was more intricate than her already wild imagination was conjuring up for her. The meal was lasagne with four vegetables; she raised her eyebrows at that.

What she thought might be a bit of a search for Doris's food wasn't at all. She simply asked Doris where her dinner was and the dog bounded into the small conservatory and happily danced around a giant sack.

'I've heard of buying in bulk but seriously?'

Doris was throwing her head about in excitement. Beth found her food bowl and put a couple of handfuls into it, which Doris seemed to inhale before the bowl had properly touched the floor. While the dog nudged the now-empty bowl around the kitchen, Beth went in search of spare bowls and something to put some food in; there was no way she was dragging the giant sack across the village green. She found a cereal box in the recycling, filled it from the sack and took it, along with a spare bowl and Doris's beanbag. If he was away another night there was no way she was sharing her bed with Doris again. Before she left, she washed up Doris's used bowl and the plate, cutlery and glass from the table so it no longer looked like the cottage version of the *Marie Celeste*.

Beth's phone beeped when she was struggling across the village with a large beanbag that constantly changed shape as it tried to escape from her clutches, a cereal box at arm's length containing Doris's food, and Doris at full stretch trying to get her nose into the cereal box. When she reached the village store, Shirley was shuffling out trolley first. The dog spotted it instantly and no amount of shaking of the cereal box was going to distract Doris from her arch-enemy the wheelie trolley.

Doris chose the route behind Beth's back as the quickest and spun Beth round inelegantly as the cereal box contents flew over Shirley and the beanbag finally made good its escape.

Shirley looked alarmed when the lolloping mass that was Doris dived onto the wheelie trolley.

'Mittens!' shouted Shirley.

'Bugger!' shouted Beth, dropping the cereal box and bowl and making a dive for Doris. She missed. Doris, however, had landed with her front paws on the trolley, which was a four-wheeled variety, and was moving away because Doris appeared to be pushing it along. As it gathered pace so did Doris.

'Stop her!' shouted Shirley. 'She's got my mittens in there!'

A pair of mittens was the least of Beth's worries because Doris and the trolley were heading towards a parked car. Beth sprang into action and ran after the renegade pair. People had now stopped to watch and laugh as the comic scene played out. Doris, who was still trotting along on two legs, had been distracted by the morsels of food on the top of the trolley but when she licked up the last of them she detached herself from the trolley just as Beth caught up. As soon as Doris was no longer pushing the trolley it slowed to a stop millimetres from the car's bumper.

A spontaneous smattering of applause echoed across the green from the few locals who had witnessed the event and Beth waved her appreciation. Beth was breathing heavily from the short sprint, as was Doris from the excitement. At least Doris wasn't barking, thought Beth, keeping a tight hold on Doris's collar with one hand and the errant trolley with the other. That was when she felt it. She didn't see it, she just felt the sharp pain when something scratched her knuckles. Beth darted a look at her hand in time to see the small white paw shoot out of the edge of the trolley lid and have another swipe at her.

Shirley appeared at her side. 'There's a cat in the trolley?' said Beth, feeling uncertain of her own words.

'Mittens!' said Shirley, as she huffily took back the trolley. Doris remembered why she hated the trolley so much and started her usual barking onslaught at a retreating Shirley. Beth shook her head and started to drag Doris back to where she'd dropped the beanbag.

'Bonkers, this village is totally bonkers,' she said but she was smiling broadly as she said it.

Beth was glad to be back inside the cottage at last with the empty cereal box, a dented bowl, a muddy beanbag and a hyper Doris. She put the kettle on and ran her scratched hand under the cold tap. It was only a minor mark but it stung all the same. At last she sat down with a cup of coffee and checked her text messages.

At the station be with you soon C x

Beth stared at the message, then she checked the date and finally she checked previous texts from Carly.

'Bugger,' she said out loud. Today was the day Carly was coming to stay because she had pantomime rehearsals in Gloucester. As if on cue there was a knock at the front door and, although her shoulders sagged, Beth felt a spike of joy as she rushed to open it.

Beth gave Carly a hug and any uncharitable thoughts instantly disappeared. Her friend had come to stay and, even though it had slipped her mind, she knew they would have a good natter and the world would feel better for it. Doris was very interested in Carly's wheelie case but thankfully quickly assessed that, surprisingly, it did not contain a cat so she returned to her blanket.

A few cups of tea later and they had slipped back into their comfortable chatter and, although the subjects weren't the most uplifting thanks to Nick, talking things through always helped to put life in perspective.

Beth explained the previous night's drama, and how she had been sure it was Nick banging on the door, and the subsequent revelation that Jack had signed the Official Secrets Act.

'Ooh, so he's yummy *and* he's dark and dangerous,' said Carly, her eyes wide as she peered over her large mug of tea. 'He's perfect for you.'

'No, he's not. I've had enough of dark and dangerous, thank you very much. And anyway he works in IT.'

'Oh, that's clearly a cover. I bet that right now he's climbing up a mountain to infiltrate a villainous gang, or rescuing vital information or shooting a baddie.'

Beth blinked hard. 'You watch too many films. I bet he's sat looking at a computer screen and retrieving someone's boring emails. The real world is a lot less exciting than the movies.'

'He is yummy, though.'

'I'm surprised you can remember.' Beth laughed at the memory of a drunken Carly crashing out on Jack's sofa.

'I wasn't that bad! I liked how he smiled with half his mouth, sort of crooked but quite endearing,' said Carly, followed by a sigh.

Beth didn't like where this was heading. She changed the subject quickly. 'And how is the wonderful and delicious Fergus?' she asked.

Carly let out an even bigger but far less dreamy sigh. 'It's all turning to poo.'

'What's happened?'

'Nothing major. It's not one big thing, it's loads of little things. We're annoying the hell out of each other, basically. I can feel him slipping away and it's happening really fast. He's going out more and more so we see each other less. He avoids eye contact which makes it very hard to have a conversation with him without it feeling very deliberate and forced.'

'Everyone has rough patches, Carls. I'm sure that's all it is.'

'I'm not,' said Carly, her face a picture of sadness.

Carly and Doris bonded while Beth changed her bed, as Carly would have to share a bed with Beth. She came downstairs with the sheets bundled up in her arms, hoping that Carly wouldn't work out that she'd forgotten she was coming to stay.

'She's a total darling, isn't she?' said Carly, rubbing Doris's middle as the dog stretched out on the grubby beanbag. Doris looked like she was in heaven.

'We're getting used to each other,' said Beth, giving Doris an affectionate rub on the head as she went by.

'I see you've not found a hairdresser yet,' said Carly, joining Beth in the kitchen as Beth rammed the things into the washing machine.

'Blimey, that's harsh,' said Beth, with a half-laugh.

'No, you still look lovely. It's just not how you used to look with your salon-perfect hair and manicures and stuff.' Carly inspected her own flawless nails.

'I don't need it, it's not who I am. It was like this costume I used to wear.' She paused and Carly was now watching her closely. 'I like this costume better,' she said, pointing at her dungarees and giving a cheesy grin for emphasis.

Carly didn't look convinced. 'The cottage is looking a million times better.'

'You've not seen the bathroom yet. That's still a horror.'

'But this is fabulous,' said Carly, spreading out her arms in the small kitchen.

'Yeah, it's great. Jack and Simon did a great job …'

'You've had the lovely Jack getting all hot and sweaty in here?'

'Yes,' said Beth, refusing to rise to the innuendo. 'He and another local guy fitted it for me in exchange for custard creams and dog-sitting.'

'Oh,' said Carly, 'they're not a couple are they? Jack and Simon?'

'No!'

'Good. That would be a terrible shame,' said Carly, her expression quite serious. 'So Jack's handsome, mysterious and handy. He gets better and better.' Carly clapped her hands together.

'Don't go getting ideas. I'm off men for a while and not only for my sake but for Leo's as well.'

'I do get it,' said Carly. 'But I want you to be happy.'

'I don't need a man for that to happen,' said Beth. 'Can you watch Doris while I go and get her some dog food from Jack's?'

'No, I'm coming too. I'm not missing a chance to have a nose around a spy's house. Ooh, do you think he has a gun?'

Beth rolled her eyes good-humouredly. 'Come on, then,' she said as she directed Carly towards the door.

Chapter Nineteen

At Jack's, Beth had quickly refilled the cereal box with dry dog food and was waiting by the door ready to leave.

'Carly, what are you doing? He might have spy cameras all over this place, you know?' Beth chuckled to herself.

'Bloody hell, do you think so?' Carly peered down the stairs.

'Carls, you can't go snooping about. If he notices something's been touched he'll think it's me!' There was no answer. 'Carly!' Still no response. Beth put down the cereal box and reluctantly went upstairs.

The cool minimalism continued to the next floor but it somehow still felt homely; perhaps that was the nature of cottages with their low ceilings and traditional fittings. She peeked into the bathroom as she passed. It was long and thin and he'd managed to get a separate shower cubicle in as well as a bath, and she found herself nodding her approval.

Beth found Carly in the master bedroom. 'Look. No photographs,' said Carly, her voice barely a whisper.

'So?'

'It's weird, isn't it? There's nothing personal here. Nothing to tell you anything about the man that lives here.'

'Come on, Miss Marple,' said Beth, shaking her head as she nudged Carly towards the door.

'Look at this.' Carly took Beth's arm and walked her into the spare bedroom. It had a simple table-like desk with a large computer screen, a keyboard and two laptops on it. There was a cross trainer, a state-of-the-art exercise bike and weights bench. Carly pointed to them each in turn.

'He works in IT and he likes to keep fit. So what?'

Carly silently pointed across the room. A large built-in cupboard dominated the end wall.

'No,' said Beth, guessing Carly's next exploration.

'Just a sneaky look.'

'I'm leaving,' said Beth, who was feeling increasingly uncomfortable. Carly crept over to the cupboard and tentatively gripped the handle.

'Argh!' yelled Beth for a joke and Carly almost fell over with the shock.

'You bloody idiot!' Carly spluttered through a nervous laugh. Once she was a little calmer she opened the cupboard. It was completely empty. A series of shelves were all clear. 'Now that *is* odd,' said Carly, pointing at the empty cupboard. A quick look in the other side revealed a lot of box files and that was Beth's cue to be a little more forceful with Carly and hustle her out of the room and out of the cottage before she took her amateur detecting too far.

The afternoon whizzed by in a flurry of natter. Carly caught up with Leo over a game of Top Trumps before they headed to the Bleeding Bear. They had dinner at the pub because Beth still only had the two chairs, and then went on to choosing budget furniture from the Internet via Beth's phone whilst sipping wine. Sadly, the solid wood half-circle coffee table was well out of Beth's price range so it would have to wait until the next property she renovated. Her plan was to reuse the furniture to dress each place for sale so she needed statement items. It was all about selling people the lifestyle; a little slice of a lifestyle she used to live back in London.

When Beth was still awake in the early hours she mulled over whether Doris was a better bed partner than Carly. At least Doris had stuck to her side most of the time, even if the snoring and doggy breath had been a bit much. Carly seemed to roll up against Beth regardless of how many times she rolled her back.

The next morning Carly was up quite early and was full of excitement at meeting the cast and minor celebrities of the panto. By nine o'clock she had been whisked away in a taxi. There was still no contact from Jack. Nevertheless, Beth had his business card and wondered about calling him but didn't know where he was or what he was doing or even if he was allowed calls. She'd got used to seeing him each morning when he dropped Doris off; he had become part of her new routine and so it felt odd that he was suddenly not about. Surely she wasn't missing his playful teasing and general usefulness? Despite her best efforts to keep her imaginings in check, Beth was starting to wonder about Jack. He had been helpful to her, kind even, but she actually knew very little about him. Could he be a spy? And, if so, where was he right now?

With Doris tired out after a brisk walk and now safely in her dog cage at Jack's for a couple of hours, Beth did a lunchtime shift at the pub which she enjoyed. It was more about taking food orders than it was about the drinks and everyone was friendly. Over the course of a few shifts, she had added names to some faces she had seen around the village and now, when she left the cottage, more and more people called her by name.

Beth borrowed a chair from the pub so that the three of them could at least eat together and decided to make her sweet potato and coconut curry while Leo and Carly took it in turns to update her on their day. Doris was sitting next to Beth and leaning into her leg as she prepared the sweet potatoes.

'... and the Romans ruled our country for nearly four hundred years! The Romans lived here in the Cotswolds too. Me and Denis are learning partners and we're going to build a Roman fort!'

'Wow, the Romans were cool!' enthused Carly.

'They had battle plans and their army was the best,' added Leo, nodding sagely as he did so. 'They brought new plants with them, too, that still grow in this country.'

Beth turned round. 'Which ones?'

'There was one with yellow flowers and one that was just green leaves. I'll go and see if we have any in the garden.'

'Coat!' instructed Beth, making Leo do a pirouette in the kitchen. He dashed past seconds later with his coat half on and Doris at his heels carrying the latest of a series of destroyed footballs in her mouth.

'He likes it here,' observed Carly.

'He's definitely more enthusiastic about school. The small class really seems to help bring things alive for him.'

'That's really good. By the way, the panto is hilarious. You must come.'

'Tell me all about it, then.'

'It's the usual *Snow White* story: pretty girl, handsome prince, cute little people, singing and dancing with some modern gags for the grown-ups.'

'Does the prince still kiss Snow White when he thinks she's dead? That bit creeps me out now I'm an adult ...' but Beth noticed Carly wasn't listening. 'What's up?' she asked as she checked the rice.

'I've not heard from Fergus. I've been texting him on and off all day but he's not replied.'

'Are you worried?'

'Nope, I think he's sulking.'

Beth looked at Carly's pouting lips and long face. 'What are you going to do about your relationship?'

Carly stared at the kitchen floor. Beth liked looking at the newly oiled floor too. She saw something different in it each time she studied it but she doubted that was what was holding Carly's attention. 'I don't know,' said Carly eventually, and when she looked up tears were already escaping.

After two bottles of wine, another night sharing a bed with Carly didn't seem so bad but for some reason Doris was uneasy. She had stayed close to Beth all day and, although Beth didn't credit her with a great amount of intelligence, she did feel that Doris was missing Jack. When she scratched at the door for the fifth time, Beth relented and let her in. Doris dived onto the bed and settled down with her glum face resting on her paws. Beth attempted to shove her a bit further down the bed and then tried to curl up in the remaining quarter of it. It was going to be a long night.

It was an odd sound that woke Beth, a sort of snapping noise. She tried to ignore it but its rhythm told her it wasn't the local wildlife and she had to investigate. She groaned as she extricated herself from the overcrowded bed, slipped into her unicorn onesie and went to investigate. She was scratching her head as she looked out of the living-room window. It was difficult to see but there appeared to be someone doing something to the willow tree. She walked to the hall and let out a huge yawn as she opened the front door.

'I'm sorry, did I wake you?' asked a chirpy Jack.

'Shh,' said Beth pointing up to her bedroom window. 'They're still asleep. What are you doing?'

'Pruning the willow,' said Jack, as if it was the most normal thing ever. She must have left the bedroom door open as Doris came hurtling out of the house and cannoned into Jack who, Beth noted, was strong enough to catch her and absorb the impact. Had it been her she would be lying on her back like at her first encounter with Doris a few months ago.

'She must have heard your voice,' said Beth, aware she was

stating the obvious, but it was early. Jack was fussing Doris and half wrestling with the delighted mutt.

'Coffee?' said Beth, as she shuffled back into the cottage emitting another seismic yawn.

Coffee was drunk in virtual silence as Doris sat directly in front of Jack with her chin in his lap gazing up at him with a look of total adoration.

'It must be nice to be loved that much,' said Beth, then instantly wondered why she'd said it out loud.

Jack grinned his lopsided grin. 'Yeah, but does she appreciate it?'

Beth was grateful to him for deflecting her statement with humour.

'I think we may have solved the mystery of why Doris hates Shirley's trolley.' Jack looked intrigued and tilted his head expectantly. 'Shirley pushes her cat, Mittens, around in it!'

'Mittens is still alive?'

'And still quick on the draw,' said Beth, showing him her scratched knuckles.

Jack snorted a laugh. 'That explains a lot. No wonder Doris goes nuts every time she sees it.' Doris pricked up her floppy ears as much as she could at the mention of her name and Jack resumed the ear rub.

'Is it safe to assume that whatever was so urgent with work is all sorted now?' She had to ask.

'Yeah. All sorted,' he said flatly.

Carly suddenly appeared at the bottom of the stairs and hurried into the kitchen, pulling her jumper down to cover her pyjama shorts. 'What is it exactly that you do then?'

'IT consultant,' said Jack, his voice even as he broke eye contact and continued stroking Doris's dark floppy ears.

'We kinda thought that was your cover,' said Carly, flicking the switch on the kettle. 'You know, so people don't think you're a spy.'

182

'We?' said Beth. 'Leave me out of this little fantasy.'

Jack chuckled lightly. 'I'm not a spy.'

Beth sipped her drink. 'That's exactly what a spy would say.'

Jack's smile was rueful. 'True, but I'm not one. It's technical surveillance. I have some specialist expertise that gets called on from time to time.'

Beth was nodding but she wasn't sure why. 'I have no idea what that means.'

'Nor me,' said Carly, making herself a cup of tea.

He stopped fiddling with Doris's ears and gave the women his full attention. 'The Ministry of Defence has the single largest computer network in Europe. Their systems log more than one million suspicious incidents every twenty-four hours. There are thousands of cyber-attacks every day and each day they get more complex. Occasionally, they have a close call and I join the GCHQ team to get it resolved quickly. I'm on contract to them.'

Carly had joined in the nodding. 'GCHQ, that's in Cheltenham; that's near here,' she said. 'I don't know how I know that. Is it okay that I know that?'

Jack snorted. 'Yeah, that's fine, it's not a secret.'

'Do you get to meet real James Bond types?' asked Carly, as she came to rest on the wall near to Jack, her jumper riding up a little.

Beth noted that Jack averted his eyes. 'No, not really. Anyway, in real life James Bond would be behind a desk doing loads of paperwork.'

'But what about having a licence to kill?' asked Carly.

Jack shook his head.

'You're deliberately spoiling it now!'

Carly and Doris went home and things returned to some semblance of normality. A few days later, Beth's living-room carpet was finally fitted as were some inside shutters for the windows as Beth hated curtains. Shortly afterwards, the furniture she had ordered online arrived. Two simply styled deep purple sofas now dominated the living room. She still didn't have a coffee table but it wasn't an essential. She had bought an ornate photo frame a couple of weeks ago and now Elsie and Wilf's photo had pride of place on the windowsill. Leo was desperate to have a television again but she wanted to save the money she'd earned at the pub for Christmas. But would Christmas be Christmas without a television? It was a double-edged sword. For now she'd stick to the plan and perhaps she could get a television in the January sales.

A busy lunchtime shift had Beth realizing that flat shoes were the way to go. She was waiting on the other side of the bar for Petra who was making up her wages. As she leaned on the bar and eased her feet out of their shoe prison, she moaned with relief just as Jack appeared.

'You all right?'

'My feet are literally killing me. I think they are starting by eating my toes and then working their way up.'

He chuckled. 'Can I get you a drink or is this the last place you want to be?'

'A drink would be great. An orange juice, thanks.'

They found a table and slipped into an amiable chat.

'How are the feet?'

'Relenting but they're not looking forward to another shift tonight. Apparently it'll be a busy one because they're switching on the Christmas tree lights.'

'Annual event on the green,' said Jack. 'Is someone taking Leo?'

'I can't and Petra is working too, so Leo and Denis will be in here.'

'I could take them both, if you like?' said Jack, with a shrug.

'Thanks. They'd love that.'

'What are your plans for Christmas?' asked Jack, sipping his Diet Coke.

'Presents first thing, then lunchtime shift here followed by a late dinner and too many chocolates. How about you?'

'I'd not thought about it until you mentioned the lights switch-on. I guess I'll come here with the other waifs and strays.'

'What about your parents?'

Jack looked like he was considering his answer or perhaps he was considering whether to answer or not. 'It was only ever my mum and she's with a guy that … well, we don't get on. I'll drop by on Christmas Eve and we'll swap presents but that's all.'

'Family can be complicated like that,' said Beth and they both nodded and took synchronized sips of their drinks.

'How about your mum and dad?'

How could she tell him that she was giving them a wide berth in case it tipped off Nick as to her whereabouts? She went for a censored version of the truth.

'They're away for Christmas, making the most of retirement, so we'll catch up with them some other time.'

'What about Leo's father?' asked Jack, as casually as he'd asked about Christmas.

Beth felt her pulse quicken; this was a piece of her past that she rarely shared. 'He's not with us any more. He was killed before Leo was born.'

'Killed?'

'He was a soldier. Mortar attack.' She found sticking to facts made it somehow easier to explain. Their relationship had been tragically cut short but nearly seven years later she had moved on, taking the fond memories with her.

Jack's face looked pained. 'I am so sorry. I shouldn't have asked.'

'It's okay. I mean, it wasn't okay, but you carry on. I was lucky I had Leo to focus on.' They exchanged knowing nods. Beth finished her drink. 'I'd better get going. Thank you for the drink.'

'Sure. I'll pick the boys up from here just before six then.'

'Great. Thanks, Jack. That will make their day.'

It was almost midnight and Carly was on the sofa in the flat watching every juddery tick of the clock. She'd been stewing

185

gently all evening and, now that Fergus was nearly an hour later than he'd said he would be, she was coming to a perfect simmer. The front door clicked and she stood up ready to ambush him. Fergus tried to hold onto the door as he staggered inside, grinning inanely. He was drunk.

'Carly!' He swayed precariously towards her. 'Carly Wilson. I love you.' He emphasized the point by wagging a finger in her face. If she hadn't built herself up into such a strop she might have laughed. He started to frown and leaned forward. The smell of drink was overpowering. 'Did you hear me?' he said. 'I love you!'

Carly started to sign and Fergus closed his eyes. 'Not reading, not reading!' he chanted. 'If you're telling me off, I don't want to know.' He opened one eye. Carly had stopped signing and was giving him a long hard stare. When she lifted her hands to sign again he quickly shut his eyes tight. He looked quite childlike and vulnerable as he stood there swaying slightly. He was still grinning as he tentatively opened an eye. Carly was not seeing the funny side of the situation. She knew it was funny but she wanted to be cross with him, though she wasn't entirely sure why.

'Come on, Carls. Where's the fun gone?'

He was right. The fun had gone. She hadn't noticed it slip away but somehow it had. When did he start going out and getting drunk without her? When did she start clock-watching and gaining a sense of gratification when he was late? This wasn't how they used to be but she wasn't sure how to put things straight. The silence seemed to close in around her as she started to realize everything that was at stake.

'I don't know,' she said, and he read her lips.

Fergus steadied himself and came towards her. He pulled her tenderly into a hug and they both cried gently as he rocked her in his arms. 'I don't know either, Carls. I wish I did.'

After a few minutes they pulled apart and studied each other's tear-stained faces.

'This is crazy,' said Fergus very quietly as he pushed his fingers through his wayward hair.

Carly nodded. He was right. 'You sit down and I'll get you a strong coffee.'

When she returned there was no sign of Fergus but she could hear a noise like a frantic burrowing badger coming from the cupboard.

'Found them!' called Fergus, before he marched into the room with a box under one arm and dragging the artificial Christmas tree behind him.

Carly raised an eyebrow and placed his coffee down a safe distance away.

'Let's decorate the Christmas tree,' he said enthusiastically. Carly stood quietly watching him and thinking. She was thinking about the other years they had done this and reminisced about the year gone by. This year's memories weren't going to make it such a fun occasion. She watched as he put up the tree and, with his hands on his hips, surveyed it proudly, even though it was the easiest thing to erect. 'Come on, Carls, let's do this together,' he said, taking her hand.

Chapter Twenty

The Christmas tree on the village green was now lit up every night and its multi-coloured lights and flashing star on the top were a sight that warmed the most 'bah humbug' of hearts. Ernie had taken to standing in front of it for at least thirty minutes at a time until someone took him off for a cup of tea and a warm-up. Every time Beth passed the tree, she felt the little sparkle of Christmas glimmer inside her as well as the usual growing anxiety that she wasn't ready for it yet. The few shifts at the pub were bringing in enough money for their day-to-day needs, leaving her depleted savings to pay for utilities and the remaining work on the cottage. Thanks to Beth grabbing her glue gun when she left Nick, she had a way to make Christmas presents for people and she always felt that homemade gifts were so much nicer – something that Nick had flatly disagreed with. Now that the Christmas meals were in full swing the tips were adding up, too. Perhaps a TV wasn't out of the question.

Beth's phone rang. It was Carly. 'Fergus has gone ...'

'What?' Beth quickly digested all that this could mean.

'I was at work and he texted to say his grandmother had been taken ill and he was going to Ireland.'

Beth felt a sense of relief that it wasn't one of the more disastrous scenarios her mind had conjured up.

'But he'll be back when she gets better.'

'I don't think so. He's taken some of his computer stuff from the playroom. Not all of it but don't you think it's odd to take stuff like that if you've been called to a sick relative?'

Beth pulled a face. 'I don't know.'

'He's taken his ukulele. I think he's left me, Beth.'

And there it was, the statement Beth had been dreading. 'I think he would have said if he was going to do that. What else did he take?'

'Some clothes, including three jumpers. That's excessive, isn't it?'

'No, not at all. When I went to Ireland I would have been glad of three jumpers. Very wise I'd say. I think you're going all Miss Marple again and overthinking this.'

'We put the Christmas tree up together the other night. We had Christmas songs playing and it was lovely. I thought things were looking a little brighter and now this …' Carly's voice was getting quieter with every word and Beth suspected she was fighting back tears.

'Come on. This is Fergus we're talking about. He's one of the good guys. I know things have been a bit rocky but he wouldn't lie about his grandmother being ill, would he?'

'I guess not,' said Carly, followed by a sniff.

'If you're in any doubt, ring his family, offer your best wishes and ask someone to let you know when he's arrived.'

'It'll look like I'm checking up on him.'

'No, it won't. It'll look like you care. Okay?'

'Yes. Good idea. Thanks, Beth.'

Beth was still reflecting on Carly's phone call when she opened her front door to a large tree.

'Rockin' around the Christmas tree …' sang Jack from behind the foliage.

'Are you branching out, Mr Selby?'

'Very funny. Can I come in? It's brass monkeys out here,' said Jack as he shoved the tree into the hall. Beth barely managed to hop out of its way.

'It's huge! If you've stolen this from the village green people will notice, you know.' She was grinning at her own joke.

Jack's face bobbed from behind the tree. 'Someone I know was selling them cheap so I got two.'

'Who buys a spare Christmas tree?'

He propped the tree carefully against the wall. 'I usually have one in the living room and one in the conservatory,' he said, rather haughtily. 'But this year I thought maybe you would like it. And, to be honest, I couldn't be bothered to decorate two.'

'Ah, now we have the truth. What do I owe you?'

'Nothing. It's your Christmas present from Doris.'

'Then how could I refuse? Please thank Doris for me.'

'Hang on,' said Jack as he nipped outside and quickly returned holding something up. 'You'll need a stand.'

'You think of everything. It's a lovely tree, thank you. That's another Christmas job I can tick off my list. Still need to get decorations though.'

'I've had an idea about that,' said Jack. 'There's a Christmas Fayre on this evening not far from here. I thought you and Leo might fancy going. It'd be a chance to get some decorations. Just a thought.' He was rubbing his hands together and shifting about uneasily.

'Yeah, that'd be great. One condition.'

'Name it.'

'You have to help decorate this afterwards,' she said, pointing at the tree.

'Deal,' he said with a broad grin.

* * *

190

The chill in the air had made the Christmas Fayre extra Christmassy and thanks to Jack's charm and haggling, they had come away with lots of sparkly things for Beth to glue to some plain picture frames to make them bespoke and special, as well as a bumper selection of decorations. The decorations were all handmade, some more rustic than others but, as they were each allocated a place on the tree, they all seemed to work together. The three of them stood back to admire their handiwork. Beth frowned at the tree.

'Something missing?' asked Jack as Leo gave him a playful nudge.

'Yeah, we forgot a tree topper. You know like an angel or a star. Never mind, we could make one,' said Beth, turning to face Jack and Leo. She looked from one to the other. 'What's going on?' She narrowed her eyes.

'We got you something,' said Leo. His enjoyment at the secret he was clearly sharing with Jack was palpable.

'We?' questioned Beth, turning her stare onto Jack.

He shook his head. 'He chose it!'

'He paid!' countered Leo.

Beth put her hands on her hips and a giggling Leo presented her with a brown paper bag. She opened it carefully to reveal a twig reindeer with a light-up red nose. Leo and Jack were already high-fiving each other and staggering about holding their sides as they laughed.

'It's fab. I love it,' she said, bringing them to an abrupt halt. She got onto the chair they had been using to put on the higher decorations and placed the reindeer at the very top. A quick flick of a switch and the reindeer's nose started to flash. 'Perfect.'

She climbed down and stood with Jack and Leo as they admired the tree. It was a job well done. A tap at the window made them all jump but they quickly relaxed when they saw Ernie's face peering inside and giving them a big smile as he pointed at the tree.

'What does Ernie do at Christmas?' asked Beth as she watched through the window as Ernie walked away.

'Mmm. Good question. He used to spend it here with Wilf. The last couple of years I know Petra has brought Christmas dinner over from the pub, so I think I'll see if I can convince him to come to the pub with me.'

Leo gave his mother a pleading look but didn't say anything.

'If you don't mind having a late dinner, you and Ernie could always eat here with us,' said Beth. She tried to sound casual but for some reason it seemed like a big thing to be asking.

Jack was scratching his head and biting the inside of his mouth, which made for an unusual sight. 'I think Ernie would like that.'

'I'd like it too!' said Leo. 'Doris is invited too, isn't she, Mum?'

'Yes, Doris is invited too.'

'Cool!' said Leo. His eyes wide, he looked towards Jack awaiting his definitive answer.

'Yeah, okay then. Thanks, I'd love to come,' he said as he leaned in and kissed Beth lightly on the cheek. In that fleeting moment she could smell his aftershave, feel the roughness of his chin against her cheek and feel something stir inside.

The next few days whizzed by in a frenzy of glue gun crafting, last-minute shopping, school plays, shifts at the pub and late-night present-wrapping. Carly was calling every evening with an update on the Fergus situation as well as his grandmother's health. The old lady had suffered a stroke and some other complications so things were not looking promising. Fergus had told Carly he was struggling with his deafness as none of the family could sign apart from his little brother who had learned a little Irish Sign Language from a friend, swear words mainly, but still. The trouble was, Irish Sign Language differed to the British Sign Language that Fergus was used to so it was all proving to be a struggle. His lip-reading had improved but it was still not perfect so he had been reduced to asking people to write things down which Carly knew was always a last resort as it made him feel like an idiot and he hated that feeling.

The good thing seemed to be that they were missing each other. They were texting each other constantly, which was a big improvement. So, despite Carly's fears, he didn't appear to have left her. They had also exchanged apologies for the last few months and were now making plans for Christmas. Maybe absence really did make the heart grow fonder after all?

Beth had made reassuring noises on each phone call with Carly and hoped, as Carly did, that Fergus was missing her as much as he said he was. When the phone went on 23 December, Beth knew who it would be.

'Hiya, Carls, happy Christmas Eve Eve!'

'And to you. What ya doin'?'

'Removing giblets from a turkey,' she said as she balanced the phone precariously between her ear and shoulder. 'How about you?'

'Euw!' said Carly with feeling. 'I've put the last of the presents under the tree and poured myself a large glass of wine.'

'What's the latest?'

'No change is all the hospital will say so the family are still on high alert and keeping a bedside vigil. He's sent me some lovely texts, I think he really is missing me and not only as a BSL interpreter.'

'That's good, and are you missing him?'

'More than I thought possible. I just want things back how they were. I don't need a proposal but I do need Fergus. I know that for sure.'

'Great. What's happening about Christmas?'

There was a deep sigh from Carly's end. 'He says he'll be home for Christmas even if he has to get leprechauns to carry him but I'm not so sure. I spoke to his mum tonight whilst he was at the hospital and she was all apologetic that he wouldn't be back for Christmas and asked if I had considered flying over there!'

'So, what are you going to do?'

'I don't know. I really don't know.'

'It's Christmas Eve tomorrow, Carls, you're kind of running out of time.'

'I know, but I don't want to spend Christmas surrounded by his family. And I don't want to be on my own. I want it to be just the two of us here.'

'Then you'd better hope those leprechauns are fast runners!'

Christmas Eve brought its own answers as Beth and Leo woke up to a village painted white with snow and it was still falling fast. Leo was beside himself with excitement and went through three pairs of trousers in his enthusiasm to make snow angels and snowmen in the garden. Beth watched him and Denis through the window as they chased each other with handfuls of snow as it continued to fall at a steady pace. Snowballs suddenly started to fly out from the willow, which was now a cascading beauty in sparkly crystallized snow. The boys were stunned for a moment until they saw Ernie's grinning face as he peeped through the willow's frozen fronds to see if his missiles had hit their target. The boys' excitement went up a notch and a full-on snowball fight ensued. When an errant snowball smashed against the living-room window Beth decided to intervene; it wouldn't be long before someone got hurt and she would like to avoid any pre-Christmas injuries if she could.

'Okay, snowball fight over. There's hot chocolate if you come in now,' she said as she dodged a snowball that hit the doorframe and shattered spectacularly above her head, dousing her in tiny droplets of snow. There was a lot of giggling as Leo, Denis and Ernie all trooped inside.

Beth was very proud of herself for getting the real fire going as it made the living room come alive and it also generated a lot of heat. The boys were rattling off all the things they wanted for Christmas and Beth tried to ignore the worries that were sweeping over her that Leo would be disappointed with his pile of gifts this year, as it bore no comparison to previous years'. There was a knock at the door and she was instantly distracted. Something made her hesitate before going to answer it.

Chapter Twenty-One

Beth braced herself and opened the front door. A very smiley man stood on the doorstep with a clipboard and Beth immediately relaxed but also felt her charitable side decline; she didn't need someone trying to sell her something on Christmas Eve.

'Ms Browne?' he asked.

'Yes,' said Beth, anticipating the inevitable awkward moment.

'Sign here, please,' he said, handing her the clipboard. He turned and walked away, which was when Beth noticed the large delivery van parked by what was left of her picket fence. She stood still for a moment as confusion reigned. She hadn't ordered anything so what could it be? She glanced over the paperwork on the clipboard for a clue. One word jumped out at her at the same time as a large box was heaved from the van and the faces at the window identified the package. 'TELEVISION!'

Beth started to panic. This had to be a mistake and it was bad enough that Leo was spending Christmas without a television, let alone having one wafted under his nose and then cruelly taken away on Christmas Eve. She strode out into the snow to intercept the deliveryman.

'I'm really sorry, there's been some mistake. We haven't ordered a television. This isn't ours.'

The man who had come to the door was still holding on to his end of the large box. He opened his mouth and tilted his head towards Beth so he could get a look at the paperwork. 'But you are Ms Browne?'

'Yes, but …'

'And this is Willow Cottage, The Green, Dumbleford?'

'Yes, but …'

'Then this is where we're delivering it,' he said with certainty. 'Come on,' he said to his colleague who looked like he was close to dropping the large box, although they now did both look rather Christmassy with their light coating of snow. As they marched the parcel into the hall, the whoops of delight from the living room were deafening and Beth's heart sank.

Beth heard a car pull up behind the van but she was too busy speed-reading the delivery documentation to see if there was a number she could call.

'Helloooooo!' called a familiar voice.

Beth spun round with a frown etched on her face. 'Carly?' What was going on?

'Ooh, it's beaten me here. That's good service. I only ordered it last night. Had to pay extra, obviously.'

Beth used the clipboard to point from Carly to the deliverymen who were now heading out of the house. Carly took the clipboard from her, signed her name and handed it to the deliverymen as they passed.

'Merry Christmas,' they all chorused and Carly and her wheelie case carried on into the cottage as Beth watched the taxi and delivery van crawl slowly out of the snow-covered drive.

Eventually, Beth came to her senses and went inside. Ernie was sitting on one of the sofas hugging his empty mug and grinning from ear to ear as Leo and Denis ripped apart the box. Carly was in the hall, taking off her shoes and coat.

'What's going on?' asked Beth, closing her eyes briefly as she tried to make sense of everything that was perplexing her.

'All flights to and from Ireland are cancelled because of the snow. I've got hardly any food in because I didn't know what was happening so I thought I'd surprise you and come for Christmas,' Carly said, with a beaming smile. 'Surprise!' she added belatedly.

'And?' Beth gave one firm finger-point in the direction of the cardboard massacre that was occurring on the new living-room carpet.

'If you think I'm spending Christmas here without a telly you're very much mistaken.' She gave Beth a kiss. 'Merry Christmas. It's your present for this year and the next gazillion years too!'

'But I thought Fergus said he'd be home for Christmas, come what may?' said Beth. However Carly wasn't listening – she was already helping the boys to set up the television.

Christmas morning was a frenzy of vegetable preparation and wrapping paper as Leo opened his presents and Beth tried to work out what to feed an unexpected vegetarian for Christmas dinner. Beth was mightily relieved that Leo loved his presents and especially the giant Lego set. It was the biggest she could afford and it had gone down a storm. He even seemed pleased with the new jeans and tops that she'd got him which were actually things he'd needed but had made for extra presents to unwrap. Carly was officially the best godmother ever as the television was an afterthought; she had also bought him a tablet, which was now charging in the bedroom.

Ernie appeared mid-morning and Leo thrust a present under his nose as soon as he came in. They'd agreed that the adults would open theirs together in the afternoon but Ernie was the exception to the rule and was allowed one now. Ernie had sat down with the neatly wrapped gift resting on his knee for a while before he eventually gave in to Leo's pleas for him to open it. Ernie carefully picked at the edges and gently unfolded the paper to reveal his present. Leo lost interest as soon as he saw what it was and quickly returned to his new toys.

Ernie was transfixed by the gift for a long while and when he eventually looked up he had tears in his eyes. Beth felt a prick at the back of hers too.

'Do you like it, Ernie?'

He nodded and swallowed hard. 'I lost my owinge scarf,' he said at last.

'Now you've got a new one,' said Beth, fighting back the tears. Ernie put on his bright orange scarf and smoothed down the ends. He sat with it on, nursing a cup of tea as he watched Leo play.

Carly seemed to be keeping her distance from Ernie and Beth sensed that she wasn't that comfortable around him. She had to admit that she had been cautious of him at first and it registered with her how things had changed since the day he'd chased them away from Willow Cottage.

Beth came downstairs, having changed ready for her shift at the pub, and was putting on her flat shoes when Carly slunk out of the living room.

'You're not seriously leaving me here with Leo and him?' said Carly in a low voice.

'If you mean Ernie, he's fine. He doesn't say much so he's a good listener, you'll love him,' chided Beth.

'Beth!' said Carly, her tone aggravated. 'He's a strange old man who thinks he lives under a tree. Anything could happen. You read about it in the papers!' Her eyes were wide and she was nodding frantically.

'Look, Miss Marple, you are quite safe with Ernie. Give him tea and he'll be fine. But if his tea runs out make sure he's not near the poker,' said Beth as she put her coat on and tried to hide her smirk. Carly stuck her tongue out.

'Bye, Leo, bye, Ernie. See you later.' She pulled on her gloves and hat. 'Carly, stop fretting, I'll be back in a couple of hours and don't forget to baste the turkey every hour!' she said as she left.

'But I'm a sensitive vegetarian!' Carly protested to the closed door.

The pub on Christmas Day ran like a well-oiled machine. All the menu choices had been given in weeks before and the meals were timed to perfection. Beth got to pull a cracker and have a glass of champagne so it was not exactly the hardest shift she'd ever done. Everyone was on fine form and the pub was filled with chatter, laughter and crooning from a dodgy Christmas CD. Most of the patrons were the elderly of the village, Shirley included, but there were also a few tables of visitors who were treating themselves to the luxury of someone else cooking their Christmas dinner for them.

Beth lost count of how many bottles of champagne she poured, but everyone was happily merry and the tips were plentiful. When Shirley suggested that they put the Queen's Christmas message on the TV and demanded that everyone should stand for the national anthem, Petra gave Beth the nod that she could leave. She left with a doggy bag from the chef, two bottles of wine from Petra and Shirley's rendition of 'God Save the Queen' ringing in her ears.

Beth texted Jack to let him know she had escaped, and he and Doris arrived as she was knocking the snow off her wellies.

'Merry Christmas, Beth,' Jack said, giving Beth a gentle kiss on the cheek that took her slightly by surprise and made her blush.

'And to you,' she said. Their eyes fixed intently on each other for a second before Doris jumped up and very nearly knocked her over. 'Oh, and to you too, Doris!' She gave the dog a fuss as Jack brought her in. He whipped out a small towel and wiped the snow off Doris and dried her paws.

'Wow, I'm impressed. I hope you're as well house-trained,' teased Beth.

'Couldn't risk ruining your new carpet,' said Jack. 'And you'll have to wait and see if I'm house-trained or not.' There was a flicker in his eye and she wasn't sure if it had been a wink. She wanted to demand an action replay but he had already kicked off his shoes and was heading into the kitchen with two more bottles and a large bag. Doris went charging into the small living room and completely misjudged everything with all the people, a half-completed Lego set all over the floor and a large tree. She careered into everything and everyone.

'Doris!' yelled Leo as she trampled over his Lego instructions and then trod on and skidded off the shiny surface of the presents by the tree.

'Argh!' shouted Carly as Doris clambered across her and the sofa. Ernie managed to save his tea and avoided any spillage but the might of Doris was too much for the Christmas tree as she sideswiped it and it toppled over, luckily missing everyone.

Beth surveyed the devastation as Jack ran to her side and Doris looked about her in amazement as if to say, 'Who made all that mess?'

'She looks even bigger from this angle. You could put a saddle on her,' said Carly, making room as Doris trotted past her. At first Carly didn't seem to notice that she was leaning towards Ernie but when she did she stood up quickly. 'I'll give you a hand with the tree.'

'No, you're okay. I'll put it straight,' said Jack, lifting the tree and the stand upright.

Doris sat next to Beth and watched as Jack put the tree back together. She gave Beth a forlorn look. 'I know you didn't mean it,' she said, as she rubbed her head and Doris rested her face against her leg.

Once Beth was happy that everything was under control in the kitchen and the living room had been put back in order, she handed out drinks to everyone and announced a toast. 'To friends and family, wherever they may be.' Everyone nodded and clinked glasses. Even Ernie had a small glass of fizz; he didn't look impressed when he tasted it, but he raised it to the photo of Elsie and Wilf all the same.

'Presents!' said Beth, and Leo dived towards the gifts which now looked slightly scraggy thanks to their encounter with Doris. Leo read out the labels and passed them round. Jack produced some gifts too and handed his out, and a frenzy of opening commenced. Doris started to bark; she was very excited by all the noise and especially the large ball-shaped present that Leo had placed in front of her.

Leo had a similar-shaped present from Jack. Unsurprisingly it was a new football.

'Because she keeps putting holes in your others,' explained Jack.

'Cheers,' said Leo, and he gave Jack a spontaneous hug. Jack became a little awkward but he looked touched as the embrace ended. Leo helped Doris unwrap her present, which was a large red ball.

'It's indestructible,' said Beth, and Jack nodded his approval.

'Well, if anyone can prove that wrong it will be Doris,' he said. Leo immediately donned his coat, hat and wellies and took Doris outside to road-test her new present.

Beth carefully unwrapped her gift from Jack. It was a slate house sign that said Willow Cottage. 'I love it, thank you,' she said and she meant it. And for a moment she held his gaze.

Jack was taken aback by his canvas print of a photo Beth had taken of Doris in front of the willow tree. 'Wow, you never told me you'd taken this,' he said, beaming broadly.

'Duh, that would have been a rubbish surprise,' said Beth, and she was pleased with Jack's reaction and watched him as he kept eyeing it. Carly pulled faces when she unwrapped an idiot's guide to the Internet from Beth but was very pleased with her sparkly picture frame that Beth had embellished herself. Ernie was surprised to get another present and was again overcome when he opened a small version of the Elsie and Wilf photograph also in a sparkly frame. He pointed at his and back at the original on the windowsill but couldn't seem to find the words. Beth gave him a brief hug, which he self-consciously reciprocated.

'What did you get from Fergus?' asked Beth.

Carly disappeared to rummage in her handbag and Beth followed her. Carly pulled out a gold box and took it into the kitchen where Beth watched her open it. Beth could feel her pulse rate quicken as the lid came off. Carly took out a piece of paper and shook the box to see if there was anything else, but that was it. She read out the handwritten message.

'Merry Christmas, Carls. Embankment Pier at eleven a.m. I love you. Fergus xx'

Beth looked over Carly's shoulder to check the message herself. 'Was that eleven o'clock today, then?'

'I guess so but he wasn't there, was he? He's stuck in Ireland so that was pointless.' She folded up the note and placed it back in the box.

'What do you think the present was?' asked Beth. She couldn't picture what was near Embankment Pier apart from, very obviously, the Thames.

Carly shrugged and looked up at the ceiling as she thought. 'I don't know. There's nothing open on Christmas Day apart from a few restaurants. I bet it was Christmas dinner out somewhere. Yeah, that'd be it.'

'Oh well,' said Beth as she put an arm round Carly, 'never mind. You can be my kitchen slave instead.'

Chapter Twenty-Two

Christmas dinner was held on Simon's borrowed paste table, which was sturdier than most and well disguised by tablecloths from the tearoom. The chairs were on loan from Jack and Beth had borrowed two large serving bowls from the pub. But, wherever it was from, when it all came together it worked. There was plenty of food for everyone and they all joined in and wore their paper hats out of the crackers. By the time they all pushed their pudding bowls away, everyone was looking decidedly stuffed, which was exactly as it should be on Christmas Day. Leo was keen to watch a film on the new mega television so he made good his escape.

Ernie stood up and all eyes followed him. 'Thank you,' he said, pointing to his bowl and then stroking his scarf.

'You're very welcome, Ernie,' said Beth as Ernie went to put his coat on. Jack jumped up and pointed after him to indicate that he'd see him out. She watched as Jack chatted to Ernie in the hall and they very formally shook hands before Ernie ventured into the swirling snow outside. Jack rejoined the adults, got more wine from the fridge en route and topped up their glasses.

'Have you left your boyfriend for good this time then, Carly?' asked Jack as Beth gave him a stern look.

'He's visiting a sick relative in Ireland.'

'Sorry,' said Jack, pouring wine into Carly's glass.

'To be honest we needed some space,' said Carly, 'time to re-evaluate things.'

'Sounds like you've been reading self-help books to me.'

Carly frowned. 'I might have been,' she said. 'Ugh,' she added dramatically, 'he spends all his time on this stupid computer game and talking to other nerdy people about it. It's taken over his life.'

'Which game?' asked Jack, now looking a lot more interested in what Carly had to say.

'*Minecraft.*'

'Sound,' said Jack, nodding with approval.

'Do you play it?' asked Beth, a little smirk escaping at the thought of Jack being into kids' games.

'Yeah, but not seriously. I dabble now and then. It's quite complex with all its different servers, dimensions, worlds, mining and crafting.'

'It is!' said Carly. 'See, I told you.' Carly turned to Beth. 'How am I meant to understand conversations about zombie pigmen in the nether. It makes no sense at all. I mean who has a T-shirt with *I'm The Ghast Blaster* on it?'

'They were a big seller this Christmas but I like this best,' said Jack sheepishly, as he lifted up his Christmas jumper to reveal a blue T-shirt with two eyes and a large square red mouth lined with white teeth.

'Squid!' shouted Carly, pointing at it in alarm.

'iBallistic Squid, to be precise,' said Jack. 'He's a *Minecraft* YouTuber as is The Ghast Blaster but nobody knows who The Ghast Blaster is. It's this big mystery.'

Beth was looking blankly at him. 'It was all over social media, did you not see it?' asked Jack. Beth and Carly shook their heads.

Jack blinked repeatedly in dismay and started fiddling with his iPhone. 'Here you go. This is one of his videos. He plays *Minecraft* and explains insider tips and tricks, then posts it on

YouTube. But unlike most of the other YouTubers you don't see his face so people all over the world have fallen in love with his voice.'

He handed the phone to Carly. Beth casually leaned over her shoulder to watch as the game popped up and a little pixellated man was wielding a pickaxe. The YouTuber's voice oozed from the phone – it was a slow melodic purr of a voice with a lilting accent. 'I'm looking for resources in the nether, in particular ghast tears …'

'Fergus!' squealed Carly and Beth together.

The revelation that Fergus was an Internet sensation dominated the rest of Christmas Day discussions; carrying on through more wine, clearing the table, the washing up, evening television and finally brandies in front of the fire. Throughout this Carly had been trying in vain to elicit a response from Fergus. The last text she'd received on Christmas Eve read:

I WILL see you Xmas day. Hope you like ur present F x

Finally Carly rang his mum in Ireland and Beth and Jack could tell by the frequent blinking and headshakes that things weren't going well. When she'd finished the call she came in and slumped onto the sofa. Jack handed over her refreshed brandy glass.

'He was on the last ferry out last night. It was coming into Liverpool. There are no trains today so she has no idea how he was meant to be getting to London. And he's left his phone charger in Ireland so he's most likely run out of battery by now.'

'Bugger,' said Beth eventually. 'He did know you were coming here though, didn't he?'

Carly shook her head. Beth and Jack both gave her confused looks. 'I thought if I told him I was coming here he would try to persuade me to stay at the flat in case he made it home, which he was never going to do, and then I would have been all on my own for Christmas.'

'But he did make it,' Jack stated, and received a harsh stare from Carly.

'We don't know that,' she said. 'He could still be in Liverpool.'

'He's a famous YouTuber so I'm guessing he's pretty loaded. He'd be able to find a way of getting from Liverpool to London,' said Jack, as he took a sip of his brandy and breathed out the fumes slowly.

'Loaded?' laughed Carly. 'I don't think so. He might be famous on the Internet but he doesn't make any money.'

Jack was looking at her quizzically. 'He has over seven million followers and his own app. Every time someone watches a clip on YouTube, or upgrades on the app, he gets paid. I think you'll find he's earning far more than you or I ever will.'

The stunned silence was only interrupted by a large crack from the last log on the fire as it gave way and crumbled into the red glow of the hearth.

'Oh,' said Carly, jumping up and going for a rummage in her handbag. She came back with an envelope. 'I just remembered this. It was in our letter box. I guess it's a Christmas card.'

Beth regarded the innocuous white envelope now on her lap. She recognized the writing instantly. It was from Nick. Jack and Carly had started talking about exactly how much money Fergus might be making, so Beth quietly slid the envelope down the side of the sofa cushions. She would deal with that another time.

Jack and Doris stood up and stretched when Carly announced that it was now 12.05 so it was officially Boxing Day and Beth went to make herself busy in the kitchen. She wasn't sure why but she had drunk quite a bit since lunch and she didn't want to make a fool of herself if he did the cheek-kissing thing again. Jack strode into the kitchen with Doris at his side.

'Happy Boxing Day!' Jack said, as he pulled Beth into a hug. He hugged her for a little longer than she was expecting. He'd drunk quite a bit too. He eventually stepped back but still had hold of her arms, perhaps to help keep his own balance. 'Thanks for a brilliant day, we loved it.' He nodded towards Doris as he spoke and she lifted her tired head as if in agreement.

'Good, I'm glad. Take care, it'll be slippy outside,' said Beth, trying to turn away. Jack still had hold of her arms and she instinctively went to pull free. As she almost toppled backwards, Jack grabbed Beth and stopped her from falling. Beth's heart was racing and she was feeling uncomfortable sensations like the many times that Nick held on to her a fraction too long to show he was in control. Beth knew Jack wasn't Nick but her body was reacting in exactly the same way. Now their faces were uncomfortably close and Beth's pulse was racing for a number of reasons. But when she looked into Jack's eyes it wasn't fear she felt at all, but an undeniable attraction.

'Are you okay?' asked Jack, his voice breathy and his gaze fixed on her lips.

Beth took a deep steadying lungful of air. 'Yeah, sorry. Too much alcohol. I think we all need to sleep it off.' She raised a smile and tapped his arm gently.

Jack blinked hard and let go of Beth. 'Okay.' He didn't look certain but he gave her a brief kiss on the cheek and left anyway, whispering his goodbyes to an already sleeping Carly who had nodded off on the sofa. Beth wasn't sure what had just happened between her and Jack, but she knew that it could go no further.

Beth walked back into the living room and was about to wake Carly when her mobile chirped and she sprang awake. It was a text from Fergus:

So I'm guessing that you've left me then. F x

'Shit,' said Carly.

Beth left Carly exchanging frantic text messages with Fergus and went to bed. She didn't hear Carly come up, but was aware of a bum nudging into her back at six the next morning so Carly had evidently turned in at some point. Beth lay still for as long as she could and then decided she needed coffee so padded to the kitchen. It was tranquil and dark outside and it had stopped snowing, but there was still a good layer of the stuff on everything.

She thought back to the previous day. She had enjoyed it far more than she ever thought she would. Leo had been pleased with his presents, and the television had been a deciding factor in how much he enjoyed Christmas. It had been lovely for her and Leo to spend it with Carly, and she'd liked having Ernie and Jack there too. She dwelled on thoughts of Jack for a moment; he was easy company and, almost without her noticing, he and Doris had become a part of her life.

She warmed her hands on her mug. There was something about Jack, something that was pulling her closer to him. Now was not good timing. She was fresh out of an abusive relationship and had no plans to stay in Dumbleford long-term, so she needed to make sure she kept Jack at arm's length.

A yawning Carly broke Beth's thoughts as she flopped onto one of the chairs and made it screech as it juddered across the kitchen floor. They were adding their own marks to the patina, thought Beth.

'How are things with you and Fergus?' Beth was scrunching up her shoulders as she asked the question.

Carly pouted. 'We're okay.'

'But are you still together?'

Carly smiled for the first time. 'Yes, we're all sorted on that front. We've both been idiots but this new year that's just a few days away is going to be our year.'

'That's terrific, I'm really pleased for you both,' said Beth, giving her a hug. 'What about not meeting him at Embankment yesterday?'

'He said not to worry about it. We can do it some other time.'

'That's a relief then.'

Carly nodded. 'Fergus is such a sweetheart. Thankfully, he understood why I'd hot-footed over here for Christmas.'

'What's the plan now?' asked Beth.

'I need tea and then I'm going back to London.'

'But there's no trains today,' pointed out Beth.

'I know. Fergus said to get a taxi. Turns out Jack was right, Fergus is loaded.'

'You're kidding me?'

'Nope, he admitted it all in our marathon text exchange last night. He knew I wasn't interested in the gaming so he never mentioned it.

'I'm really going to make it work this time, Beth. No more dreaming about proposals and weddings, I'm focusing on the two of us being happy just as we are,' said Carly, and she looked like she meant it.

So much for keeping Jack Selby at 'arm's length', thought Beth when she found herself with his arm casually draped round her waist on New Year's Eve. In fact, Jack's arm had made its way round her waist a number of times during the evening. They had spent the whole time together in the overflowing pub. Granted, she had been working but Petra was a great boss and Beth and the other bar staff had each managed to catch breaks throughout the evening. Petra had even closed the bar temporarily so that everyone could join in the countdown to midnight. Leo and Denis barrelled into the bar just in time and made their way to their respective parents. Leo squeezed in between Jack and Beth as the count reached its climax.

'... one, zero! Happy New Year!'

Beth picked Leo up and kissed him. He was always the first person she kissed at midnight on New Year's Eve. Even when he had been a baby and had been sound asleep, he was always her first kiss of a new year. Leo quickly squirmed away and he and Denis disappeared again. Petra was next with a hug and kiss for both Beth and Jack followed by one of her theatrical winks.

Jack gently steered Beth to the edge of the room. The noise around seemed to ebb to a mutter as Jack spoke. 'So, here we are. A brand new year.'

'I wonder what it holds,' said Beth, as she looked into Jack's eyes. She marvelled at the colour; they were the palest grey-blue and quite mesmerizing this close up. Jack reached out and took her hand. Beth followed his gaze and they both watched as their fingers perfectly knitted together. She looked up and he was smiling. He really was gorgeous especially when he smiled, and she felt her pulse start to quicken. Despite all her protestations, right now she wanted him to kiss her. It was New Year's Eve, she was completely sober, and she wanted to be kissed.

Jack was looking at her intently. 'Happy New Year, Beth.' He gradually bent forward and placed the gentlest of kisses on her lips. The noise of the pub was now replaced by her own pulse thrumming in her ears as every fibre of her being focused on the kiss. For so many reasons she had been fighting this but right now it felt completely right. Beth had her eyes closed but, more than that, they were screwed up like those of a child awaiting a surprise. And this was a surprise. His firm but gentle kiss was sending ricochets around her body. She felt herself naturally relaxing against Jack. She was considering how to take the kiss further without looking like a hussy when a tap on her shoulder ended the moment abruptly.

'Sorry,' said Petra, 'bar's opening now.'

Jack gave a disappointed eye roll as Beth sighed and drew away. What had just happened between them? There was a post-midnight frenzy behind the bar as punters eagerly awaited top-ups. When the rush had died to a trickle, Petra beckoned Beth out the back and she followed.

Petra took a deep breath and splayed out her hands. 'This is not my business but I feel I should say something,' she said, her accent sounding stronger somehow. Beth was a little taken aback at the ominous start to the conversation. 'I don't like to see people get hurt or let down, okay?'

'Of course,' said Beth, wishing that Petra would spit it out.

'Jack's past has not been good. Did you know?'

'No,' said Beth, with a brief shake of her head.

'Then it's not for me to tell you the details, that's for Jack. All I will say is that domestic violence is a terrible thing. He's getting his life back together but still it was a big thing in his past … Do you understand what I'm saying?'

Beth felt sick and she swallowed hard. 'Loud and clear.'

'I wouldn't want to see people I care about get hurt.'

'Of course not.' Beth tried to smile but failed.

'You okay? I've not said the wrong thing?'

'No, you've said exactly the right thing. Thanks, Petra, I appreciate it.'

Petra looked surprised and relieved in the same moment. 'Oh, that is good then. Phew. I was worried. Anyway, back to work.' Petra disappeared and Beth gave herself a moment to compose herself; her hands were shaking. She had to get through the next hour and then she could escape back to the cottage. Until then it was stiff upper lip territory.

Beth kept herself busy, racing past the other members of staff to serve customers, collecting glasses, chopping umpteen lemons – anything rather than have to speak to Jack. Jack spent most of his time drinking Guinness and laughing; whenever he glanced over he had a look in his eye. It was a deceptively gentle look that an hour ago would have melted something inside Beth but now it had the opposite effect. A core of steel was growing inside her. How could she have been so gullible for a second time? She was furious with herself for not being more on her guard. When Petra eventually said she could finish for the night she collected a reluctant Leo and disappeared quietly out the back way. Beth swallowed the lump in her throat and blinked away the tears. She couldn't face Jack right now and she didn't know when she would ever be able to again.

Chapter Twenty-Three

Leo was back to his old self with the television blaring in the background and his face glued to his tablet. All was right in his world. Beth brought him a drink of juice and put it on the windowsill for him.

'This is for you, Mum,' he said as he pulled out the rest of the white envelope that was sticking up from the side of the sofa cushion. Beth's stomach churned. She took the envelope from him, went to the kitchen and shut the door. She sat down and thumbed the envelope; she could feel that there was a card inside. Beth knew from the writing that it was from Nick; perhaps it was just a Christmas card. She could destroy it without opening it; fling it in the open fire tonight when Leo had gone to bed. It was a tempting thought that she could watch it burn but could she cope with not knowing what was inside?

In an instant she answered her question as she ripped it open. It was a Christmas card; simple and classy. She held it in her hands and noticed they were shaking ever so slightly. She opened the card and something fluttered to the floor. She left it there for a moment while she read what was written inside.

Dearest Elizabeth and Leo,
   Wherever this finds you I pray you are safe and well.
Love always
Nick

Beth read it again. There didn't appear to be any hidden message or any threat and most importantly no hint that he was coming after them. She leaned down and picked up what had fluttered out of the card. It was a newspaper clipping. She turned it over in her fingers to identify which side was relevant and then she spotted it.

SOCIAL MEDIA — FINDING THE MISSING

She speed-read the short article and nausea swirled in her stomach. One sentence in particular struck her: *Social media has become a useful tool for the families of missing people and the police in helping to locate them.* It went on to give various examples and how even celebrities had got involved with sharing and retweeting photographs to raise awareness and jog people's memories. Beth slowly and deliberately screwed up the newspaper clipping until it was a tight ball in her hand. On top of the revulsion, she felt an uncomfortable sense of pleasure that she had known Nick well enough to second-guess that it would be something more than a Christmas card.

She remembered how she'd brushed over the fact that Nick used to open her mail. Everything would be still in the envelope. He appeared to have slit the envelopes neatly for her as a thoughtful thing to do ever since she'd ripped into one and got a paper cut. An innocent gesture, she had thought at the time. It was only later that she realized things were going missing: the social invitations, bank cards and the odd personal letter. It became clear that Nick was reading her mail when he questioned why she had visited certain shops or knew about an engagement party for a friend that had moved away.

The paper clipping was a clear threat, she knew that, but instead of fear she felt anger. She was angry that he thought he was still in control of her. Beth stood up, folded the card roughly and shoved it into her jeans pocket. There was a knock at the door and Leo was unlikely to stir so she went to answer it. If her face was stony when she opened the door the frown that appeared would have done nothing to enhance her expression of welcome.

'Hiya,' said Jack, 'I hadn't seen you about so I thought I'd check you were okay.' He was smiling. Beth wasn't. All the sensations generated by the newspaper article were washing around inside her. She didn't speak. 'Are you okay?' asked Jack with a concerned raise of an eyebrow.

Beth swallowed hard. How could she have fallen for another charmer? Was she a complete idiot? She studied his face for a moment. There were no clues there. He looked completely normal. In fact he looked relaxed, casual and gorgeous and she, like a fool, had fallen for it. How was she to know he was *another* abuser? He was staring at her and she knew she had to say something. Leo was in the other room so she had to be careful. 'Yes, fine, thanks. Was there anything else?' Her tone was brusque and her expression remained sombre.

'Er, are you sure you're okay? And Leo?' Jack half looked past Beth and she instinctively stepped forward to block his view into the hall. Jack pulled back, scowling. 'There is something wrong, isn't there? What's up? Tell me.'

'Nothing, and it's really none of your business anyway.' Beth shut the door. She closed her eyes and took a deep breath. Shutting Jack out was what she had to do. But then why did she feel so bad about doing it?

'Beth!' Jack banged on the door. 'Beth, what's wrong? You're worrying me.'

Leo shuffled into the hall clutching his tablet. 'Is that Jack?' he asked as Jack continued to raise his voice outside. Beth nodded, leaning against the door as if shielding Leo. 'Why can't he come in?'

'Because, because …' Beth did not want to have to explain this. 'We fell out and we're not friends any more. You know that sometimes happens.'

Leo nodded his understanding. 'Why did you fall out?'

'Oh, nothing serious. Would you like a hot chocolate?'

Leo smiled and followed his mother into the kitchen as Jack continued to thud on the door. He eventually gave up and left Beth and Leo to have their drinks in peace and for Beth to start to think. She hadn't actually begun a relationship with Jack so in theory keeping his involvement in their lives to a minimum should prove to be straightforward. However, the problem with theories was that they were often disproved. She liked Jack, that was the bottom line, and now she had to un-like Jack and it was not as easy as it was on social media. She needed to reset her emotional gauge where he was concerned. He was now a no-go zone and she couldn't kid herself that she wasn't more than a little sad about that. She gave herself a shake. She shouldn't be feeling sad, she should be elated that she'd had a lucky escape this time. Perhaps that feeling would take longer to materialize.

There was also the question of Doris. She was meant to be dog-sitting again from tomorrow. She hated the thought of going back on a deal and whatever Jack had done in the past he had made a good job of her kitchen. But unlike Simon and his acceptance of a couple of packets of biscuits and a free-flowing supply of tea while he worked, there had been no end date pinned to the dog-sitting agreement. Beth had surprised herself by getting used to having Doris about the house while she worked and even enjoying her company. Leo considered himself to have a part ownership in the dog, flinging his arms tightly around her when he got in from school and using her as a stand-in playmate when Denis wasn't about. But despite how Doris may have wheedled her way into their lives, Beth knew what she had to do.

She sat and stared at her fifth attempt to write a note to Jack.

She really wished she didn't have to do this, which made it that much harder to write. She sighed and gave it a final read.

Jack,
I am really sorry but I am no longer able to dog-sit for Doris. Leo and I have loved having her here but as I move on to the next stage of getting Willow Cottage ready for resale it won't be possible to look after her any more.
Sorry.
Beth

Beth put what she hoped was a polite and well-worded note through Jack's door as quietly as she could. She had almost made good her escape when the door opened and she heard his footsteps jog up behind her.

'Beth, talk to me. What's going on?' Jack's voice was soft behind her. People like Jack knew when to play the charm card and when to apply pressure.

For once Beth had thought through her response. 'I'm sorry, but I need to be able to work on the hallway and it will mean having all the doors and windows open and I can't risk Doris running away. Anyway, it was never meant to be a permanent arrangement, was it?'

Jack's head twitched a no response. 'You're having all the doors open in this weather?'

Beth glanced around her as if only noticing for the first time that it was January. The snow had almost gone; all that was left were stubborn dirty lumps of ice here and there. 'Got to get on. I want the cottage back on the market by Easter.' She knew it was over-optimistic but she liked to set goals and stress to Jack that she was not a suitable candidate to set his sights on, since she would be moving on as soon as she could. Putting distance between them might help to heal the damage he'd done. She'd actually started to trust him. That was what hurt the most.

'Oh,' said Jack, fumbling in his pocket for his phone and frantically pressing buttons. 'Did you hear about this?'

Beth was scowling. She didn't want to get caught up in chitchat; self-preservation was key on a number of levels. 'I need to get going …'

'This guy hired a boat on Christmas Day to sail up the Thames and get Tower Bridge to open,' he said at high speed as he glanced between Beth and his phone. 'He was going to propose to her but she never turned up. Do you think it was Fergus and Carly?' Jack thrust the phone under her nose.

Beth's neck snapped back in surprise. She forcefully pushed the phone away and tried to keep a hold on her racing pulse. He wasn't trying to hit her, but it was a swift movement and it had put her on high alert all the same.

'I doubt it.' She turned to leave.

Jack rubbed his chin and his face reflected his utter confusion. 'Have I done something to upset you? Because if I have then … I'm really sorry.'

She turned back and briefly studied his face. He did look sorry but then that was all part of the charade. She'd seen Nick play out his role as wounded hero so many times. Petra had said domestic violence was in Jack's past – she had an opportunity to give him the benefit of the doubt, maybe he had changed, but she simply couldn't take a risk like that. She felt a strange sense of loss although it was something she had never really had.

'It's just that the New Year brings renewed focus, that's all. I need to get on. Bye Jack.' Tears pricked at Beth's eyes and she had to turn away quickly.

Later that day Beth was thankful that she hadn't heard anything further from Jack but she couldn't help a sidelong look at his cottage as they walked past on the way to school. She wondered if Doris was shut in her dog cage or if Jack had found someone else to have her. Leo and Denis dashed into school, leaving Beth to her thoughts as she walked home. Another glance at Jack's cottage on the return trip revealed nothing. She found herself sighing as she let herself into Willow Cottage. Right, now I really do need to get some work done, she thought.

Carly tapped Fergus's arm. They were sitting in the back of his dad's old Mini. Although, Fergus was more sort of folded into the back seat with his head only a fraction off the roof lining, which he bumped with monotonous regularity every time they hit a pothole, which was frequently. Fergus turned to look at her. An advantage of having a deaf partner was that instead of whispering she could simply mouth something and he would be able to lip-read it. He wasn't the best at lip-reading and strangers were particularly tricky, but with Carly he understood every time.

'What the feck is going on?' she mouthed. Fergus snorted a chuckle and his dad glanced into the rear-view mirror.

Fergus signed back to her. 'Going to see Granny.'

'I thought that's what he said. But she's dead.'

Fergus snorted again and Carly gave him a nudge in the ribs.

'Is your man all right back there?' asked Mr Dooley in his thick Irish accent.

'We're both fine, thanks, Mr Dooley,' replied Carly as she was signing to Fergus to stop snorting.

'Ah, now you want to be calling me Cormac,' said Mr Dooley.

'Okay,' said Carly as she took in what Fergus was signing in reply.

'… it's traditional that everyone goes to spend some time with the deceased …' he signed.

Carly knew her wide eyes would be sufficient response. Fergus patted her thigh and then took her hand in his and squeezed it gently, and she tried very hard to relax.

'Cormac?' said Carly tentatively, not wanting to distract him too much from his erratic pothole swerving.

'Yes, love.'

'Are there family flowers we can contribute to or do we need

220

to buy our own wreath? We weren't sure which would be the right thing to do.'

'No, no, you don't need to worry about that. You see, Granny requested no flowers at the funeral on account of her pollen allergy,' explained Cormac, his tone serious as he nodded at the rear-view mirror.

'Oh, I see,' said Carly, forcing herself not to dissolve into inappropriate hysterics.

They arrived at Granny's house and peeled themselves out of the tiny car.

'I'll be back in about an hour,' he said, looking at his watch.

'An hour?' asked Carly, a fraction louder than she meant to. She was guessing there was nowhere she could get a black chai tea.

'Did you want longer with yer granny?' Cormac asked Fergus.

Fergus thankfully shook his head. 'An hour's fine, Da. Thanks.' He put his arm round an anxious-looking Carly and led her inside. The small terraced house was dark and silent. They entered the front room where a vast amount of heavy drapes adorned the windows. As her eyes adjusted to the poor flickering light cast by numerous candles, Carly caught a glimpse of an open coffin before the door was closed behind them.

A sudden movement caught Carly off guard and she had to stifle a scream. 'Ahh, Fergus. Good to see you, just awful sad about the circumstances, but yer granny would be glad you made it,' said a short man as he left a chair next to the coffin and threw himself into a bear hug with Fergus. The man stood back to appraise him.

'You look well, that English piss-like beer must be suiting you then?' he guffawed.

'They have Guinness there too, Uncle Padraig.' She was impressed; Fergus's lip-reading was better than she'd thought because she could barely understand the mumbling man with his heavy Irish drawl. 'You remember Carly?'

'Still a beauty, you are. Is he looking after you, now?' he said, pulling her into a tight squeeze. Carly opted for copious amounts of nodding and grinning and hoped that would be enough of an answer to whatever it was he'd said. He turned to Fergus. 'You need to get a ring on that there finger, so you do,' he added, waving Carly's left hand at Fergus, making her feel like a puppet.

Uncle Padraig let go of her and with an arm round Fergus ushered him to a corner for a private chat. She noticed Fergus gently reposition his uncle in front of him so he could lip-read and ask him to repeat what he'd said.

Carly didn't want to look like she was eavesdropping so she turned away and then had a nasty surprise when she realized how close she was to the open coffin. She took an involuntary sharp intake of breath but steadied herself.

Granny was laid out in a simple dress and cardigan and looked just like she was asleep although as Carly cast her eyes towards Granny's feet she had to stifle a chuckle. Granny was wearing rather fetching bootee-style slippers. Carly was fighting hard to control the giggles that were starting deep inside her. She was desperate to drag Fergus over but he was still deep in muffled conversation. There was lots of backslapping from the men and they joined her at the coffin.

'Ahh, she's sleeping peacefully now. Bless her,' said Padraig as he put his arms round Fergus and Carly. 'Now, will you do me a wee favour and translate to me laddo here?' he asked Carly.

'Of course.' Carly faced him but now he was fiddling with his phone.

'Hang on … just a minute there,' he said slowly as he scrolled up and down the phone's screen.

Fergus took Carly's fingers in his and held them with the lightest of touches, and when she looked at him he was smiling. She squeezed his hand. It was an odd place to have a moment, but a moment it was. They could have been anywhere; it was just the two of them acknowledging the other one's closeness.

'I'm so glad you're here,' whispered Fergus.

'And me,' signed Carly, with her free hand. Fergus's fingers tightened their grip and Carly felt something ping deep inside. *This* was what she wanted; she wanted to feel that closeness between them that she had feared was slipping away. Fergus turned his head to look at Granny and, mirroring him, Carly did too.

Suddenly Granny's voice echoed around the sparsely furnished room. 'Can you hear me?' she said. Carly gripped Fergus's hand and he looked at her with the same relaxed smile because he couldn't hear it. Carly shot a look at Granny. 'Now that you're here I wanted to say a few words ...' Granny's lips were definitely not moving and Carly was sure she'd never been a ventriloquist.

'Are you not going to be telling him what she's after saying?' Uncle Padraig was looking mildly irritated as he waved his phone. Carly opened her mouth and then closed it again because she was feeling a little queasy, but she managed a nod. Padraig rolled his eyes. 'I'll start it again then,' he said, as he fiddled once more with his phone. Carly let out a deep sigh and tapped Fergus's arm so he was ready to read what she signed.

Thankfully it was a short message that Granny had recorded a few months ago, at her birthday gathering, saying what a good life she'd had and how proud she was of all of her family. She finished with an odd sentence. '... and remember: it's easy to halve the potato where there's love.' Carly knew she was frowning but she couldn't help it. What was the woman talking about?

Fergus started to laugh and Padraig joined in. 'I'll leave you to your prayers,' said Padraig, his face abruptly becoming sombre. He patted Fergus on the shoulder and left the room. Fergus stood for a while with his head bent and his eyes closed and Carly did the same until she'd run out of things to pray for. She had another look at Granny in her bootee slippers and it made her smile. Maybe that was the idea? You never knew with the Irish, they were always up for the craic.

The Irish seemed to have a good balance when it came to death, thought Carly. The funeral was a long drawn-out and sad affair, as funerals often are, where many cried and a few wailed, which took Carly by surprise at first but a steadying hand and a few words about Irish traditions from Cormac had her under-standing it all a little better. Once that was over it was all about celebrating Granny's life, all the things she had done and achieved. And while it wasn't the most adventurous or high-achieving existence, everyone had high praise for her as a mother, grand-mother, friend and neighbour, and to the people who knew her best that was what really counted.

Carly managed to lure Fergus away from a riotous drinking game.

'It's noisy in there, are you okay?'

He shrugged. 'They're all family, they know about my deafness and that it makes no difference to who I am.'

'Doesn't stop it being noisy?' said Carly.

'No, but it does stop it bothering me.' He put his arm round her shoulder, pulled her to him and kissed the top of her head.

'I saw you signing with that lady in the navy dress earlier. That was nice.'

'No, it wasn't,' laughed Fergus. 'Mary is something like me mam's third cousin twice removed and she learned to sign years ago when her donkey went deaf.'

'What?' said Carly, starting to laugh.

'Well, she thinks she knows some sign language but I think she's making half of the signs up so it was either her donkey or her neighbour that she signed and I'd like to imagine it was the former!'

When their laughter had dwindled Carly remembered some-thing she wanted to ask. 'What did Granny mean about the halving of a potato?' she asked. She had been puzzling over it ever since.

'It's easy to halve the potato where there's love,' repeated Fergus. 'It's an old Irish proverb …' Carly started to snigger. 'It is! And it means that if you're surrounded by love then however little you have it's easier to share it.'

Carly stopped sniggering. 'That's actually quite sweet.'

'I know,' said Fergus emphatically and he kissed her softly.

The lady in the navy dress approached and signed to them both that there was 'chicken cake' if they'd like some. Fergus started to giggle as Carly kindly signed back that they would love some 'lemon cake' although *she* used the correct sign for 'lemon'. Confusing the two was an easy mistake for a novice signer to make.

Chapter Twenty-Four

Petra was being attentive during Beth's lunchtime shift and she figured that she must have spoken to Jack. When it was time to go, Beth was zipping up her coat when Petra came over to her. 'Are you sure you are okay? I am a little worried,' she said.

'I'm fine, honest.'

'Good. Then I won't ask again. What is the next project at the cottage?'

'Oh, decorating mainly but at some stage I need to tackle the stairs. They are missing a few spindles and that sort of craftsmanship is expensive so I'm not sure what I'll do with them. But I'll think of something.'

'What about a night class? They do them at the college. I can have Leo and you can borrow my moped. All you need to do now is find one that gives you these skills. Okay?'

It made Beth smile at how quickly Petra seemed to solve her problem. 'Okay, I'll look into it.'

'Good, you must do this.' Petra squeezed her arm for emphasis. Beth couldn't help but be touched by her support. The feeling that someone local had become a friend and was keen to offer suggestions to help her achieve her goal was heartwarming and despite everything else that was going on it made her feel calm.

Back at the cottage over a well-earned cup of tea Beth found herself searching the internet on her phone for carpentry courses. By the time she had reached the bottom of her mug she had found a local wood-turning course that ran one evening a week and was suitable for beginners. There was even a possibility that she was eligible for the concessionary price. Beth decided to join Petra on the school pick-up run to check that she really did mean it about the pink moped. Beth hadn't ridden since university but her motorbike licence was still good and Petra said she'd let her know about insurance costs.

Beth and Petra were chatting as they passed Jack's cottage and heard Doris's plaintive whines and barks. Beth felt a twinge of guilt. Leo unexpectedly shoved his mother in the ribs. 'That's your fault, she's shut in a cage! You've made her sad and I hate you!' he shouted before running off. Petra looked sympathetic but Beth didn't have time to comment as Leo was running at full pelt towards the road. He stopped as he reached the edge of the pavement, giving Beth time to catch up with him and escort him across.

'Leo, we don't push people around however cross we get.'

'I don't care!' he shouted and he ran off once more, this time across the green towards the cottage. Beth rubbed her side. He had pushed into her with some force but it wasn't that that was hurting. It was the fact that he thought it was acceptable to treat his mother that way. One more thing to loathe Nick for, she thought. She hated to see Leo upset like this; he and Doris were unfortunate victims of her self-imposed ban on Jack. She knew she was doing the right thing; she had to protect Leo, but that didn't stop her feeling guilty for being the cause of his distress, and for that matter Doris's.

In between arguments with Leo, Beth managed to make a phone call to the college and enrol herself on the wood-turning course. It was a brief interlude in an otherwise dreadful evening where Leo stropped about ignoring his mother while she repeatedly explained to him the importance of respecting other people.

Breakfast was frosty both inside the cottage and out. Leo's jaw was rigid as he glowered at his porridge. Beth couldn't help but worry about what else Leo had vicariously picked up from their time with Nick.

The walk to school was brisk, as Leo appeared keen to get away from his mother, and Denis was almost running to keep up. They were through the gates before she had a chance to say goodbye and she knew there would definitely be no backward glance from Leo today. She watched for a moment to check that he went inside and saw Jack greet Leo at the door. Leo threw himself at Jack and although the situation was awkward there was little Jack could do but let the child cling to him. All reason left Beth as she stormed across the tarmac.

'Get away from my son!' she said firmly in hushed tones so as not to create a scene as she tried to pull a now sobbing Leo away from Jack.

Jack put his hands up in surrender. 'He's upset but it's nothing I've done.'

'You fell out and now Doris is sad!' shouted Leo as he twisted to address both the adults in turn. He rubbed roughly at his teary eyes with his coat sleeve.

'Did we fall out?' asked Jack.

'Irrelevant,' said Beth to Jack before crouching down to Leo's level. 'Doris is fine, isn't she, Jack?' Her expression willing him to reassure the child.

'Er, oh, yeah. You know what she's like, Leo. She sleeps most of the time.'

'But we heard her crying yesterday,' said Leo, his bottom lip pushed out, reminding Beth of when he was a toddler.

'Well, yesterday was different as I was out all day but I'll take her for a walk at lunchtime. Do you want to come?'

'Yeah!' squealed Leo, immediately brightening as his mother tried to control the fear and anger that was instantly coursing through her veins.

228

'No, I'm sorry, Leo. You have to stay on school premises at lunchtime. Doesn't he, Jack?' The look that accompanied the sentence was instruction enough.

'Oh, yeah. Silly me. No, you can't come but I'll tell you how she is and I promise you she'll be fine. Okay?'

Leo nodded glumly as he pulled himself free from his mother's grasp and sulked off into the school, dragging his rucksack behind him. The adults watched him go and Beth's heart melted for her son. When he was out of sight, Jack ran his hand through his hair and gave a self-deprecating smile. 'That was a bit tricky. I didn't—'

'What the hell do you think you're doing hugging my child and then inviting him out of school?' Beth felt the emotion catch in her throat and she fought hard to stay in control. The last thing she wanted to do right now was cry but the mixture of suppressed anger and unhappiness was a volatile cocktail. How had everything turned so suddenly from picture perfect to an utter nightmare?

'Wow! Slow down with the accusations. That is not what happened and you know it.'

'Stay away from my child or I will report you, Jack. I'm not the pushover you think I am.'

As Jack stood looking bewildered and confused in the doorway, Beth walked away, struggling to see as the hot tears blurred her vision.

Beth had a horrid day. She spent most of it replaying the scene at the school and going over and over what exactly had been said and whether she should speak to the head teacher. She had finally resolved that whatever Jack had done in the past he was now holding down a responsible job and she knew the support he provided to the school was invaluable. She decided instead to make it clear that if she had any cause to feel that Leo was threatened then she would be shouting it from the highest point in the village, which was most likely the Bleeding Bear pub sign.

She was very glad to leave a sulking Leo at the pub, don Petra's helmet and escape to her first evening class. She took with her one of the broken stair-rail spindles so that she would have a template to make replicas, and popped this inside her coat. Beth had memorized the best route and knew that, even on the ancient moped, it should only take about twenty-five minutes to get to the adult education centre where the classes were being held.

January rain lashed at Beth for most of the journey and she felt vulnerable as a large lorry had overtaken her only leaving a narrow corridor of space between her and its thundering wheels. As she arrived at the centre a small sign pointed her into the car park and an allocated area for motorbikes. She parked the small pink moped between two large motorbikes, locked it up and jogged over to the steps that led to the entrance and provided some cover. A quick look at her watch showed that she had made good time and was a little early.

Beth was about to take off her helmet when a familiar figure came striding towards her. Her heart pounded in her chest and she found she was clenching her fists and gripping the spindle tightly. What the hell was Jack doing following her here? She started to struggle with the strap in her haste to take the helmet off quickly but even as she struggled she realized although Jack was heading towards her he was looking straight past her. She followed his gaze inside as he strode by without even a glance. Beth stood still for a moment and found she could undo the helmet strap in one easy movement if she wasn't panicking.

Keeping her helmet on, she followed Jack inside, keeping a safe distance back, and discreetly picked up a leaflet as she went by the stand so that she could pretend to read that if he looked round. He turned a corner and then bounded up a staircase two at a time. As she reached the top of the stairs there was no sign of him and her helmet had almost completely steamed up. She stood, looking along the corridor, wondering if she should take

230

her spying mission any further as curiosity nibbled at her conscience.

'Oh, my word. You gave me a start!' squealed an older lady in a very shiny blouse. She peered a bit closer at the tinted helmet. 'Are you all right?' she said slowly as if Beth was deranged. Beth had a quick glance down the corridor to check there was still no sign of Jack before she removed the helmet.

'Yes, sorry. I didn't mean to make you jump. I was following someone …'

The woman gave her an old-fashioned look. Rumbled, she thought.

'I thought they might be going to the same class. What classes are up here? IT?' she ventured. It was most likely that Jack was running a course rather than attending one.

'Oh, no classes on this floor, it's all local meeting groups. What class are you here for?'

Bugger, thought Beth. 'Wood-turning.'

The woman looked taken aback. 'Then you need to be in the workroom outside. Come with me.'

'Don't I need to sign in or something?' Beth strained a last look up the corridor as the woman put out an arm to guide her back downstairs. She gave in as her shoulders sagged and she trudged after the woman, leaving a trail of drips off her coat as she went.

The workroom was very tidy with a series of low benches on one side of the room and six workstations on the other side. Each station had a wall of tools all very neatly hung up. Two men were already seated at the front bench so she went to the one behind and sat down. They stopped talking as she approached and smiled kindly at her. Beth was introducing herself as someone marched into the room, creating a draught. The larger-than-life figure put her in mind of a ginger and slightly less hairy version of Hagrid from *Harry Potter*. He marched to the front of the class and clapped his hands astonishingly loudly. Beth instantly wanted to clap her hands together to see if she could get the volume anywhere near close. She sat on them instead to stop herself.

'Hello, hello, welcome, welcome. New recruits and old favourites,' he bellowed as he waved to two more men entering the room behind her. He was a bear of a man with a voice to match. Despite his size and volume Beth found she quickly warmed to Tollek, who explained that he was originally from Norway but had fallen in love at university in Bath and had stayed, despite having his heart broken. Beth found herself doing a head tilt at the romantic story and then, noticing that nobody else looked remotely interested, she sat up a bit straighter.

As she had suspected she was the only woman in the group with five men. Her bench partner was a homemade-jumper-wearing fifty-something called Ray who made lots of notes. The first half of the lesson whizzed by as Tollek provided a brief history of the craft of wood-turning and explained his own qualifications, which included coming from a long line of wood-craft devotees in Norway. He also ran through the course syllabus and placed a lot of importance on health and safety and the rules of the workroom. Beth eyed the machinery with longing. She really wanted to have a go.

'Enough of me. Let's have a break for coffee and a bit of socializing and then we will acquaint ourselves with the lathe,' said Tollek with another handclap, which Beth was sure had set off a mild case of tinnitus. Ray scuttled round the bench to join the other men and Beth found herself following behind all the way to the refectory like a lost sheep.

She was rummaging in her purse for change when she heard Jack's voice and forced herself to remain still and with her head down. She slowly turned to watch him leaving the break area with a young man. They stopped to chat outside the gents' toilets and when the young man went into the toilets Jack walked away towards the stairs.

Beth pulled a receipt from her purse and prepared herself. As the young man came out she pounced.

'Hi, sorry. The man you were with dropped something.' She waved the receipt in front of him vaguely and he was momentarily distracted like a cat with a feather. 'Which class is he in?' She was desperately keen to know what Jack was doing here. It was none of her business but simple curiosity was getting the better of her.

The man reached out his hand. 'I'll give it to him if you like?'

That was the obvious thing to offer, she really hadn't thought this through.

'Oh, okay,' she handed over the receipt. 'Is it good? The class or meeting you're going to, because I wondered if I might switch.'

He was frowning deeply now as he shoved the receipt into his pocket. 'Sorry, it's not a course. Look, I'd better go or I'll be late.'

'Oh, of course, yes. Enjoy yourself,' said Beth, feeling like a total idiot. Was he shaking his head as he went up the stairs? She wouldn't have blamed him. She sloped back into the break area, got herself a tea from the machine and went to read the notice-board. There was a brochure of all the courses and she sprang on it, took it to a nearby table and started to look through it. Each course also had details of the room and floor it was on. The men from her course got up and left. She checked her watch: time to go back. A woman was wiping down the tables and Beth sidled back in.

'Excuse me. Do you know which groups are meeting on the first floor tonight?' It was a long shot.

'Er, Tuesday, is it?' said the woman and Beth nodded. 'Knit and natter – actually no, that's moved to a Thursday. Adult dyslexia support and domestic violence support,' she said and then carried on wiping.

Beth knew she was frowning. Either Jack was dyslexic or there was something very sinister going on that he was attending a domestic violence support group. Beth wandered back to her class and sat at her bench and tried hard to listen to Tollek but her mind was distracted by what she'd just discovered and the uneasy feeling that was breeding in her gut.

After a lengthy discussion about tools and sharpening and a quick refresh of the health and safety they all moved over to the machine side of the room. Tollek ran them through the basic principles of the lathe, put on a safety mask and did a demonstration. Beth forgot about Jack for a while, watching Tollek intently as he rounded off a piece of wood. The machine had a low purr as Tollek expertly ran the chisel across its surface. Wood shavings curled away from the wood and filled the air with a fresh scent. She watched him cut in to make a specific groove and demonstrate the importance of keeping tools sharp. She was fascinated.

When the students had a go themselves Beth had to stop herself from running to a lathe in her excitement. Tollek came to each of them in turn and checked that their piece of wood was secure and got them started. Beth knew she was grinning as she rested her chisel on the tool rest and felt it make contact with the wood and change the tone of the machine's purr.

'Stay firm and smooth with your actions,' said Tollek. 'Good start, Beth.'

As she worked the wood her mind drifted back to Jack. Her curiosity was piqued and she wanted to find out more. He was either attending the dyslexic group or the domestic violence support group; she really hoped it was the former even though she hadn't spotted any signs that had led her to think he might be dyslexic. But just because she hadn't noticed anything that didn't mean he wasn't. Yes, it had to be that. Her foot slipped off the motor pedal and the lathe ground to a halt. She'd lost concentration.

Tollek was soon at her side and got her started again and this time she stared hard at the wood to maintain focus. A few seconds later her mind had wandered off again. If it was the domestic violence group *why* was he there? Was he scouting for his next victim? She felt a shudder go through her and immediately banished the thought. Surely nobody would be that twisted and surely not Jack, although she knew too well that just because someone was pretty did not mean they were good. Perhaps the support group was for reformed abusers? she thought. But if it was, that was an odd thing to need support for, wasn't it?

Tollek suggested that they stop working and inspect their handiwork. She was so pleased she almost gave herself a clap. Despite her wandering thoughts she had actually made something that looked pretty good.

When it was time to leave she had visions of replacing every spindle and setting up her own wood-turning business. Everyone was buoyed by the experience and now they were all chatting, the gender barriers had been removed – they were one happy band of novice wood-turners.

As Beth waved her goodbyes she headed for the motorbike parking area and there she spotted Jack. He was on the phone and looking over the pink moped. What was he up to now?

Chapter Twenty-Five

Beth gripped the helmet tightly, pulled back her shoulders and strode over to Jack.

'Problem?' she asked.

'Ah, ignore this message, Petra, Beth has turned up and I think that solves the puzzle. Bye.' He ended the call and looked apologetically at Beth. 'Sorry, I recognized the moped and thought someone had stolen it, because I knew Petra was working. But I'm guessing you've borrowed it.'

'Well, I haven't stolen it if that's what you're thinking!'

Jack's expression was pained. 'I didn't think you had.' He slapped a smile on his face. 'So are you doing an evening class?'

'Yes, wood-turning.' She watched him closely for a reaction.

'Wow, that's a real skill.'

'How about you?'

He looked at the ground. 'Just a meeting, nothing as much fun as wood-turning. Anyway I'd better get back.'

Beth took a deep breath as he was about to walk away. 'So are you dyslexic?'

There was a pause as Jack slowly spun back to look at her, his face crumpled in thought. 'Er, no, why?'

'In that case it means you must have been at the domestic

violence support group.' Beth stepped forward; she wasn't sure why but she felt like she was going head to head with him. His facial expression changed rapidly in a few short moments.

'Bloody hell, Sherlock, you're good.' He tried to laugh it off.

She felt her pulse quicken. Her worst fear realized. She tried to read his face for some clues as to how he felt about being rumbled.

'You don't deny it?' she asked. He shrugged and shoved his hands into his trouser pockets. 'So how does that work then?' She was interested to see how he was going to explain himself.

'We just meet up and talk. That's it really.'

Beth knew she was scowling. He was fidgety but otherwise quite calm. 'So is it you and lots of people that have been abused?' She felt nausea swirl in her stomach.

Jack was looking increasingly uncomfortable. 'Look, we shouldn't really discuss this out here,' he said, looking furtively around.

'Where do you suggest then?' she asked as she stopped herself from suggesting the local police station.

'Machine coffee?' he said as he nodded towards the main building. Beth checked her watch. She could spare five minutes, this was important.

They went inside to the deserted refectory and Beth sat at a table while Jack got the drinks. Her brain was humming along with the coffee machine. She glanced across to see the fire alarm was nearby and gained a strange comfort from it. If he lashed out, as he might now he was cornered, she could summon help quite quickly.

Jack gave a brief smile as he brought the drinks and sat down. 'So what do you want to know?'

Beth licked her lips self-consciously. This was like facing Nick, although it wasn't him, obviously, but all the questions she wanted to fire at Nick were marauding through her brain as well as the unwelcome associated emotions.

'Why? Why are you here doing this?'

Jack puffed out his cheeks and blew out air calmly. 'Because sometimes it's difficult to move on.' His sad expression was at odd with his words.

'Do you regret it?'

Jack narrowed his eyes as they darted about. 'How do you mean?'

Beth was frowning; something wasn't adding up. 'I don't understand. You get these abuse victims together and then what?' Beth's voice was going wobbly and as she lifted her drink to her lips she realized her hand was shaking.

Jack pulled a leaflet from his back pocket and handed it to Beth. 'Perhaps this can explain better than I can. I set the group up a while back. We're a bit of a minority.' He pointed to the title on the leaflet as he spoke. It said: *Support Group for Male Victims of Domestic Violence.*

Beth kept her eyes downward, the heat rising in her cheeks as her brain tried to unscramble all the assumptions she'd made. She started to grind her teeth and then stopped herself; it was the first time she'd returned to that habit in a while. 'I think I owe you an apology for these last few weeks. I'm sorry.' She looked up and met his gaze. She felt truly awful. She had jumped to a very wrong conclusion about Jack. She was an idiot.

Jack was smiling. Then it slipped and vanished. 'You knew before tonight?'

'No, not exactly. I mean, I had heard about you being involved in an abusive relationship but when you hear that a man is involved in domestic violence …' Beth ran out of words and her eyes dropped to the leaflet she was still clutching.

So Jack finished her sentence. 'You assumed that *I* was the abuser?'

Beth shook her head but she couldn't lie as that was exactly what she had thought. It was what she had taken Petra to mean when she warned her off. 'I made the wrong assumption about you. I'm really sorry.' Why wasn't there a stronger word than 'sorry' for moments like this? she thought as her stomach churned.

'You thought I was capable of domestic violence?' His jaw was tight and his hand movements jerky.

'I didn't think it through …' She actually felt sick.

'But you were happy to accept that I was the person beating the crap out of someone else. Well, thank you, Beth. It's good to know what you really think of me.' Before she could respond he was already standing up and striding away.

'Jack, I'm sorry!' she shouted belatedly as a couple of teenagers charged through some double doors sniggering. She shoved the helmet on her head to hide her embarrassment and marched out to the moped. How had she got it so very wrong?

'So what did you do?' asked Carly as Beth finished retelling the events of the previous night.

'I got on the moped. I was hardly going to run after him to see if he wanted to compare notes.' Beth switched the phone to her other hand as her palm was sweating from holding on to it for so long. She had gone over and over the whole thing and whichever way she looked at it, it was a mess of her own creating. If only she had questioned Petra more perhaps all this could have been avoided.

'You could swap stories. At least he would understand,' said Carly. 'Ooh, it could be the thing you have in common.'

'I can think of a million better things to have in common other than domestic violence!' The irony of the situation wasn't lost on Beth.

'Okay, sorry. The thing I don't get is why did Petra warn you off him?'

'It's a good question and one I'm hoping to get answered at work later on. Anyway, how are things with you and Fergus now you're home?'

'We're fine. I know the trip to Ireland was for his granny's funeral but being away has definitely helped. We are happy and we are ticking over nicely.'

239

Sounds like Shirley's old car, thought Beth with a smile. 'And is ticking over enough?'

'It is. I am living in the now, not in a fantasyland.'

'I'm proud of you, Carly, I think that's a healthy approach.'

'Do I need to bring sleeping bags when I come to stay for the panto at the weekend?'

'No, it's okay. You and Fergus can have my bed and I'll sleep on the sofa. We'll be fine.'

'I'm looking forward to doing the signing at the panto, especially now that Fergus is coming too.'

It was nice to hear that their relationship had steadied itself and they seemed at last to be over their bumpy patch, thought Beth, which was more than she could say for her own relationships. She cared about them both and they seemed well suited when they weren't annoying each other and that was just something they would have to learn not to do.

Beth stepped out into the ice-cold rain and trudged the few short steps to the pub, bumping into Shirley on the way. She had her plastic-bonnet-covered head down as she battled against the elements.

'Hi, Shirley. Hello, Mittens,' said Beth trying to peek into the trolley.

'She's deaf!' said Shirley, shaking her head at Beth as if she were potty.

'At least she's dry in there,' said Beth as the rain started to lash down harder. 'I'd better go.' She made a run for the cover of the pub doorway. The pub was quiet, the rain and wind keeping both visitors and regulars away. When there was nobody nearby and Petra had stopped polishing glasses Beth saw her opportunity.

'Petra, you know on New Year's Eve when you warned me about Jack's past? I think I might have got confused. Can you run through it again, please?'

Petra sighed. 'I don't want to speak out of turn.'

A bit late for that, thought Beth. 'What did you mean exactly?'

Petra looked hopefully around the bar but there were no customers to use as a distraction so she returned her eyes to Beth. 'You are both my friends. I like you both. I could see you getting close and I know how much Jack has been hurt in the past. And I know how you are always telling me that soon you will be leaving, that you cannot stay. I did not want him to be hurt again. He was hurt very badly by someone he cared about.' She made a face that made her look a little like a chimpanzee eating an orange and Beth expected that was her being conciliatory.

'So when you said that he was involved in domestic violence, you didn't mean he was hitting someone?'

Petra looked shocked; her hand flew to her mouth and it was a moment before she spoke. 'No, not Jack, of course not. His girlfriend, she had problems,' she tapped the side of her head for emphasis, 'and she would throw things at him and she would ...' She stopped talking. 'I have said too much. It is not for me to say. But no, *he* was the one getting hurt, not the other way around. I am sorry, did you think?' Beth nodded. 'Did you say this to Jack?'

'Not exactly but ... I may have implied it,' said Beth, wincing at the thought.

'What now?' said Petra.

'I'm not entirely sure. But you were right about me planning to leave, so thank you for that. A relationship with anyone is not what I need right now.'

Petra shrugged. 'Uh, it is a shame as you would make such a cute couple.' She winked as she stepped past her to serve a lone wet customer.

The pub door opened and in with the chill air came Jack wearing a heavy coat with the collar turned up. Beth froze. A thousand unspoken words passed between them as they exchanged looks. Jack stood for a moment before lowering his eyes, turning around and leaving. Beth caught Petra watching her and she shrugged her shoulders. She'd made her decision not to get involved, possibly not based on correct information, but it was the right one. However, that didn't mean she wouldn't regret it.

The cottage felt smaller somehow with Fergus in it. Perhaps it was watching him duck every time he switched rooms? They were Beth's first planned guests and she was pleased with her efforts to make things feel homely. Willow Cottage was still very much a work in progress but all major works had been completed with the exception of the disastrous bathroom and the hall and the dining room and the gardens … so maybe not all major works then, she pondered. There was also a large flashing question mark over the boiler, which seemed to have a serious attitude problem and only worked when it felt like it. The other jobs on the Willow Cottage list were time-consuming but low cost and nothing she couldn't do herself if she put her mind to it. The garden would have to wait until the spring but there was enough inside to keep her busy until then. Perhaps she could even say she was over the halfway mark?

Willow Cottage looked a whole lot better on the outside with the rambling plants long since removed and the door and window frames repainted. It was now a bit of a mismatch with the unkempt front garden, rickety fence and missing gate. The willow looked slightly odd after its haircut but she knew it wouldn't be long before spring came and it would start to grow again. Pretty much like her hair that she had finally managed to get cut in Stow. She had decided against colouring as that was a luxury she couldn't afford, and she'd warmed to her natural golden coffee tones.

The back garden wasn't a lot better than the front with the grass worn bare in patches thanks to Leo and his football and the odd hole that Doris had dug. The plants seemed to be more self-regulated here and although they were full they hadn't yet taken possession of the lawn.

After the pleasantries and the oohs and ahs at how the cottage was looking had been dispensed with, the conversation moved on to Leo.

'He's doing really well. He has made friends and there's another single mum …'

'Petra at the Bleeding Bear,' said Carly as she signed.

'The bloody bear?' chortled Fergus, deliberately misreading the sign.

'It's the pub, it's called the Bleeding Bear,' explained Beth. 'Petra's son Denis and Leo get on really well, so that has definitely helped him to settle.' She let out an involuntary sigh. 'He got very fond of Doris, Jack's dog, but as I don't dog-sit any more he's missing her. I don't want to admit it but I think he's missing Jack too.' She had never really explained to Leo what had happened, which was good because now she would have to explain that it had all been a mix-up, but it still meant that Leo had lost Doris and Jack from his life without explanation. Beth pushed her hair off her face as she thought about the situation, the guilt still intruding on her thoughts.

'I'm sure I can get a ticket if you want to ask Jack to come this afternoon?'

Beth shook her head. 'I don't even think the panto could recover his sense of humour,' she said with a brief pout.

'Oh yes it can,' chanted Fergus. He was standing in the doorway watching them. 'You seem concerned about what this guy thinks.'

Beth gave a non-committal shrug. 'He was kind to me and I wish I hadn't upset him.'

Fergus came over and sat down. 'It's always fixable you know.'

Beth sat back in her seat. 'There isn't a lot of point in fixing it because I'm not looking for a relationship and I'm not staying in Dumbleford long-term.'

Fergus nodded his understanding. Carly excused herself and went upstairs to the toilet. Fergus sat down and started signing at Beth.

'You know I'm not good with signs, but I heard the toilet door lock so she can't hear you if that's what you're worried about,' said Beth as she signed 'heard toilet door, Carly gone'.

Fergus tilted his head to one side. 'See, you know more signs than you let on.'

Beth grinned and signed 'Woman. Loch Ness Monster. Roller-skates. Sunset. Biscuit. I love you.'

Fergus stared blankly at her. 'What?'

'They're my favourite signs.' She grinned. 'Actually, that's pretty much my whole repertoire!'

Fergus shook his head. 'We don't have long before she comes back. I need your help and it's top secret. Not a word to Carly, okay?'

Beth leaned forward. 'Not a word.' She mimed zipping her lips as her eyes beamed at him expectantly.

'Good, you see for a while now I've been planning to—' started Fergus but the toilet door opened upstairs and Beth waved at Fergus to stop talking. That had to be the quickest wee in history but she couldn't really blame Carly for wanting to leave the oppressive bathroom of doom.

The first half of the pantomime was highly entertaining with lots of audience participation and innuendo. It was quite sweet to see how Fergus gazed at Carly most of the time with only the occasional glance at the cast on stage. He definitely knew the story of *Snow White* so that wasn't why he was glued to her. Leo was loving his first pantomime experience and especially the fact that it was quite acceptable to shout at the top of your voice when the baddie came on stage.

As soon as the curtain came down for the half-time interval Fergus was up and heading for the ice-cream queue with Leo in hot pursuit. Beth was checking her phone messages when Carly joined her and flopped down into Fergus's seat.

'Well done you, that was brilliant!' said Beth, waiting for her messages to pop up.

'You don't know what I was signing, it could have been rubbish!'

'I know a few bits.' She'd had a crash course from Carly some years ago and added to what she'd learned since Carly and Fergus had been together. She knew enough to get by.

'You know more than you think you do,' said Carly.

'Perhaps. But seeing as Fergus was laughing in the right places I'm guessing you were okay.' Carly gave her a friendly nudge. Beth felt her breath catch in her throat as she read a message from Jack.

'What's up?' asked Carly, looking over at the phone.

'Nick,' was all she could say. Her mouth had gone dry. She frantically searched the crowd for Fergus, who was lolloping back with a stack of mini tubs of ice cream.

'What's happened to Nick?' asked Carly and her concerned tone had Beth distracted for a second.

'Not nearly enough,' snapped Beth, wishing that he would slip under a bus or train or any large moving vehicle.

'Fergus!' Beth shouted in vain; he was looking around and waiting for some people to move out of his way. Leo looked up and she instantly felt self-conscious. The last thing she wanted to do was alarm Leo.

She stood up and beckoned to them but Fergus was now looking at Carly, who was signing to him. Fergus made his apologies and squeezed past the slow-moving people to get back to his seat.

His face was now looking suitably concerned. 'What's up?' he asked, as Leo was settling himself into the seat next to his mother. Beth said nothing but swapped the tubs for her phone and let him read the text from Jack. When he looked up she spoke. 'Can you look on Twitter for me?' He nodded and pulled out his phone.

Within seconds the full horror of what Nick had done was scrolling before Beth's eyes. She could barely take in the number of messages as Leo's photo shot past again and again.

'Missing person?' said Carly, and Beth widened her eyes and

shook her head in a silent attempt to stop her revealing anything to Leo. Carly nodded her understanding. 'Why would he do that?'

Beth's fury escaped in Carly's direction. 'Because he's a lying, manipulating bast—' She modified her language for Leo's ears. '... person, who is trying to track us down by any means possible.'

Chapter Twenty-Six

Carly rested her hand on Beth's arm and looked at Fergus. Beth was shaking as total confusion reigned. Her head was pounding. She felt like she was being watched by everyone in the theatre. She couldn't think straight. Leo was tucking into his ice cream, thankfully oblivious to the drama unfolding next to him. Beth's mind was a fuzz of fear and questions. How long before someone locally responded and their location was revealed? How long before Nick was back in their lives?

Beth looked from Carly to Fergus. 'What do I do?' She was pale and felt dizzy with the panic.

'Call the police,' said Fergus. 'Report Nick for what he did and explain what he's doing now. I'll go online and see what the social media sites can do to help us.'

Leo looked up at the mention of Nick's name. 'You okay, Mum?' he asked, with his plastic spoon poised.

'Yes, it's fine. There's nothing for you to worry about,' said Beth, trying to summon up a reassuring expression. Leo seemed to take his mother's word happily and he carried on with his ice cream.

As Fergus was frantically messaging on his phone Beth turned to Carly. 'How can I report him after all these months, they won't believe me.'

Carly gripped her hand. 'It doesn't matter how long you've left it. A crime is still a crime. Call them.'

Beth was pacing in the theatre foyer after being put through to a number of people and told someone would call her back. She was fast losing hope of gaining any support from the police. However, within twenty minutes a female response officer was on the phone. She was very reassuring and confirmed that they would speak to Nick directly about the incident back in London and tell him to take down the missing persons request on social media. The officer gave Beth her details, which she scribbled down on the back of an old receipt, and explained that someone would be in touch to follow up the case. Then the call was over. There was nothing more Beth could do and it was a desolate, helpless feeling that engulfed her.

Despite the heater in the theatre foyer she felt frozen from the inside out. She could hear the laughter coming from inside the auditorium and knew that Leo would be part of that. He was safe with Carly and Fergus and she was grateful that for now he was unaware of what was going on. She looked out at the dark-ness of the evening sky, which was somehow seeping into her, and took a deep breath. If Nick wanted a fight then that's what he'd get because she would do whatever it took to keep Leo safe.

Back at Willow Cottage the mood was drained. The three adults had been overly jovial to try to hide things from Leo and now he had gone to bed they had been able to shut the living-room door and discuss the situation at length. The good news, if there was any, was that Nick had only put his missing persons plea on social media sites and had not officially reported Leo missing via the correct route, which was the police. This meant that none of the official missing persons websites were supporting the search.

Fergus's quick thinking in reporting the violation to Twitter had enabled them to close down the account that Nick had set up so the original message was deleted. However, the retweets and copied details that had been shared were already over a thousand and growing as unsuspecting members of the public thought they were helping to find a missing child by sharing Leo's photograph and Nick's heartbreaking plea.

A knock at the door made Beth and Carly jump. Fergus looked alarmed at the reaction of the women in the room.

'Door,' signed Carly and Fergus went to answer it.

He pulled the door open briskly to a startled-looking Jack, who took one look at the stranger in the doorway and started shouting, 'Beth! Beth! Are you all right?'

'Hey. Calm down,' said Fergus, his usually melodic accent a little harsher than usual. Beth appeared behind Fergus.

'Jack, it's all right. This is Fergus,' said Beth, stepping forward and touching Fergus's arm so that he would know that she had joined him.

Jack threw his eyes skywards. 'Bloody hell, you had me worried there!' he said, as he wiped his hand across his mouth.

Fergus was frowning at him, unable to lip-read his words, but he said nothing. Over Jack's shoulder Beth watched the few people leaving the pub, scanning the dimly lit area for any signs of Nick.

'Right, well this is awkward. So, I think I'll go,' said Jack, pointing a thumb over his shoulder.

'Sorry,' said Beth, refocusing on Jack.

'I just came to check that you and Leo were all right.' In all the drama Beth had forgotten to reply to Jack's original text alerting her to what was spread across the internet. She suddenly felt bad.

'Yes, thanks, we're fine …' said Beth at the same time as Fergus spoke.

'They're fine, we're staying overnight.' The two voices jumbled together.

Jack was narrowing his eyes as if sensing there was something wrong. Fergus was showing none of the usual signs of apology that you emit when you talk over someone.

'Come in, it's cold,' said Beth to Jack.

Jack stepped inside and looked at Beth for an answer to his puzzlement. She shut the door and registered his questioning look; the penny finally dropped. 'Oh, Fergus is deaf.' She tapped Fergus's arm so he would look at her and she signed, 'He didn't know you're crazy.'

'Crazy?' said Fergus with a chuckle.

'I said deaf!'

'Not quite,' said Fergus and he proceeded to show her the difference between the two signs.

'Hello,' signed Jack. 'That's all I know I'm afraid,' he said.

'You're better than Beth already,' said Fergus and the men shook hands. Beth and Fergus headed into the kitchen and Jack into the living room. Carly jumped up to give him a hug.

'Hi, how are—' started Carly before Jack raced to speak over her.

'So that's The Ghast Blaster?' whispered Jack, his face filled with childlike glee.

'Apparently so,' said Carly, this revelation very much old news to her. 'No need to whisper.'

'Oh, yeah, right. I think I'm having a fan-boy moment!'

Carly looked instantly bored and flopped back onto the sofa as Jack hovered in the doorway waiting for the internet celebrity to return.

When Beth and Fergus came back with teas and coffees they all settled in front of the fire that was spitting ferociously as it devoured a fresh log. After a round of silent sipping Jack spoke first.

'Who posted Leo as missing?'

The other three exchanged uncomfortable looks. Beth sighed; it was down to her to explain. 'It was Nick, my ex-boyfriend. I left him and moved here.'

Jack was nodding encouragingly but Beth had stopped talking. 'You didn't tell this Nick where you'd moved to then?' asked Jack.

'No, because we moved to get away from him,' said Beth, her voice slow and deliberate, her discomfort palpable.

'I never liked him,' said Fergus and all eyes shot in his direction. 'What?' He shrugged. 'Call it my deaf superpower if you like but I didn't warm to him.' He gestured to Beth with a rather full mug and the liquid sloshed about. 'You were always tense around him. I could see it and I could sense it. And, however he spun it, he always got his own way over everything.'

Beth pondered what Fergus had said. 'Turns out you were more observant than I was then,' she said. 'Anyway, the police are dealing with the false missing person stuff now so all we can do is hope nobody responds and gives away our location.'

'At least it's not summer,' said Jack. 'This time of year we don't have as many tourists swilling around,' he explained for Fergus and Carly's benefit. Fergus glanced at Carly and she signed an appropriate expression for 'swilling'. They both nodded their understanding.

'So what's the big deal about him finding you?' asked Jack, taking a drink from his mug.

'Sorry, I'm really not comfortable discussing this,' said Beth, her voice brittle.

'No, I'm sorry. I didn't mean to pry,' said Jack with a brief smile and they all concentrated hard on the contents of their mugs.

Beth's phone rang and when she saw who was calling she stood up quickly, 'Shit, my parents!' She answered the phone and went to the kitchen, leaving the others with just the crackle of the open fire.

'You've done a nice job with the kitchen,' said Fergus to Jack.

'Cheers, I enjoy that sort of thing to be honest. This ex-boyfriend of Beth's, is he dangerous?'

Carly shot Fergus a warning look which he ignored.

'Yes, he is. The worst kind. Utterly charming on the outside, rotten on the inside.'

'Right,' said Jack, raising his eyebrows as he studied the flames that were now overwhelming the log in the fireplace. 'That's good to know.'

After a few minutes Beth appeared and hovered in the doorway. She gave a badly acted yawn as Carly and Jack watched her. Fergus was watching the fire. 'I think I'm going to turn in,' she said, giving Jack a look that she hoped conveyed she'd like him to leave. After a short delay he stood up.

'Right, I had best be off then. If you need anything you know where I am,' said Jack softly. He gave Carly a brief air kiss, shook Fergus's hand and joined Beth in the hallway.

Jack turned as he reached the door and Beth realized she was very close behind him. She put up her hands as if to stop herself bumping into him and he gently took them in his. Her pulse started to quicken and she had to concentrate not to pull away.

'Look, Beth, can we …' But Beth was already shaking her head.

'No, Jack. I'm sorry about the mix-up, really I am, but the truth is I have to move on soon, so …'

Jack was nodding. 'Okay. But we can still be friends. Friends that watch out for each other, yeah?'

Beth forced down the lump in her throat. 'Yeah,' she said, but it came out more as a squeak. He let go of her hands and left and as the front door clicked closed behind him Beth let out a sigh.

'I need a drink!' she said, flopping onto the sofa.

Carly was giving her a look. 'I thought you were going to bed?'

'No, I just said that so that Jack would leave.' She felt awful admitting it out loud but it was the truth. 'It's all very awkward after the whole domestic violence mix-up.'

'That wasn't his fault,' said Carly. 'You jumped to the wrong conclusion.'

'I know.' Beth closed her eyes, feeling the embarrassment and regret resurface. 'I think I need to retrain my brain or something because I'm still getting uneasy feelings whenever he's around. I

think I pigeonholed him under dangerous and now I can't …'
She was trying to think of a word.

'Unpigeonhole him,' offered Carly.

'Precisely.'

Fergus was looking at Carly as he clearly hadn't been able to lip-read her last words. 'There is no sign for that one,' she said and he smiled.

Carly eventually gave in and went to bed and when Beth went to follow her Fergus tugged her arm and stopped her getting up from the sofa.

'Has she gone?' asked Fergus, shutting the living-room door anyway.

'Yes, she's gone.'

'I need some help with something,' he said, his face lit by the dying embers of the fire.

'Anything.'

'Can you come and stay with us over Easter?' His face was expectant.

Beth took a deep breath. 'I don't know. After what's happened today I don't think that would be a good idea.'

Fergus hung his head. 'I know it's a lot to ask but I tried to sort something out myself at Christmas and it turned to poo so now I'm thinking that having an accomplice might work better.'

'Accomplice?' Beth was sitting up straight now. What was he suggesting?

'I'm going to propose to Carly,' he said, his face breaking into a huge grin.

'Oh. My. God!' said Beth, her mouth muffled by her hands.

Fergus pulled her hands away. 'Good idea or bad idea?'

'The best idea ever! I'm so pleased for you,' said Beth, launching herself into his hug. 'Oh,' she said, covering her mouth to stop the squeals again and then realizing how annoying that was for someone trying to lip-read. 'Sorry. Was that you with the boat and Tower Bridge at Christmas?'

It was Fergus's turn to look startled. 'Yes, it was! Does Carly know?'

Beth waved her hand and signed for him to speak quieter. 'No, I don't think so. I've not said anything. It was Jack that put two and two together.'

'Smart guy. I watched Carly talking to you on the phone a while ago and she said she wanted the world to stop for her just once. I figured I couldn't stop the world but I could stop a small section of London when the bridge was up.'

'That's perfect. Are you doing it again?' Beth was going dreamy-eyed at the thought of Carly's reaction.

'No, that's the thing. I had to pull in a load of favours to use the boat and get the bridge opened up so I can't do it again. Any other ideas how I can stop the world or a small portion of it?'

'Mmm,' said Beth, her brain working overtime, 'leave it with me.'

'Will you come to London, so I can be sure that whatever we come up with Carly will actually be there?'

'Of course,' said Beth, her heart speeding up a fraction at the thought of being within a five-mile radius of Nick. It was for her best friend. What else could she say?

Chapter Twenty-Seven

February brought with it a cold snap as the temperature plummeted and the sky resolutely maintained its dull grey tinge. Leo had been outside almost as much as he had in the summer as he was obsessed with providing food for the birds. Homemade fatballs and a birdfeeder made from an old pop bottle with wooden spoons stuck in it were hung up proudly and closely monitored. There was also a hedgehog house, although the only obvious indicator of what the wooden crate and earth pile was meant to be was a sign Leo had painted that said Hog House.

The back garden looked less intimidating now that most of the foliage had disappeared and when the frost clung to the bare bushes it made them sparkle like Christmas. It was easier to see what plants there were and also how much cutting back was needed. There was a rose with a stem more like a trunk which Beth took a hacksaw to one morning and instantly filled up the dustbin and freed up a whole corner of the garden. Beth was still filling her time with any and every job that needed doing. Things may have calmed down after the social media scare but it was still dominating her thoughts.

The local police had been to visit Beth and had taken a statement and thanks to them and the social media sites Leo's wanted poster had withered to a trickle. Fergus, under his pseudonym of The Ghast Blaster, had made a concerted effort to make people aware of the dangers of sharing things on social media that you didn't know were genuine and had found himself spearheading an internet safety campaign. The cold snap had kept both Shirley and Ernie indoors and Beth had been doing fewer shifts at the pub because it had been so quiet.

It was early as Beth shuffled into the kitchen, and it was freezing. She checked the radiator and it was stone cold. She pulled on her floral print beanie hat, puffed out her cheeks and went to look at the boiler. Beth didn't know what she was looking for but the boiler was old and had been struggling. It appeared that it had now finally died. Now was not good timing as the great outdoors had been reset to arctic, nor was it an ideal time for something expensive. She bundled up a grumbling Leo, completed the school run and then headed straight for the pub.

Petra gave her an odd look. 'You're not working today.'

'No, I'm in need of help,' she said, pulling off her hat and letting her static hair dance wherever it wanted to. 'Boiler's died. I don't suppose you know of anyone that could replace it without it costing me hundreds?'

Petra pondered for a moment and flicked on the coffee machine as she passed. 'I make us coffee to help warm our brains and help us think, okay?'

'Yes, that would be very okay,' said Beth, pulling up a bar stool and rubbing her hands together.

'You know what? I might just know somebody.'

'Yeah?' said Beth hopefully.

'Since Leo's picture was all over the internet I have questioned any new faces that come in just in case they are up to no good and one was a retired plumber. I'll track him down.'

'Thank you for checking people out. The pub is one of the first places you'd go to ask.' She felt reassured to have Petra on her side.

Petra nodded. 'I won't be able to grill them when the summer rush starts but for now I am like police officer!' She laughed at her own joke. 'Coffee!' she said, rattling cups, and the machine burred into life.

That evening the cottage was starting to warm up nicely and Beth was handing over twenty-pound notes to a very short Welshman. Petra had made a few calls and finally tracked down someone who restored boilers, and for a bottle of brandy and cash in hand she now had a reconditioned boiler that worked. Beth was pleased with herself for sorting it out without Jack's help. He hadn't been to the cottage since the awkward evening with Carly and Fergus, although she had seen him regularly in the village and at college. She knew it was daft but she could barely make eye contact with him and that wasn't all about the misunderstanding. What Petra had said about her getting close to Jack and then leaving the village had rung true and she was keen to protect her own feelings as much as his. She *had* been getting close to him, she knew that. They seemed to get on well together and easy relationships like that were hard to find. She needed to move their relationship back to where it was when they were easy-going friends without them getting too involved. Beth wasn't even sure that it was possible but she wanted to try.

As February drew to a close Beth found herself excitedly locking up the moped at college and almost skipping into class. Tonight they were each choosing a specific item they wanted to make using the lathe and Beth was going to try to recreate a spindle that would hopefully match the others attached to the banister at the cottage.

Tollek was incredibly helpful and kept a watchful eye on her as she secured her wood, or square, in place and set the rpm for the lathe and rested her carefully chosen chisel on the tool rest. She had used the calipers to measure her wood and mark where she needed to work. She took a deep breath and began.

By the time they got to break, Beth was ready to break something. She had been building up to this for the past few weeks and had been encouraged by what she had achieved but it appeared that tooling a spindle to a specific pattern was quite different, and very much harder than going freehand with your designs.

She had almost completed two and each time she had come to the final delicate beading at the end she had made a mistake and the spindle was ruined. If Tollek hadn't been so patient and calm she might well have thrown the spindle across the room. She trudged off to the break area behind the others in her group. They had all given her their sympathies but nevertheless seemed to be doing very well with the things they had chosen to work on. Beth reminded herself that for them this was just a hobby or an opportunity to learn a new skill to keep them out of the wife's way during retirement. For Beth this was virtually work, she needed to make these spindles or she couldn't finish the staircase. It was that simple.

She pressed 'hot chocolate' on the drinks machine as she needed the extra sugar and watched as the brown sludge foamed into the plastic cup.

'Hiya,' said a voice behind her.

Beth gave a quick look over her shoulder but she knew who it was. 'Hello, Jack,' was all she could manage. She took her drink and went to find somewhere to sit away from people. She was grumpy and it was best that she didn't inflict that on anyone else. Even the sight of a smiling Jack couldn't pull her out of this mood although the fact that he'd spoken to her did cheer her a fraction. It was only a spindle, well, two to be precise, and what she needed was practice; nobody was instantly amazing, you had to work at it, she told herself. Beth took a sip of the hot chocolate. It was not hot and there was little to indicate that it had ever seen a cocoa bean. She puffed out her cheeks and let out a frustrated blast of air.

'Boy, you sound fed up. Can I join you?' asked Jack, sitting down.

'I'm not sure you want to do that. My grumpiness is probably contagious, you know.'

'I'll take the risk,' he said with a brief smile. 'What's up?'

'I'm a shit wood-turner.'

Jack's eyebrows shot up; it was rare to hear Beth swear. 'I'm guessing there isn't a type of wood called shitwood?'

She looked up through her eyelashes, seeing he was mocking her. 'No, there isn't.' She stared at her drink.

'So you're just shit then?' He tilted his head.

She smiled. 'Utterly. The spindles for Willow Cottage are super tricky and I keep ruining them.' Her voice was speeding up.

'You'll get the hang of it.'

'Oh, Jack, I'm rubbish at it and I need to get very good very quickly. Another spindle on the stairs splintered the other day,' she said, her voice returning to its morose tone.

'Could you ask for extra lessons?'

'Money's a bit tight.' She pulled her bottom lip between her teeth, since it felt uncomfortable to admit this.

He nodded and pulled an understanding face. 'Could you make simpler spindles for the whole of the staircase?'

She shifted forward in her seat. 'That is a possibility but it would be a lot of work and a lot more wood.' She eyed him hopefully; she could see he was thinking up more suggestions and trying to help her solve the problem.

'Or have alternate ornate ones and plain ones? Or move them around and have plain ones on the landing where nobody will notice.'

'That could work,' said Beth. There was a pause and they were both looking intently at the other. Beth felt something ping in her gut and quickly picked up her drink to distract herself. They squished their plastic cups together in an impromptu toast. A moment's silence followed but for some reason it didn't feel uneasy.

'I saw Mittens this morning,' said Jack, his face creasing into a grin.

'In or out of the trolley?'

'On the windowsill at Shirley's. You know it's not struck me before but that cat's markings are quite unusual. I took a photo.'

Beth was pulling an intrigued expression as Jack found the picture on his phone and passed it to her. 'Remind you of anyone?'

Beth studied the photo of the mainly white cat with a black splodge on its head over one ear which reminded her of a lopsided beret. As she took in the black smudge under Mittens's nose she gasped with laughter.

'Hitler! She looks like Hitler!'

Jack was bobbing his head as he laughed. 'I know! There's even a website for cats that look like Hitler. I'm thinking of posting Mittens on it.'

'She could be the next internet sensation,' said Beth as the laughter subsided but the grins remained.

'I had better get back,' he said, downing the contents of his cup and standing up.

'Thanks, Jack,' said Beth. She was feeling a million times better after talking it through with him. He was a good person; it was ridiculous to have ever doubted it.

'You're welcome,' he said as he turned and walked away.

Beth returned to the class with a renewed sense of enthusiasm and a plan. Tollek was at her lathe. She put on her protective goggles and joined him.

Tollek looked up. 'This design is beautiful. Early Victorian I think but it is tricky.'

'That's exactly what I just said to a friend.' Beth felt her cheeks flush as she said it. It was a nice feeling to think of Jack as being her friend again.

'But it can be done,' said Tollek, leaning down and picking up two perfect spindles in his large hand.

Beth was close to jumping up and down on the spot. 'They're amazing!'

'Thank you. Stand behind me and I will show you how I am working the wood. Then you will try, okay?'

'Definitely!' said Beth, full of excitement. She only needed nine more and she was good to go!

Beth went to bed with a silly grin on her face. She knew it was silly because it was the grin she had always had until Nick had pointed out that a smile without showing your teeth was so much more refined. She blew a raspberry to Nick and settled down to sleep and tried to ignore the headache that had most likely been brought on by too much excitement.

'Pinch and punch!' said Leo as he jumped on his mother's bed and assaulted her bare arm.

'Ow!'

He giggled and ran downstairs. 'Oh, wow, these sticks are cool!'

'Noooo!' shouted Beth as she hopped about in one slipper and one arm in her onesie. She dashed downstairs as Leo was waving a spindle about in the manner of a *Star Wars* light sabre. 'That's delicate, please put it down. It took me ages to make.'

'You made them?' He put it close to his eyes and studied it. 'That's really cool.'

'Yes. Yes it is,' said Beth proudly.

Outside it was as if nature had realized it was March and that it should be warming up. The bitterness was gone from the wind but it had unfortunately been replaced by rain. This was not ideal as, having stripped off most of the layers of paint from the staircase, Beth was hoping to get on with sanding the remaining spindles, rail and balustrade. Despite wearing gloves her fingers got sore very quickly from the repeated movement of sanding the delicate spindles with fine sandpaper and the dust was getting to her too.

She was thinking about taking a break when Fergus's face

popped up on her phone. FaceTime was a great way to communicate apart from when you were covered in dust.

Fergus started chuckling. 'You've aged since I saw you last!' he said.

Beth gave her hair a shake and a shower of white dust softly fell around her. She positioned the phone so that Fergus could see her clearly. 'You can bugger off!' she said with feeling.

'Sorry, couldn't make that out. You know I can't lip-read swear words,' he lied.

'What do you want, you idiot?' she signed to him as she said the words.

'That's better,' he said with a grin. 'We're almost ready for Good Friday. You are still coming, aren't you?'

'Yes, I've got my train tickets and Leo is looking forward to a sleepover at the pub.' It had been her compromise, as she couldn't risk taking Leo to London. In Dumbleford they had managed to avoid Nick and his stupid internet missing person hoax but in London she wouldn't be able to relax if Leo was with her. She didn't like leaving him but she felt Dumbleford was the safest place for him to be.

Some mid-March sunshine had the children playing on the village green again as the daffodils and crocuses did their best to survive the odd misaimed football. The tree blossom was in full bloom, giving the centre of the village a soft pink hue. Beth loved the springtime. She never expected it to be sunny so was always very pleased when it was. So far there had mainly been rain but today the sun was forcing its way through the crumbly clouds and making everything feel alive as if waking from hibernation. Beth was sitting on a wooden bench watching the boys while she read a book and tried to ignore a niggling headache. She took in a deep breath; the air was clean and scented slightly with a trace of fresh dew. The early signs of spring made Beth feel optimistic but also concerned for how much she still had to do on the cottage, though with the change in season came a new sense of purpose, of starting again, and she began to reorder her to-do list in her mind as she watched Leo dart about.

'I'm too hot, Mum,' he complained as he dropped a tangled coat on the bench next to her. She could no longer leave Leo to play outside with Denis, she needed to be with him or be certain he was with someone she trusted to be alert. Nick and his nasty games still dominated her thoughts however hard she tried to push them to the back of her mind.

Her train of thought was broken as Doris barrelled into her. Doris's wet paws were all over Beth as she scrambled to try to get her paperback to safety.

'Doris, you great lump,' she laughed as Doris jumped onto the bench next to her and lay down on Leo's coat with her head in Beth's lap and inelegantly lifted a leg so that Beth could stroke her tummy.

Jack sprinted across the green and came to a halt in front of Beth. 'Sorry,' he panted. He must be very fit, thought Beth, as just a couple of deep breaths and Jack was breathing normally again. 'Doris, get down,' he instructed with a wave of his hand and a reluctant Doris slunk to the floor and lay on Beth's feet instead.

'Ow, she's heavy,' said Beth. Jack took hold of her collar but Beth touched his arm. 'No don't move her. She's fine.' Beth felt a pang of guilt for the dog too, she must be even more confused than Leo was about the whole situation. 'Nice day,' she added, then instantly wanted to curl up and disappear – how dull did she sound?

Jack raised an eyebrow. 'Yeah, it is. Do you mind if I sit down?' He pointed to the bench.

'No, of course not, watch out for giant wet paw prints.' She bundled up Leo's coat so there was space.

They sat silently, watching Leo and Denis chase after the football. 'How are things?' asked Jack with some tension in his voice.

'Okay, thanks. Bit of a headache but … did you mean me or my ex or the cottage?'

'All of it really.' Jack gave a half-smile.

'I think we're getting there on all counts.'

'Good,' said Jack with a nod and they returned to the silence.

'Oh,' said Beth, 'you were right about the whole Tower Bridge proposal thing on Christmas Day. That was Fergus.'

'I knew it,' said Jack, looking chuffed. 'Wow, that guy has style.'

'Yeah, but he's come up with an even better plan B to propose to her,' said Beth, twisting on the bench so she was facing him more.

'And he's told you?' Jack looked surprised.

'I've helped him and I'm going to London next weekend to make sure everything goes to plan.' Her voice changed and she moved back to watch Leo. 'It'll be weird being back in London after all this time.'

'Do you miss it?'

There was a pause before Beth answered. 'I did miss it, when we were first here. But now, not so much.' She hadn't thought about it recently and seemed to drift off for a moment. 'Anyway, it's only for two nights and Petra is having Leo and they have pizza and Nerf gun wars planned so I'm sure it will be fine.' She glanced at Jack.

'You don't look convinced,' he said, his tone matter-of-fact.

Beth's shoulders dropped. 'I'm dreading it,' she said with a small shake of her head. 'I daren't take Leo with me and I can't bear to leave him. But not going isn't an option either after what happened to the Christmas Day proposal.' Her speech was speeding up as she explained her predicament.

Jack reached out a tentative hand and placed it on her forearm. 'Can I get you a coffee?' She felt something when he touched her and whatever it was it had brought warmth to her face. It was a nice feeling.

'Yeah, that would be good, thanks.'

Jack reappeared shortly afterwards with two takeaway coffees from the tearoom. 'I like your hat,' he said as he sat back down.

'Cheers. It's another charity shop find,' she said as her hand instinctively adjusted the grey engine-driver's peak.

'If you like I can keep an eye on Leo while you're away. He and Denis can walk Doris with me.' Doris lifted her head momentarily and then flopped back onto Beth's feet. 'If the weather's nice I might organize a penalty shoot-out on the green ...'

'Thanks, Jack, but ...'

'No, I want to. And you need to be there for Carly and help make her dreams come true.'

Beth felt a smile spread. 'Well, if you put it like that, what else can I do?'

Chapter Twenty-Eight

Beth felt like a child as the automatic announcement on the train told her she was arriving at Paddington station. She was filled with a mix of excitement and trepidation. Most parents longed for time off from their children but she and Leo were close. They always had been, and since Nick and his shenanigans there had been an even stronger pull. Beth was already standing in the aisle adjusting her Merlot-red fedora when the train finally came to a halt. She carried her bag off the train and headed for the tube. Nothing had changed about the Hammersmith and City or Northern lines. The trains looked and smelled like they always had done, the people on them looked exactly the same and the 'mind the gap' message was unchanged. It should have been encouragingly familiar but it wasn't. Every time the train pulled into a station Beth found herself searching every face for Nick. She kept telling herself the further they got from Paddington the less likely she was to bump into him but still the sense of unease grew. There was no reason why he would be on the tube and the chances of him being on the same one as her were infinitesimal but it still didn't stop her worrying or her skin prickling.

Beth almost ran out of Kentish Town tube station. Her heart was racing and the enormity of what she might be facing was weighing heavy. What was she thinking coming to London? Exactly what would she do if she came face to face with him? Beth took a huge gasp of breath; she needed to pull herself together. He was a nasty piece of work but as far as she knew he wasn't a murderer and he probably wasn't psychotic – she needed to calm down and get a grip. Leo was safe. It was her overactive imagination. Beth took another large gulp of air and set off at a steadier pace towards Carly and Fergus's flat.

What *would* she do if she met him? The more she thought about it the angrier she became. All the analysis she had done over the months had given her so much material and so many reasons to despise Nick. He had been manipulating her and controlling her all along. From the outright 'No, you can't do that' to the far more subtle 'Baby, for me let's not'. She hated him and would happily shove him in the Thames and hope he swallowed enough germs to wipe out a small nation. But she also hated herself for not spotting it sooner, for brushing away the minor doubts and for believing it would all be all right in the end because he loved her.

Beth realized she was breathing heavily and stepped out of the flow of people and took another moment to calm down. This had to stop. She was done with being on edge, she was done with worrying. If she bumped into him she would stand up to him and tell him straight and then she would call the police and run like hell. She gave herself a congratulatory nod; she had a plan and she felt better for it. Beth held her head high as she turned the corner and approached Carly's building, her breathing returning to its natural rhythm.

When the hugging and excited yelping had eased Fergus stepped forward and gave Beth a hug. 'Thanks for coming,' he said, giving her a sly wink. The afternoon was spent in a pub nearby, the torrential rain keeping them inside. They chatted about everything and nothing with Carly stepping in as interpreter whenever she was needed. Beth noticed how attentive

Fergus was, the odd gesture, a touch of the hand or an encouraging smile in the right place. He was a lovely person and very obviously besotted with Carly. Beth smiled to herself. This time tomorrow, she thought, Carly's going to be the happiest person on the planet.

When Carly paused for breath and went to the toilet, Fergus handed Beth a note.

'Ooh, this is like a spy thriller,' she said, taking it from him and reading it as fast as she could.

Trafalgar Square. 4th Plinth. 13.00 – not a second before or after.

'That's precise,' said Beth, folding the note and squirrelling it away in an inside pocket of her handbag where even she might never find it again, let alone anyone else.

'The company who have organized things said that it starts at one o'clock whether we're there or not,' said Fergus, his face solemn.

'Got it,' said Beth, feeling under pressure. But it was only a few stops on the tube and it would be no problem getting her there on time.

Fergus's expression returned to its usual carefree pose and Beth resisted the urge to turn round because she knew that Carly must be returning.

'Do you want to go to this gig tonight that Fergus is going to?' asked Carly almost before she'd sat down again.

'Gig?' questioned Beth.

'The Headless Rodents,' said Fergus. 'They're quite good. Each time I see them they've got a new lead singer but they play well, covers mainly but some of their own stuff too.'

'This is a band we're talking about?' asked Beth, looking confused.

'Yes,' said Carly. 'And no, he can't hear them.'

'Might be a blessing if their name is anything to go by.' Beth grinned. Fergus stuck his tongue out at her.

'I miss the music, you both know that, but being in the atmosphere when a band is on reminds me what it was like and how it feels. There's a bit of a vibration too with live music. I like the vibrations.' Both the girls sniggered.

'Filthy, the pair of you,' said Fergus, shaking his head in mock disapproval.

Beth and Carly both woke up on Good Friday with a touch of wine flu so paracetamol, lots of water and *Mamma Mia!* on DVD were called for. Fergus left the house at around 10.30 on the pretext of meeting friends for lunch and he and Beth exchanged excited looks as he left. When Carly was finally showered and dressed and looking human Beth thought it was time to head off.

'Shall we catch a tube to Covent Garden and grab some lunch?' asked Beth so casually she impressed herself.

'Tube strike,' said Carly, equally casual. 'Let's have lunch at the deli round the corner, they do these amazing—'

'No!' said Beth, the force of the word making her jump a fraction. Carly looked startled. 'I mean, I miss London so much and I've been looking forward to sitting outside.' Beth glanced out of the window and clocked the rain falling liberally from a heavy grey sky. 'Or inside at Covent Garden. How about a taxi?'

'On Good Friday with a tube strike on?' Carly pulled a face.

Various swear words ran through Beth's head but nothing useful. 'We could walk,' she said eventually, knowing it was a ludicrous suggestion.

'We'll be like drowned rats by the time we get there!'

Beth looked at the red-rimmed kitchen clock; at a guess it would be about an hour's walk. It was more than doable but it was now all about finding the incentive that would propel Carly out into a rain storm.

'Cleopatra's needle!' exclaimed Beth and Carly looked at her suspiciously. 'Leo has been doing the Egyptians … at school and he wanted me to take a photo of Cleopatra's needle,' she said, getting out her phone for emphasis.

'There's better stuff at the British Museum ...'

'Nope, has to be Cleopatra's needle. Then we could have lunch in Covent Garden afterwards ... after I've taken the photo. Come on,' said Beth, picking up her black mock croc patent hat that was ideal for rainy weather.

'It's nice to see you back in hats,' said Carly, linking arms with her friend. 'They suit you.'

'Thanks,' said Beth and she mentally prepared herself for the journey.

Beth checked her watch on the sly for about the fifth time in as many minutes. She was finally back on track and it was all going to plan. For the first mile or so Beth had set the pace and found that made Carly too suspicious. They were also covering ground too quickly and in danger of having an hour to kill in Trafalgar Square. They picked up a quick bite to eat in Chinatown and now Carly was wittering on about whether or not she should go back and buy the shoes she'd seen half an hour ago. Beth was only half listening, so she hoped she was saying yes and no in the right places. As they passed the National Portrait Gallery, the stress started to diminish. They were very close to Trafalgar Square now. A few more steps and Beth could really start to relax.

'Oh, hang on,' said Carly, stopping dead. 'I think we could have come a better way for Covent Garden.'

'What?' was all Beth could manage; her mouth had gone dry.

'Yes, let's go this way.' Carly turned right and started to walk away. She stopped and looked back as Beth stood motionless with eyes wide as if she'd just received an unexpected injection. 'Are you okay?'

Beth blinked quickly. She really needed her brain to be on form. 'Actually, no. I don't feel right.'

'Oh dear. Let's find somewhere to sit down and have a cup of tea,' suggested Carly, moving off again.

'NO!' shouted Beth, making Carly spin round looking worried. 'It's okay. I think what I need is to cool my feet down in the fountain in Trafalgar Square.' It wasn't the best plan she'd ever come up with but after a stressful morning it was all she could muster.

Carly giggled then stopped. 'Are you serious?'

'Absolutely! Come on,' said Beth and she walked off towards Trafalgar Square hoping that Carly was following her. She daren't look back until she was on the square and could see Nelson and the lions. Carly did a little trot to catch her up.

'Are you sure you're all right? You've gone all weird.'

'I'm okay. I want to look at the fourth plinth.' The fourth plinth had a long history – it had been the only plinth without a statue for some 150 years, but a few years ago a project had started using it to display works of art for a few months at a time.

'Okay,' said Carly, following Beth as she strode off to the fourth plinth. She stood nearby, ostensibly studying the art installation intently but instead she was scanning the crowd below for Fergus or at least a sign that everything was in place. No matter how much she scanned she could only see a hubbub of tourists milling about aimlessly, some climbing on lions and some taking photos.

Carly huffed at her side. Beth checked her watch; she had about three minutes to kill. They were going to be the longest three minutes of her life. 'Do you like it?' asked Beth.

Carly gave the object on the fourth plinth a cursory glance. 'It's all right, I suppose.'

'They were going to put up a statue of King William, I forget what number William he was, but they ran out of money you know,' said Beth, wishing she had paid more attention when they had visited in year six. She had only returned for the odd New Year's Eve celebration and never paid any of the plinths any attention for that matter.

'Mmm,' said Carly, her tone bored. 'Come on, let's go.' She

turned and started back the way they had come. Beth's heart rate sped up. She was so close.

'No, come on. Let's paddle in the fountain,' said Beth and she walked past the back of the plinth and down the steps. If Carly would only follow her she would be almost in place. Beth kicked off her shoes and rolled up her skinny jeans as far as she could.

Carly was staring at her. 'You'll get arrested,' she said, subconsciously scanning the square.

'No, it's fine, are you coming in?' said Beth as she climbed onto the edge and stepped into the ice-cold water. She gasped and tried to smile through it, which made her look like an overexcited chimpanzee. One last look at her watch. They were now bang on time. It should happen now ... or now ... or now ...

Beth slowly turned round and looked across Trafalgar Square, as she started to lose sensation in her toes. There were lots of people but there was no Fergus. She could feel the prickles of sweat break out on her forehead and top lip. In direct contrast to her feet, her head was overheating. This was not good.

'Beth?'

'I think I feel a little faint,' whispered Beth and she wasn't lying. She sat on the side of the fountain with her feet still sloshing in the cold water, got out her bottle of water and took a long slow swig. That killed another two seconds, she thought desperately. Carly was looking at her intently.

'You don't look well. Maybe we should go back to the flat?' Beth looked past her and it made Carly turn to look too. 'What is wrong? You are acting really strangely, Beth.'

'I think it's the heat. If I sit here for a little while I'll be fine.' She was starting to sound like Shirley. Before she knew it she'd be pushing a deaf cat around in a wheelie trolley swigging sherry. Old age in Dumbleford had a few perks, she thought.

'Um, what heat?' asked Carly. 'It's been tipping it down most of the morning and from the looks of it your feet are turning blue.'

They both eyed Beth's feet as a crisp packet floated past.

'Not raining now though,' said Beth, 'and it's not too bad when you get used to it.' She wriggled her toes and took a sly glance at her watch. Two minutes late. Fergus said he would be bang on time, no margin for error he'd said. How much longer could Beth keep Carly in Trafalgar Square?

Jack was killing time jogging round the green. He'd been out for nearly an hour and he wanted to make up the last few minutes. He jogged towards the pub and shook his head as a silver BMW pulled into the already full car park and blocked in two other cars. Easter weekend was always madness in Dumbleford. Everyone seemed to suddenly remember where the pretty villages were and set off en masse. As he jogged past he shook his head at the tall dark-haired man getting out of the BMW: sunglasses, crisp white shirt and chinos – the uniform of the London crew.

The pub was busy even by bank holiday standards, everyone was working flat out and Petra had just left the bar to help out in the kitchen for a few minutes. The tall stranger stood at the end of the bar and gave a slight smile in Chloe's direction. He was very handsome and not wearing a wedding ring.

Chloe worked her way down to him. 'What can I get you?'

'A soda and lime, please.'

Chloe quickly produced the drink and rang it through the till.

'Thanks. Actually a friend of mind moved to the area recently and I'm hoping to surprise her,' he said.

'That is a nice surprise,' said Chloe, admiring his neat appearance and good looks although he was far too old for her.

He gave a modest smile. 'Her name is Elizabeth. Do you know her?'

Chloe thought for a moment and tried hard to ignore the pensioner rapping their fingers on the bar. 'Sorry, don't know an Elizabeth.'

'Oh well, thanks anyway,' he said sipping his drink before standing up and taking it outside.

There was clattering in the hallway followed by a peal of giggles as Denis and Leo ransacked the crisps. The giggling stopped suddenly, there was a muffled discussion and Denis stepped behind the bar as if he'd been shoved. He eyed the back of the dark-haired man's head wearily as he shut the pub door behind him. Petra reappeared from the kitchen. Denis kept his eyes on the door as he walked to his mother's side and tugged at her dress.

'A moment, Denis,' she instructed with a hand gesture. He stood silently at her side, staring at the door. 'Yes, Denis. What is it? I'm busy.' Denis beckoned his mother to lean down to his level and he whispered in her ear. Petra's head jolted in the direction of the now closed door but her expression had changed. 'Okay, Denis, you both go upstairs and I will be up in five minutes.'

She served another customer and then told Chloe that she was taking a quick break. She was doing all she could to appear calm.

Petra exited the bar and scurried upstairs, shutting doors behind her. She rushed into the living room but there was no sign of the boys apart from the abandoned Lego pieces on the floor. 'Denis? Boys?' A head popped up from behind the sofa. Denis and Leo were hiding. 'Come out, it is safe. I promise.'

Leo was fighting hard to stifle sobs and Denis looked both concerned and embarrassed in equal measure. Petra took hold of Leo's hands. 'Denis told me who you thought you saw in the bar. Are you sure that it is him?' she asked in a soft voice.

He nodded and sniffed back a tear. 'It's definitely Nick.'

Petra tried hard to hide her alarm. 'Did he see you?' she asked. Leo shook his head and she sent up a silent prayer. 'Okay, we'll sort this. Please do not worry.' She pulled Leo into a bear hug and picked up the phone.

Chapter Twenty-Nine

It was a short but highly charged call from Petra and as Jack ended it he jogged across the green. He took a sly photo of the silver BMW on his phone and then a swift elbow to the wing mirror had its alarm blaring. In a few strides Jack was hiding behind the trunk of the willow tree where he watched and waited. Within seconds Nick was up off the picnic bench and striding towards the car where he scanned the car park and cancelled the alarm. Lucky guess, thought Jack. Nick gave the vehicle a cursory look over, checked his watch, got in and drove away, leaving his unfinished drink on the table.

'All clear, Petra. He's gone,' said Jack into his mobile before he made a series of other calls.

Beth rubbed her eyes and checked her phone. There were no messages and no sign of Fergus. She splashed her feet about in the fountain; it wasn't too bad once she'd got over the shock of the initial temperature. Carly was stood over her looking anxious. 'Do you think you could be having some sort of breakdown?'

Beth gave a weak smile. Carly might be right but it was not being caused by what Carly thought it was. Then, out of the corner of her eye, Beth saw something. Someone about twenty feet away wheeled in a large black box. As long as it doesn't contain a Hitler lookalike cat we could be in business, thought Beth.

Carly put her hands on her hips. 'It's not that warm and you've been wearing a hat all morning, so I don't think you've got heat stroke,' she said, as music started up behind her. Beth felt the sense of relief wash over her like poured honey. Carly was still looking at Beth but as Beth stood up and looked past her into the square she turned and followed her gaze.

A single girl stood on her own a few feet in front of the box as it played 'Moves Like Jagger' by Maroon 5 and she was moving in time to the rhythm. As soon as she started into a simple dance routine two more girls joined her and they continued dancing in perfect time with each other. Every few seconds more dancers joined in. Two men came and stood near Beth and Carly and they were watching too.

'Watch your bag,' said Carly cautiously.

'Okay,' said Beth and she started to clap along. The music changed to 'Call Me Maybe' by Carly Rae Jepsen and the two men ran and back-flipped into the routine.

'Wow!' said Beth, as at least thirty people were now dancing.

'Is this one of those flashy thingies?' asked Carly, turning to look at Beth who was stepping along in time to the music, splashing water everywhere.

'Flash mob!' said Beth, still unsure how Carly had managed to survive this far into the twenty-first century without being addicted to the internet.

'Right,' she said. 'They're very good.'

'Yes, they are,' said Beth, her excitement at full tilt. 'Keep watching!' she urged, pointing back at the display, as the last thing she wanted was for Carly to miss the crucial moment.

The current dancers went into a free dance section where they bounced about in a less coordinated fashion and pushed the crowd back to grow their space.

'I think it's finished,' said Carly.

'No, I don't think it has,' said Beth.

The music changed to 'Uptown Funk' by Mark Ronson and half of the large crowd moved in time to the new routine and the dance troupe instantly grew to more than a hundred people.

Carly's eyes were on stalks. 'How do they all know the steps?' asked Carly.

Beth was beyond being able to answer, she just kept clapping. When the next tranche joined in the whole of Trafalgar Square was either dancing or stood captivated by the spectacle.

'We're so lucky being here at the right time,' said Carly, at last looking like she was impressed and enjoying it.

Thank goodness for that, thought Beth.

The dancers suddenly shuffled backwards and were all bunched together as the music changed for the last time and 'Marry You' by Bruno Mars blared out of the speaker. Beth stopped clapping and watched Carly. She loved that Carly had no idea what was about to happen. She was smiling and jigging about a little in time to the music, watching the dancers so intently that when they waved their arms in a cascade motion, parted into two groups and a corridor opened up between them she didn't seem to notice who was walking down it and towards her.

Doing a little dance of his own came a tall man carrying two giant bouquets of brightly coloured gerbera. The dancers were now stood signing the words of the song while their hips all moved in time to the music …

> Cause it's a beautiful night,
> We're looking for something dumb to do.
> Hey baby,
> I think I wanna marry you.

The bouquets parted and Fergus was grinning as he walked up to Carly. Carly's face was a picture, she went through so many emotions in only a few moments: surprise, shock, thrill and lastly totally overwhelmed as Fergus got down on one knee. She started to cry, big body-wrenching sobs.

'Carly Wilson. I tried to make this little corner of the world stop for you today. I love you so much. Will you be my wife and spend for ever with me?' He opened a small Tiffany-blue ring box and a glint of sunlight caught the diamond at exactly the right moment, making it sparkle beautifully.

Carly was uncontrollably blubbing and Beth was feeling slightly smug as she handed her a handful of man-size tissues from her bag. 'Yes,' spluttered Carly as she launched herself into Fergus's arms. The music changed to 'Happy' by Pharrell Williams and the dancers starting waving signs that said *She said YES!* Fergus picked Carly up and swung her around and around. Beth was having her own little celebration as she splashed water in all directions and whirled her hat round her head. The two male dancers from earlier kicked off their shoes and joined her in the fountain. Fergus put Carly down and she looked overawed by the whole event as dancers and watchers alike all thronged round to congratulate the couple and they disappeared in the multitude of well-wishers.

When the crowd eventually ebbed away Carly saw Beth and her little gang drenched to the skin in the fountain and she started to laugh as Fergus guided her over.

'Congratulations!' shouted an excited Beth as she soaked the pair of them in a clumsy hug.

'Was this all just for me then?' asked Carly, her hand on her chest as she shook her head.

'Yep,' said Fergus, his shoulders back and a look of total pride on his face.

Carly turned quickly to point a finger at Beth. 'You!' she shouted before giving her a pretend whack on the arm. 'I thought there was something wrong with you!'

'There was! I needed you to be in the exact right spot at the right time!'

'That was bloody amazing!' said Carly as Fergus thanked the dancers and organizers. Everyone started to mill away. 'I'm engaged!' shouted Carly and Beth and Carly started to screech at the top of their voices. Fergus signed, 'You're screaming aren't you? I'm glad I'm deaf,' but nobody was looking at him.'

When the screaming had reduced to the odd squeal and they were opening champagne back at the flat, once Beth had dried off and warmed up, they watched the whole thing back on Fergus's computer.

'Look at my face!' said Carly, shaking her head. 'I can hardly believe it happened.'

'Who was filming?' asked Beth as she sipped her champagne and watched the events unfold for the third time.

'Loads of people! It's all over YouTube,' said Fergus, grinning. 'But this version was the guy from the flash mob company, it was part of the deal.'

'I loved it,' said Carly, going all weepy again. 'It was the best proposal ever …' She sniffed but couldn't continue. She slumped onto Fergus's lap and he wrapped one arm around her while he high-fived Beth with the other.

'You two have a few hours to make yourselves even more beautiful, while I make myself scarce, then we have an engagement party to go to!'

Carly pushed herself up from Fergus's chest. 'I get the feeling you're not stopping.'

'No way!' said Fergus. 'I'm showering and changing into that new shirt I got and some smart trousers,' he looked proud of himself, 'and then I'm meeting Ryan and Budgie at some bar.'

'Deaf club mates,' explained Carly to Beth.

Beth pulled Carly to her feet. 'Come on, let's get cracking, there's a lot to do!'

Carly blew a raspberry at Beth but followed her anyway. When she glanced back, Fergus had a soft look on his face and he was holding up his right hand with his ring finger and middle finger bent into the palm and his remaining two fingers and thumb splayed out in a sign.

'I love you too,' said Carly.

Curled up on the sofa, wearing dressing gowns with their hair in towel turbans, Beth and Carly were concentrating on painting each other's nails.

'I still can't believe it,' said Carly, wiggling the fingers on her left hand. She turned sharply, making Beth splodge the varnish.

'Carls! Keep still!'

'Tell me you didn't suggest this to Fergus?' Her face was serious.

Beth tilted her head to one side. 'Don't be daft, he'd had it planned for a long while. He just needed help with getting you in the right place at the right time. It's all his own work. He really wants to marry you.' Carly visibly relaxed again. 'Heaven knows why,' muttered Beth with a grin and Carly jogged her again. Carly watched Beth for a moment.

'You know you don't have to tell me but I'm guessing the night you left Nick wasn't the first time he'd hit you. I just wish you'd told me, that's all,' said Carly, reaching out a hand and stroking Beth's arm.

The comment took Beth by surprise and she breathed in slowly. 'No, that was the first and the only time he hit me.'

'Really?' said Carly rather too quickly.

'Yes.' She let out a deep sigh. 'It was almost a relief when it happened, like confirmation that he was the person I thought he was deep down and not the charming facade he put up most of the time.'

'Right, I guess I just thought when you said he'd been abusive for a while that, you know …' Carly didn't finish the sentence but tilted her head to one side.

'There was a time when I also thought that if someone was being abused it had to be physical but I've learned the hard way that it comes in many different forms.' Carly squeezed her hand. 'With Nick it was all about control and to do that he needed to strip me of my friends, my self-confidence and anything that didn't fit into his picture of how I should be – like calling myself Beth instead of Elizabeth or wearing hats.' She patted the fedora on the arm of the sofa next to her.

Carly was still looking puzzled. 'Did he shout at you, call you names? That sort of thing?'

'Not really. I know this is hard to understand, Carly, it's taken me ages to piece it all together and see it for what it really was. All the times he pleaded with me not to go out was about controlling me, all the times he put down my friends, didn't pass on their messages or deleted emails was about distancing me from other people. When he bought me new clothes and packaged up some of my old favourites for the charity shop he wasn't being thoughtful, he was exercising more control. The times he looked sad or sulked were all about getting me to behave how he wanted me to. Putting Leo into private school, signing him up for every after-school club and having someone to take him and pick him up from school wasn't about helping me manage my time, it was about keeping me and Leo apart. He wanted him to go to boarding school but I refused, which caused a blazing row. I've never seen anyone that cross; I thought he was going to hit me then although he didn't. He was unbearable for weeks but on that one I held my ground – I couldn't bear to send Leo away. Things got worse and worse after that, like he wanted me to pay for my decision to keep Leo at home with us. I think he saw Leo as a rival for my time and affection.'

'That's ridiculous!'

'Not to Nick. His behaviour became magnified, he criticized everything but always very subtly: the underhand comments, the tuts, the looks of disapproval. He got onto Leo about anything and everything, pushing his buttons and making him retaliate. He was even talking about taking Leo to a psychiatrist because he was trying to convince me there was something wrong with him!'

'I didn't realize,' said Carly, tears welling in her eyes.

'Nor did I for a long time. I put it down to him being overprotective but it's not. His behaviour isn't normal, his need to control is unnatural and at times quite frightening. He would only have to look at me in a certain way and my insides would knot up. I found myself checking everything I said and did so as not to upset him. I was worrying all the time about silly little things, almost afraid to start a conversation in case it would trigger one of his moods.' Beth forced a brief smile onto her face. 'So, he did only hit me the once but he hurt me every single day and that was why when he did hit me it confirmed everything I had been feeling for months and that was my cue to get me and Leo as far away from him as possible.'

Carly threw her arms round Beth and sobbed. Beth felt her own tears trickle down her cheeks but she somehow felt lighter for having voiced all the fears she had been carrying around like a stagnant rucksack for so long.

Carly pulled away from Beth, wiped her eyes and blinked hard. 'You have been so brave.'

'No, I was stupid not to trust my instincts. The signs were there but I chose to ignore them because he loved me – the sad thing is a love like that will only do you harm.'

'I wish you'd shared some of your worries with me, I would have understood,' said Carly, running a finger under her right eye and collecting more tears.

'I wish I had too,' said Beth and stood up. 'But now we have to change you from a puffy-eyed wreck into a glamorous fiancée. It may take a while.' She grinned as Carly pouted at her.

As Carly was doing the finishing touches to her hair Beth made a swift call to Petra. 'Hiya, how's things?'

'Hi, Beth. We are all very fine and well, thank you. How did it go?'

Beth wasn't sure if she heard tension in Petra's voice or if it was just that some people weren't that relaxed when they spoke on the phone. Ignoring it, Beth launched into an account of the proposal and directed her to it on YouTube.

'That sounds amazing.'

'It truly was. I'm so happy for them both. Thanks again for having Leo. Is he about?'

'Yes, of course. Hang on. Leeooo!' Beth pulled the phone away from her ear as Petra shouted.

There was a pause and muffled sounds as the phone was passed over. 'Hi, Mum,' said Leo and Beth had to stop the emotion that welled up.

'Hiya, mate. Are you behaving yourself?'

'Mmm,' said Leo in bored tones.

'What have you been doing?'

'Stuff.'

'Leo, come on, a bit more info needed here, please.'

Leo sighed down the phone. 'We took Doris for a walk and played football and watched *Star Wars* on DVD. Tomorrow Jack is taking me and Denis to a climbing wall,' he said as he started to succumb to his own enthusiasm.

'Oh, so you've been with Jack then?' The mention of him made his image spring to mind and she suddenly wanted to share with him the spectacle in Trafalgar Square.

'Yeah, he's been here all day and he's staying with us tonight. I need to go. Jack's ordering pizza and I want peper—'

'Hi,' said Petra. 'Sorry, the call of food was too strong. But he's fine. Please don't worry.'

'I'm not,' said Beth, although she now felt a twinge of something a lot like worry and she wasn't sure why.

'This is good. You enjoy yourself and we will see you tomorrow.'

'Thanks, Petra.' Beth took a deep breath when she came off the phone. Everything was okay. Leo sounded fine and there was nothing to worry about, so why did she have an odd sensation that there was something she should be worrying about? Beth pushed the niggle to the back of her mind. It was Carly's night and she didn't need a paranoid mum spoiling things.

'Come on!' called Carly. 'Cab will be here in a minute.'

Apparently it was traditional for the newly engaged person to get the drinks in all night so Fergus found himself back at the absurdly crowded bar. The long thin room was packed out but they had found somewhere to stand at the back. He'd had two pints so this was his absolute last one because there would be champagne at the restaurant later and he didn't want to be legless at his own engagement party. He stood patiently at the bar as people jostled around him. He was pleased he was tall as it was an advantage in getting noticed and therefore in getting served. The harassed barman blinked upwards to indicate it was Fergus's turn to order.

'Pint of Guinness, pint of bitter and a Coke, please,' shouted Fergus above the hum of the bar. A well-built man a few feet away started to swear his annoyance at being overlooked for service yet again. The barman started to get Fergus's order and he put his hand up in apology to the squat man further down.

Eventually Fergus paid and was able to carefully balance his three drinks and start to make his way through the hordes of people. It was slow progress and he had to keep stopping. A woman in front of him was on the phone and she couldn't seem to hear his polite request to get past and he had no free hands to tap her with, so he stood and waited. Fergus didn't hear the not-so-polite request from the squat man behind him who was carrying two bottles of beer.

'I said pissing well excuse me!' he repeated loudly. When there was no response he nudged Fergus in the back. Fergus turned and gave the squat man a smile and nodded his head in the direction of the woman by way of explanation.

'Get out of the way, dickhead!' shouted the man and people around Fergus started to look. Fergus didn't react; he was now watching the woman and was lip-reading her side of an interesting conversation. He was lost in the discussion about online porn from what appeared to be a very prim and smartly dressed woman in her thirties.

'This is your last warning, dickhead. Pissing well move!' yelled the man as he bumped Fergus.

Fergus turned round to see that the man was speaking.

'What's wrong with you, are you bleedin' deaf or sumfin'?'

'Yes,' said Fergus with a smile, 'I am.' He turned back to catch up on the woman's increasingly interesting conversation.

Fergus felt the sudden blow to the back of his head, but at first he didn't actually feel any pain, he felt wet as the contents of the shattered beer bottle cascaded over his head. The squat man dropped what was left of the smashed bottle as two men grabbed him and pulled him away. Fergus saw the look of horror on the woman in front's face as she screamed and stepped back. It was then the pain registered but he was already falling forward. My new shirt's ruined and I'm going to spill my Guinness, he thought, as his knees gave way and everything went black.

Chapter Thirty

As the taxi pulled up Carly's mobile rang. She could see from the screen that it was Ryan calling. Beth stepped forward to get in the cab and Carly held her back. She would have ignored the call except she immediately knew there was something very wrong because, like Fergus, Ryan was deaf and a deaf person would never make a phone call.

'Ryan?'

'Hi, is that Carly?' said a stranger's kind voice. The background noise was loud but she knew she wasn't speaking to Ryan although it was someone using his mobile phone.

'Yes, who is this?'

'My name is Charlie and I'm a paramedic. Do you have someone with you, Carly?'

'Oh God, what's happened?' asked Carly, suddenly feeling sick. Beth was looking concerned.

'Is there someone there?' Charlie repeated.

'Bloody hell. Yes, there's someone here. Tell me what's happened!'

'Fergus Dooley has been involved in an accident and we're taking him to hospital.'

'What sort of accident?' asked Carly.

'Shit,' said Beth with feeling as she grasped what was going on from the one side of the conversation she could hear.

'He was involved in a fight and—'

'A fight?' butted in Carly. 'Fergus wouldn't be involved in a fight if his life depended on it.'

The paramedic was ominously quiet on the other end of the phone.

'Sorry. How bad is it?' asked Carly as her head started to spin and a sense of dread crept up her spine making her shudder.

'He's unconscious. Look I wouldn't normally do this but his friends are deaf and somebody needed to tell you what was going on, which is why I borrowed one of their phones.'

'Fergus is deaf too,' said Carly, her voice almost a whisper.

'That's good to know. We're taking him to University College Hospital, so if you can make your way there they will be able to tell you more. Okay?'

'Yes, thanks. Bye,' said Carly and she ended the call, her legs feeling unsteady. Beth instinctively clutched Carly's arm as she wobbled.

Carly leaned into the open window of the waiting cab. 'University College Hospital as quick as you can, please.'

Carly paced the linoleum floor as best she could in heels as Beth sat slumped in a plastic seat. Shortly before one o'clock they had made the decision to operate and now, five hours later, they were still waiting for news. Beth had tried everything the hot drinks machine had to offer with the exception of the chicken soup, having seen someone else walk away with what looked like hot bubbling vomit. She checked the time; it was a bit early to call Petra but she had to update her soon as it was unlikely Beth was going to be on the 11-something train out of Paddington. She couldn't leave Carly until she knew that Fergus was going to be okay and he had to be okay because anything else was unthinkable.

She dialled the pub flat. 'Er, hello,' came a very sleepy male voice.

Beth's eyebrows shot up. Petra was a dark horse and Beth was feeling instantly uneasy about the fact that she was horsing around with Leo nearby.

'Hello, is Petra there, please?' She was tempted to add, 'She'll be the dark-haired beauty lying next to you in case you didn't catch her name?'

'Beth, it's Jack,' came the slightly more lucid response. Beth had the sensation of drifting and had to pull herself back to the moment. What the hell was going on? Perhaps it had always been going on? Which would explain why Petra had warned her off. 'Beth, are you still there?'

'Yes, sorry. Look, I'm going to be delayed. Fergus got hit over the head with a bottle in a bar last night and he's being operated on now.' She realized then how matter-of-fact and callous it sounded but there was no easy way to pass on something so serious. 'I can't leave until I know how he is.'

'That's awful. Is he going to be okay?' asked Jack tentatively.

'Nobody knows, he's lost a lot of blood,' said Beth and she had to quickly get her emotions in check as they risked bubbling to the surface. 'Is Leo all right?'

'Don't worry about Leo, he's fine here with us. You take care of Carly and keep us posted, okay?'

'Okay, thanks,' said Beth but all she could think was 'us'. He used the word 'us' when he was referring to him and Petra and it suddenly seemed like a very big word indeed.

As she came off the phone Carly handed her a plastic cup and she stared at the liquid inside. 'Are we playing guess what the hot drinks dispenser has bestowed upon us this time?'

'It's meant to be tea,' said Carly, 'but it's like no tea I've tasted before.' They both took a sip and winced. Whatever it was, it was the colour of old lady tights, lukewarm and frothy.

They sat down and gave each other reassuring looks. They had run out of conversation hours ago. When they had first seen Fergus, his bloodied clothes and unconscious state had been a shock but the doctors and nurses had been reassuring as he had been whipped away for a series of tests. The initial panic had been replaced by practical activity as Beth had called the restaurant where the engagement party was going to be and they had told the guests the situation. It was a blessing that the party was only a small group of friends and that no family had been invited as Fergus had rightly assumed that it would be best to tell them the good news face to face. He also didn't want them to know before Carly.

Carly had been forced to call Fergus's parents to explain what had happened and advise them about the operation. Carly didn't know too much, only that he had lost a lot of blood and there was also further bleeding that was putting pressure on the brain and needed releasing. The doctor had made it all sound straightforward but Fergus had been in theatre a while now. They'd had very little information about what exactly had occurred at the bar as neither of Fergus's two friends had actually seen what had happened. They had only been involved in the aftermath and now Carly was keeping them updated by text.

The door release clicked, automatically opened and an unsmiling doctor came through. Carly reached out and clutched Beth's hand in hers, spilling her drink, but Beth didn't care.

If Carly and Beth had been expecting a conclusive report from the doctor they were disappointed. He explained in detail what they had done and Carly grew paler by the second; she was more than a bit squeamish. They had performed a craniotomy, which he explained was when a section of the skull is temporarily removed so the surgeon can access and remove the haematoma, and he believed the operation to have been successful but time would prove that theory right or wrong.

'He'll be in recovery for a while yet but once he's regained consciousness we'll move him and you'll be able to see him. Any questions?' he asked.

'Definitely no brain damage?' asked Carly.

'The MRI was clear with the exception of the subdural haematoma, which we've removed, so it's a matter of waiting for the brain to settle itself now. A nurse will be up once he's awake.'

'Thank you, Doctor,' said Carly and he disappeared.

As the automatic doors clicked shut Carly burst into tears and Beth pulled her into a hug. 'He's going to be okay,' she whispered into Carly's hair.

'I know ... that's why I'm crying,' she sobbed as a strangled laugh escaped too.

'You silly bugger,' said Beth, blinking back her own tears. Their elation kept them going for the next hour but when a glum-faced nurse walked in they knew something was awry.

'Miss Wilson?' asked the nurse as she sat down opposite Carly and Beth. 'We're about to move Fergus from recovery.'

'So he's awake?' asked Carly.

The nurse shook her head. 'His vital signs are stable but he hasn't regained consciousness as yet.'

'Why not?' asked Beth.

'It's difficult to tell with head trauma and after an anaesthetic sometimes the brain takes a little longer to right itself.'

'Should I be worried? Because I am,' said Carly.

'Some people take longer than others to come round. He's being moved to intensive care where he'll be closely monitored and you can sit with him.'

Carly gave Beth a fleeting look and Beth gave what she hoped was a reassuring smile.

'Is he in a coma?' asked Carly.

'He's just taking his time to come round,' said the nurse and Beth got the feeling she was choosing her words carefully. She put a hand on Carly's shoulder and guided her out of the room. 'Come and sit with him in ICU and talk to him. It helps for patients to hear their loved ones' voices; they are often still aware although not awake but the brain takes it all in so ...'

Silent tears were rolling down Carly's face and Beth gripped her hand. When they spoke they spoke together. 'He's deaf.'

ICU was quiet, serene almost. Carly lifted Fergus's hand from the white sheets and gently arranged his fingers, flattening down his ring and middle fingers into his palm to make the sign for 'I love you'. She moved her plastic chair nearer to the bed and it scraped on the floor, the sound cutting jaggedly through the peace of the small bay of hospital beds. Fergus's heart monitor beeped reassuringly behind her as the ventilator for the man opposite burred at a different pace. She watched as Fergus's chest rose and fell. He was breathing on his own, a good sign. He could be sleeping if it weren't for the wires and the tubes attached to him.

Carly took a slow deep breath and eyed the clock. It had been hours since she'd had a cup of coloured water from the inappropriately named 'hot' drinks machine. It was odd how it tasted of nothing but scorched creamer when you drank it but it left a harsh metallic taste that lingered for hours. She'd kill for a proper cup of tea right now.

She took his hand in hers again and made his fingers flat and then repeated the arranging of his fingers. She knew in her heart he was aware that she was there, his deaf super sense would tell him that, she thought. The door opened almost silently and Beth came in. A shower and change of clothes had perked her up but she still looked tired around the eyes.

'Come on, relay,' she said, handing Carly the flat keys.

Carly shook her head. 'I can't leave him.'

'Carls, look at you. When he wakes up you're going to scare him. Your make-up has run and smudged and your up do, well it's no longer on the top of your head and, I say this as a friend, generally you look like shite.'

It had the desired effect and raised a smirk from Carly. 'Tell it how it is, why don't you?'

'The doctor said he's not in danger. He's just taking his time to come round. You go and get freshened up and I'll stay with him. I promise I won't even go for a wee, I'll get them to fit a catheter if necessary.'

Carly shook her head and chuckled. 'Okay, but if he so much as blinks an eyelid you call me. Got it?'

'Absolutely,' said Beth, giving a feeble salute.

Carly stood up. 'Oh, and I've been …' She lifted Fergus's hand gently to show Beth how she had been moving his fingers into a sign.

'Oh, great, I'll see how many swear words I can spell out on his fingers!' said Beth, sitting down in the newly vacated seat.

Despite everything Carly felt herself laughing. Perhaps it was a release valve because it wasn't that funny but as Beth set to work in spelling out 'fart' on Fergus's hand Carly turned to leave. She pressed the door release button and waited for the slow doors to open. She gave one last look over her shoulder and walked through.

Despite rushing round the flat like an escaped balloon she felt she was away too long and the relief to see Fergus and Beth exactly as she'd left them almost started her crying again. Beth was right, she did feel better for a shower and a change of clothes and she'd brought a few things from home for Fergus too which made her feel hopeful.

Beth gave Carly a brief hug before shuffling into the next seat so Carly could sit down. They both breathed in and slowly let out synchronized sighs. This was going to be a waiting game.

Fergus's parents could be heard bickering long before the doors opened and they rushed into the Intensive Care Unit. Carly was grateful for the few moments' notice as she slipped the engagement ring off her finger and slid it into her jeans pocket before she intercepted Cormac and Rosemary and guided them to Fergus's bed where all but his head, shoulders and pale chest were covered by a white sheet.

'Dear God, what have they done to my baby boy?' said Rosemary as she tried to embrace Fergus and set off an alarm as one of his monitoring wires was disconnected. A nurse was quick to intercept and the alarm was reset.

Cormac greeted Carly and put his arm around her. 'How are you bearing up?'

'I've been better. But really I'm fine,' said Carly.

'She's exhausted,' butted in Beth.

'Cormac and Rosemary, this is my friend Beth, she's been here the whole time,' said Carly, as her voiced cracked a little. Beth gave her hand a squeeze.

'Nice to meet you both, I'll grab some fresh air and be back in a while,' said Beth and she disappeared to give them a chance to get up to speed and for her to search for a proper coffee shop that did a decent takeaway coffee.

'He's a strong one, you know he'll be fine, so he will,' said Cormac. Rosemary was clutching at Fergus's hand and talking to him and Cormac stepped forward to pull her into a hug. She broke down completely and sobbed into his shoulder. 'Ahh, now come on. You're making a mess of your face there. Remember he's a Dooley, he loves to sleep, sure we're world-famous for it,' said Cormac with a wise tilt of his head. He sounded relaxed and together but his face was etched with pain and Carly's heart went out to them both. There was an odd sense of comfort in someone else hurting the same as you did because you cared for the same individual, but it didn't make it feel any better. If anything it highlighted the feelings Carly had been fighting to keep under wraps for hours.

Cormac gave a half-smile. 'Now, I have another arm so if you were wanting to have a wee sob too, that would be fine,' he said, his voice a deeper version of his son's. Carly felt something dissolve inside her and she stepped into Cormac's hug. 'There, we're all in this together, so we are. And we're all here for the boy.' He held the women as he watched his son lying motionless apart from his slow rhythmic breathing. 'We're all here for the boy,' he said as his eyes swam with tears.

When Beth returned with four quality brand hot drinks she could see that tears had been shed, which was quite a relief as Carly had spent too long being brave.

Beth had brought a selection of coffees that would hopefully cover most people's preferences. Cormac and Rosemary took a drink each as Beth pulled up a chair next to Carly and squeezed her free hand.

'You need to get back to Leo,' said Carly without moving her gaze from Fergus.

'I know and now you have company I feel a bit better about leaving you but I'll stop a bit longer,' said Beth, feeling the emotions rise up in her; she swallowed hard. They all sat in silence and watched Fergus breathe, his chest rising and falling at a steady pace. His mother kept patting his hand as if trying to stir him from his deep slumber, but Fergus didn't respond.

Chapter Thirty-One

The lead-grey sky was weighing heavy when the train pulled in. Leo ran across the platform to meet Beth and she was warmed by his open show of affection. Jack gave a forlorn smile in greeting. Her mind was filled with images of him and Petra together and she had to work hard to force them away. She knew she should be pleased for them both but right now she was struggling.

She sat in Jack's car as the rain streaked across the passenger window in a wind-driven formation. Droplets making good their escape, some being caught up in a merge of drips to create a rapid stream. All jumping slightly like Fergus's heart monitor when the car hit a pothole. Beth didn't feel like talking so it was handy that Leo was keen to share everything he had been doing as well as all the plans he and Denis had made for the rest of the school Easter holidays. It was good to see Leo so positive, she thought whilst she tuned in and out of what he was saying as Jack drove them home.

'… and we got to play darts in the bar before the pub opened and I got it on the board every time. Denis says I can be in the darts team when I'm bigger and Jack is letting Doris sleep at ours for a while to keep us safe and there's an Easter egg hunt in the village …'

Beth twisted in the passenger seat to direct her response at Jack. 'Why do we need Doris to keep us safe?'

'Nick was in the pub,' said Leo. 'Can I do the Easter egg hunt, Mum?'

Beth knew it was true when she saw the expression on Jack's face as his eyes darted in her direction. 'Nick was here?' she asked, her voice weak.

'He came in the pub yesterday, said he was looking for a friend. Leo saw him but he didn't see Leo. He left none the wiser,' said Jack.

Beth felt like she was having a hot flush as heat rushed through her body. 'How do you know he didn't see Leo?'

'He didn't, Mum. I was playing behind the crisp boxes in the hallway.'

'He spoke to Chloe and because he asked if she knew someone called Elizabeth she didn't make the connection so I think we put him off the scent,' said Jack. 'I thought having Doris about might make you feel …'

Beth turned back to face the road. 'Why didn't Petra tell me?' asked Beth, her voice hushed.

'Because we talked about it and decided there was nothing you could do. Leo wasn't in any danger and it was best to wait until you came home,' said Jack.

Beth was jerking her head about as her expressions mocked his explanation. 'What do you mean, not in any danger? You have no idea. It wasn't your decision to make, Jack. You should have called me.' She was seething and couldn't let rip because Leo was in the car and the last thing she wanted was for Leo to see how scared she was. Her brain was whirring. Dumbleford was no longer safe but the cottage wasn't ready to sell.

'He's not been back. If he thought you were there he would have come back,' added Jack.

'Let's not discuss this now,' said Beth, with a twitch in Leo's direction, and Jack pursed his lips firmly together and nodded.

The rest of the journey was filled with a tense silence. As they crossed the ford into the village the ducks quacked in annoyance. Jack pulled up outside Willow Cottage and they all got out. Jack lifted Beth's bag from the boot and she took it from him with a firm grasp.

'Thank you,' she said. She let Leo in and stopped Jack, who was attempting to follow them inside. 'I need to pack some things, so …'

'Pack?' said Jack, running a hand through his hair. 'You can't keep running away, Beth.'

Beth was annoyed at his assumption and arrogance. 'I can do what the hell I like and I *will* do what I think is right for my child!'

'Er, Muuuuuum!' shouted Leo and both Beth and Jack lurched inside. A few steps into the kitchen and they were splashing through water; Beth instinctively lifted Leo into her arms as she scanned the room for any signs of a break-in.

'You've been flooded,' said Jack. 'Sorry to state the obvious.'

'Flooded?' Beth was standing in a giant puddle of water that was gently lapping over her ballet pumps. She swallowed hard: could this weekend get any worse?

'It's the brook, if we get a record amount of rain, like we have in the last few weeks, it can't cope and this happens.'

'It's a regular thing?' said Beth, looking around and realizing that her beautiful floor was ruined and most likely the cabinets too. She felt her mood slide even lower.

'No, not exactly. Once every ten years or so, maybe,' said Jack with a shrug.

'You can call your insurance company from my place, come on,' he said, taking Leo from her arms and leading the way out of the cottage. Beth felt bereft; she'd worked so hard and now a big chunk of that had been undone.

She had an instant headache thanks to the revelation that Nick had tracked them down and that the cottage was flooded and a large amount of her hard work had been for nothing. As she passed the living-room door she couldn't bear to open it and see what had happened to the carpet. Feeling downcast she trudged back to Jack's car, one soggy footstep at a time.

She sat in the car fiddling with her phone for the short trip round the green to Jack's cottage. There had been no update from Carly, which meant there was no change in Fergus. There had been nothing good about Good Friday. It would have been far more aptly named Crap Friday and she now appeared to be experiencing Shite Saturday. Jack opened her door for her.

'At least it's stopped raining,' he said, his cheerfulness feeling rather misplaced to Beth.

'A bit too late to save my kitchen though,' said Beth.

Leo squeezed her hand and made her feel a fraction better but he soon let go as soon as he saw Doris. Jack let her out of her cage and she and Leo started racing round the garden as if they hadn't seen each other for ages.

'How's Fergus?' asked Jack, his blue-grey eyes looking somehow greyer.

Beth shrugged and shook her head at the same time. 'Medically he appears to be okay but he's not coming round. Apparently the brain can take its time to settle after it's had a shock like that.'

'How's Carly?'

Beth gave the same shrug and headshake. 'She was on cloud nine one minute and then dumped on her backside the next. Fergus's parents seem nice so at least she's got some support.'

Jack put a reassuring hand on Beth's arm and gave it a brief squeeze. 'Coffee?' he asked.

'Gin and tonic would be better.'

Jack looked momentarily concerned until he saw the flicker of sarcasm in Beth's face. 'I can ask Shirley if she's got something in her trolley. I don't keep any alcohol in the house.'

Beth looked round the kitchen as if to check. He was right; there was no wine rack. 'But you do drink, I've seen you!'

'Yes, but my girlfriend. My ex-girlfriend,' he corrected, 'she had a drink problem.'

'Ahh,' said Beth. 'Is that what triggered the ...' Jack was already nodding so she didn't have to finish the sentence. 'I think I'll skip anything out of Shirley's trolley in case Mittens has added to it.'

'Coffee it is then.'

A phone call to the insurance company proved surprisingly helpful. They needed photographs and an assessor would be round after the bank holiday but otherwise it looked as if they would be paying out to replace anything that was damaged by the floodwater as well as providing machines to dry out the cottage.

Beth left Leo with Jack and headed back to the cottage with her phone at the ready so that she could take pictures of the kitchen. There was a rustle in the budding willow tree as she approached and she was momentarily wary until Ernie sauntered out with a smile on his face.

'Hello, Ernie, how are you?' Ernie smiled and bobbed his head in reply. It was somehow nice to see him back in the tree again; she had missed him not being about during the cold weather. He followed her to the door.

'Sorry, Ernie, there's been a flood so you'd better not come in or you'll get wet feet.'

'Brook flooded,' said Ernie. Beth wasn't sure if it was a question or a statement.

'Yes, the brook flooded and it's flooded the kitchen. I need to take photographs so we can get it all fixed.' She couldn't stop the sigh that escaped.

She went through the cottage and Ernie followed despite her warning. She took pictures from every angle as Ernie watched from the doorway.

'Come up!' said Ernie, emphasizing the expression with a sharp jab in the air with his middle finger. He was not aware of the meaning of the gesture and despite everything it made Beth chuckle.

'I totally agree, Ernie. All the floor will need replacing.' She said it more to herself than to Ernie.

'Leave 'em be,' said Ernie forcefully.

'Who, Ernie?' She instantly thought of Jack.

'Boards.' Ernie pointed to the puddle.

'The floorboards?' queried Beth, peering through the dirty water to where they were just visible. She could feel underfoot that they had warped.

'Oak boards. Leave 'em be says Wilf.' Ernie was frowning hard with the effort of getting his message across. Beth sloshed over to him.

'This has happened before, hasn't it?' said Beth and Ernie nodded vigorously. 'And Wilf left them?' Ernie was nodding so hard Beth was worried he would strain his neck. 'Okay, so if we get the water up and we leave them, they return to how they were?' Beth looked more than doubtful at her own words. Ernie nodded and grinned. 'Well, I'm happy to give it a try, Ernie.' She ushered him out of the cottage and went to check the damage in the living room.

Beth opened the door very slowly and peeked through with one open eye. She wasn't sure why but it made it all seem slightly more bearable. She needn't have worried as the living room looked exactly as she'd left it. Keeping her wet feet in the hall Beth crouched down to touch the carpet; it was dry. The small step up from the kitchen had made all the difference and had protected the other ground-floor rooms. She was relieved. The kitchen she could cope with. It would mean a few weeks of inconvenience but she wasn't looking at redoing the whole ground floor. She shut the living-room door and paused for a moment in the hall. The light shifted as something moved outside and reflected through the glass in the door panel. As she put her hand on the door latch she had a feeling – it was a sensation that left her cold.

* * *

300

Carly was becoming increasingly frustrated with Rosemary, who sat at Fergus's side reading to him out of the paper. Cormac was surreptitiously watching her.

'I'll be away to get a cup of tea now,' he said, giving Carly a nudge. She glanced in his direction and he clumsily signalled to her with his eyes.

'Oh, I'll come with you … if you like?' said Carly, her words jolty as if she was reading from an unfamiliar script.

They silently left the unit and walked along the bland corridor, where it was hard to distinguish where floor met wall.

'You see, our Rosemary, she needs to be doing something,' explained Cormac. 'She can't sit in silence and watch our boy like that.'

Carly's shoulders sagged. 'I know, I do understand, really I do, but talking to him is so pointless.'

'Ah, now you don't know that for sure,' said Cormac, pulling his wallet out as they reached the coffee shop.

'Cormac, he's deaf. Even if he was awake he wouldn't be able to hear a word she's saying. Being unconscious won't have improved that!'

'No, but we humans, we have a sixth sense. So on some level he may know that she's there.' Carly went to speak and he halted her with a tilt of his head. 'And even if he doesn't it's helping Rosemary.'

'How so?' said Carly, listening but at the same time scanning the drinks menu that she knew off by heart.

'He's our youngest, the babby of the family, and as his mother she cannot just sit by with her two arms the one length.'

Carly turned to look at him. 'But there is nothing else to do,' she said flatly. The tiredness and the emotional exhaustion were draining her of her fight.

'No, Carly, there is always something you can do. Always something.'

Carly's head felt like it had been plugged into the mains as she walked back carrying her hot drink. Cormac had annoyed her. She wasn't sure if that had been his intention but it had certainly fired up her grey matter and as well as silently remonstrating with Cormac's endless optimism and Rosemary's futility she was also racking her brains for what she could do. Was there really something she or the hospital had overlooked?

As they turned the corner the button for the door into ICU had just been pressed by Fergus's doctor and he greeted them warmly.

'Excuse me, Doctor, do you have a moment?' asked Cormac.

'Of course,' he said, ushering them into a small office.

'I'll deliver this and I'll be back in a jiffy,' said Cormac as he marched off with Rosemary's tea. When he came back Carly and the doctor were half-heartedly discussing the weather. Cormac sat down and placed his tablet computer on his lap.

'Thank you, Doctor, we were after an update really. Nothing seems to have changed since we got here,' he said.

'Well, no, I'd say he's about the same,' said the doctor, but when there was further expectation in Cormac's eyes he added, 'Fergus's vital signs are still encouraging.'

'I see. Well, I've been looking on the internet,' said Cormac, holding up his tablet computer as evidence, 'and it says patients usually come round within twenty-four hours, so why hasn't our boy woken up yet?'

'It's difficult to say. Every patient is different and every head injury affects them in different ways,' said the doctor.

'What else could we all be doing to help him? Is there something you could do to speed him up a little?' asked Cormac, snapping his tablet cover shut.

'Unfortunately, there is no treatment we can use to bring a person round when they're comatose. Likewise, there is no test to predict when they will come round,' said the doctor.

'Coma?' said Carly, leaning forward in her seat, her face the picture of stunned.

The doctor nodded. 'He's comatose and we're monitoring him constantly.'

'Since when was he comatose rather than being unconscious or just not come round yet?' said Carly, her speech rapid.

Cormac clutched her hand. 'What we want to know is when did he deteriorate?'

'He hasn't deteriorated. He's stable. It's a way of categorizing his level of responsiveness,' explained the doctor. 'I didn't mean to alarm you.'

'Ah, but you did all the same,' said Cormac, his voice curt despite the soft accent.

As they left the office Cormac whispered to Carly, 'Not a word to Rosemary.'

'Okay,' said Carly, thinking that despite the doctor's protestations she did feel that Fergus had somehow taken a backwards step. They both gave Rosemary slightly exaggerated smiles as they sat down at the bedside.

Rosemary paused mid-paragraph about the rugby. 'What did the doctor say?'

'No change,' said Carly as she looked over her shoulder for Cormac's concurrence.

'He's doing grand. Just grand,' said Cormac and Rosemary smiled before adjusting her glasses and looking for her place on the page.

Cormac opened up his tablet and started stabbing at the keys with his sausage-sized fingers.

'Actually, could I borrow that for a while, please?' asked Carly. She knew very little about computers and the internet but she figured now was as good a time as any to learn.

Chapter Thirty-Two

Beth knew there was someone on the other side of the front door. Her heart rate quickened as adrenalin coursed through her. She sidled over to the living-room door to peek through the gap but the angle was all wrong and all she could see was a slice of the inside of the room. If she went into the room anyone that came to look in the window would see her immediately.

She crept upstairs and into her bedroom. Her head started to pound. She stood behind the scrunched-up curtains and peered down onto the front garden. There was a faint shadow being cast, which meant she wasn't hallucinating. There was someone at her front door but they hadn't knocked. Did that mean they had seen her go in and were waiting for her to come out? Or perhaps waiting for her to open the door before they rushed inside.

Beth fumbled in her pocket for her mobile and gasped as she almost dropped it. Clutching it tightly she crafted a text to Jack.

Think someone outside cottage can't leave.

Her thumb hovered over the Send button. What was the point in sending that message? Apart from making her look, at best, a bit of a wimp and, at worst, a total head case what was she expecting Jack to do? He couldn't come storming over because he had Leo with him and if it was Nick outside then the last thing Beth wanted was for Leo to have to face him again. She deleted the message and had another peek at the shadow. It had gone.

Beth crept out of her bedroom and across the landing into Leo's room. The bare walls reminding her that she really needed to get round to decorating his room. A cautionary peek out of the window showed no signs of anyone in the back garden and the horses were munching away in the field, which was a sure sign that there was nobody about as they were the first to investigate anyone's presence in case it meant food.

She took a deep breath and gave herself a mental shake. She must have imagined it. Her head was throbbing hard now and the nausea increasing. She came quietly down the stairs then sneaked into the living room just to be totally sure there was no one hanging about. Nobody was. She took a deep breath and went to the front door, undid the latch and opened it a fraction keeping her foot propped against it on the inside in case she needed to slam it shut in a hurry, but there was no need. There was no sign of anybody. She stepped out, shut and locked the door and had a good look round. Nope, it was her overactive imagination or perhaps it had just been Ernie?

Beth kept an eye out as she walked across the green. But she was already feeling like a bit of a fool.

'I thought you'd got lost,' said Jack with a chuckle when she walked in.

She gave him a look. She could bluff it out, make something up or she could be honest with him. The trouble with honest was that you could make yourself look like an even bigger idiot. 'I'll tell you later,' she said, rubbing her forehead. 'Have you got any tablets?'

'Headache?'

'Migraine I think. I've not had one before, so I'm not entirely sure,' said Beth as she popped two tablets out of the packet Jack offered her and downed them with a glass of water.

'Do you feel sick? Dizzy? Flashing lights?'

'A bit sick, that's all,' said Beth.

'Drink this,' said Jack, handing her another tumbler of water. 'Why don't you go and have a lie-down upstairs?'

'Ahh, I don't know …'

'Go on. Leo and I will take Doris out and they can play in your back garden while I take the foot boards off the cabinets so they don't soak up any more water. Then perhaps when you wake up we could watch a film and order takeaway?'

'Yay!' came a shout from the garden.

'That child's hearing is awesome,' said Jack. 'Come on, the rest will do you good. I'll bring you up a coffee in a couple of hours,' he said as he shooed her to the stairs.

'Thanks, Jack. This is really kind.'

'I am,' said Jack with a lopsided grin.

He was actually starting to look even cuter now that he was taken. That grin had a boyish charm and coupled with his good looks and caring nature he really was a very good example of the male specimen. Oh well, thought Beth, he's the one that got away but at least it was for mostly the right reasons.

'Beth …' Someone was whispering her name and it made her smile. She was dreaming about sleeping in a hammock and the voice grew louder and fainter as she swung. 'Beth, cup of coffee here.'

She opened her eyes and saw a very smiley Jack looking at her. 'Hello.'

'Hello. How's the head?'

She closed her eyes again and had a check. 'It's fine now.'

'And the sickness?'

'Gone.'

'Are you up for a Chinese then? That's what Leo fancies, he's chosen about eight dishes.'

'As long as he has chicken chow mein on the list it's all good with me.'

'Me too,' said Jack and he left her with her coffee.

They sat surrounded by the debris of the Chinese meal and the remnants of a bottle of wine. Leo had taken himself to bed and with Jack's help had set up camp in the spare room in Jack's sleeping bag. Doris had sneaked up shortly afterwards and settled next to him in the hope of getting to sleep upstairs for a change. A film was on the television but neither of them were really watching it.

'Don't worry about your kitchen. It'll be easy to sort out,' said Jack.

'Huh, you know I remembered something from the original auction details today that I thought was a typo when I read it. It said there was a stream running through the property. They weren't joking, were they?'

Jack laughed a hearty laugh. 'I thought the brook was the boundary but I guess it is on your land … and a bit under the cottage too!'

'Ha, ha,' said Beth. 'Ernie seemed to think it happened a lot?'

'From asking around we think it's pretty rare, about eight years ago was the last time.'

'That's good, I won't be here for the next one then,' said Beth with a snort.

Jack wasn't laughing, his cheek twitched. 'So what took you so long at the cottage?' he asked, dividing out the rest of the wine between their two glasses.

'Now don't laugh!' said Beth, which set the scene and Jack's face was already trying to control a smirk. 'It's silly really but I thought there was someone outside the front door so I had to creep about and check out of all the windows before I'd dare open the door.' She was smiling at her own stupidity but Jack's smirk had faded.

'Why did you think there was someone there?'

She shrugged. 'I got this feeling. It was horrible really but as I touched the door latch I thought I saw a change in the light through the glass in the door but with the sun shining on it it's difficult to tell. It was probably a cloud or something.' She took a sip of wine and tried to look nonchalant.

'But you thought it was Nick?'

Beth nodded. 'I know it sounds crazy.'

'Why are you so scared of him?' Jack's gaze was intense.

'Because he said if I left him he would find me and kill me.'

Jack looked suitably shocked. 'And do you think he's capable—'

'No! He's all talk. He's manipulative and a liar but I don't think he's capable of murder.'

'Still, it's a very nasty threat.'

'Well, he's a very nasty guy.' Beth took a long slug of wine. 'Not a lovely guy, like you.' As she realized she'd said it out loud her eyes widened. She felt such an idiot. Jack was giving her an odd look and she knew colour was rising from her neck.

'You're lovely too, Beth,' said Jack, his voice husky, and he tentatively laid his hand on hers. Her eyes darted in the same direction as her heart started thumping wildly at the unexpected contact.

She pulled her hand back. Jack was with Petra now, that ship had sailed. 'I think I should go to bed. Alone,' said Beth, retrieving her hand.

A big grin spread across Jack's face. 'Okay. Watch out for marauding dogs.'

'Yes, right. I'll do that,' she said, pointing firmly at him. He was still grinning at her. 'Good night,' she said decisively and headed for the stairs.

'Night, Beth,' said Jack, and he watched her disappear.

Rosemary had nodded off and the newspaper was a crumpled mass in her arms as she was slumped against the side of Fergus's bed. Cormac was reading a magazine on photography that he had found in one of the waiting areas. Carly's phone vibrated again as yet another text came in. She ignored it. She had been glued to the tablet for the past hour or so. So much for the internet; it hadn't provided her with anything useful about bringing deaf people out of comas, or whatever the doctor had called it, all it had done was distract her with videos of cute kittens. She was close to giving up and returning the tablet to a fidgety-looking Cormac but Cormac's words had bugged her into action. 'There's always something you can do,' was what he had said and despite the doctor reassuring them that everything was being done she was on a mission to do something herself. She hadn't known what that something would be when she had started to search randomly on Cormac's tablet but as she clicked on a link she realized she might have found a very small and tenuous something. Carly scanned the screen and tried to take in all the details.

She scrambled around in her handbag, almost dropping the bag as she pulled out a small notepad and pen, then copied down pages of information from the screen in fast scrawly writing and handed the tablet back to Cormac.

'Now what are you up to?' asked Cormac with a shrewd look in his eye.

'It's what you call a very long shot,' said Carly. 'I'll be just outside making some calls.' She leaned over and kissed Fergus, being careful not to knock any wires. She took his hand and signed 'back soon' and left his fingers in the 'I love you' sign.

The first few numbers she tried either couldn't help her or were answer machines where she had left messages but had little hope of a response – it was bank holiday weekend after all. This was the longest of long shots, the River Nile of long shots she thought, and it made her smile. Her smile was fading when she turned the page of her notepad to see that she had tried all the numbers she had written down. She thumbed through the pages; each number had a neat tick or a cross next to it. That was it, that was all her long shots fired into the darkness.

She walked the few steps to a seating area and slumped onto yet another plastic chair and looked at her phone. There were a couple of messages from Beth, all encouraging and none of them asking for an update because she knew as soon as there was news Carly would be in touch. She sent her a quick 'there's no change' message and then placed her phone on the notebook and put them on the empty plastic chair next to her. Carly gave a big stretch, her neck sore from leaning over the tablet and her back aching from sitting in the same position for hours.

She closed her eyes and tried to clear some space in her brain to think. She was also trying very hard to not think about what Fergus being comatose really meant. Was it the same as a coma? She wasn't sure. She couldn't let herself consider all the people that spent months or years in a coma or those that simply slipped away. Her thoughts were broken by the jarring sound of her phone vibrating off the notebook and onto the plastic chair. She answered it quickly.

It was one of her long shots returning her call. The brief conversation was much simpler than she had thought. Once she had explained the situation the man on the phone offered to meet her outside Warren Street tube station in about twenty minutes. Carly ended the call with her faith in the kindness of strangers a fraction restored.

Thirty minutes later she was dashing back into ICU clutching a small plastic bag. Cormac stood up as she came in. 'I'm doing a tea run, did you want one of those fancy pants cuppas that you usually have?'

'Wait a minute, I might have something,' said Carly, touching his arm for a second. 'It's only a small something, but it's worth a try.'

Rosemary came to as Carly fussed around Fergus. 'What's wrong?' She looked at Cormac.

'Nothing's wrong, Rosie, we're trying something out for our boy, here,' he said and they both watched as Carly fiddled with a small white device, placed it on Fergus's chest and then plugged its cable into Fergus's iPhone. Carly stared at the screen for a moment until she had located the icon that said *Music*, clicked it and then chose one of Fergus's playlists. She knew they were still on there because he often reminisced about his love of music and the playlists he had made for each and every occasion. He didn't have one for this situation so she went with 'best tunes' and pressed Play.

She couldn't hear anything, which was good because none of the patients in ICU would have welcomed a blast of music at this time of day. She placed her hand on top of the device to check it was working and she could feel it vibrating. Carly sat back down and Cormac and Rosemary followed her with their eyes.

'So, will you be explaining what that wee box is?'

'It's a vibrating speaker,' said Carly proudly. 'If it was attached to something hollow you would be able to hear it but, well, as Fergus is …'

'Dense?' said Cormac with a chuckle.

'Precisely. The sound is a vibration and hopefully one that he will recognize. It's a long shot …' said Carly.

'But it's something,' said Cormac, his eyes glistening as he patted Carly's hand.

Chapter Thirty-Three

Easter Monday dawned and Beth was woken by an overexcited camper jumping onto the bed, still encased in Jack's sleeping bag like a giant marauding caterpillar. 'Oof, Leo!' groaned Beth as Leo rolled across her bladder; there were more pleasant ways to be woken up. She reached out a hand to the bedside cabinet and checked her phone to see if there was anything from Carly but there wasn't.

'It's the Easter egg hunt today!' said the caterpillar, unzipping itself and bouncing back across Beth before flying out of the bedroom. There was the sound of clinking mugs downstairs followed by the thud of large paws on the stairs as Doris bounded into the bedroom and jumped on top of Beth.

'Seriously?' she said as Doris tried desperately to show her love by washing any body parts that Beth had foolishly left uncovered.

'Doris, down!' commanded Jack and Doris slunk off the bed and out of the room. 'Coffee?' said Jack, placing the mug on the bedside cabinet. 'How's the head?'

'The migraine is long gone now. Thanks for the coffee.'

'I meant after the wine last night but either way that's good to hear. Leo's helping me make pancakes so I'm thinking you're probably safest up here until we serve them, okay?'

'Okay,' agreed Beth, picking up her mug and hugging it. She was thinking how lucky she was to have a friend like Jack and then her mind started to wander and she thought how much luckier Petra was to have a boyfriend like him. Although he was lucky too because Petra was a lovely person and obviously very understanding if she was happy for another woman to stay the night.

After pancakes she and Jack tidied up the kitchen and then went to join the throng of people that had gathered on the village green. A large area had been roped off for the Easter egg hunt and Easter egg bunting swung jauntily between the posts. Leo made straight for Denis and they went to add their names to the list and pay their entry fee as Petra came to join Beth and Jack.

'How's the headache?' asked Petra.

'It's fine now, thanks.'

'And the cottage?'

'Don't ask! After the egg hunt I'll go and have another attempt at tidying up.'

'It's drinks in the pub afterwards. It is traditions,' said Petra, taking in Beth's pained expression. 'But if you want to clean up I can have Leo.'

'I'll be going to the pub after the egg hunt,' butted in Jack, 'so he'll be fine.'

'Thanks, guys, that would be great.' Beth noticed the looks that passed between Petra and Jack but couldn't quite make out what they were alluding to. The now familiar woman from the WI and her leather trousers stood on a makeshift stage of a few hastily arranged pallets and took the microphone.

'Welcome to Dumbleford Easter Egg Hunt. Thankfully the weather is a little drier than it has been but to be on the safe side you are going to be looking for these.' She held up two coloured plastic eggs. 'These can be exchanged up to a maximum of five with my colleague Shirley over there.' Shirley and the wheelie trolley were positioned behind a table that was stacked up with

313

Easter eggs far higher than Shirley's headscarf. 'The colour of the egg denotes the size of egg you collect from Shirley.' The crowd of excited children muttered happily. 'Three, two, one, go! Happy Easter!' she bellowed, causing the microphone to screech as the bunting was cut and the children charged into the previously out-of-bounds space. Thanks to the long grass the eggs weren't as obvious to find as you would have thought. Beth was laughing at the children's uncoordinated approach.

'I would be sweeping up and down so I knew where I'd looked,' said Beth.

'Nope, I'd be exactly the same as those two,' said Jack as he watched Leo and Denis sprinting in random directions and diving into the grass regardless of whether there was an egg there or not.

'Thank the Lord for the washing machines,' said Petra as Denis stood up with a huge grin on his face, a yellow egg in his hand and green and brown streaked down the front of his outfit.

Leo was fifth in the queue to exchange his five coloured eggs for chocolate ones as the WI lady joined Shirley to give her a hand. He left the table with one good-sized egg, three different bite-sized ones and a bag of mini chocolate eggs. Beth took his photo as he approached; it was a picture of happiness. 'Did you see, Mum? Did you see, I beat that boy to the red egg and it was for a big one.' He held it up proudly. 'It's for you!' he said, giving her the egg.

Beth tried hard not to cry. She didn't want to be the embarrassing mum but it was tricky when they caught you unawares like that with a spontaneous show of affection. 'That's really kind, thank you, Leo. How about we share it?'

'Okay,' agreed Leo quickly. 'I'll look after it.' He took it back as Denis appeared out of the crowd with a similar armful of chocolate swag.

They all walked off the green together and Petra, Jack and the boys peeled off to the pub as Beth waved to them and walked on the few extra yards to sort out her kitchen. Once inside she realized she must have stepped over the post when she had come in, so she picked it up and headed down the hallway. Beth looked around at the state of her once-perfect kitchen, surprised to see that the water had receded and a very wet silt-strewn floor with warped oak boards was left in its place. It wasn't anything different to what she was expecting but it still gave her a twinge of irritation. A brief sort-out of the post gave her a pile of bills, another of junk mail and the makings of another headache.

Beth got out all the things she would need to clean up the kitchen as her headache cranked up a notch. She got a tall glass of water and some painkillers from the cupboard. She swore as she stumbled a little on the small step as she left the kitchen. She felt so tired all of a sudden and a bit sick if she was honest – perhaps this was what a migraine felt like? In the calmness of the living room she took two tablets and a long slug of water before putting the glass and tablet packet on the windowsill and sitting down. The sofa was a welcome relief as she arranged the cushions into a pillow and curled up for a quick nap. She'd managed to sleep it off so perhaps she could do the same now? Despite her pounding head she quickly drifted off.

Jack watched Leo make the few steps from the pub to Willow Cottage and disappear from sight thanks to the willow tree that was now in full blossom, its furry-looking catkins giving it a white ethereal hue. Jack knew Beth was in the cottage so he was happy that Leo was being safely handed over. He strolled back inside the pub.

'Come on, what is it?' asked Petra as he slid back onto his bar stool.

'What?' said Jack.

'The thing that is weighing you down, I can tell.'

Jack straightened his back in a half-stretch. 'I don't know … actually, I do know. It's Beth.'

'One minute,' said Petra as she went to serve a customer. Jack watched as she took down the long food and drinks order. After a few minutes she came back.

'You are worrying about Beth. This is not a surprise,' said Petra as she busily sliced a lemon. 'She is not herself right now. I think she has too much worry and this gives her the headaches.'

Jack was pondering what she'd said. 'Yeah, she has had a lot of headaches recently.'

'It is the stress,' said Petra, waving the small knife. 'You and I never have the headaches because we have no stress and the fresh air it helps too,' she added. 'She is cooped up in the cottage working for too many hours.'

'Yeah,' said Jack slowly. 'You know I did have a headache.' He was trying to think exactly when it was because Petra was right, it was a rare thing for him to have one. 'I was taking off the foot boards on the cabinets in Beth's kitchen.' He leaped off the bar stool and sprinted for the door.

'What's wrong?' called Petra.

'That bloody boiler!' he yelled back as he flew out of the pub. His heart was pounding as he dodged round the cars in the car park, jumped through the willow tree and ran to the cottage. Thankfully Ernie wasn't there or he would have scared the life out of him. Jack tried the front door and when it was locked he started banging on it. 'Beth! Leo!'

He darted to the side to look in the living-room window and the sight he saw made his pulse instantly quicken. Beth was lying on the sofa looking pale and unconscious.

'Beth! Beth!' he shouted as he slammed his hand on the glass. There was no response.

Chapter Thirty-Four

It was early and the hospital and ICU ward were still peaceful. Cormac and Rosemary had arrived looking slightly less weary having spent the night in a nearby hotel, although they were both quiet and subdued. Rosemary had a paperback with her and she began reading silently as Cormac scanned a newspaper. Carly was sitting at Fergus's side scanning his music collection; she had been playing his music through the vibrating speaker all night. There had been no change in Fergus. Not a flicker of an eyelash or a twitch of a finger – nothing.

Carly let out a huge yawn; she was exhausted. Sooner or later she would have to accept that she needed to go home for a proper sleep in her own bed. Nobody had said as much but she was starting to realize that this was only day three of what could be very many days at his bedside. She didn't want to think about it but she knew she had to. Everything had changed so suddenly – what was meant to have been one of the happiest times of her life had quickly become a nightmare. It was still unclear why some lout had smashed a bottle over Fergus's head and she wondered if he had any idea of how quickly that action had changed so many lives.

Maybe it was the tiredness but she felt like a layer of bubble

317

wrap surrounded her and numbed her senses. She almost couldn't believe this was reality. Each time she thought, *This can't be happening*, the beep of the machines reminded her that it was. Watching the man she loved lying there still and lifeless sent shivers of fear down her spine. How long would they have to play this waiting game? The hours spent watching Fergus looking pale and unresponsive put everything into perspective. All she needed was to have her indestructible Fergus back and everything would be right again. Carly wiped away a tear, only half aware of them now as they seemed to start without her noticing. She looked up and spotted that the middle-aged man from the bed opposite had disappeared in the night and she convinced herself that it was because he had recovered. She couldn't bear to think about the alternative.

Carly looked through the photographs on Fergus's phone; she especially liked all the silly selfies they had taken together. They looked happy in every photo, even the ones where they were pulling sad clown faces. Fergus looked different lying there in the hospital bed. It was like she was looking at a different person. She couldn't explain exactly what it was, perhaps the lack of his smile or his mischievous eyes, she wasn't sure, but there was definitely something missing from the man who lay motionless in the bed next to her.

Carly needed something to distract her tired mind so she pressed on the music icon. She was really getting the hang of the iPhone now, having struggled to start with, and she thumbed through the playlists and albums like an expert. Something caught her eye and she scrolled back.

'Fergus, you dark horse,' she mumbled to herself. Selecting the album, she pressed Play. She put her hand on the small vibrating device she had bought to check it was pulsating on his chest and it was. Carly picked up his hand and started to sign what was playing. It took a while for her to spell it out in finger signs. '*Mamma Mia* album first song "Honey, Honey".'

She started to giggle. It was probably a mixture of anxiety and the ridiculous but the giggles took over. Cormac rustled his newspaper and Rosemary placed her bookmark in her current page and put her book down.

'What is it?' asked Rosemary, her laughter lines enhanced with concern.

Carly waved a hand as she tried to control her tittering. 'Fergus and I don't like the same sort of music but I've found some Abba in his music collection and I'm force-feeding it to him.'

'Do you think the vibrator works?' asked Rosemary in all innocence. Cormac coughed and Carly started to giggle again. 'What?'

'Tha' wee thing there is a vibrating speaker, so it is,' said Cormac, rolling his eyes. 'Not a vibrator!'

'It's the same thing!' protested Rosemary.

'No, no it's not!' said Carly through her laughter.

'Eejit,' muttered Cormac, returning his eyes to his paper.

'Do you think it works?' asked Rosemary again, still not getting the joke.

Carly composed herself. 'I honestly don't know. I hope so because when he comes round it'll be cool if he can get some pleasure from music again. He's really missed it.' In her head as she said the word 'when' another small voice said 'if' and Carly had to swallow hard to keep her emotions in check. She couldn't think like that, she had to stay positive.

'When he was a wee lad he loved his music. I used to think he'd glued those headphones to his head,' said Rosemary chuckling at the memory. 'He really liked that Cheeky Girls song.'

Cormac eyed them over the top of the paper and shook his head but a smile played on his lips. Carly was frantically pressing icons trying to work out how to download new music.

'This is brilliant, Rosemary. What else did he like?'

Carly and Rosemary hatched an eclectic playlist of the songs from Fergus's youth. They enjoyed putting it together but when it was on its second repeat, and there was still no reaction from Fergus, the excitement of the new playlist dwindled. She watched what was starting to play on the iPhone screen and spelled it out on his hand: 'Sound of the Underground' by Girls Aloud.

Without warning Fergus's hand slowly closed around hers. Carly gasped and looked at Fergus's face but there was no sign of any movement. Her stomach was tumbling over and she tried to quell the feeling of elation. She didn't want to get her hopes up unnecessarily but this was a good sign. It had to be. The silent tears trickled down her cheeks and she hardly dare make his parents aware in case it broke the spell. She waved her left hand frantically and Rosemary glanced up from her book.

The words were hard to get out. 'He's holding my hand,' said Carly, her voice lost in the deep emotion as she blubbed helplessly.

There was a moment before the sentence registered. 'Mary, mother of God!' exclaimed Rosemary, barging past Cormac and around to Carly's side of the bed. Cormac followed her and they all stared at Fergus's pale hand clasping Carly's. Cormac wiped away a tear and put his arms around the two women. 'He's always liked to take his time has this one. Always liked to take his time,' said Cormac, giving Carly's shoulder a squeeze.

'Nurse!' called Cormac. 'I think we have a few more vital signs that need checking out over here.'

The nurse came over and they explained excitedly what Fergus had done. She took Fergus's hand from Carly and Carly wanted to hit her.

'Hey! Do you have to do that?' asked Carly, rising to her feet. She wasn't a violent person but the sensation of having the contact taken away so abruptly made something primal flare up inside her.

'Calm now, she's just doing her job,' soothed Cormac, and he beckoned Carly to sit back down.

The nurse didn't look fazed; she most likely faced a lot worse on a regular basis. 'I need to check a few things, okay?' she asked but she was going ahead and checking them anyway. She went through the usual routine and jotted down her findings on Fergus's notes. Carly sat back down and took Fergus's hand in hers. She squeezed it but there was no response. She waited a moment and squeezed again.

'He's not gripping any more,' said Carly, looking frantically from the nurse to Cormac and Rosemary.

'Could have been a spasm,' the nurse explained with a look of commiseration.

'No.' Carly shook her head. 'No, he held my hand for maybe half a minute?' She felt the tears start to fall afresh as she looked to Rosemary for backup and Rosemary nodded briefly.

'Okay,' said the nurse kindly. 'Let's hope he does it again.'

Jack thumped on the front door of Willow Cottage. 'Leo! Open the door!' he shouted but there was no response. He went back to the living-room window.

'Beth!' he yelled as he repeatedly smacked his hand on the glass but there was no movement from her. She remained curled up on the sofa deathly still. A thought struck him and fear shot through his insides like his first-ever vodka shot – he might already be too late. He pulled out his phone, dialled 999 and ran to the back of the cottage to see if he could easily get in that way. Jack pulled at the stable doors and checked the windows but everything was securely locked up.

The 999 operator answered and Jack asked for an ambulance, explained that he thought Beth was suffering from carbon monoxide poisoning and gave the address. The operator was asking questions but Jack slid the phone into his pocket. He needed to get inside and fast. He pulled off his T-shirt, wrapped it around his elbow and with a sharp jab he smashed in one of the small sections of the kitchen window. He quickly brushed away the glass fragments with the T-shirt, threw it to the floor, put his hand through and released the window catch inside.

Jack pushed open the window, leaped onto the windowsill and was soon inside crouched on the worktop. 'Leo!' he hollered but there was no reply. Where was Leo? Had Beth been able to let him in? And if she hadn't where had he gone and where was he now?

Jack's primary focus had to be Beth. She was the priority. If he was right about the boiler and the carbon monoxide poisoning then he was fast running out of time. His heart was pumping hard and without thinking he took in a deep breath. A spike of a headache shot through his temple. Ignoring it he jumped down onto the damp and distorted floorboards, then hurried out of the kitchen and into the living room.

'Beth!' He dropped to his knees and gently patted her cheek. There was no response. He pressed his fingers to her neck and checked her pulse. She was still alive. The sense of relief was immense although he knew she wasn't out of the woods yet. He scooped her up into his arms and carried her to the front door. He struggled with the front-door lock with Beth in his arms because he couldn't see what he was doing. He felt odd, like he was floating, but it was not a pleasant sensation. Jack shook his head only to find that aided the dizziness and nausea that were gripping him. He lifted Beth higher into his arms and turned so he could see the lock properly. His head was pounding. He gripped the key and it turned clunkily in the lock. Jack reached for the latch but his vision was blurring and his first attempt to grab it missed so that his fingers closed around air. He reached again and this time he had hold of it tightly. He released the door and pulled it open. His head felt heavy and his knees started to give way. Jack lunged forward out of the cottage, turning as he fell so that Beth would land on top of him and be protected from the ground. He was barely aware of the impact as he landed hard on the path and everything went black around him. His last thought was Leo.

* * *

322

There was something on his face and Jack pushed it away. He could feel the cold of the stone path on his bare back but there was something soft, like a pillow, under his head. He was unsure what was going on and his memory was sketchy.

'Hey, you need that, pal. It's oxygen,' said the paramedic, putting the mask back in place. Jack opened his eyes and tried to focus; it took a few attempts. 'I'm Clark,' said the ordinary-looking paramedic and Jack managed to raise an eyebrow.

'Yeah, I know, my parents had a sense of humour. But you've been the real Superman today ...'

Jack's memory came flooding back to him. 'Is she all right?' he asked. His throat was dry and the words were barely a croak. He tried to lift his head and the pounding increased.

'She's on her way to hospital, she's not conscious yet but they're working on her. You did good, pal. You need to take some steady deep breaths for me. We're flushing the carbon monoxide out of your system with oxygen, okay?'

Jack did as he was told and took in a deep lungful of oxygen. He looked around him and saw another paramedic was at his side setting up a stretcher. Beyond him a police car and a fire engine were parked near the pub and a policeman was keeping rubberneckers away.

'Nice steady breaths, that's great,' said Clark. 'We'll move you in a minute and get you properly checked out at hospital.'

Jack took another deep breath and felt his body start to revive. He still had the pounding headache but his brain was starting to fire up. 'Leo!' he said into the mask, forcing himself upright.

'Hey, you want to be lying nice and still. Whoa!' said Clark as Jack wrenched off the mask.

'Leo is missing, he's six years old, he could be in there,' Jack explained, breathlessly pointing towards the cottage.

Clark tried to reattach the oxygen mask. 'Nope, it's all clear. We alerted the fire service and they've been in and checked. There's nobody else in there.'

'Then he's missing,' said Jack, struggling but failing to get up.

'Whoa there, mister. You're going nowhere,' said Clark, taking hold of Jack's bare arm and easing him back into a lying position. 'Let the police handle it,' he added, waving them over.

A rather serious-looking police officer jotted down everything Jack told him. Jack passed him his mobile and guided him to the picture of Nick's silver BMW.

'This guy may not have anything to do with it but in case he does,' said Jack. He had no idea where Nick was; he was most likely back home in London but he couldn't take the risk. Leo was missing and Nick was the prime suspect.

Chapter Thirty-Five

The hospital corridors were busy again with visitors trooping in and out. Rosemary and Carly were waiting in the queue in the canteen. Neither of them wanted to eat anything but both knew they had to. Cormac had decided to skip lunch because he'd had a large muffin with a coffee not long ago so had sent the women off to eat together. Carly didn't know Rosemary that well. Fergus's parents flew over to London a few times every year but visits were fleeting and Carly often found she was there mainly as an interpreter. She didn't mind, it was Fergus they came to see, she knew that, but it did encroach on any conversation she might have had with his parents. They hadn't said much to each other since they had been sharing the bedside vigil – the music conversation had been the most they had interacted.

Rosemary looked at Carly's bowl of soup, which was rapidly going cold on the tray. 'You still a vegetarian?' she asked. Rosemary must have been struggling for things to talk about too.

'Yep, still a veggie.'

'Not much choice, is there?' said Rosemary, poking her packet of unappealing sandwiches.

They paid for their food and found a recently wiped-down table to unload their trays onto.

'How long are you staying?' asked Carly. 'I'm thinking that Cormac will need to be back at work tomorrow, won't he?'

'He will. But I can't leave Fergus.' Rosemary shook her head as she wrestled with the sandwich carton. Carly held out her hand and Rosemary passed it over. Carly opened the carton and handed it back. 'Thank you.'

They ate in silence. The soup was still warm and surprisingly tasty. Carly realized that she hadn't eaten anything substantial since she and Beth had walked through Chinatown, which now seemed such a long time ago. An incident like this put all your usual structures out of kilter; drinks and food were grabbed randomly through necessity at any time of the day or night, hours passed and time lost any meaning. Carly had a very real fear that something might happen, good or bad, when she was away from the bedside, which had become an overwhelming power that made her not want to leave. She had gone hours between toilet breaks in case something happened while she was away.

Rosemary pushed the remains of her sandwich back into the carton. 'Would you mind if I stayed with you when Cormac goes home?' she asked, and Carly's eyes shot up from her soup, a spoonful suspended en route to her mouth. 'It's just that I'm none too keen on staying in a hotel on my own, you see.'

'Yes, of course,' said Carly, recovering herself. 'It'll be company for me too.' What else could she say?

'Now, you're sure you don't mind?'

Carly's mind flashed back to the flat. She had barely noticed anything when she had gone back to change but she knew the sofa was still a made-up sofa bed that Beth had slept on. Their bedroom was chaos; she had flung her clothes on the bed on top of the numerous outfits she had previously left there when she had been deciding what to wear to her engagement party and there was definitely no milk in the fridge. Rosemary was waiting for a response.

'I don't mind, but you might. It's a bit of a tip because …'

She suddenly wanted to tell her about the engagement because if she didn't tell her now when would there ever be a right opportunity? Her hand instinctively went to her pocket to check the ring was still there and it was; the shape of it under the fabric of her jeans reassured her.

'Oh, that doesn't matter. I quite like to tidy up, that'll be something I can do to help you,' said Rosemary, leaning across and laying her hand on Carly's. 'Perhaps we could have a rota so there's always someone with Fergus.'

Carly wrestled with her conscience. Fergus wanted to tell his parents about the engagement face to face, she knew that, but when would that be? Beth came into her mind. She knew what Beth would say. She would tell her to stop and think. And she was right, now was not the time. Any pleasure at sharing the engagement news would be short-lived because Fergus wasn't able to celebrate with them. She'd have to wait. She turned the ring over in her pocket and left it there as she put her hand back on the table.

When they returned to ICU Cormac pretended that he hadn't recently woken up. Carly noticed the curtains were drawn around a nearby bed where a teenage motorcyclist had been since last night. She could hear muffled sobs from his family and feared the worst. The thought that at any moment that could be them struck her like a falling tree.

Rosemary retook her place next to Fergus and Carly stood totally still, staring at the drawn curtains. 'Are you all right?' Cormac asked, looking concerned.

'No. There must be more we can do. We can't just sit here waiting for him to …' She knew there were two ways she could end that sentence. 'You said there was always something!' She jabbed a finger at Cormac although she knew he wasn't the source of her frustration. They shouldn't have to be working out where Rosemary was going to stay or how she was going to speed-tidy-up the flat so that his mother didn't think she was the slovenly sort. They should be planning a wedding and arguing over guest lists and seating plans, not working out a rota of who was going to sit with Fergus in case he woke up or … She felt crosser than she ever had before, with the possible exception of the time when Fergus was juggling with the flat keys and managed to drop them down a drain. She wanted Fergus back and she wanted him back now.

'Is there something you want to do?' asked Cormac gently.

'Yes, I want to do something! Argh!' Carly was tired and beyond frustrated. She marched round to her side of Fergus's bed thinking that she and Rosemary must look like a pair of statues or, worse still, gargoyles.

She picked up the iPhone and scrolled back to the teenage Fergus playlist they had put together earlier, selected 'The Ketchup Song' and pressed Play. She took Fergus's limp fingers in hers and spelled out the track for him. She squeezed his hand but he didn't respond. She clutched it tightly and tried her best not to cry.

Cormac was watching her closely. He walked round to her and crouched down. 'You're a lovely girl, Carly,' said Cormac, his face sincere. 'You've brought back the old Fergus.' He spoke slowly and melodically while Carly stared unblinking at Fergus. 'After the illness he wasn't himself, he took the hearing loss hard. In shock he was, to tell the truth. Lost his job and his self-confidence. Terrible thing to watch something like that happen to your child.' Cormac shook his head as if remembering. 'And then you came along with your kick-up-the-bum attitude and he was determined to learn sign language so that he could talk to you.'

Carly turned to Cormac, still crouched at her side. 'Did he say that?' she asked, engrossed in the alternative side of the story she knew so well.

'He did. You put the fire back in his belly, so you did. We couldn't ask for a better girlfriend for our boy.' Cormac opened his arms and Carly leaned in for a hug. She didn't mean to cry but she didn't seem entirely in control of the tears; at the moment they came and went at will as the emotions ebbed and surged.

A strained voice from the bed made them spring apart. 'Fiancée. She's my fiancée.'

Jack was sitting on the back step of the ambulance when Rhonda pushed past the police and ran to him.

'A customer came in and said there was an ambulance, a fire engine and police.' She waved her arms about, just missing Jack's head. 'What the hell has happened here?' continued Rhonda, scanning the front garden and taking in Jack's naked torso. Jack went to lift up his mask and Clark wagged a finger at him so he left it in place.

'It was the boiler. It must be faulty and it's poisoned Beth,' he said. Rhonda's hand shot to her mouth and she looked back at the cottage. 'They've taken her to hospital. Petra went with her. They tell me she'll be fine.' Jack gave a sideways glance at Clark, who saw his cue to join in the conversation.

'Proper hero he is. Saved her life, risked his own. Mind you, that wasn't so smart.' He handed Jack a clipboard and paper. 'There you go, you need to sign that if you really won't let me take you to hospital.' Jack scrawled something similar to his signature on the bottom of the form.

'If he says you need to go to hospital, you should go!' said Rhonda, putting her hands on her hips.

'Leo is missing,' said Jack, his voice anxious.

Rhonda looked like someone had slapped her. 'Are you sure?'

'He was with me at the pub but he wanted to put his big Easter egg somewhere safe at home. I should have walked him to the door instead of watching him because once he was past the willow tree I couldn't see him and I assumed—'

'It's not your fault,' said Rhonda, cutting him off. Her eyes alternated from his face to his ripped torso.

329

'It *is* my fault,' said Jack, standing up. He held on to the ambulance until he was sure of his steadiness.

'Go to your GP tomorrow, ask for a blood test to check your carboxyhaemoglobin level,' said Clark. 'Take this with you.' He tore off a carbon copy of the form and handed it to Jack.

Jack saluted him, took off the oxygen mask and swapped it for the form.

'What shall I do?' asked Rhonda.

'We need to search the village.'

'I can round a few people up to do that.'

'Great. If Leo's here we have to find him fast because when Beth comes round he's the first person she's going to want to see.'

'If he's here?' questioned Rhonda, her forehead creased into a deep frown worthy of someone far older.

Jack didn't want to share what was going through his head and as Rhonda's expression changed to horror it appeared he didn't need to. Dark thoughts were dominating his mind. He guessed it was down to the carbon monoxide but he could still picture Beth lying on the sofa and the awful sensation that had accompanied it when he had feared he was too late to save her. Question was, was it too late to save Leo?

Jack splashed his face with water. He was tired and dirty. His body ached and his head still throbbed. He'd left Rhonda checking for Leo at the last few houses and gardens on the village green while he got himself a T-shirt. It appeared that the sight of him topless had rendered a couple of women speechless and was definitely distracting Rhonda. Doris was very pleased to see him and was nudging her food bowl round the kitchen hopefully. Jack went upstairs to get a clean top and Doris followed him, then peeled off to the spare bedroom where he could hear her making odd little grunting noises. He pulled the top over his head and took a peek at what Doris was up to. She was rolling on the sleeping bag with her legs in the air.

Jack smiled at her. 'Come on, Doris. Does it smell of Leo?' Doris got up and trotted past him and down the stairs. Jack looked from her to the sleeping bag – he had an idea. After a full two minutes of waving the sleeping bag under Doris's nose, feeding her a treat and repeating 'Leo' countless times he felt they were ready to give their experiment a go. He clipped on her lead and they set off in search of Leo.

The police were now stepping up their interest and another patrol car had parked by the green. Leo had been missing for nearly an hour and nobody had seen him since he left the pub. Jack was mentally berating himself for not having waited a few more minutes. If he had would he have seen that Leo couldn't get inside? Would he have found Beth sooner? Whatever way he thought about it he knew Leo would be safe if he hadn't taken his eyes off him and the guilt made him feel sick.

A picture of Beth laughing flashed through his mind but was instantly replaced by a picture of her lying motionless on the sofa. His heart clenched when he thought of her in hospital. The thought of losing her scared him more than he thought possible. He pushed it out of his mind; he couldn't be in two places at once so he needed to deal with each problem in turn.

He headed for the tearoom; if anyone had a handle on the latest news it was Rhonda and Maureen. He opened the door and the bell announced his presence. 'Any news?' he asked.

Rhonda shook her head while she loaded a tea tray with cups and saucers and Maureen plonked down a full teapot. 'Nothing,' said Rhonda, her eyes surveying his clean T-shirt. 'There's two groups and they've searched all round the green and now they're spreading the net wider.' Rhonda sounded like she was giving a report on *Crimewatch*.

'One lot have gone towards Henbourne,' said Maureen, her usual gruffness somehow softer.

'The others are doing a wider house-to-house,' chipped in Rhonda. 'We'll do tea for them all when they're back.'

Doris was pulling to get inside, drawn by the smell of cake that was wafting out. 'Great, thanks, ladies.' He pulled Doris back and set off towards the cottage. He stopped by the willow tree and parted the fronds to peer inside, but there was no sign of Ernie. Come to think of it, Jack hadn't seen Ernie all day. He told Doris to sit and because he had a treat in his hand she obeyed instantly.

'Leo. Doris, find Leo.' He gave her a treat, she inhaled it and wagged her tail. He stood up straight. 'Find Leo,' he repeated. Feeling like a prize idiot he checked no one was watching over his shoulder. Doris certainly didn't look like a sniffer dog but he had to try. Doris stared at him hopefully but remained sitting and lifted a paw. 'This is useless. Come on.' They set off past the pub and down to the ford. Two groups of parents were sitting on the grass nearby where a few children were running about in the water and some others further up were feeding bread to the ducks.

'Have you seen a young boy here today? Six years old, dark hair?' he called. They all shook their heads. He marched on over the small footbridge and out of the village. He'd walk his usual jogging circuit as he didn't have the energy or lungpower to run right now.

Chapter Thirty-Six

Beth balled up the cloth in her fists and pulled hard at the sheet she was lying on. Leo was on a conveyer belt being propelled away from her and towards Nick who stood on the other side of the canyon, his arms folded and his expression smug. She felt something up her nose and she tried to dislodge it but someone took her hand away from her face. Her eyes popped open and for a moment all she could see was white light that emphasized the pain in her head and made her blink hard. Her eyes darted about her alien surroundings and she saw nothing that was familiar to her. She was suddenly confused and still had the uncomfortable sensation of something up her nose, but her hand was being held down.

'Can you hear me?' said a soft voice to her left. Beth turned to look, trying to clear the fuzz that was currently occupying her head and stem the anxiety she felt rising inside.

'I'm a nursing assistant, you're in hospital,' said the voice.

A frown burrowed across Beth's forehead as she tried hard to focus on the rather young person in blue seated on her left. Confusion turned to panic. She tried again to reach her nose and was thwarted by the warm touch of the nurse's hand.

'It's oxygen,' she said. 'It's helping you. You're going to be fine.

333

Your friend will be back in a minute. I'll go and tell Staff Nurse that you're awake.'

Beth was trying hard to make sense of what was going on. Was she still dreaming? Her mind would have been a blank had it not been filled with something akin to swirling marshmallow. She felt sick and she wanted to sleep but she also wanted to know what the hell was going on. She closed her eyes until the sound of someone moving the chair next to her forced her curiosity and she opened an eye. She watched Petra's bottom jiggle about as she moved her bag and coat off the seat.

'Petra?' said Beth, her voice barely a croak. She was still totally confused but pleased to see something she recognized even if it was Petra's behind.

'*Dovraga!*' Petra held on tight to her paper cup and cursed in Croatian. 'You're awake! I was here for ages and I only left for the toilet and this,' she said, waving the cup. 'Oh, but this is very good that you wake up, even if I am not here.' She gave Beth a kiss on the cheek before sitting down. 'How do you feel?'

'Rubbish,' said Beth, her hand reaching up to touch the tubes that were uncomfortably violating her nostrils. She tried to swallow but her mouth and throat were too dry. 'Leo?' He was always the first thing on her mind, even when her mind was a blur of confusion.

'He's fine,' said Petra sharply and she began fussing with Beth's covers.

'What's going on? Why am I here?' She gazed around to check her surroundings again but still nothing rang any bells – she had no recollection of how she had got there.

'Your boiler is leaking gas. It made you very sick and you collapsed.'

Beth stared at Petra while her addled brain attempted to take in the information.

'The boiler?' said Beth. Her head hurt and her brain felt like it was on a go-slow. Nothing was making sense.

'Jack got you out. I came with you in the ambulance.'

'Ambulance? I don't remember,' said Beth, shaking her head a fraction. It was a frightening feeling that something serious had happened and yet she had no recollection of any of it.

'I am sorry. I think the plumber was a not very good one. Jack worked it out and ran out of the pub and I wondered what ...'

'Where is Jack?' asked Beth, scanning the busy area as the many moving people and accompanying chatter in the busy hospital ward started to register.

'I don't know,' said Petra, sipping from the paper cup and breaking eye contact. Beth could sense the tension in her voice. 'Still at the cottage I think.'

'Petra, you're a terrible liar.' Beth spoke slowly. 'What's going on?'

She winced. 'When they bundled me into the ambulance with you Jack was with the paramedics.' Petra's expression was one of grave concern.

'Paramedics?' Why couldn't she recall any of this herself? The effort of trying to remember was making her head pound even more.

'He was lying on the ground. He wasn't conscious.' Petra shook her head.

'Why? What's wrong with him? What happened?' Beth fidgeted in the bed, getting impatient with the drip-fed story.

'When he was rescuing you he was also poisoned by the gas,' said Petra, closing her eyes.

Beth sensed the seriousness of the situation but without any recall it was difficult to comprehend what exactly had happened, like switching on a murder mystery part way through. But there was one thing that was suddenly very clear to her.

'Who's looking after Leo?'

Carly spun round in her seat to check she wasn't imagining it. Fergus was blinking slowly and a smile played on his lips.

'Oh my God, you're awake!' Carly forgot the wires and threw herself onto Fergus, setting off alarms all over the place and two nurses came running over.

'Oof,' said Fergus. 'Mind the spam!'

Rosemary clutched his arm and cried silent tears, her lips moving in hushed prayer.

Cormac stood up, leaned over and clasped Fergus's hand in both of his. 'You took your time there, son.'

Carly moved out of the way while the nurses reconnected wires and started checking Fergus over. Fergus appeared more than confused by the tears and attention.

'Hello, Fergus. I'm a nurse and you are in University College Hospital. Can you remember what happened to you?' Fergus stared at the nurse's moving lips as she spoke.

'I got engaged?' he said, looking happy but still confused.

'Is the boy delirious?' asked Cormac, swinging his head round to address the older of the two nurses now engrossed in jotting down information from the surrounding machines. The nurse gave Cormac a hard stare.

'Fergus is deaf, would you like me to translate?' asked Carly. With Carly's help the nurse asked Fergus a few simple questions and his correct answers had her ticking boxes with a flourish.

'He needs to rest,' said the nurse to Cormac. 'Maybe come back in a while?'

'Ach, are you serious? I've been sat here so long my bum's gone numb and now he's finally woken up you want me to leave?' Cormac was laughing in between his words but the nurse wasn't registering any humour.

'You scared us all, you big eejit,' signed Carly and Fergus grinned back at her.

'I have no idea what's going on but I feel like I've had a massive spliff,' said Fergus, his voice a little wobbly.

'Tell him his mother's here!' said Cormac, losing his whimsical air and pointing to Rosemary still praying at Fergus's side.

'I know she's here. Hiya, Mam, are you okay?' He tilted his head as far as it would go to the right so that he could see her.

Rosemary smiled and patted his hand while fresh tears rolled down her cheeks. 'I'm fine now, son.'

'Will someone tell me why I'm here or is this one of those weird dreams where I'll suddenly be naked and …' He lifted the sheet and grinned. 'I'm na-ked!' he said in a sing-song voice.

Carly started to frantically sign to him. 'It's not a dream. You were attacked with a bottle in a bar when you were out with Budgie and Ryan. You've been unconscious for three days.'

'What?' said Fergus with a beaming smile, which soon faded as he registered the looks on his parents' faces. Eventually his gaze rested back on Carly, her eyes red with tears, and he took her hand. 'Seriously?'

Carly nodded. 'We thought you were going to die.' It was the first time she'd said it out loud; the words seemed to unleash yet more emotion and a sob escaped.

'Hey, it's okay. Look, I'm fine,' said Fergus, smiling again.

'You're on a strong intravenous painkiller and when that wears off you may think otherwise,' said Carly. She decided she would keep the news about the surgery until a little later as he already looked astonished by the information overload.

'What day is it?' he asked cautiously.

'Easter Monday,' replied Cormac, moving round to be next to Rosemary. 'This'll do nothing for your Messiah complex, so it won't.' He shook his head but he was smiling broadly, now standing behind Rosemary with his hands on her shoulders.

'Easter Monday,' repeated Fergus.

'Look, maybe the nurse is right. Perhaps we should leave you to rest,' suggested Carly, looking across the bed.

Cormac nodded his agreement. 'She's right. We're all pretty knackered too. We'll be back in later to see you.' He and Rosemary kissed Fergus's forehead in turn. 'Shall we wait for you outside?'

said Cormac to Carly and she nodded. They watched Cormac and Rosemary grip hands tightly as they left.

Fergus studied Carly, her face red and puffy from the tears. His eyes refocused on her left hand and as he rubbed his thumb over her ringless fingers, a frown darted across his forehead and he narrowed his eyes. She could see he was trying to work out what had happened.

She very gently touched his chin so that he would look up and see her speak; she was suddenly exhausted and too tired to be bothered to sign. 'The ring is safe in my pocket. I didn't want your parents to find out when you were ...' She tailed off.

'So I didn't imagine that you said yes?'

Carly started to grin as she remembered Trafalgar Square. 'No, you didn't imagine that.'

He pulled her to him and kissed her. 'Thank heaven for that. My head is all spaced out.'

'It's bound to be, you've been through a lot.'

'And the weirdest thing. I've got these songs going round in my head.' Fergus was puzzled.

'Oh yeah?' said Carly, getting to her feet and trying hard to hide a smirk. 'What songs?'

Fergus chuckled. 'Really crap ones!'

'How odd. I'd better go, your mum and dad are waiting. I love you.'

'I love you too,' said Fergus.

Carly left the ICU with her hand held up in the 'I love you sign' and Fergus grinned as he watched her leave. He looked around and picked up the unfamiliar device that was on his bed. He turned it over in his hand, feeling the vibrations, and followed its cable to his iPhone.

'What on earth is this?' he said to himself. He scanned the screen of his phone and saw that it was playing 'We Are the Cheeky Girls' on repeat. 'Bloody hell! Were they trying to finish me off?'

* * *

338

Jack was trying hard not to panic but, between him and the two volunteer search groups, they had checked everywhere there was to check in the village and there was no sign of Leo. Doris had been next to useless but she appeared to have enjoyed her long walk and she trotted along keeping pace with Jack. He was racking his brains for an idea, a clue to where Leo could be, but each thought was hijacked by the fear that he was wasting his time, that Leo was no longer in Dumbleford. He stopped for a second and took in a great lungful of air. He needed to think. Who had he not asked? Jack broke into a speed-walk, which took Doris by surprise as her lead yanked her forward. Jack was heading for Ernie's. Ernie was the only person Jack hadn't seen all day; he hadn't been there at the Easter egg hunt, he wasn't in the willow tree when the drama all kicked off and there'd been no sign of him since everyone had been searching for Leo.

What was a short walk seemed to take far longer than usual because, when Jack quickened his pace, his whole body ached thanks to the after effects of the carbon monoxide poisoning. A few minutes later he was at Ernie's, calling through the letterbox and banging on the door. There was no answer – Ernie was missing too. Jack went and knocked on the neighbour's door, which was quickly answered.

'Hello, Jack, come in and have a cuppa, won't you?'

'Sorry, Audrey, I can't stop. I'm trying to find Ernie. Have you seen him today?'

Audrey looked momentarily disappointed but she soon recovered and pondered the question. 'I saw him leave about ten-ish I think. No, it was before ten because afterwards the news came on the radio …'

'Thanks, Audrey,' said Jack and he pulled an inquisitive Doris away and walked to the corner of Ernie's road. He stood there for a moment catching his breath as if he were unfit. The carbon monoxide had taken its toll; he hoped its effects would soon wear off. His mind darted to Beth and it spurred him on. He needed to find Leo and for some reason he felt finding Ernie would hold some answers. He needed to think like Ernie and that gave him a sense of despair, for who knew how Ernie thought? It was hard to tell. He understood most things, it was communicating he struggled with, especially since Wilf had died. Wilf, that was it, thought Jack. Where would Ernie and Wilf have gone if they were troubled? He had no idea but he knew someone who might.

'Stop the bloody banging!' yelled Shirley moments before she opened her front door. 'Oh, it's you, what's up?' she said, standing in front of him with a limp cat under her arm. Jack looked at Mittens and felt the panic rise as he squinted at Doris, who was engrossed in sniffing the doorstep. Jack pointed elaborately at Doris and then Mittens, who had already clocked the large dog in her vicinity and was now starting to do something akin to the backstroke in mid-air.

'Shut the door,' said Jack softly.

'Why? Don't be ridiculous, they're fine,' said Shirley but Mittens made a break for it over Shirley's shoulder and the movement and flash of white landing in Doris's view kicked off World War Three. Doris charged into Shirley's house and Jack had to let go of the lead as it was yanked from his grip or risk knocking Shirley over. Shirley shook her head. 'Well, you'd better come in,' she said, the reluctance evident in her voice.

Jack didn't have time for this. His mind was a throbbing whirl of worries. There was no word on how Beth was. The thought of anything happening to her concerned him more than he cared to admit. He dared not ring Petra because the first question would be, 'Where is Leo?' And the sick feeling that was overpowering him was less to do with the poisoning and more to do with the creeping fear that Leo had been abducted. The pain that would cause Beth was too much to comprehend. She would never forgive him.

Jack shot past Shirley and she shut the door as a high-speed

Mittens came skidding across the polished parquet floor. Shirley scooped Mittens up into her arms and the cat clung to her cardigan like Velcro, her tail the size and colour of a bleached toilet brush. Doris came to a halt in front of them and proceeded to bark her excitement.

'Now stop,' said Shirley and she bent her small frame forward and rested a bony finger on Doris's wet nose. Doris stopped barking and went to lick the finger, her eyes shooting to the cat who was now very close indeed. Jack went to grab Doris's collar. 'No!' said Shirley firmly. 'They need to sort this out between the two of them.'

Jack struggled to think of a worse idea. 'I think they said the same about Germany and Poland and look how that turned out!' He agitatedly ran his hands through his hair. Shirley gave him an old-fashioned look. 'I'm kind of in a hurry,' said Jack, checking his watch and wishing he hadn't as it reminded him of how long Leo had been missing and that it would soon start to get dark.

Shirley ignored him and carried Mittens off into the kitchen with Doris trotting after her in silence. Jack stood in the hallway shaking his head. This was getting him nowhere and precious time was ticking away. He could now see a glimpse of the madness of Dumbleford that Beth referred to.

The kitchen door reopened. Shirley came out and carefully closed the door behind her. Jack gave her a quick once-over with his eyes but she appeared to be all intact – no scratches, no bite marks.

'Don't worry about them. What was it you were in such a hurry for?' asked Shirley.

'Yes, right,' said Jack, reordering his thoughts. 'Wilf and Ernie, was there somewhere they liked to go? Or perhaps a place they played when they were children?'

Shirley was staring at Jack like he'd gone loopy. 'Why?'

'Leo and Ernie are missing.'

Shirley drummed her fingers across her lips while she thought.

'They used to play at the farm, we all did,' said Shirley, her face softened by a smile as her eyes wandered off to somewhere over Jack's right shoulder.

'Bramble Hill Farm?' asked Jack, his mind whirring away trying to work out his quickest route there.

'Yes, we had such jolly good fun up there, me and the boys,' said Shirley with a girlish giggle and Jack's eyes widened.

'Anywhere else?'

Shirley gave a pout as she thought. 'On the green, obviously, and the farm and all the fields around and about.'

Jack felt his shoulders sag. Fields and countryside surrounded the village; it was impossible to cover it all before dark but he started towards the front door all the same. A thought struck him. 'Was there anywhere that was a sanctuary, Shirley? Somewhere you would escape to?'

'The pillbox,' said Shirley without a flinch.

'Pillbox?' Jack was squinting at her.

'Yes, on Bramble Hill not far past the farmhouse. After the war we used to hide in it, even into our teens, such japes!' said Shirley with a giggle.

'That old concrete box thing in a mound in the field?'

'Yes, it's a pillbox, those were our war defences, what do they teach you in school these days?'

Jack didn't like to point out he hadn't been a pupil in school for some years. He gave her a clumsy hug and he hoped beyond sanity that she had supplied the answer to the nightmare. Shirley was still giggling as Jack raced out of the door.

'Hey, what about your dog?' she called but it was too late, Jack was gone.

Chapter Thirty-Seven

Jack found some energy from somewhere and he sprinted off towards the farm. His heart was racing and his lungs were burning but all he could think about was finding Leo. His phone started to buzz in his pocket but he ignored it. The uphill climb to the farm pulled at his thighs and he started to understand what Clark the paramedic had been trying to tell him about the effects of too much carbon monoxide in his blood. He dragged in deep lungfuls of air through his mouth as the farmhouse came into sight. A few more strides and he could glimpse the grey concrete pillbox, partly obscured by a mound of grassed-over earth that was piled up on one side, which Jack guessed had been a crude attempt to hide the structure when it had first been built. He climbed over the fence and into the field, and crossing the meadow his stride lengthened.

'Leo! Ernie! Leo! Ernie!' he shouted breathlessly, drawing closer. He ran up to the pillbox and peered into the dark hole at the front. 'Leo?' There was no answer.

'Leo, it's me, Jack. I'm on my own. Everything is okay, you're not in any trouble,' he said, walking round the side to find an open entrance. It was pitch black inside. Jack pulled his phone out of his pocket and tried to ignore that he'd had a missed call from

Petra. He switched on the torch and shone it into the darkness. The wall twisted away like a snail shell and he followed it round. It was a creepy, dank place with an unpleasant, pungent odour and it was becoming increasingly unlikely that Leo would be here. What would drive a six-year-old to hide somewhere like this? Jack's footsteps echoed as the wall opened out into one small room.

Jack swept the light around and almost jumped out of his skin when it lit up Ernie.

'Bloody hell, Ernie!' remonstrated Jack, his heart pounding fiercely in his chest at the sudden shock. Ernie was standing in front of a bench and he held up his hand to shield his eyes from the light. 'Ernie, Leo is missing – do you know where he is?'

'Beth wouldn't wake up,' said Ernie, still shielding his eyes.

'I know, it's okay, she's in hospital, Ernie, where's—'

'Mum's in hospital?' said a small voice and Leo stepped out from behind Ernie.

'Oh, thank God,' said Jack, stepping forward and lifting Leo into his arms. 'She's going to be okay, mate. Come on, let's get you out of here.' Jack shone his phone to light the way out of the pillbox. 'You too, Ernie!' shouted Jack over his shoulder. When he got outside he put Leo down; he was about to hug him but Leo was frowning hard.

'You okay?'

Leo nodded quickly but he looked like he was fighting back tears.

'Ernie, come on!' called Jack.

'Man was there,' shouted back Ernie.

Jack's eyes darted about as he tried and failed to make sense of what Ernie was saying. 'What man?'

Leo shrugged his shoulders. Ernie shuffled out to the entrance and his eyes searched the field at speed.

'Man was there,' repeated Ernie, wringing his hands in agitation.

'What man?'

'Near the pub.'

'What did he look like?' asked Jack gently.

Ernie shook his head hard. 'Black hair. Stranger. Laughed at me.' Ernie briefly made eye contact with Jack then hung his head as if exhausted.

'It's okay, Ernie. Don't worry, there's no man about now. We need to get Leo back to Beth.'

'Stranger looking for Eliz-a-beth,' said Ernie, struggling to pronounce the name.

Jack patted Ernie on the back. 'Thanks for keeping Leo safe, Ernie, you did great. Let's get you both home.' Ernie was agitated but he took hold of Jack's hand and walked with him across the field.

Jack, Ernie and Leo walked back to the village and dropped Ernie off at his bungalow on the way. He didn't say goodbye, just unlocked the door and went in.

'Leo, you had everyone worried. We've been hunting for you everywhere. What happened after you left the pub?'

'Sorry,' said Leo with a shrug. He clearly had no idea of the drama that had unfurled. 'I went to the cottage and knocked on the door but Mum didn't answer. She was asleep on the sofa. Ernie was hiding in the back garden and he came round shouting about a stranger.'

'Did you see this stranger?' asked Jack.

'Nope. But Ernie was all panicky and really scared and that made me kind of scared too. Ernie said we needed to get away and he took me to that dark room.'

'What did you do there all that time?'

Leo looked thoughtful. 'We ate my big Easter egg and I told Ernie about the Romans. It was weird in the dark but I wasn't scared,' he said, jutting out his jaw defiantly.

'I'm sure you weren't,' said Jack, giving his shoulder an affectionate squeeze.

'Are we going to hospital to see Mum now?' asked Leo.

'I don't know, mate.' Jack remembered the call he had missed when he had been searching for Leo. He took out his phone and called Petra back. After a brief conversation with her the phone was passed to Beth.

Jack covered his mobile and turned to a concerned-looking Leo. 'Your mum doesn't know about you going missing, okay?'

'Are you going to tell?' asked Leo, narrowing his eyes. Jack shook his head and handed over the phone.

When Leo had chatted to his mum and brightened up considerably he passed the phone back to Jack. Jack felt Leo's hand snake into his and he smiled.

'I hear I owe you a thank-you,' said Beth, her voice weaker than usual. Jack smiled to hear her.

'Ah, it was nothing.'

'No, Jack, don't go all modest on me. You saved my life and …' Her voice cracked and she cleared her throat. 'Thank you.'

'You're very welcome,' he said, mirroring her sombre tone. 'But you know me, all-round saint,' he added with fun in his voice.

'Are you going to lecture me on the reconditioned boiler?'

'Not now, but I will,' he said. 'We could have lost you.' He found he was gripping Leo's hand as he spoke.

'But I'm fine thanks to you. Is Leo okay?'

'Yeah, he's brilliant,' he said, glancing down at the small boy staring up at him. 'Don't worry about him, I won't let him out of my sight.'

'I'm very grateful, Jack. And are you all right? I was worried because Petra said you were unconscious when she left.'

'She exaggerates, I'm fine …'

Leo pulled at his hand and pointed to an elated-looking Rhonda waving at them from outside the tearoom. 'I've got to go. You concentrate on getting better and don't worry about a thing. Promise?'

'Promise,' said Beth, her voice sounding full of emotion.

They said their goodbyes, Jack ended the call and carried on across the green. Rhonda gave Jack and Leo very tight hugs and Leo rubbed her wet kisses off his cheek with his sleeve. Jack gave Rhonda money to cover the costs of the tea for the search party and the police who were now all looking relieved that the drama was over. Jack promised to come back for celebratory cake later despite Leo's pleas to get cake now.

Jack was beyond thrilled to have found Leo safe and well; the feelings he had experienced when Leo was missing were very new to him. He'd lost sight of Doris at a beach once but that didn't come close to the terror of imagining Leo had been taken. He wished he knew for sure who the stranger was who had freaked Ernie out so much that he had run off to the pillbox but perhaps he'd never know. For now he was going to concentrate on keeping Leo safe and looking forward to seeing Beth fit and well again.

Leo started to head towards Jack's house.

'We need to pick up Doris first.'

'Why? Where is she?' Leo asked, quickening his stride to keep pace with Jack.

'She's on a play date but you'll never guess who with,' said Jack with a grin. They walked across the green together and up to Shirley's house.

Leo scanned the huge door. 'There's no doorbell.'

'Yeah, there is,' said Jack, lifting up Leo and showing him the iron rod and handle at the side of the door. 'Pull that.'

Leo did as he was asked and was delighted by the resulting peal of bells that came from inside.

Shirley opened the door and a smile danced momentarily on her lips when she saw Leo. She turned her attention to Jack. 'I thought you'd forgotten the dog,' she said, stepping aside and letting them into the large hall. She shut the door and they followed her. 'They're in the snug,' she said over her shoulder and Leo giggled.

Shirley opened the door to a small wood-panelled room with a real fire crackling in an ornate fireplace. On the heavily patterned rug in front of the fire lay Doris and Mittens back to back. Jack and Leo stared for a minute. The two animals looked up but neither showed enough interest to actually move.

'I don't know how you did it,' said Jack to Shirley, 'but you're a marvel.'

'Like all of us they needed to learn a little tolerance,' said Shirley wisely, 'and I find the tiniest smear of pâté works wonders too.' She sat down with a thud in a large wing-backed leather chair. 'You'll see yourselves out, won't you?' she added and she picked up a hardback book and started to read.

'Shirley, one question. Does Mittens remind you of anyone?' asked Jack.

Shirley looked at the cat. 'Like who?'

'A certain moustached dictator.'

'Oh, yes, I see what you mean.' She nodded wisely. 'But I didn't know you'd met my sister Miriam.' She hid her wry smile and turned back to her book. Jack looked more puzzled than ever.

'Come on, Doris,' said Leo and the dog yawned and stretched. Doris stood up, then paused for a moment to sniff Mittens, almost as if she were kissing her goodbye. Jack held his breath but Mittens just closed her eyes and went back to sleep.

'You need to calm down because you're giving me another headache,' said Beth, only half joking as she tried to speak over a very agitated Carly.

'I rang to tell you the amazing news that Fergus had come round and your phone was answered by some woman from the tearoom who told me you'd been carted off to hospital in an ambulance. And I've spent the last two hours trying to find out if you're dead or alive …' Carly paused for breath.

'I'm alive.'

348

'I know,' said Carly, her voice dissolving into tears. 'But for a moment I thought you weren't. I thought I'd got Fergus back only to lose you.'

A corresponding sob escaped from Beth. She knew exactly how she would have felt if the tables had been reversed. 'I'm sorry you had a fright. But I'm okay, honestly I am.'

'I don't know what I'd do without you, Beth,' said Carly, followed by a loud sniff, her voice now gentle and childlike.

'And I don't know what I'd do without you and you're making me cry now, which won't help anything. Although it is meant to be good for your skin.'

'You daft sod,' Carly spluttered through more tears.

'I'm so pleased about Fergus, that is such good news.'

'He's still in hospital or I'd be on the next train, you know that, don't you?'

'I do and that's lovely of you but they're just keeping me in for observation and I'll be home tomorrow.'

'Okay but you can't go back to the cottage, it's dangerous.'

'Apparently Jack is sorting everything out for me. He's even found an emergency plumber who will replace the boiler today. He's been really kind.'

'The woman from the tearoom said he was like a superhero saving your life and risking his own. Seriously, what does this guy have to do to get you to snog him?'

Beth laughed. 'He is pretty amazing but I'm afraid I missed my chance there, he's with Petra now and ...'

'The lucky cow!' said Carly with feeling.

'And my head really is starting to throb ...'

'Okay, I can take a hint. Call me when you can. I love you, Beth.'

'I know and I love you too.'

Beth was smiling when she ended the call. Poor Carly, she must have had a nasty shock. Beth could imagine how dramatic Rhonda would have made the whole episode sound; she was probably the worst person for Carly to have spoken to. Beth closed her eyes and tried to remember what had happened but the last thing she could recall was being at Jack's and then the next thing she remembered was seeing Petra's bottom at her bedside – there was nothing in between which was frightening in itself. What she really needed to come to terms with was the fact that she could have been killed. Every time someone mentioned it she was quick to point out that she hadn't died but the truth was that the only reason she was alive was thanks to Jack.

Denis and Leo watched from the car as Jack and Petra helped Beth unlock the cottage. Petra was gripping her arm while Jack tried to guide her.

'Stop fussing!' said Beth but she wasn't cross, it was quite pleasant to see that they genuinely cared about her. 'Really I'm fine, thanks to both of you,' she went on, although she was staring directly at Jack, whose eyebrows did a little hop before he looked away.

'I'll keep fussing until I'm sure you are all better,' said Petra with a small frown, ushering Beth inside the cottage.

'I'll be back to work later,' said Beth.

'No, you will not!' Petra put her hands on her hips for emphasis.

'I don't think that's wise,' said Jack, taking the slightly less confrontational stance.

'The hospital said I'm fine. No lasting effects. There's no reason I can't do a shift. Well, at least let me come in and see how it goes?'

Petra snorted. 'Tomorrow perhaps. Now I make you tea. The British are right about one thing – tea fixes everything.' And Petra disappeared into the kitchen leaving Beth and Jack looking awkwardly at each other. They exchanged smiles and turned away.

'Thanks again, Jack. It was really brave of you to come in here when you knew the dangers.'

Jack shrugged. 'Anyone would have done the same.'

'That's as maybe but I am truly grateful.' She leaned forward a little and hesitated before giving him a brief kiss on the cheek. Jack's face reddened and he took a small step back.

'Right,' he said, rubbing his chin. 'I'll show you how to work the new boiler later on and there are three carbon monoxide alarms: one in the kitchen, one in the hall and one on the landing.' He pointed above his head and Beth spotted the small white box on the ceiling next to the fire alarm. 'It makes a loud beeping sound if there's too much of the gas about. The cottage is clear of the lethal stuff now so you're quite safe.' He took a much-needed breath and puffed out his cheeks.

'Great, thanks,' said Beth, feeling something was amiss but she couldn't sense what exactly. 'You need to let me have the bill for the new boiler,' she added.

'Yeah, I'll drop it round.' He slapped his arms on the sides of his legs. 'Right, I'm off. Call if you need anything.'

Petra emerged from the kitchen with a large mug of tea, which she handed to Beth. 'Like he says, call if you need anything.'

'I will,' said Beth and they both gave her disbelieving looks. 'I will! Now go,' she said, shooing them out of the cottage.

Petra and Jack walked to the end of the garden where the remains of the old gate now lay in a small stack.

Petra pulled a face. 'What?' he said.

'I don't like that we haven't told Beth about Leo going missing,' said Petra.

'I know, but it seems like an extra worry that she doesn't need right now, especially when we found him safe and well.'

'Still,' said Petra with a shrug.

'If Leo tells her that's up to him,' said Jack.

'And this mystery man that Ernie saw worries me.'

'Me too but we don't know it was Nick. It could have been a tourist,' said Jack, looking doubtful. 'I wish she would listen and stay with me for a while.' He briefly glanced back at the cottage as he spoke.

'I know, I have offered for her and Leo to stay at the pub but she refuses. She is an independent woman, what can we do?'

'Keep one eye on her and another one looking out for this Nick character.'

'I wish I knew what he looked like but if there's anyone suspicious I will call you straight away,' said Petra.

'Here's the car keys,' he said, handing them over. 'You and the boys have a fab afternoon at the wildlife park.'

'Thanks, Jack, we will,' said Petra with a light squeeze of Jack's arm. Her eyebrow jolted upwards. 'You are still working out I see,' said Petra with a cheeky grin as she gave his bicep a harder squeeze.

'Ger off!' Jack batted her hand away light-heartedly. 'Come here,' he said, giving her a fleeting hug. 'Thanks for … well, everything.'

Petra kissed his cheek then rubbed at the lipstick mark she'd left. 'Always my pleasure.'

'Right, I'm off to work. Have fun,' he said and they waved to each other and went their separate ways.

From the shadows of the living room Beth watched them leave, feeling a small pang of jealousy at witnessing their familiar exchange.

Chapter Thirty-Eight

After a very bubbly bath, to hide the grim avocado tub, and a snooze in her own bed, Beth felt almost human again. She lay on the sofa and made a new list. There was virtually no money left and she still had quite a bit to do before she could put the cottage up for sale. She needed to use her initiative if she was going to get it finished quickly and back on the market. She was puzzling over her lack of options when her mobile rang. The screen showed a number she didn't recognize, which immediately concerned her. Beth pressed the Answer Call button and listened.

'Hello? Beth, are you there?'

The sound of the familiar voice sent a wave of relief over her. 'Hiya, Carls, what's with the odd phone number?'

'I've bought myself a new iPhone and you can stop laughing. I thought it was time I caught up.'

'Well done you, I am impressed. How are things with you?'

'We're both fine. They've moved Fergus to an ordinary ward and they're very pleased with his progress. But how are you feeling?'

'That's great news about Fergus. I'm fine now I'm out of hospital.'

'You were going to call me when you were home. Has the

boiler leak affected your memory?' asked Carly with genuine concern in her voice.

'No,' chuckled Beth. 'I've not been back long. I was about to call you, honest.'

'You're not in that deathtrap of a cottage are you?' said Carly, alarmed.

'Yes, I'm in the cottage but it's no longer a deathtrap as you so delicately put it. The boiler has been replaced and I have carbon monoxide detectors coming out of my ears thanks to Jack. It's quite safe now, thanks.'

'I wish I was there to take care of you.'

'But I don't need looking after, really ...'

'Perhaps lovely Jack could nurse you back to health. I bet he has an exquisite bedside manner,' she mused.

'You're naughty! I'm fine and like I said Jack is out of bounds so stop searching for the fairy tale.'

'Okay,' said Carly, followed by an unhidden sigh. 'But I do want to come and see you soon, once Fergus is fully recovered.'

'Of course, that would be lovely. You'll love the village this time of year. I swear there's a load more crocuses sprung up on the village green in the last twenty-four hours!'

'It is such a pretty village, Beth, it would be a fabulous place for a wedding,' mused Carly.

'It would, there's a sweet little church up the hill between Dumbleford and the next village, and I can see why it's popular for weddings in the summer.'

'Oh, do strangers get married there?'

'Strangers?' chuckled Beth. 'I hope not, but if you mean people that don't live in the village, then yes. Petra was telling me she's catered a few of them. People seem to get married wherever they like these days.'

'Ooh,' exhaled Carly, 'I might suggest that to Fergus, how much fun would that be? A wedding in Dumbleford!'

Beth was pulling a face and she was glad she was on the phone.

'It's a bit of a trek for Fergus's family and pretty much everyone apart from me!'

'I guess,' said Carly, her voice losing its exuberance.

'If you're thinking about venues does this mean you've set a date for the wedding?'

'No, not really. We're both agreed on a summer wedding but Fergus thinks next year would be too much of a rush to organize everything.'

'But you'd have over a year!'

'I know but he doesn't do anything at speed doesn't our Fergus.'

The next morning Beth let out a huge yawn as she opened the front door and Doris trotted in followed by a smiling Jack.

'You're early,' said Beth, forgetting her manners.

'Good morning to you too!' said Jack. 'I thought I'd walk Leo to school so you can go back to bed or do whatever it is you unicorns like to do to relax.' He was grinning at her onesie, which clearly never failed to amuse him.

Beth stifled another mammoth yawn. 'That is kind of you but we're fine. I was about to go and get dressed.'

'Ohhhh Mum! Can Jack take me for a change? Please!' came the plea from the kitchen and a spoon was dropped into an empty cereal bowl.

Jack pulled a smug face and tilted his head to one side awaiting her response. Leo joined them in the hall and she now had two sets of pleading eyes boring into her.

'Okay, okay, I give in,' she said, raising her hands in surrender while Jack and Leo high-fived each other.

'Did you have a good time at the wildlife park yesterday?' Jack asked Leo.

'Yeah, it was awesome! We heard a camel fart!' said Leo, collapsing into giggles.

'Excellent,' agreed Jack with a snort. 'Anything else good or was the camel fart the highlight?'

'We saw zebras doing yoga,' said Leo with a pout.

'Really?' asked Beth.

'That's what Petra said they were doing but I think they were having sex.'

'Okay, time to get ready for school,' said Beth, keen to end the discussion.

'I need to do my teeth and get dressed,' yelled Leo, racing upstairs.

'It's okay, no rush,' called back Jack before turning his attention to Beth. 'Sounds like we missed out on a fun afternoon.' Jack was grinning like an idiot.

'You know, I thought moving to a quaint village like this I'd miss the high culture of London but not at all,' said Beth and they both started to chuckle. 'Are you okay to pick up Denis en route, it's just that I always do.'

'Yep, I've got it all covered. You have a relaxing day.'

'Okay, then I will. Thanks,' said Beth, her eyes darting over his face. They had settled back into an easy friendship and she was truly grateful for it but a part of her was starting to feel that she had missed out on the chance of something very special with Jack.

Over the next few weeks things started to get back to normal for both Beth and Carly. Beth went back to work at the pub and spent her spare time stripping doors with a borrowed blowtorch. Jack and Petra had been terrifically supportive with Jack even turning up with a load of groceries to save Beth taking the bus to the supermarket.

Fergus had returned home and despite the loss of a large chunk of hair he had made a full recovery and he and Carly were closer than ever. Tiny balls of fluff had briefly appeared on the pond and had been quickly shooed back under cover by their protective parents but the first ducklings of the year signalled new life in the village and that spring would soon become summer.

Everything felt like it had settled back into its rightful place and the normal rhythm of life had been restored.

Waiting by the school gates Beth laughed at another autocorrect text fail from Carly, who was struggling to get to grips with her new mobile phone. Apparently she had been baking and was keeping muffins in her new underwear – Beth suspected the message was meant to read Tupperware instead of underwear but the thought of the former was too funny.

She was still giggling to herself when Leo appeared at her side. 'Ja … Mr Selby wants a word with you,' he said, taking Doris's lead before continuing a conversation with Denis about which animals fart the loudest.

Beth looked up to see a very smartly dressed Jack waving at her while he was simultaneously pointing children in the direction of their respective parents. Beth walked over as the last child skipped down the steps.

'Hi,' said Beth, feeling strangely coy now she had his full attention. He was totally gorgeous when he was dressed like that. What was it about a man in a good suit? Or perhaps it was just Jack.

'Hi. Haven't seen you for a few days so I wanted to say … well, hi,' said Jack, shoving his hands into his pockets.

'Hi,' repeated Beth, feeling self-conscious. She kept a watchful eye on Leo, Denis and Doris.

'What have you been up to?'

'Oh, you know, working my way through the never-ending list of stuff that needs doing at the cottage.'

Jack nodded encouragingly while she was speaking. 'What're you working on right now?'

'Doors mainly. I'm sure most places don't have as many as Willow Cottage seems to have.'

'Need a hand?'

'Thanks, Jack, but I know you're busy.'

'I'm done here,' he said, nodding over his shoulder at the school. 'The joy of helping out is that I don't have all the additional work that comes with full-time teaching. I could be with you within the hour.'

'Great, but you must stay for dinner – my way of saying thank you. It's only pasta, which is probably not the best thank-you but ...' She realized she was gabbling. 'Anyway stay for dinner as long as that's not going to cause any issues.'

Jack smiled from the corner of his mouth. 'No issues. That would be perfect. See you in a bit.'

Beth watched him disappear inside.

'Come on, Mum!' shouted Leo, who had now decided to sit on the ground next to Doris. Beth hurried over and as they set off she felt a flicker of excitement that Jack was coming over.

Like he promised Jack appeared about thirty minutes later wearing some paint-splattered joggers and a fitted white T-shirt and set straight to work stripping off the paint from the bathroom door with the blowtorch. Because they only had the one blowtorch, which was Jack's anyway, Beth was working on getting off the residual bits of paint from her bedroom door that she'd stripped earlier. She found she was glancing over at Jack now and again and watching the taut muscles in his arms as he carefully edged the melted paint away from the door. She may have ogled at him one too many times because Jack suddenly turned towards her and Beth quickly looked away.

'You okay?' he asked.

'Oh yes, me, I'm fine. Thank you ... for asking,' she said, wondering why she sounded like a 1940s radio presenter all of a sudden.

'Muuuuuum, I can't do my homework, it's too hard!' shouted Leo from the kitchen.

'What subject is it?' called back Beth.

'Maaaaaaths,' called back Leo, managing to convey his despondency in the drawn-out word.

Beth felt her shoulders sag. Helping Leo with his homework

invariably turned into an argument because basically he didn't want to do it and any minor setback was his cue to give up. Jack was watching her closely.

'I'll go if you like?' he said. Beth pulled a face. She would very much have liked Jack to take over but he was already helping her with the doors. As if reading her mind, Jack spoke. 'I don't mind. I like maths and I like Leo.'

Beth couldn't help but smile. 'I am really taking advantage of you,' she said.

He switched off the blowtorch and handed it to her. 'Not at all, chance would be a fine thing,' he said, jogging downstairs. Beth narrowed her eyes after him. Was he flirting with her? Or was he implying that Petra was not taking enough advantage? Or perhaps she was reading far too much into the innocent comment. She decided on the latter and picked up where Jack had left off on the bathroom door to refocus her mind.

The giggling that came from downstairs warmed her heart. Jack and Leo got on well. It was good for Leo to have a strong male role model around and she knew he would miss Jack when they eventually sold the cottage and moved on. She swallowed hard when she thought about how much she would miss Jack too.

'I'm pregnant!' shouted Carly from the bathroom. She ran out of the room clutching the white tester stick and rushed into Fergus's playroom.

'Whoa!' he said, good-naturedly pausing his game.

'You okay?' he asked as he watched Carly literally bounce up and down in front of him.

Carly steadied herself and tried to appear serious. She studied Fergus; apart from the patch where his hair still needed to grow back and his accompanying short haircut you wouldn't know what had happened to him. He was sitting at his computer in a T-shirt and lounge trousers, the picture of health with a hint of laziness, but she loved him just as he was.

Carly went to put the stick in her pocket to leave her hands free to sign but remembered that she'd recently peed on it so she carefully put it down behind her on Fergus's desk.

Carly waved her hands like a conductor about to direct an orchestra and Fergus chuckled at her. 'Is this charades?' he asked. 'I'm very good at charades.'

'You cheat at charades!'

'It's not my fault that people can't help but mouth the words they're trying to act out,' he said, trying to look innocent.

'Anyway,' she said and she started to sign very carefully and deliberately. 'I have important news …' She left a dramatic pause. 'I did a test and …'

'You're going to grammar school?' teased Fergus.

'Fergus!' admonished Carly and he signed 'sorry'.

'You're going to be a daddy!'

Fergus looked puzzled. 'I'm going to be naughty?' he said and it made Carly question her signing. She'd definitely used the right sign but she tried another tack.

'No, I'm pregnant!' she signed and emphasized it with her lip movements but Fergus was staring at her hand moving over her stomach as she signed 'pregnant'.

'You're a stomach?' he said. 'Are you poorly?'

Carly's frustration was rising. 'No, we're going to have a baby!' She repeated the sign for baby, cradling an imaginary infant in her arms and rocking it from side to side – this was a sign nobody could confuse.

'I know,' he said calmly. 'I saw the predictor stick when you came in. I'm deaf, not blind!' He chuckled and she whacked him on the shoulder. 'But it was dead funny watching you sign it in forty different ways!'

'Oooh! You git!'

He pulled her onto his lap. 'This is amazing, I'm ridiculously happy right now,' he said, nuzzling into her neck.

'Me too. Argh! We're going to be parents!' squealed Carly and she started to bounce again making the chair rock precariously.

'Argh!' said Fergus, copying her bounciness. 'Can you move the pissy stick off my accounts, please?' he asked as he cuddled her.

Carly was laughing as she stood up but when a thought struck her the smile slid from her face. 'Oh shit! This isn't good at all.'

'What's wrong?'

'My nan will know we've had sex before marriage!'

All Fergus could do was laugh.

Chapter Thirty-Nine

'Beginning of June?' screeched Beth into her mobile a bit louder than she intended. 'You're getting married in four weeks' time?'

'I know!' said Carly.

'Why would you put yourself through that stress? What's the big rush?' Although Beth was already feeling excited at the prospect.

'I simply can't be a fat bride,' said Carly calmly.

There was a momentary pause while Beth made the connection and screamed, 'Oh my God! You're pregnant!'

Carly and Beth exchanged squeals of delight then returned to normal volume. 'I can't believe it's happened and Fergus is as thrilled as me!'

'That's the best news ever, I'm over the moon for you both. You'll be amazing parents,' said Beth and a stray happy tear sploshed off her chin. 'You've made me cry now.'

'You soft sod!'

'How many weeks are you?' Beth blinked hard to try to stop the happy tears.

'Four and stop counting backwards, that's a very intrusive thing to do,' said Carly haughtily.

'Too late. You little minx, Fergus could only just have been out of hospital!'

'You're as bad as him, he keeps saying I took advantage of him in his weakened state.'

They both laughed. 'I am so happy for you, Carls.' Beth knew how important having children and being part of a family was to Carly and it filled Beth with happiness for her friend that her wishes were coming true.

'Thanks, and now it's full steam ahead on sorting out a wedding in beautiful Dumbleford for the first weekend in June.'

'Dumbleford? You're bonkers! How will you organize a wedding in four weeks at a venue that's a hundred miles away?' said Beth, but she was already working out the answer.

'With your help,' said Carly, her excitement palpable. 'I'll do most of it over the phone and on the internet.'

'Internet? You?'

'I'm getting better with my new phone apart from the fact when I type something it becomes something completely different.'

'Autocorrect,' said Beth but Carly wasn't listening.

'… and Fergus will help too.'

'There's still loads to organize though,' said Beth, already wondering how much of this madness would fall at her door. She didn't mean to be uncharitable but her aim was to get Willow Cottage finished in the next few weeks, not plan a wedding. She wanted to get it on the market by the end of June at the very latest in the hope that she could move in the school summer holidays and Leo could start at a new school at the beginning of the new term in September. She knew there were a lot of variables that could, and most likely would, impact on her plan but at least it was something she could aim for.

'So you'll help me?' asked Carly, her voice small and a tad pathetic.

'Of course I will!' said Beth. 'We'll make it the best wedding ever. What's our budget?' she asked, rapidly warming to the idea of spending someone else's money.

'Pretty much whatever we like, within reason,' said Carly, followed by a small squeal. 'Fergus has shown me his bank accounts and he's raking it in!'

'Excellent!' said Beth, metaphorically rubbing her hands together.

'It also means we can investigate buying a house. We need more room and a garden for when the baby arrives. But we're focusing on the wedding first.'

'Okay, you write out a list of what you want and we'll see what we can do. You know you'll have to compromise on some things?' Beth didn't like being the voice of caution but she felt it was better to manage expectations early.

'Beth, it's fine, I get it. The important thing is that I'm marrying Fergus Dooley and having his baby. We could get married in a shed for all I really care!'

'Now that level of compromise I like to hear. A shed I can definitely arrange!'

Beth opened her front door to Jack holding aloft a bottle of wine and a box of Maltesers. 'Supper?' he said and Doris trotted past him and into the cottage uninvited.

Beth smiled; she'd had a busy day preparing the hallway to be painted and had pretty much nothing at all to show for all her hard work as it looked exactly the same as when she started with the possible exception of the scuff marks from the sandpaper on the skirting boards.

'Hang on a second,' she said, trying hard not to be a party pooper. 'Does Petra know you're here?' The last thing she wanted was to upset her friend.

Jack screwed his face up in amused bewilderment. 'No, why?'

'Don't you think you should check?'

'Again. No and why?' said Jack, looking even more entertained.

Beth's shoulders sagged. 'I would hate her to get the wrong impression of our friendship.'

364

'Would you?' Jack was frowning over one eye, making him appear quite quizzical.

'Yes,' said Beth earnestly. 'I like Petra and I'd hate us to fall out if she did get the wrong idea.'

'Right,' said Jack slowly. 'What would be the wrong idea?'

'That we like each other … like that …' said Beth, feeling the colour rush to her cheeks and cursing her mother's genes for that particular family trait.

'Like what?' asked Jack, his mouth twitching mischievously.

Beth pushed her hair behind her ear, breathed in and held it for a moment while she thought how to answer without getting herself into a worse mess. 'Like more than friends that like each other's company.' She was rather pleased with her diplomatic response.

'And that would be an issue because … ?'

Beth's eyebrows shot up in alarm. Was he suggesting an affair? Her mind was a swirl of questions and her tummy was swirling with butterflies. 'Because it would be morally wrong and I couldn't betray Petra like that however much I might … or might not … I simply couldn't. I wouldn't. I'd feel awful.' She was pointing at him now and struggling with how to finish her monologue. 'And worse still would be if you guys split up.' She pointed her index fingers from herself to Jack.

'Split up,' repeated Jack, relaxing against the doorframe.

'Yes,' said Beth taking a deep breath.

'Me and Petra?'

'Yes.'

Jack's lopsided grin was mocking her. 'Petra's not my girl-friend.'

Beth was confused. 'But you stayed over … and she touches you … a lot.' She was thinking out loud. 'You're not together?'

'Nope.' Jack shook his head. 'We were once, very briefly, ages ago, but there wasn't that spark, you know?'

'Yes. Right. Okay.' She found she was nodding at him slowly while the information sunk in.

'Can I come in now, please?'

Beth blinked as if coming out of a trance. 'Of course, sorry.' She stepped out of the way, feeling like a prize idiot; her ears were now actually burning with embarrassment, but she was also feeling a tiny sense of relief too. 'That looks like my kind of supper,' she said, trying to distract herself by taking the wine and Maltesers from him and thinking that a few months ago she would have been mentally calculating the calories and sugar content.

'Sorry about the whole Petra thing. I could see you were close and I assumed … which I shouldn't have done,' continued Beth while Jack took off his hoody and stood in the kitchen doorway.

'It's okay, we are quite close I guess. She's not had it easy bringing Denis up on her own. It's tough being a single mum.'

'Don't I know it,' said Beth with empathy in her voice. 'But it must be harder being in a different country away from family and friends.'

'Yeah,' said Jack slowly. 'She came here to study. She was young and naive, which in a new country makes you vulnerable. She got badly hurt by someone …' Jack paused briefly. 'Petra's had more to endure than most but she's a fighter and I love that about her.'

'Me too,' agreed Beth, tipping the Maltesers into a patterned bowl and handing them to Jack. She got the feeling that there was a lot more to Petra's story but she wasn't going to pry.

She picked up two wine glasses and Jack followed her into the living room. 'Oh, I gave Carly your phone number, I hope you don't mind,' said Beth as the thought struck her. She passed Doris a dog treat, which she devoured in one gulp before settling herself in front of the sofa so that Beth had to climb over her to sit down.

'I know, she rang earlier,' said Jack. 'What's with the high-speed wedding planning? And why here?'

'I don't know exactly, apart from her being pregnant!' said Beth happily, pouring out the wine.

'Ahh, that explains it. Lovely news. Here's to baby GhastBlaster!' he said, raising his glass. 'Still not sure why it's in Dumbleford.'

'Once she gets her mind set on something, there's no swaying her.'

'I've been allocated cars, marquee management, and I'm introducing the readings in church but at least I get an invite to the wedding,' he said before taking a slow drink.

'You've got off lightly, I may have to delegate some of my tasks to you!'

'Hey, I've got a business to run.'

'I've got a cottage to finish,' said Beth, taking her drink and placing it on the windowsill.

Jack's light mood seemed to have changed. He patted Doris's flank but she didn't move. 'What are your plans once it's finished?' he said, his eyes still fixed on Doris.

'Put it up for sale, hope I make my money back plus a bit more and then buy the next place,' said Beth. 'Hopefully, second time will be easier.'

'Will it be around here?' He gave a glance in her direction. 'Because there's talk of the old gatehouse going up for sale. It was once attached to the manor house but—'

Beth could sense Jack's intentions so she cut in. 'I don't think that would be wise, Jack. What with Nick sniffing around the pub it's made me a bit jumpy and the plan was always to move on.'

'How many times do you think you can do that?' He was looking uneasy.

'As many as it takes.' She picked up her wine glass and took a sip. 'Nice wine, thanks.'

He nodded. 'At some point you will have to face whatever it is that you're running from.'

'I'm escaping, there's a difference. The film wasn't called *The Great Running Away*, now was it?' She was keen to lighten the increasingly heavy mood.

Jack shook his head. 'Better to face it head on, I think. Whatever or whoever it is will catch up with you sooner or later. Our demons always do.'

'Then I'll face them when it happens.' Beth was starting to feel slightly uncomfortable with the interrogation. 'Jeez, there must be something else we can talk about.'

Jack didn't answer.

'What about you, Jack? What troubles you?'

There was a long pause. 'Rebecca,' said Jack quietly, his focus on stroking Doris.

Beth pulled a face. 'The book?'

'No, my ex-girlfriend,' said Jack. Beth's eyes widened a little but she kept quiet. 'She was an alcoholic …' He took a slow and slightly juddering inward breath.

'Oh,' said Beth, surprised by the change of direction. Jack rarely shared anything personal.

Jack briefly smiled at her and returned his attention to Doris. 'I didn't know when we got together but it turned out she'd been fighting it for years and nobody knew … Once you've spotted the pattern it's obvious. She would get drunk and get into these rages.' He took a deep breath and leaned back into the sofa, his eyes skyward. 'She used to lash out and it was me that she directed her temper at.' He went quiet.

Beth gently squeezed his forearm. 'I'm really sorry, Jack, it must have been an awful time for you.'

'I couldn't understand why she was doing it but then you realize it's not them, it's the alcohol, the addiction. It's an illness.' He closed his eyes; it was clearly hard for him to share his story and Beth really felt for him.

'You don't have to tell me this,' said Beth gently.

'I want to. Nobody knows what it's like unless they've been through it. It's not just the physical scars, although I have plenty of them, it's the mental stuff.' He tapped his index finger against his temple. 'I felt weak for taking the blows time and time again

368

but what could I do? I was never going to hit back, although sometimes she wanted me to.' He pulled up the side of his T-shirt and Beth wondered for a moment what he was doing, then she saw the scar. A blob of crumpled red skin in a familiar shape.

Beth reached out to touch it but stopped herself, her fingers suspended inches away.

'I asked if I could help with the ironing,' said Jack with a sardonic laugh and Beth realized what the familiar shape was.

'She burned you with the iron?'

'Yep, that was probably the worst thing she did to me and it was also the last straw. There had been many broken ribs, a broken nose and wrist and I lost a couple of teeth and split my lip when she hit me with a chair.'

'A chair!' Beth was horrified.

'Funnily enough I could cope better with the physical abuse, it was the verbal stuff that got to me more. The constant put-downs and the blame. I felt useless for not being able to help her and worst of all I felt worthless.' He hung his head and Beth's heart went out to him.

'It wasn't your fault,' she said softly.

'I know,' he said, turning to look at her. 'But after a while, however strong you think you are, it seeps into your subconscious and you start to believe it. You start to take the blame. Even after we'd split up I couldn't shake off how it had made me feel. That's why I started the support group. I figured there might be some other poor sods out there like me and it turns out sadly that there are.'

'How long has it been?'

'Nearly two years. I still miss her. That's twisted, isn't it?' Beth shook her head but she was inclined to agree with him. He snorted, 'You know what? Her side of the wardrobe is still empty, exactly how she left it. I moved bedrooms but I still can't put anything in her space.'

Beth recalled the empty cupboard at his house that Carly had discovered. 'Are you waiting for her to come back?'

369

He shook his head. 'She's not coming back, and it wouldn't be right for either of us if she did.' He let out a sigh. 'I really must put stuff in that part of the wardrobe, it's daft.'

'I agree, storage space is a valuable commodity, you should utilize it,' said Beth, releasing her hold on his arm and giving it a pat instead.

Jack chuckled. 'Wise words indeed.'

'I know,' said Beth, finishing the rest of her glass of wine and immediately picking up the bottle to pour some more; she needed another drink after Jack had bared his soul. She knew too well what he'd been through.

He took a drink of the refreshed glass. 'What's your story? Is it something similar?'

She feared this was where the conversation was going to go. An *I'll show you mine if you show me yours* moment.

'I feel a bit of a fraud now you've told me all that. Nick only hit me once but it was the fact that he was about to hit Leo that made me leave.'

Jack looked shocked. 'I didn't realize. It explains why Leo was so scared.'

Beth tilted her head. 'Oh, when Nick turned up at the pub?'

Jack appeared slightly wrong-footed. 'Yeah, that's right.'

'That last day in London was the climax if you like, our whole relationship had been building up to that. It was a series of tiny doubts all coming together like droplets of water that eventually become a stream. Of course I didn't see it at the time. I feel such an idiot now, thinking back.' She gave a hollow laugh. 'He was controlling everything but he did it in such a way that it made me feel special … I sound ridiculous, don't I?' Beth felt an overwhelming sense of embarrassment at opening up to Jack but in a way she was confronting what she'd been through by voicing out loud what she'd been over and over many times in her head. She hadn't even told Carly all the details, mainly because it had taken her separation from Nick to work them out.

370

'You don't sound ridiculous. It's complicated when someone you love hurts you whether they mean to or not.'

'You know that's the thing,' said Beth, getting animated. 'I honestly don't think Nick meant to hurt me. It's the way he is. He has to control things and if those things don't want to be controlled that's when he gets bent out of shape. Argh! The times I felt bad for making him cross. It makes my blood boil that I took the blame for his behaviour!'

'Here,' said Jack, holding up a cushion. 'Give that a thump, you'll feel better.'

'Violence is not the answer,' said Beth, taking the cushion and playfully whacking him over the head with it.

'How's Leo about it all?'

'He noticed it first. I am such a bad mother …'

'Now you are being ridiculous. You're a great mum!'

'No, I was caught up in my career. I thought the job bought me babysitters and childminders but what it was really doing was forcing us apart. And that was what Nick wanted; he didn't want to share me with Leo and he never tried to connect with him. He even said he didn't want to replace Leo's dad and I thought he was making some gallant gesture!' She chuckled at her naivety. 'He was simply telling me straight. He shuffled Leo off to this private school with long days and extra lessons and after-school clubs and I went along with it. I thought it was about getting the best education for Leo, opening him up to new opportunities and experiences, but it was about putting a distance between us.'

It was Jack's turn to reach out a reassuring hand. He ever so tenderly placed his warm hand on top of Beth's and his fingers gently gripped hers. She looked up at him and smiled at the gesture. 'And the sad thing is that deep down somewhere I had an inkling about his motivations but I chose not to act on it. I was selfish because I had an attractive man who made me feel like the most special woman in the world. How shallow is that?'

'But you did see through it and I don't think there's any lasting damage where Leo's concerned.'

'I hope not,' said Beth, stretching out her legs, touching Doris with a toe in the process. Doris stretched and farted loudly. Jack and Beth started to giggle and the heavy mood was broken.

Chapter Forty

Seated in the tearoom on a drizzly Wednesday, and with the help of three cups of coffee, Beth and Rhonda appeared to have nailed the catering for the wedding. It had turned into a hard-nosed negotiation where Rhonda saw herself as the authority on buffet food and Beth needed to drag her away from all that was wrong with 1980s cuisine.

'So we're still a maybe on the vol-au-vents,' said Rhonda, checking her own list.

'No! No vol-au-vents,' said Beth, trying to keep hold of her remaining shred of patience. There had been a moment when she was tempted to tell Carly that they were going retro and it was an eighties-themed buffet; it would have been a whole lot easier.

'Any particular flavour for the crisps?' asked Rhonda. The crisps and nuts had been Beth's concession.

'A mixture, you choose,' said Beth, downing the last of her coffee and feeling a sense of achievement at completing one of the bigger items on the wedding to-do list. She stood up to leave. 'Let me know if you have any issues sourcing anything, okay?'

'It'll be fine, the cash 'n' carry is very good,' said Rhonda and

Beth looked taken aback. 'Ha, got you, only joking!' said Rhonda with a hoot of a laugh.

'Very funny,' said Beth, absent-mindedly rubbing her forehead.

'Are you still having problems after the carbon monoxide poisoning?' asked Rhonda, leaning in as if about to get a scoop on any ongoing health issues.

Beth was aware that it had been the most exciting thing to happen in Dumbleford since it was mentioned in the Domesday Book as 'Four villagers and two smallholdings'. 'No, I'm completely recovered, thanks.'

Rhonda started to shake her head. 'Jack was amazing that day. It was like something out of a film how he risked his own life to rescue you and rallied everyone despite being poisoned himself,' she said, her hand splayed across her chest when she spoke like she was taking some sort of oath.

'He did a great job,' conceded Beth. 'I dread to think what might have happened to me. Anyway, I best get going.'

'And Leo, of course. Anything could have happened to Leo, him running off like that. Jack was marvellous, he had virtually the whole village searching for him. Proper manhunt it was,' said Rhonda, now in full amateur dramatics mode. 'Anyway, how is Leo?' she asked, returning to normal again.

Very slowly Beth sat back down.

Nick slowed his pace but kept an eye on Carly as she walked along oblivious to his presence on the other side of the road. She was talking on her mobile; he wasn't close enough to hear what she was saying but she was beaming with happiness and he could see she was admiring something on her left hand. He couldn't be sure but it was possible she was wearing an engagement ring.

Nick wasn't stalking her, she just happened to be going the same way he was. He was rarely over this side of town but he liked the deli in Kentish Town and he was planning on picking up a few things from there. It had crossed his mind that he might bump into Carly or Fergus which, after his last encounter with them, didn't fill him with optimism, but he was now interested in the development in their relationship. A recent engagement would mean an engagement party. Perhaps Elizabeth would be back in London for that? Carly turned a corner and he had to cross the road, dodging the traffic to keep her in his sights.

Okay, now he had to concede that he was following her – the deli was in the other direction. There were not that many people about so he had to keep his distance or risk being spotted. When Carly crossed the road and checked over her shoulder he thought he had been rumbled but she was laughing when she reached the opposite pavement and she didn't show any signs of having seen him. He looked about him; he was pretty sure that Carly was now heading for the hairdresser's. He followed at a much slower pace. If she was going to the hairdresser's she would be in there for ages.

Nick toyed with the idea of waiting for Carly and asking her to go for a coffee but after their last meeting he feared she would decline and given Fergus's parting warning to him it would most likely be a fruitless excursion anyway. He turned the corner and could see the hairdresser's salon clearly with Carly inside hugging one of the staff. He leaned against a wall and watched for a bit while his mind wandered off to the deli and what he might choose when he got there.

Carly handed something over and the member of staff read it and started to jump up and down with Carly. It was like watching a children's television programme; Elizabeth's friends were all juvenile. Whatever it was they were both excited about it, so it was probably the engagement party. Nick's interest resumed and he watched the two of them closely. One more hug and double air kisses and Carly was heading for the door.

Nick slunk back round the corner and went into the first shop, which was a bookshop. He walked to the back and pretended to peruse the shelves.

'Hi, can I help you?' said a bright young man in his late teens.

'Er, yeah. Do you have anything for an unruly six-year-old boy?' he asked, pleased that the shop assistant was blocking him from being seen from the window and he watched over the young man's shoulder as Carly went past.

He left the bookshop and walked round to the hairdresser's. Through the glass he could see that what Carly had handed over had been an invitation of sorts and it was now pinned to a board behind the reception desk. He strolled inside and gave the receptionist a fleeting smile.

'Hi, my partner, Elizabeth Thurlow-Browne, comes here and I wanted to buy her the products she usually uses for a present but she's away on business and has taken them all with her. Would you be able to let me know what they are?' he asked. The young woman started to witter on excitedly about what a nice thing that was while he moved himself into a better position to view the invitation. It was a wedding invitation. He returned his attention briefly to the prattling woman.

'Money's no object but I want to get the right thing. You ladies are very particular about hair products.' He gave a conspiratorial chuckle and the woman started merrily tapping away on the computer. While she was busy printing him off a list he leaned over and managed to see some of the inside of the card.

Carly Wilson and Fergus Dooley request the pleasure of Danny & Greg at 1:30 p.m. on Saturday 3rd June at St Botolph's Church, Dumbleford.

He almost smiled but the thought of having to return to that village filled him with a sense of unease. It was far too close to Cheltenham for his liking. Nick tuned back in to the babbling female.

'The list is great, thanks. I'll take it home, have a peruse and get back to you, if that's okay?' he said, taking it from her and clutching it gratefully.

'Sure, bye,' said the woman and she watched Nick stride out of the shop smiling to himself.

Beth had already opened the door of Willow Cottage and stepped outside before Jack had been able to knock.

'Hiya, I was about to …' started Jack.

Beth nudged Jack back down the path and he went ahead of her. 'What's up?'

'When the hell were you planning on telling me that Leo had run away?'

Jack's jaw contracted; this was the moment he'd been dreading. 'He didn't exactly run away, he was with Ernie and—'

'Rhonda blabbed and Leo has told me the less dramatic version of events. He said he was petrified because Ernie had seen a man that sounded like Nick. Was it Nick?'

Jack shrugged. 'I don't know.' He wiped his hand across his lips. 'Beth, I am really sorry but the last thing I wanted to do at the time was worry you, what with you being ill in hospital and the boiler and everything.'

'He is my son. There is no excuse for not telling me when he goes missing!'

'To be fair when he first went missing you were unconscious, so technically …'

Jack realized his error when Beth's cheeks changed to a deep shade of red. 'You had no right to keep this from me for this long!'

Jack held up his hands in surrender. 'You are quite right. That bit was unforgivable. I'm truly sorry. But in my defence Leo was completely fine, he hadn't got himself injured or been kidnapped.'

Beth froze. 'Oh my God. You thought Nick had taken him. You actually thought he'd been kidnapped. Didn't you?'

Jack wasn't sure how he had painted himself into this particular corner and was even less sure how he could make Beth see that the bottom line was that Leo was unhurt by all of it.

'Honestly?' He tried to buy himself a moment's thinking time.

'Honestly,' said Beth, her hands now resting on her hips in full-on challenge mode.

Jack took a deep breath. 'A million and one scenarios went through my head that afternoon and, yes, the fact that someone, possibly Nick, may have taken him was one of the conceivable explanations,' he said, speaking in cautious bursts. Beth was shaking her head and grinding her teeth. Jack frowned but carried on. 'But this is Dumbleford and at the end of the day, nothing terrible happens here. With the exception of the WI fashion show.' He sniggered at his own joke but taking in Beth's steely expression he coughed and continued. 'We live in this safe little bubble.' He indicated a bubble shape with his hands.

'And one day some bad guy is gonna come along and burst it.' Beth took Doris's lead from Jack and led her up the path. Beth was shutting the door when Jack stepped forward and put a hand on it to stop her.

'Honestly, I was doing what I thought was best for everyone,' said Jack, his eyes conveying his regret. Beth paused for a moment, gave a cursory nod and closed the door.

Beth found she was able to paint at double-quick speed when she was still cross about something and had a deadline hanging over her. She had seen the estate agent and they had agreed that they would come round and take photos in three weeks' time. By then she needed to have pretty much everything sorted and anything that wasn't quite ready they simply wouldn't photograph. It would be on their website a few days after that, a sign would go up and the marketing would commence in earnest. She was on the downward slope of the renovation of Willow Cottage and she should have felt good about it but it was difficult because she was still using all her emotional energy to deal with Leo running away. It had been a shock to hear it from Rhonda and she couldn't help feeling that Jack was wrong to have kept it from her. Losing Leo was her worst nightmare. Keeping him safe was all that really mattered, and she kept repeating that in her mind.

She tried to turn her attention to the decorating; she had chosen a light but warm shade for the hall, stairs and landing and it was making the space look clean, fresh and welcoming. She had to admit that what had drawn her to the shade had been the name, not the actual colour, as it was called Pointing and it had reminded her of how little she had known when she had started this project and how much she had learned. She was on her knees doing the lower part of the wall and her hair was getting in the way. She put down her paintbrush, rolled her hair up and stuck it underneath her baseball cap with the peak facing backwards.

Doris sauntered over, sat next to Beth and leaned against her shoulder. Beth gave her a cuddle. She wasn't sure if Doris could sense it but Beth was already starting to feel sad about having to leave Dumbleford. She never thought she would feel that way but the people and the village and even this huge lolloping dog had wheedled their way into her heart and, however much she tried to deny it, she knew it was going to be a wrench to leave. But what choice did she have?

She eventually took a break and made herself a sandwich in the kitchen. After paying back Jack for the new boiler she had virtually no money left and the part-time work at the pub was barely enough to cover her bills. But she liked a thrown-together sandwich of leftovers and she had a good feeling about leftover bacon and peanut butter with jalapeños. She sat down at the small table and studied the floor while she ate. Ernie was right about the oak floorboards; they had almost returned to normal now that they were drying out. Beth turned her attention to her two to-do lists; one was headed up 'Willow Cottage the last leg' and the second 'Carly's wedding'. There was a lot on both lists and a glance at the calendar told her she was fast running out of time. She needed to come up with a much better plan than the one she currently had, which was to muddle on regardless. She went to the living room to get a pen to jot down some options and when she returned Doris was lying under the table, her big dark eyes full of guilt, and Beth's sandwich had gone.

Beth had been on the phone so long she thought her ear must have those funny little wrinkles you got on your fingers from being in the bath too long.

'... on top of the cake disaster I can't find a florist that is free and within a fifty-mile radius as apparently everyone in the Cotswolds is getting married that weekend!'

When Carly paused for breath Beth saw her opportunity. 'I've had an idea. Now listen before you dismiss it because it's not as bad as it sounds,' she began.

'Really selling it to me there, Beth,' said Carly with a small huff.

'The WI.'

'The Women's Institute! Are you having a laugh? My nan belongs to that! It's all curly perms and bitching about soggy bottoms!'

'Is that listening before you dismiss it?' said Beth, her voice going all schoolteachery, and she acknowledged she had a bit of a habit of doing that.

'No,' said Carly, sounding like a sulky teenager.

'Right. Petra is a member of the local WI ...'

'Petra!'

'Ahem!' Beth coughed her annoyance at the interruption.

'Sorry,' said Carly.

'Yes, Petra is a member. It had a revamp not long ago when they brought two WI groups together so it covers a few villages and hamlets.' Carly groaned on the other end but Beth ignored her. 'It's a real mix of ages: mums from school, people who work, some who are retired, and the one thing they have in common is that along with embracing all that is good about the WI and its pledge to educate women they mainly drink wine and eat cake.' Beth was happy with her summary. She had been along once with Petra and she would have gone more often but even going halves on a babysitter was a cost she couldn't stretch to right now.

'Okay, but how exactly does that help me?'

'The WI has lots of women with lots of skills and links to lots of local businesses. I know that Petra does favours for the other members and I'm wondering if we could tap into that. I'm sure at the very least they could whip up a lovely Vicky sponge,' said Beth with a chuckle.

'Bloody hell! I want more than a soggy-bottomed Victoria sandwich for my wedding cake!' said Carly but at least she was laughing too.

'So shall I ask the WI?'

'Nothing to lose,' said Carly. 'See if any of them do flower arranging too.'

'I will, good idea!'

Chloe, Petra's barmaid, had a sister who was a very responsible sixteen-year-old, although Beth feared that was an unlikely combination. Anyway she had been persuaded to leave Leo, along with Denis, in the girl's care in exchange for free-flowing fizzy drinks and crisps, on the strict instructions that she call immediately there were any problems. Jack had offered to take them climbing but Jack was still in Beth's bad books and she wasn't ready to swallow her fatty lump of pride just yet.

And if Beth wanted the help of the WI the least she could do was turn up to one of their meetings and ask her favours face to face. Beth had a jacket on, another charity-shop find that she had become rather attached to, and a mulberry flat cap although even for a May evening it was definitely starting to warm up.

They walked up the hill to the church hall that sat firmly

between Dumbleford and Henbourne-on-the-Hill and Beth took a proper look at the church for the first time. It was really rather pretty in neatly cut Cotswold stone with a square tower that was topped by an unusual pitched roof. Beth hadn't taken much notice of the church but now she was keen to get a look inside.

'Come on!' said Petra, trudging up to the church hall, which was a little further on and itself a more modern conservative building. When they opened the doors the noise struck Beth; a lot of high-pitched chatter was emanating from inside. She followed Petra in and paid her money to attend as Petra's guest and dutifully bought a raffle ticket although she had no idea what the prize was and didn't like to ask. Petra headed to the hatch through to the kitchen area where wine glasses were rowed up. The bright lights were momentarily blocked when Maureen appeared on the other side of the hatch. Beth looked at her for a moment, studying her expression. She was almost expecting her to growl.

'Two glasses of white wine, please,' asked Beth, handing over a note.

Maureen poured out the drinks, handed back the change and pointed to a tray of gooey brownies. 'Help yourself,' she said with what Beth hoped was a smile but it was hard to tell with Maureen. Beth smiled back, scooped up two brownies and handed them to Petra while she carried the wine glasses.

Seats were all set out round the room. They found a couple of free ones and sat down. The brownies soon disappeared and after a good mouthful of wine Beth's taste buds had returned to normal. She was about to ask, *What happens next?* when a woman in her thirties with short dark hair stood up and clapped her hands. The noise level reduced and she began to speak. 'Good evening, ladies, tonight is Strictly WI and we are learning salsa ...'

Beth wasn't sure what was said after that because she was having some sort of panic attack. She had come along to ask for some help with cakes and flowers. What was going on?

Despite her protestations Beth found herself flung, literally, into learning some basic salsa steps and an hour went past at lightning speed. She was on her second glass of wine, laughing along with some other women of a similar age, when Petra tapped her on the shoulder and she followed her to the front of the room.

'Ladies, this is my friend Beth. She is new to Dumbleford and the WI but she learns fast,' said Petra, pointing at the wine glass, and a small cheer went up. 'She is helping organize her friend's wedding here at St Botolph's Church and she needs our help.' Petra stepped back and gestured for Beth to continue.

Beth cleared her throat. 'Thanks, everyone. It's my friend Carly and she's getting married on the first Saturday in June which is three weeks away and surprise, surprise all the key things we need we can't have because they're already booked up. I'm in desperate need of people to help with flowers for the bride, the church and table centres, a cake and hang on …' She took a folded list out of her jeans pocket. 'Chairs and tables for inside the marquee, photographer, butterflies – she wants to release some as she comes out of the church, a band … actually, no, don't worry about that one,' said Beth, realizing that that was one of the things she really should keep a tight rein on, but the ladies of the WI were already chattering away. 'Anyway, if anyone can help with anything you usually have at a wedding, please let me know. Oh and of course the happy couple are going to pay you.' This last piece of information seemed to send the volume back up again. Beth sipped her wine and waited.

As she had hoped women started coming over and introducing themselves and she ended up jotting down her mobile number on several serviettes. When it was time to go Beth was feeling very pleased with herself and she handed over her empty wine glass to Maureen with a smile. 'I'll do the cake,' said Maureen. It sounded very much like a statement of fact rather than an offer.

Beth was still taken aback by the gruffness of Maureen's voice even after all these months. 'That would be terrific, Maureen, thank you. There was another lady … Barbara, I think it was, that said she could decorate the cake but wasn't a confident baker. Could you two work together do you think?' Beth was feeling very brave after all the wine.

Maureen shrugged and took the wine glass to the sink. She wasn't sure if that was a yes but Beth didn't like to question her further.

Chapter Forty-One

One minute Beth was glossing the skirting boards and the next she was looking at a very elderly man's photos of his partially bald parrot.

'And here's one of him on top of his cage ... and this is the new road sign they put up. Is that one blurry? It could be my eyes, you see I'm waiting for a cataract operation ...'

Beth failed to stifle a yawn. 'Have you ever photographed a wedding?' she asked, already nodding her head more in hope than anything else.

The old man copied the head-nodding. 'Yes. I took snaps at my grandson's wedding last summer.'

'Great, have you got any of those?' Beth tried hard to muster some enthusiasm.

'Not had the film developed yet because there's still a couple to take on there but I could pop them round when I have if you like?' Film! When was the last time anyone used that? Beth was thinking that the poor old soul might curl up his toes before he got to the end of his camera film.

This was going to have to be a 'no', it wasn't even a 'maybe in case we get desperate', and Beth wasn't good at this sort of thing. 'Thank you for coming round and showing me your photos,' she said and the old man sat up straight making it all the harder to let him down. 'They were lovely and very interesting but I really think we need someone with a digital camera because my friend lives in London and she'll want the photos emailed to her. I'm really sorry.'

'That's okay, lovey, it was nice to see what you've done to old Wilf's place. I would have knocked it down myself but you've clearly worked very hard and it's looking grand.'

Beth was surprised by how much the kind words meant to her. She *had* worked hard and it was lovely for someone that knew Wilf to give her their seal of approval. 'Thanks, there's been a lot to do,' she said, showing him to the door.

'Yes, but you've made yourself a cosy home here and that's something to be proud of. Cheerio,' he said and he shuffled out into the May sunshine.

With just over two weeks to go until Carly's wedding Beth's living room was full to bursting with her amassed gang of wedding helpers. She laid the mobile phone on the arm of the sofa while everyone shuffled forward in their seats. 'Can you hear me, Carly?' she asked.

'Loud and clear,' came the reply from the carefully balanced phone.

'Great. We need to take it in turns to speak because she won't be able to hear us if we all speak at once, okay?' said Beth and everyone nodded, which meant they'd understood but wasn't very helpful to Carly on the other end of the line.

'Right, my update is that I think I've found a bridesmaid's dress for you, Beth,' said Carly, followed by a small squeak of delight. 'I'll send you a photo when I've worked out how to do that, all right?'

'Great.' Beth was wondering how they were going to check it fitted ahead of the wedding, but she simply added it to the already very long list on her lap. 'Maureen and Barbara, let's have a cake update,' she said.

'Too early to bake a sponge,' said Maureen.

'I've been making rose petals all week,' declared Barbara, clapping her hands together and leaving them there as if in prayer. 'I've discovered how to make gerberas and I'm having a go at those this week!' Barbara looked excited at the prospect; Maureen rolled her eyes and huffed. Beth nodded encouragingly at them both.

'Jack, how about you?'

He put his fingers together in a steeple and pursed his lips. Beth felt tension in her shoulders. 'I can't get a big marquee, I've tried everywhere and there's nothing available …' There was a gasp from the phone, which was helpful because it reminded Beth that Carly was still there. 'Sooo I spoke to this guy I know and he hires tents and yurts for festivals; glamping, that sort of thing, and he had a festival booking for that weekend but they've let him down saying they hadn't pre-sold enough tents.' Jack noticed the glazed expressions around him and the silent phone. 'Anyway I thought perhaps we could link a load of tents together, what do you think?' Belatedly he pointed at the phone and the eyes in the room moved in the same direction.

'Really, there's nothing else?' asked Carly, her voice almost a whimper.

'I think it could be really cool and different, in a good way,' said Beth, looking at Jack, who nodded earnestly. 'Could we string up bunting and fairy lights?' Beth asked.

'I can make bunting. It's really easy with a sewing machine and I always keep spare bits of material,' said one lady and a chorus of 'me too' followed.

There was a small but positive disembodied voice from the phone. 'I like bunting and fairy lights.'

'Sure, we can make it fabulous, Carly. Trust me?' said Jack, leaning forward and addressing the phone directly.

'Okay,' came the same small voice.

'Great. My other thing is cars and I'm … um, still sorting that one out,' said Jack before mouthing to Beth, 'It's not good. I'll talk to you later.' Beth gave him a look that she hoped conveyed that she would reluctantly speak to him. She knew she was punishing Jack for far too long over not telling her about Leo's disappearance but keeping Jack at a distance seemed the sensible thing to do, especially when she would hopefully be moving out of Dumbleford very soon, and Jack was a potential complication she could do without.

One of the ladies on the sofa glanced up from her mobile phone. 'I've got WI Craft Club onto the bunting, they'll keep making yards of it out of scraps until we tell them to stop,' she said, looking rather pleased with herself.

'Scraps!' came an alarmed squeak from the mobile phone.

Chloe stood up. 'I need to get back to the pub but my boyfriend has the videoing all covered. He's borrowing some state-of-the-art camera from college, which is all above board before you ask,' she said, tipping her head in Petra's direction. 'And he's going to wear a GoPro; that way you'll get some really cool angled stuff too that he'll edit in afterwards.'

'GoPro?' came the flabbergasted voice from the phone. 'This is a wedding, not an extreme sport!'

'It is when you try to arrange it in four weeks,' said Beth coolly into the phone. 'Right, moving on to …' She checked her sheet and scrutinized the four women huddled on one sofa. 'Sally, Kath, Donna, Julia and the flowers.'

Flowers seemed to be all over the place with each of the four ladies having their own ideas about bouquets and church flowers and none of them fitting particularly well with Carly's thoughts of simple, pretty and scented. Ernie seemed to lose interest at this point and left and Beth vowed to find something that he could get involved in.

Next up were Rhonda and Petra who between them had the catering and drinks all sewn up.

'If we're having tents how about a Boy Scout campfire theme, hot dogs, sausages, chipolatas, that sort of thing?' suggested Rhonda, nodding her head excitedly, and there were murmurs of agreement in the room.

'God, no!' said Carly. 'We're vegetarians!'

'Oh,' said Rhonda, instantly dispirited. 'Not even little vegetarian cocktail sausages?'

'No!' Carly was obviously close to the mouthpiece because it came out as a shout and everyone jumped. She sounded like she was in full-on bridezilla mode now.

Beth picked up the phone and took it off loudspeaker. 'Hang on a mo,' she said, leaving the room, and the buzz of disgruntled chatter rose behind her.

'Carls, come on, these people are doing you a huge favour …'

'But I don't want favours, I want the perfect wedding, well, as near perfect as we can get in four weeks. I am seriously compromising here already,' said Carly, sounding quite rational. 'Rehabilitated festival tents, scraps for bunting and a GoPro video,' she added to emphasize her point. Someone knocked at the door and Beth headed in that direction but still speaking to Carly as she went.

'I know,' said Beth, 'and it will be perfect. Perhaps you need to use a bit of imagination.'

She opened the door to Ernie. 'Shirley's got a camera and car,' he said loudly and she had to move the phone away from her ear when Carly let out a frustrated shriek.

Beth had just dropped Leo at the pub so she could go to her evening class when Jack intercepted her heading for the moped. 'Hiya, Beth. Did you want a lift to college?'

389

'Thanks, but I'm fine,' said Beth, keeping it civil but not over-friendly.

'Oh, come on. I wanted to talk to you about the wedding and if I'm going to college too ...' Beth turned to look at him. He was wearing dark fitted jeans and a black T-shirt and he'd shaved, which was a change from his often rough stubbly appearance that she quite liked. 'It's not good for the environment, two vehicles doing the same trip,' he said, followed by his usual lopsided smile. Beth felt herself smiling in response and stopped herself. What was it about Jack that made her want to smile?

'You're right,' she said. 'I hate it that you are right, by the way,' she added, walking past him and over to where his car was parked on the edge of the green. The trees had scattered their blossom all over it as if there had already been a wedding.

Beth liked the longer days and she watched the ducks having a bath in the ford as Jack joined her and unlocked the car. The first couple of minutes of the journey they sat in silence and Beth was for the first time thinking how close you were to someone when you were in a car and how nice Jack smelled. It was a mingling of freshly washed man and aftershave and it was making her stomach tighten. She chuckled to herself.

'What?' asked Jack.

'I had a text from Carly earlier. She's struggling with autocorrect.'

'Was it a howler?'

'Totally. She doesn't like the smell of the new colon Fergus has bought for the wedding and his shit doesn't go with his tie!' Beth spluttered out the last few words as both she and Jack dissolved into giggles. She took out a mint to take her mind off the close proximity of Jack. 'Want one?' she said, offering the packet under his nose.

'Please could you get one out for me?'

'Sure.' Beth eased the mint out of the wrapper and was about to pass it to Jack but instead of holding out a hand to take it from her he opened his mouth. Beth felt her spine go rigid. *He wanted her to put the mint in his mouth,* which suddenly felt like a very intimate thing to do. Stop being an idiot, it's a sweet, thought Beth crossly and she quickly threw the mint between Jack's parted lips.

'Aw,' said Jack, 'you hit my tooth!' He laughed.

'Sorry,' said Beth, feeling like her awkward teenage self.

'Wedding cars.'

'Yes, where are you with those?' asked Beth, thankful for the conversation to distract her.

'We don't have any.'

'Jack! We are running out of time. Actually, we've run out of time, the wedding is in eight days.'

'I've been thinking, I could put some ribbon on my car and take Fergus and his best man to the church. What was the best man's name again?'

'Budgie,' said Beth. She was frowning as she waited for the punchline that didn't come.

'And for the bride how about a quintessentially English vintage vehicle?'

'From where?' asked Beth, her voice full of suspicion.

Jack glanced at her with a huge grin. 'Shirley's Morris Minor!'

'Bloody hell, no! Carly will kill me!'

'No, she won't, think about it. It's a beautifully kept classic car.' He glanced across at Beth's crumpled face, which showed she was far from convinced. 'Now try to picture it without Shirley at the wheel.'

Beth felt a small amount of fear diminish. 'Who would drive it?'

'Simon says he will and I've found a chauffeur's hat on eBay for three quid to make him look the part.' Jack sounded very pleased with himself. He gave another brief head-turn in Beth's direction and something in his eyes made her want to kiss him.

Pull yourself together, she told herself.

'Okay, not sure about the cheap hat but at least we should get there in one piece if Simon is driving. And you're right, it is a lovely little car, even if it does smell of vinegar,' she conceded and she opened the window to let in some cool air.

'Is that a yes?' asked Jack, his face looking younger somehow since he'd shaved.

'Go on then, but I'm not telling Carly. We'll just show her when she gets here. Because I think if she sees the car she'll love it too.' She was smiling now, there was no way to quell it any longer. She was happier when she was with Jack. There was something about him that switched on something inside her and made her sparkle.

'Brilliant. Now can we talk about toilets?' asked Jack and the moment was gone.

They were outside college still discussing where to place the temporary toilets that came with the tents the yurt hire company were supplying when Tollek arrived and walked over to them. They paused their conversation. 'Good evening, Beth. Hello, I'm Tollek,' he said, offering his hand to Jack.

'I'm Jack. I've seen you in the canteen at break and Beth showed me your spindles, they look amazing.'

Beth suppressed the silly urge to giggle but it did sound a little like a euphemism. 'I can't take credit, she is a natural. I am simply a guide,' said Tollek.

'Ooh, before I forget are there any photography classes on here?' asked Beth, having had the flash of inspiration that perhaps there would be someone who might make a suitable trainee wedding photographer.

'No, we run day courses in photography but I am a photography enthusiast, I'd be happy to answer any questions,' said Tollek with an innocent smile.

Beth and Jack stared at each other, their eyes wide with glee as they both turned to face Tollek, who looked slightly unnerved.

* * *

392

A week later Beth opened the door to an almost pale-green Carly who dashed past her and up the stairs to the bathroom while Fergus lugged in three large cases and two suit carriers.

'Morning sickness that lasts most of the day,' he said, nodding towards the stairs. 'Anyway, hello, fabulous wedding coordinator and bridesmaid, how are you?'

'A bit stressed out but otherwise okay. It's good to see you looking better,' said Beth, pulling him into a hug. The memory of his pale figure lying in a hospital bed a few weeks ago still vivid in her mind. 'That's a whole lotta luggage you've got there!'

'Wedding,' he said, pointing at the suit carriers. 'Honeymoon,' he pointed at the two largest cases, 'and stuff for the next couple of days,' he said, pointing at the last case.

Beth peered behind him. 'I thought your best man was coming with you?'

'Budgie has gone straight to the B&B; he was on the night shift so he's knackered. He'll be right for the rehearsal though.' Fergus stepped into the hall. Beth paused for a moment when she saw the estate agent's car pull up outside. He got out and waved.

'Okay if I put the sign up now?' he called.

Beth swallowed hard. The estate agent had been round yesterday and taken the photos; he'd gone on a lot about the impact the ancient bathroom would have on the price but there was nothing she could do about that now. And here he was knocking in the For Sale sign. Leaving Willow Cottage had suddenly got very real.

'The cottage is looking terrific,' said Fergus behind her. 'Does it have a ghost? That could be a great selling point.'

Beth retreated into the cottage and shut the front door.

'Thanks, and no, there's definitely no ghost.' They heard the toilet flush upstairs and Carly reappeared looking very ghostlike and far from the epitome of the blushing bride. 'You look …' started Beth and with a tilt of her head Carly willed her to lie to her … 'like shit,' finished Beth and Carly started to laugh.

'I feel it too,' she said as they hugged each other. 'Why aren't the tents up on the village green yet? Will the flowers be wilting if they start making them today? Have you checked if this photographer is any good? And what's happening with the cars?'

'Whoa!' said Beth. 'Champagne and elderflower fizz first then we'll talk about the wedding but it's all under control. Please relax and enjoy it.'

'To be honest, it's a bit late now anyway,' said Fergus with his usual relaxed shrug and before Carly could start to protest again he pulled her into a hug and she visibly relaxed in his arms. Beth watched them for a second – *that* was what she wanted, someone who took all the stress away, who put things in perspective and had you at the top of their list. She let out a sigh and tried hard to dispel the image of Jack that had popped into her mind.

They were clinking glasses and Carly was eyeing her sparkling elderflower with a resigned frown when Jack appeared at the window. Fergus jumped up and went to greet him at the door like an old friend. There was lots of mutual male adoration before Jack came inside.

'Could you get another glass for Jack, please?' asked Fergus, lifting up the champagne bottle.

'Hiya, Carly, you look … well,' he lied. Carly and Beth exchanged looks and Beth went to get a glass for Jack. 'I just needed a quick word with Beth about tomorrow.'

'Is there a problem?' asked Carly, sounding anxious.

'No! Heavens, no. Everything is completely fine,' said Jack, his eyes darting about. He picked up the nearest cushion and plumped it vigorously.

Beth returned and along with the others watched Jack self-consciously return the cushion to the sofa. He took the proffered champagne glass, which Beth filled while mouthing, 'What's up?' Jack gave a twitch of his head. Beth was feeling uneasy.

'Happy wedding eve,' said Jack, raising his glass, and he glanced at Beth and mouthed 'cake wars'. Beth shook her head at him because Fergus was watching and if he was watching he was lip-reading.

'What was it you needed to speak to Beth about?' asked Fergus, looking mildly amused as he took a long slow sip of his champagne.

'Ah,' Jack faltered and his eyes darted between the two worried women surveying him. 'Well, the thing is …' His expression changed when he appeared to have a flash of inspiration. Beth found she was holding her breath and willing him not to announce a disaster at this, the eleventh hour. 'The thing is, Beth and I wanted to let you know that the wedding car is sorted. It is something that we –', he stepped closer to Beth and she felt his arm brush hers making the hairs on her body stand to attention, 'have arranged as our wedding present to you.'

'How lovely,' said Carly, taking Fergus's hand and squeezing it tightly.

'And because it's a present, you don't get to see it until tomorrow,' said Jack, taking a welcome slug of champagne.

'It's a surprise,' said Beth and she indicated to Jack that they should speak outside.

'That's really good of you,' said Fergus, kissing Beth and shaking Jack's hand, but worryingly for Beth he still had that faintly amused expression on his face.

'Jack, can you come and have a look at my back door, it's sticking a bit,' she lied as she took him by the elbow and steered him out of the living room, through the house and into the back garden, shutting the perfectly good stable door behind her.

'Don't mouth things in front of Fergus, he lip-reads. Did you say cake wars?' said Beth, trying to keep her voice down although the adrenalin was taking control, making it quite difficult.

Jack nodded. 'I've come straight from the tearoom. Maureen and Barbara were having a stand-up row about how to decorate the cake.'

'Right,' said Beth, already feeling relieved that there was a cake. 'Do they need me to make a decision or something?'

'Barbara's made all the flowers out of icing and wants gerberas on top, Maureen wants them cascading. Barbara wants roses round the base, Maureen hates roses and doesn't want them spoiling the cake she's spent hours making.' Beth looked bored and waved a hand to hurry him along while she gave a quick peek into the kitchen to check they hadn't been followed. 'So anyway, Barbara almost shoved a rose up Maureen's nostril, Maureen flicked it on the floor and it got trodden on. Barbara cried.'

Jack winced at the memory and Beth made a noise as she took a very sharp intake of breath. 'You're right, it's cake wars,' she said in a low voice.

'I know. I left Rhonda comforting Barbara while Maureen was knocking back a large espresso. What do we do?' asked a troubled-looking Jack.

'You stay here, talk *Minecraft* to Fergus and tents to Carly. I'll sneak off and sort it out. Okay?'

'Okay,' said Jack as Beth stepped away towards the side entry. He reached out and caught her fingers, stopping her in her tracks.

Beth turned and stared at Jack; his fingers were gripping the tips of her own – they were almost holding hands.

'Thanks, Beth. You're amazing,' he said.

Beth's pulse quickened and she suddenly felt very warm. 'Thanks. You're not all bad yourself.' She smiled and he chuckled, letting her hand slip from his own before she disappeared down the side of the cottage feeling a lot happier than she had in a while.

Chapter Forty-Two

With cake wars calmed to a cold war of stares and a cake beautifully decorated with brightly coloured cascading gerberas and the odd rosebud dotted around the base, Beth was pleased to be walking back into the cottage.

'That's my cue to leave,' said Jack, shaking Fergus's hand. He reached Beth at the door and put an arm around her shoulders, making her emit a tiny gasp. 'How did it go?' he speed-whispered into her hair.

'Fine, all sorted. How about here?'

'Great,' said Jack, kissing Beth on the cheek and releasing his grip. 'I'll see you later at rehearsals.' She opened the door for him and he turned round and put his hands together as if in prayer and mouthed 'thank you'. Beth couldn't help grinning as she shut the door.

'Shit! Shit! And triple shit!' shouted Carly from upstairs and Beth ran to investigate, closely followed by Fergus who must have sensed there was something wrong when Beth shot upstairs. Carly was sat on the bed, tears streaming down her face and a pair of shoes on her lap.

'What's the matter?' said Beth, flopping down onto the bed next to her. 'Oh, I see,' she said, spotting the problem with the once very pretty suede shoes with a silk ribbon bow. She peered a bit closer. 'What colour is that exactly?' asked Beth, pointing at the blue nail varnish that was dripping off the shoe having covered one side of one and the tip of the other – it had turned the previously pale ivory shoes into a hideous two-tone affair.

'Frisky Freeze,' said Carly with a sniff and Beth handed her a tissue from the box on the side.

'At least it's sparkly,' said Fergus from the doorway.

'Get out! It's bad luck to see anything before the day!' said Carly and she started to cry again.

'Sorry,' signed Beth. Fergus shrugged and left her to it.

'It's not his fault,' said Beth, taking the shoes from Carly.

'No, but …' She sniffed again. 'They're ruined and now I've got nothing to wear. They were the perfect height for the dress and I've been breaking them in for two weeks.'

'Yep, definitely ruined. If there's nothing to lose will you let me try something?' said Beth, studying the worst of the shoes closely.

Carly shrugged, emitted a sniff and a reluctant 'Okay'.

They were about to leave for the church rehearsal when Beth emerged from the kitchen.

Carly came off the phone. 'That was my uncle. Him, my aunt, cousins and my nan are all settled in Tewkesbury and looking forward to tomorrow and they've seen two minibuses arrive and boxes of wine being unloaded so the Dooleys have landed too!'

'Great, do you want to see what I've done?' asked Beth as she presented Carly with the bridal shoes on a tea tray. 'Now, don't touch 'cause they're not dry yet but how do these grab you?' Beth smiled at Carly and her eyebrows danced.

Carly stared at the shoes, lifted them up and scrutinized them at close range. The shoes now had a spiralling sequin and crystal design that came along the sides and finished across the toe and was identical on both shoes. 'How did you do that?'

'Got the worst of the nail varnish off with remover but it had stained so I got to work with the glue gun and the sparkly stuff I had left over from making Christmas gifts.' Unless you peered very closely you couldn't see any of the demon nail varnish and even then it wasn't obvious.

'Verdict?' said Beth, feeling a little apprehensive because Carly was still inspecting the shoes.

'I love them and I love you. You are totally brilliant,' she said and she started to cry again. Beth figured the baby hormones were getting to Carly at the moment.

'Great, that's another crisis sorted. Let's get to the rehearsal,' said Beth, putting on her shoes.

'What do you mean, "another" crisis?' questioned Carly, her face contorting.

'Oh, nothing. Come on!'

Apart from Carly having to leave twice due to the all-day morning sickness the rehearsal went okay. Leo got very bored very quickly with his job of ring bearer but hopefully he'd be okay tomorrow when he was needed to stand still and stop letting go of the ring cushion to scratch his head every few minutes. They had confirmed the hymns and Carly had given Beth a crash course in how to sign the words to 'Amazing Grace', which was more than a challenge, but she'd give it a go for Fergus's deaf friends that would be attending.

Shirley was in the church supervising the flower arrangements that were arriving like a floral relay race every few minutes as the ladies of the WI dropped them off. Shirley had sidled over to Carly like the worst spy in the west, checked the coast was clear and boomed, 'Are you up the duff?'

Carly pulled all kinds of embarrassed 'how could you even think that' faces while Fergus answered, 'Yeah, shotgun!' And got a swift elbow in the ribs from Carly. Shirley had gone back to her flower arranging giggling away to herself.

By the time they left the church the scent of freesias and stocks filled the air and pretty posies, all slightly different, were tied with ivory silk ribbon and fixed to the end of the pews, with two large cascading arrangements placed at the front of the church. It looked and smelled fabulous and Carly seemed happy apart from when she had to say goodbye to Fergus, who was spending the night at the Bleeding Bear and was very excited about the impromptu stag do that Jack, Simon and Budgie were throwing with Petra's help.

The last visitor of the day had been Shirley with some apple cider vinegar and instructions that Carly add one teaspoon to a half-pint of water and sip it. Carly decided to give it a go because she was at the point of being willing to try anything to stop the dreaded sickness that was threatening to turn her wedding day into a vomitfest.

There was no more Beth could do now but try to get a good night's sleep. Carly had sent Fergus a final text telling him she lived him very mush and that she'd see him tomato – Beth wondered if Carly would ever get the hang of her new phone.

Carly was already tucked up in bed and sleeping peacefully when Beth tiptoed through the cottage. As she switched off the light on the landing she turned towards her own bedroom door to see floating in front of her a headless woman in white. Beth's scream was involuntary and a louder noise than she thought she was capable of making. The shock made her fumble for the light switch. In those few moments all the times Leo had asked her about a ghost shot through her mind. Mid-scream realization dawned.

An alarmed-looking Carly appeared on the landing, her face almost as pale as her wedding dress that hung resplendent from the doorframe. They both stared at it.

'Whoops!' said Beth, feeling like a proper idiot. 'Not a ghost after all. Sorry. Night, night.' And she scuttled into the bedroom with the sound of Carly's groans echoing behind her.

* * *

The wedding day dawned in a perfect Dumbleford style with the dawn chorus and sunshine streaming in through the gaps around the blinds. Beth yawned and stretched. She rolled over and squinted through the window. It was early and already the sunshine was bouncing off the roof tiles and making the dewy grass sparkle. The still sky was a Disney blue apart from the rippled striations of pure white cloud that had been expertly painted on. She wasn't that familiar with the view out of Leo's window; the fields were all distinctive, each one growing something different – the grooved brown of fields nursing crops about to sprout, the cheerful yellow of rapeseed and the varying shades of grass dotted with lambs all across the rolling hills that tumbled out of sight, making her smile. It was going to be a beautiful day.

Beth blinked; she didn't have to get up yet. Having a pregnant bride at least meant that neither of the ladies were waking up with a hangover. Petra had been a star by having Leo overnight to keep the sleeping arrangements at Willow Cottage nice and simple. Beth was in Leo's room and Carly had her room because it was decorated and there was no step to trip over on the way to the bathroom. Beth hadn't slept that well with all the arrangements that had been popping up in her mind as if needing her to make one last mental check on each of them but she was stirred fully awake by a text message arriving on her mobile. It was from Petra.

Boys have nice

Beth squinted at it and smiled. Petra's English was first-rate but there were odd occasions when she got things slightly wrong that meant you could tell it wasn't her first language. A second message arrived.

Bloody autocorrect. LICE the boys have LICE!

Beth sat bolt upright in bed and rang Petra. As she held the phone in one hand she was already scratching her head with the other one. Petra answered immediately. 'Lice?' said Beth, dispensing with any greeting.

'Yes, I thought they were messing about but I have checked and they are both walking head lice nests. I have soaked them in olive oil ...'

'Olive oil?' Beth had no idea where this was going.

'It stops the lice breathing and when they are dead I will comb them out. But I have the lice too and I wondered about you?'

Beth hadn't realized she was scratching her head again. 'Bugger. I think I might. The hairdresser is due here in a couple of hours. He will freak out!'

'Come over now and we sort out each other,' suggested Petra and while Beth really wished she had a better idea at seven in the morning she simply didn't. 'Okay, give me five minutes.' She was now seriously worried about Danny the hairdresser finding a nit on her or Carly because she had heard the stories of him stopping mid-haircut and refusing to continue when he'd found lice in someone's hair once and that was the last thing they needed today.

After leaving a note for Carly, a few minutes later Beth found herself sitting on the floor of Petra's bathroom with her head tilted back over the bath, her scalp dripping with olive oil. Denis and Leo had already been treated and were in the living room with their oil-doused heads covered by shower caps.

Petra was sitting next to her, humming. 'Why are you all jolly?' asked Beth.

'I'm not sure,' said Petra, moving her eyes in Beth's direction but keeping her head still. 'It is a beautiful morning, there will be a wedding in the village and a party on the green. And above all my boy is happy, even with the nits.'

'You are funny,' said Beth. Petra definitely knew how to give you perspective on things. 'Not everyone gets the mother and son bond, do they?'

'We are indestructible. Whatever life throws at us, we can fight it because we have each other. Denis was my greatest heartache and my greatest prize.' Petra swallowed hard.

'Heartache?' asked Beth tentatively, not moving her head – to make eye contact would have changed the intensity of the moment.

Petra let out a long breath and it whistled through her teeth. 'Perhaps one day I will explain, my friend, but today is for love and happiness …'

Beth got the message and needed to lighten the mood. 'And nits! How long do we have to stay like this?' she asked.

'We don't, we can put on the shower caps but it does leak a little. Either way the nits die within a few hours.'

'Hours? We don't have hours!' Beth felt panic rapidly rising.

'Calm down. We have a metal comb and we can comb out most of the lice and next week we do it again because the eggs will have hatched by then,' explained Petra in a matter-of-fact tone.

'This is totally gross,' said Beth. 'Who wants a nitty brides-maid?'

Petra sat up and coiled her hair into one of the shower caps that were usually left with the shampoo and shower gel for guests who stayed at the pub. 'Come on, let's delouse you first, nitty bridesmaid,' she said with a giggle.

After having her hair methodically combed and the comb contents thoroughly scrutinized Beth came to the conclusion that she might actually have escaped the nits, but it was better to be safe than sorry. She had done the same for Petra and showered and washed her hair three times until it felt vaguely normal again. That said, Beth had to admit that her hair did now feel silky smooth; perhaps the olive-oil trick might become a regular part of her beauty regime, not that she had one of those any more.

Ever since she'd left London she had stopped having herself groomed because there was nowhere local and she no longer had the money for expensive treatments, but she felt better for it and more like her old self, which was definitely a good thing.

They left the boys, who were quite happy in their shower caps because they looked as daft as each other, and the longer they kept the oil on the more likely they were to have suffocated all the lice. It was all arranged that Jack would collect Leo and Denis from the pub and take them to the church with Fergus and Budgie so Beth could focus on getting the bride ready.

Leaving the pub, an amazing sight greeted Beth. The sun was now higher in the sky; most of the cloud from earlier had burned away to leave pretty wisps like cobwebs across the sky. The village green was picture-perfect with swathes of vibrant green grass and the last few blossoming trees, and even the horse chestnut was putting on a display with its cone-shaped blooms. But the most exciting thing was that the tent company had arrived. Its large vans were parked on the road, and the first tent was going up. It was nothing like Beth had imagined; her mind had conjured up the ancient green canvas tents that had been the pleasure of many a Brownie camp in her youth, but these were far different. The tent being erected, the colour of wet plaster and the shape of a giant tepee, even had wooden struts sticking out of the top. Within a few minutes it was up and the next one was being rolled out on the grass.

She spotted Jack helping to unload chairs. As she watched him he turned and looked straight at her, giving her goose bumps. She gave a brief wave and because his hands were full he nodded an acknowledgement. Beth walked back to the cottage with her heart a little lighter for having seen Jack and she had a firm word with herself that once she had left Dumbleford she really would have to get over whatever this silly crush on Jack was. But for the time being it was harmless so she was going to enjoy it, but from a safe distance of course.

404

Beth smiled when she spotted Danny the hairdresser's car parked outside Willow Cottage but her smile faded as she saw the For Sale sign in her front garden, which reminded her that she would soon be leaving, assuming of course that someone wanted to buy it. She already had two people coming to see it on Monday, which was an encouraging start – well, that was what the estate agent had called it.

Inside the cottage was a hive of activity and she was greeted by Danny like long-lost treasure. 'Beth! Lovely to see you again,' he said, instantly taking a clump of her hair in his hand. She froze. Had he spotted a stray louse? 'This has got long. Tut, tut, split ends and goodness, is this your natural colour?' Beth nodded and for some strange reason tried to have a look for herself although she knew what colour her hair was. 'Why did we ever colour this? It's gorgeous. Not bad condition either seeing as you've been fending for yourself in this wilderness.' He swept his other arm out dramatically.

Beth let out a slow sigh of relief. She had passed the nit-master test.

Chapter Forty-Three

The next couple of hours flew by with Beth making copious amounts of tea for everyone including Carly's very nervous uncle who was giving her away and was now pacing the hallway like a caged animal. Carly had felt queasy when she woke up but Shirley's vinegar remedy seemed to be keeping it at bay and all in all everyone was doing okay.

Carly coughed as she appeared on the stairs looking completely stunning. Her wedding dress was exactly what Beth had expected. It was a simple lace-covered ivory dress, knee-length at the front, and it descended elegantly into a full-length gown at the back, with a puddle train. Danny had done an amazing job on Carly's hair; it was all encased in a very neat bun style, her dark hair shining healthily.

Carly had done her own make-up and had gone for an au naturel look, which suited her and enhanced her natural beauty. Her uncle wiped away a tear, Beth handed him a tissue and he blew his nose loudly.

'You look amazing,' said Beth as Carly reached the bottom of the stairs. Carly was glowing but her expression changed to one of contemplation.

'Actually, I think I need to pee again, will you give me a hand?' she asked, turning round and heading back up the stairs.

When everyone was back downstairs Beth picked up her flowers and straightened her own dress. She was pleased with her bridesmaid's dress; it was a simple strapless floor-length gown in the palest blue and it couldn't have fitted her better if it had been made for her.

There was the beep of an old-fashioned car horn outside and Beth leaped into action.

'Right, remember to lock up and bring the key. The car will be back for you in about five minutes. Okay?' she said, fussing around Carly's dress for no apparent reason.

'I'm fine, really. I don't feel sick and I'm about to marry the loveliest man in the world,' said Carly as her voice started to crack.

'No, don't cry, you'll ruin your make-up.'

'Bloody hormones!' said Carly with a snort. 'Go!' and she waved Beth away.

Beth went to the door. 'Promise no peeking at the car until it comes back?'

'I promise,' said Carly, picking up her posy of flowers. 'Now go or you'll make me more than fashionably late!'

Beth gave her a thumbs-up and slunk out of the door just as Chloe's boyfriend was arriving with the video camera, so she ushered him inside. At least now she would get to see Carly's reaction to Shirley's car and she hoped to God that she liked it but if she didn't it was only a short walk to the church.

Shirley's little car looked marvellous. Simon had polished it and attached wide ivory ribbons across its bonnet and Julia from the WI had hung a flower garland around the inside, which was visible through its many windows. It was the perfect little wedding car, a little quirky perhaps but very cute. And best of all it no longer stank of the vinegar Shirley used to clean it with because

Simon had thoroughly wiped the upholstery with a far more modern cleaner. Actually, when Beth got inside she noticed there was still a faint hint of vinegar but the freesias were doing a good job at masking it.

As they drove past the green Beth was amazed at the finished spectacle of the assembled tents. Now a crescent shape of large tepees cascaded from the largest central one and they were festooned with pretty bunting. Half the village green was cordoned off with the colourful garlands that were flapping idly in the light warm breeze.

There were a few cars parked near the church and far more people milling about. Half the village had turned out and pretty much all of the WI, along with lots of people Beth didn't know, who she suspected were Fergus's folks. She knew the village store had sold out of confetti yesterday and had enterprisingly started to sell small bags of rice, no doubt out of date, instead.

Leo ran over clutching the ring cushion as Simon opened the door and let Beth out of the car. 'I saw the For Sale sign. I don't want to move. When do I get the rings?' he asked his mother as he bobbed up and down on the spot fuelled by his excitement but with a melancholy look in his eyes.

She kissed him and decided to focus on the wedding-related question for now. 'You can have the rings at the last possible moment,' said Beth, still fearful that they would be lost between the church doors and the altar steps.

An unexpected ripple of applause broke out when Beth stepped fully out of the car and she felt herself blush at the compliment.

'You'd better get this lot inside, I'll be back in a mo,' said Simon with a tip of his cap. Beth was pleased she'd gone with the slightly more expensive version of the chauffeur hat; it suited Simon, he really looked the part.

Beth and Leo walked away from the car and Fergus strolled over with Budgie, who was munching his way through a packet of Hula Hoops but politely shoved them in his pocket and brushed his hands together to dismiss the crumbs before he greeted her.

'You ready for the rings now, big man?' said Fergus to Leo, holding out a fist to bump, but Leo was still clutching his cushion.

'Yeah!' shouted Leo. Budgie took him to one side and they began to attach the rings to the ribbons on the cushion while Fergus introduced Beth to a ridiculous number of his relatives, none of whose names she would remember in twenty seconds' time. '... and this is my da, Cormac.'

'Now, aren't you a sight?' said Cormac, taking Beth's hand and kissing it. Beth assumed it was a compliment.

A loud bark drew Beth's attention and she saw Doris, resplendent with flower collar, trotting along with Ernie until something caught Doris's eye and she bounded off with poor Ernie jogging behind her like he was the one being controlled by the lead.

'... you've done all the organizing, Fergus tells me. Now, is there plenty of Guinness?' said Cormac with a smile although his eyes conveyed the underlying importance of the question.

'Yes,' said Beth, trying to keep the bounding Doris in her sights. 'There's plenty of the black stuff. The pub landlady stocked up especially.' But she was distracted by a commotion near the church and Budgie heading her way while signing frantically. Jack was close behind.

She hadn't seen Jack since this morning when he'd been setting up the tents and here he was looking remarkably different. He was wearing a dark suit, one she hadn't seen him in before, and coupled with his perfect dark hair and the merest hint of a smile she found herself staring – she didn't want to but she knew she was. She had a sudden urge to mess up his perfect hair and felt her heart start to quicken.

Beth blinked, quickly realizing Budgie was trying to tell her something, although filtering out all the signed swear words made it tricky. She handed her posy to Jack and started to sign with Budgie as best she could and even her rusty effort was enough to make him calmer, which thankfully made it easier to understand his signing.

'Rings, you've lost the rings,' said Beth out loud, pleased to have deciphered the message. 'Shit! You've lost the rings?'

It appeared that Doris in her urgency to get to a small rabbit on the far side of the churchyard had bumped into Budgie and Leo, sending the rings up in the air to land somewhere in the long grass.

She turned to Jack standing there holding the posy, looking a little confused. 'Call Simon, tell him to stall. He can take Carly round the green and people can wave at her a few times, anything but stop her getting here until we've found the rings!'

'Got it,' said Jack, thrusting back the posy as if he'd just remembered he was still holding it. He got out his phone and started dialling.

'Can I go and play with Denis? And those other kids?' asked Leo, still clutching the empty cushion.

'Er, no, you need to help find the rings!'

Unfortunately, Beth quickly discovered the more people you had trampling around the same small space the harder it was to find something. With Jack's help she ushered the guests into the church and she and Jack had one last search for the rings while the organ music wafted out of the church. He was crouched down next to her and she could smell his spicy aftershave, which was making it surprisingly hard to concentrate fully on the search.

'Bloody hell, how could they vanish like this?' said Beth, parting great clumps of grass at high speed. 'Ah, ha!' she said as she and Jack both lurched for the same shiny piece of metal at the same time, his hand getting there a fraction after Beth's and landing on top. They both froze. Beth could feel the smooth ring in her fingers but she could also feel the heat of Jack's hand covering hers and he wasn't moving it away. She moved her head slowly to look at Jack and he was licking his lips as if about to say something monumental. The moment seemed to hang between them.

'Beep, beep!' came the horn of the Morris Minor and Simon pulled up at the lych gate. Jack slowly took back his hand and gave Beth a faint smile.

'At least we've found one of the rings.'

'I'll keep looking for another minute or two,' said Jack.

Beth stood up, clutching the ring, her heart pounding a drum solo in her chest as she walked down to meet Carly and her uncle. Beth did her duties of sorting out Carly's dress and when she glanced over her shoulder she saw Jack tie Doris up at the side of the church, where she flopped down miserably. Beth watched him sneak inside the church ahead of the wedding party. Carly was beaming and Beth was so pleased for her but she was a little distracted by the encounter with Jack and the ring she was still clutching.

As Carly took her uncle's arm Beth tried to relax and her errant heart began beating a more stable rhythm. It was going to be all right. They walked down the aisle in time to the traditional music and when they reached the front Beth placed the solitary ring on the cushion that Leo was still dutifully holding. He grinned up at his mother and Beth felt the love and pride she had for her son swell inside. Beth looked at Jack and back at the cushion and Jack gave a brief shake of his head. Oh well, thought Beth, one ring was still better than no rings; there was nothing they could do now and she very much hoped that it would be a story they could laugh about later. She took a deep breath and began to actively listen to the vicar and enjoy the service.

But part way through that became difficult to do because Doris had started to woof outside, which quickly became an unrelenting bark. Beth glared at Jack, who twitched the piece of paper in his hand reminding her that he was about to introduce a reading so he couldn't pop out to the dog. Doris continued to bark outside

411

the church and could be heard even through the closed heavy doors, so Beth scanned the pews for someone to step in and help. Her eyes met Ernie's and she twitched her head in the direction of the church door. Ernie gave her a brief wave, excused himself from his pew and walked out very tall as he went to undertake his allocated task. Beth smiled to herself as the doors clicked shut and Doris stopped barking.

The vicar announced that the next hymn was 'Amazing Grace' and Beth and Budgie turned to face the congregation and sign the words for the deaf guests. Everyone was smiling, some were even laughing, but everyone was happy and that was what today was all about, thought Beth.

Chapter Forty-Four

Outside, Doris was assaulting Ernie in the friendliest of ways as she greeted her new companion. 'Daft dog,' said Ernie, ruffling the velvety fur around her ears. When Ernie stood up he sensed there was someone watching him and he twisted to look down the steep path. A tall dark-haired man was striding towards the church. Behind him Ernie could hear the vicar speaking and as the man reached Ernie and the church doors the vicar asked '… if anyone knows cause, or just impediment, why these two persons should not be joined together in holy matrimony …'

Ernie stood up straight and stared at the man, who tried to push him out of the way. He stood his ground. Ernie recognized the stranger; he'd met him once before and that hadn't ended well.

'No!' said Ernie firmly, holding up the palm of his hand near the man's face. Doris resumed her barking, this time at a more frantic pitch than her usual attention-seeking woof.

'Get out of the way!'

Ernie went to speak but nothing came out. He closed his eyes and swallowed hard. 'M-make me,' he said, resolute.

'I've no time for this,' said the arrogant stranger, taking hold of Ernie by the shoulder and roughly trying to move him to one side. But Ernie didn't budge, he stood solid, and while the man was looking puzzled Ernie drew back his arm and struck him on the chin with all his strength.

Doris's continued barking had been too much for Jack and he appeared through the church doors just in time to see the punch land. He quickly shut the doors behind him.

'What the hell?' said Jack, seeing Ernie nursing his right fist. Jack turned towards the stranger and instantly recognized him. 'Nick?'

Nick looked taken aback but quickly composed himself and he inspected the blood now pouring from his split lip. 'This imbecile should be locked up!' he said, trying to get past Jack.

Ernie stepped forward to stand shoulder to shoulder with Jack. 'Not stop wedding,' said Ernie, his jaw tight.

'Don't be bloody ridiculous, I'm a friend, I'm here to—'

'No, you're not,' said Jack. 'They no longer consider you a friend. I think you should leave.' Nick stood there for a moment rolling his eyes and dabbing at his lip with a handkerchief. Ernie pulled back his shoulders and lifted his fist, making Nick take a couple of backward paces, still inspecting his lip as he went.

The congregation inside the church burst into spontaneous applause and Ernie heaved a huge sigh of relief. Jack slapped him affectionately on the back. 'You did good, Ernie,' he said and Ernie puffed up with pride.

'Junior boxing champ nineteen fifty-eight,' said Ernie, holding up his fists in a boxing stance.

A few minutes later the large doors opened. Jack watched from behind the lych gate, where he had managed to convince Nick to stand so that at least he wasn't the first thing the wedding party would see when they left the church. Ernie sat on a nearby wall with Doris and she was lapping up the attention.

The bride and groom came out first closely followed by the young cameraman and Tollek snapping away while the newlyweds spontaneously kissed on the church steps. The rest of the congregation swarmed out of the church behind them and eventually Jack could see Beth. Nick had spotted her too and he was inching forward.

'Hold on, they've got photos to do, I don't want ...' But as he spoke he saw Beth searching the churchyard for someone and her face lit up when they made long-distance eye contact but the light immediately faded as she registered who was standing next to him. 'Bugger,' mumbled Jack.

Beth lifted up handfuls of her dress and strode over, her expression now more than furious.

'What the hell are you doing here?' she said, stopping abruptly as she reached them. 'What happened to your face?' she asked Nick while aiming accusatorial daggers at Jack. Jack stepped back and held up his hands in mock surrender.

'Nothing to do with me.'

'Some half-wit attacked me,' said Nick, looking doleful.

Beth turned to Jack for an explanation. 'Still not me,' he said with a cheeky smile, which did not change Beth's expression. 'Ernie,' said Jack, becoming more serious. 'He means Ernie.'

'Is Ernie okay?' she asked and Jack pointed to where Ernie was sitting with Doris and on cue Ernie grinned and waved happily. Beth slowly turned back to Nick. 'Ernie is not a half-wit, he's a friend of mine.'

Nick was pulling mocking faces but they faded as he watched Beth's reaction. 'Why are you even here?' she asked.

'I had to speak to you, Elizabeth. I miss you so much. This is all a misunderstanding. I love you, what more do you need to know?' said Nick, sounding very rehearsed.

Beth snorted. 'You are bloody unbelievable.' Nick looked genuinely surprised by her reaction. 'This is Carly's wedding and you' – she jabbed a finger at him – 'are not going to spoil it!'

'No, of course not! We need to sort things out between us. Let's talk. That's all I ask. Please?' said Nick, bowing his head slightly.

Beth bit her bottom lip and Jack noticed a twitch of Nick's cheek – even the guy's facial tics were arrogant. 'Okay. When we've done the photos I'll come down to the green ahead of everybody else. And I'll give you precisely five minutes. Then I'm expecting you to leave, Nick. Got it?' said Beth.

Nick nodded but his expression was slightly smug and Jack was momentarily tempted to split his other lip for him, but the feeling quickly passed.

'Can you take Nick to the green and keep him away from the wedding party?' she asked Jack.

'Sure,' said Jack, slapping him manfully on the shoulder. Nick shrugged him off and the two of them walked away.

Tollek was nothing if not thorough and Beth kept asking Budgie what the time was. Each time he simply added on another minute to the time that he'd told her previously though of course that could have been accurate, she wasn't sure. She felt like she was having some sort of mild panic attack; her breathing was fast and her stomach was churning and all she could think about was getting Nick to leave before Leo saw him.

'What's up?' said Carly through a fixed grin while Tollek adjusted his camera.

'Oh, it's nothing,' said Beth, slapping back on her best smile. 'Look at you, Mrs Dooley!'

'I know!' said Carly, waggling her ring hand, which was adorned with a Hula Hoop. Budgie's last-minute ring stand-in had caused a lot of amusement. She waved her hand at Beth and almost up Fergus's nose.

'Steady on there, Carls. Is it time for Guinness and cake yet?' asked Fergus.

'No, we need lots more photos of my gorgeous husband!' said Carly, almost jumping up to kiss Fergus.

'Nice signing, by the way,' chuckled Fergus as he signed something to Budgie and they both collapsed into belly laughs.

'Ignore them. I'll tell you later,' said Carly, grabbing Fergus's arm and pulling him close to her.

Leo and Denis were standing in front of Beth and still intermittently scratching their heads. Beth leaned forward a little and had a surreptitious scan for anything bug-like. 'Boys, they've all gone. Keep your hands in your pockets.' She smoothed down a tuft of Leo's unsettled hair while quelling the urge to scratch her own head.

'Leo, I need to go in a second and check on everything for the reception. You make sure you stay with Denis and Fergus. Okay, promise me?'

'O-kay, Muuum,' he said without turning round.

'Right, everybody smile,' said Tollek and everyone did their best pose as he clicked away. When he paused to check the shots Beth slunk over to him.

'Tollek, are you done with me? There's something I need to sort out.'

'Er, yes, of course, Carly tells me you have been a wonder—'

'Great, thanks,' said Beth, striding off towards the lych gate, feeling a bit bad for cutting off poor Tollek. But she had to get rid of Nick. She quickened her pace and was glad she was wearing flat shoes – they made all the difference when you were speed-walking. While she walked along she marvelled how she had changed from the last time she had seen Nick. She was no longer afraid of him. Still angry, but not afraid. She was back in control of her life and it felt good.

Beth walked past the side of the tearoom and the village green with the wonderful display of interconnected tents as they came into full view. The sun was casting a warm glow across the scene. The only shadow was Nick sitting on one of the benches in front of the tents where Jack appeared to be stalking around him. Beth hoisted up her dress so it didn't drag on the grass and marched towards them. They both looked over as she approached.

'He won't let me touch him,' said Jack, waving about a lump

417

of cotton wool and a bottle of TCP. Nick's lip was now a mess – swollen, purple and crusted with blood.

'Right, give it here.' Beth crouched in front of Nick and Jack handed her the cotton wool and TCP.

'You're beautiful,' said Nick softly, reaching out a hand to touch Beth's cheek. She dodged the contact and glared at him. He slowly lowered his hand.

'You've got five minutes,' said Beth and she glanced at Jack, who was still standing behind him. 'Time him, would you? Please.'

'Happily,' said Jack, rolling back his jacket sleeve and making a big display of scrutinizing his watch.

Nick started again. 'It's all a misund—'

'Let me stop you right there. You were about to hit Leo and you did hit me. There is no question about that. But that was simply one moment in time. The final straw, if you like. You have spent the last couple of years isolating us and controlling us. And that has made me miserable and, worse than that, it turned me into someone I didn't want to be.'

Nick met her gaze and his cheek twitched again ever so slightly. 'I am truly sorry, Elizabeth. I didn't mean any of it. I love you so much. Come back with me now and things will be different, I promise you.'

Beth dabbed at Nick's split lip and he flinched as the antiseptic made contact. 'Nick, you need help. You have a problem. People don't control and abuse people without there being something deeply wrong somewhere. You need to get help.'

Nick looked like he was going to laugh. Beth paused the dabbing and raised her eyebrows in anticipation of his inappropriate response but instead he tightened his jaw and nodded briefly. 'Okay. I will investigate that. Will you come back with me now?'

Beth shook her head. 'No, Nick, I won't. It's still over between us and there is nothing you could do that would make me want to be in a relationship with you.'

Nick's expression changed; he leaned into Beth's ear and growled his response. 'I could make life deeply unpleasant for you and Leo.'

Beth inwardly shuddered. This was the moment when she needed to hold on tight to her emotions. She was now literally facing her fears. She blinked slowly, took a deep breath and looked Nick straight in the eye.

'Yep, I guess you can but it won't change a thing. You see, you've lost your hold over me, I'm not scared of you any more.' Beth tilted her head to one side. 'There was a time when I'd have done anything to please you but I don't want that now. So, do your worst.' Neither of them blinked. She could feel the anger emanating from Nick. 'I'm done here,' she said, balling the blood-stained cotton wool in her fist and standing up. Nick stood up too and towered over her.

'Four minutes gone,' said Jack, but his voice was overshadowed by a sound nearby.

They all turned when the smash and chink of breaking glass pulled their attention. Petra stood a few feet away on the pavement outside the pub, her hands in front of her as if she was still holding the tray of glasses that now lay shattered at her feet. Her face was ashen and her eyes wide with shock. Beth looked from Petra to Nick. Nick was staring at Petra but there appeared to be no recognition in his eyes, unlike Petra's terrified stare.

'What's going on?' asked Beth as Jack strode towards Petra.

'Beats me,' said Nick with a shrug, turning back to face Beth.

'Nicholas,' said Petra in a shaky voice, pointing at him, her hand hanging in the air despite its tremor. 'Nicholas!' she repeated but this time slightly louder. Jack reached her and put his arm around her waist to support her.

Nick slowly turned back to glare at Petra and this time his expression quickly changed from a frown to one of startled recognition. Jack was still supporting Petra but his eyes were focused on Nick.

'Is it him?' he asked softly. Petra swallowed hard and nodded repeatedly.

'Definitely,' she said, her voice still shaky. Jack took his mobile out of his pocket and dialled a number.

The jumbled sound of happy voices behind them indicated that the wedding party was approaching the village green. Nick's head spun round when he registered all the faces now staring at him.

'And again. What is going on?' said Beth to Nick as Fergus jogged over to join them. Nick said nothing, pushed past Fergus and Beth and strode purposefully towards his car. Jack stepped away from Petra and walked a few strides nearer to Nick's BMW. When he was a few feet away Nick pressed the button on the key fob and Beth noticed Jack was also aiming something at Nick's car, something that looked like the remote control for a child's toy.

Nick pulled at the car's door handle but it didn't open. He squeezed the button on his key fob repeatedly but nothing happened. Beth watched Jack slip the small black remote control device into his pocket while he continued to speak into his mobile. What the hell was going on? Fergus was watching Jack intently and Beth realized he was lip-reading.

She tapped Fergus's arm so he would know she was about to speak. 'Fergus, what's he saying?' She pointed at Jack.

Fergus started to translate. 'IC1 male, circa six foot, dark hair, late twenties. Yes, that's right … wanted in connection with a rape in Cheltenham … August two thousand and eight … victim's name …' Fergus stopped speaking and his eyes darted to Petra, who was now decidedly wobbly with Jack no longer holding her up.

'Oh my God,' said Beth as she ran to Petra's side.

Chapter Forty-Five

When the police arrived Jack intercepted them and having made a citizen's arrest he simply opened the back door of the police car and shoved Nick in. He had a short chat with the officers in the front of the car before they drove off. As dramas go it was handled very discreetly. Beth was standing outside the main tepee and she watched until the police car disappeared. By now the whole wedding party had trundled down from the church and were accepting glasses of champagne from a tray proffered by Chloe. Jack strode over, picked up two glasses and handed one to Beth.

'Come on, now the celebrating can really start,' he said.

'Is Petra all right?' asked Beth, taking the glass.

'She's not great, it's been a huge shock but someone is with her and they'll call if we're needed. She's a tough cookie. She'll get through this,' said Jack, offering Beth his arm. 'Come on. You've got to dance with a budgie and I can't wait to see that!'

'He keeps laughing at me,' said Beth with a frown, linking arms with Jack.

Inside, the joined-together tents made a huge space. At one end of the crescent was the bar and at the other was an area with patterned rugs and squishy cloth cubes to sit on and a swinging

421

sign above indicated it was the chill-out zone. In a safe corner outside the chill-out zone was a pile of old crates painted and distressed in pastel colours that made the perfect cake stand to display what could only be described as a masterpiece. The cake was four tiers high with a cascade of pink and orange gerberas spiralling from top to bottom, and the bottom edge of each tier was surrounded by a halo of rosebuds. If Maureen had done half as good a job with the sponge underneath as Barbara had done with the flowers they were all in for a treat.

The main area was taken up with a number of large round tables, surrounded by simple white fold-up chairs each decorated with an ivory organza bow. The centre of each table had a chalk-board and each table had the name of a famous film couple. Beth smirked as she read them: Scarlett and Rhett, Baby and Johnny, Han Solo and Princess Leia, Carrie and Mr Big were just a few.

Above them were strung a multitude of fairy lights and yet more WI bunting with delicate posies of sweetly scented freesias dotted about – the whole thing was incredible. Beth was aware that Jack was watching her.

'What do you think of the tents?' he asked. Beth's eyes drifted over to an excited Carly who was trying out the chill-out zone with a squiffy-looking Shirley.

'I completely love them,' said Beth, turning to him and clinking glasses.

'Beth, can we talk? I've seen the For Sale sign outside Willow Cottage and before you make any hasty decisions I need you to …'

'Ladies and gentleman and members of the Dooley clan,' announced Cormac loudly to much good-natured heckling. 'The wedding buffet is now open for business.'

'Sorry, what?' asked Beth, her eyes searching Jack's for a clue to where the end of that sentence was going but Jack was already being pulled away by Rhonda.

* * *

After far too much to eat, possibly too much champagne and a bellyful of laughter at the speeches, Beth found she was one of a few that had wandered outside. She sipped her almost empty champagne flute while she gazed at the sparkling fairy lights and the spectacle of the tents all lit up against the deep blueberry night sky. She was thinking about Budgie's speech; he had signed and Fergus had translated and he had made it both poignant and comic in equal measure, quite an accomplishment. She discovered the reason he kept laughing at her was her incorrect signing during 'Amazing Grace'. Apparently instead of '… I was blind but now I see …' Beth had signed '… I was pissed …' which was an easy mistake but quite a funny one. And if nothing else it had everyone in the tent learning a little sign language just so they could repeat the joke.

Beth was suddenly aware of someone standing behind her. She knew it was Jack without even turning round.

'One question about earlier. What did you do to Nick's car?' she asked, still staring at the hypnotic fairy lights.

'I jammed the frequency of his key fob signal. Simple device really. A friend at GCHQ gave it to me and I keep it on my key ring just in case it might come in handy. I have a question for you. Who are Zack and Paula?' asked Jack, his breath warm against her neck making her whole body shudder.

She twisted to see he was standing very close. 'I'm shocked that you don't know,' said Beth, stepping back a little to give herself some space, the scent of his fading aftershave heightening her senses.

'I know they must be a couple from some romantic film but …'

Beth shook her head at him teasingly. 'They were the characters in *An Officer and a Gentleman*.'

'Right,' said Jack with a pout, looking like it wasn't ringing any bells.

'Richard Gere and Debra Winger?' said Beth and Jack nodded. 'It's such a great film about ordinary people escaping their past, achieving their dreams against all the odds and finding true love.' She realized she was gabbling. 'And the ending is perfect.' She took a sip from her empty glass and was grateful that it was dark because she knew her neck was starting to colour up.

'Huh, never seen it,' said Jack, taking a sip from a full pint of Guinness.

'Then we need to fix that sometime soon.' He was studying her intently; perhaps he could see her turning red even in this light?

'Before you leave?' asked Jack, his voice heavy. He was watching her closely.

Beth swallowed and wished she had some drink left. 'Yeah, about that ...' She was thinking on the spot and she knew that was dangerous, especially after alcohol, but sometimes you had to take risks. 'I'm guessing Nick's going to go to prison for a while ...' She took a small step closer to Jack.

There was the faintest hint of a smile on Jack's face. 'He'll be remanded in custody ahead of a trial and probably bailed but whatever happens he has to keep away from Dumbleford because Petra is here.'

'So all of a sudden Dumbleford becomes the safest place for me and Leo to be.'

Jack took a tentative step forward. They were almost touching each other. 'Does that mean you're staying?' he breathed.

'He was my reason for leaving ...' Beth tilted her head up and felt her pulse quicken.

'But do you have a reason to stay?' Jack's voice was a whisper and oh, so sexy.

'I *might* have.' Two could play at the teasing game, thought Beth as Jack lowered his lips tantalizingly close to hers.

'I could give you ...' Jack paused, his lopsided grin proving that he was rethinking his sentence to avoid innuendo. 'A very good reason to stay.'

Jack's lips brushed Beth's and she gave a little gasp.

'Then how could I refuse?' She closed her eyes and waited for his kiss.

'Hold this,' said Jack, thrusting a slopping pint at Beth, and she narrowly missed it splashing down her dress. It wasn't exactly how she was hoping the moment was going to end. She watched him run off across the green, hurdling the bunting on the way.

Carly joined her and let out a huge yawn. 'Where's he off to?'

'I have no idea,' said Beth, feeling a little wrong-footed. 'But how are you, Mrs Dooley?'

'Could. Not. Be. Happier,' said Carly emphatically, blowing Beth a kiss as she couldn't get close enough for a hug with all the drinks glasses. 'Thank you so much; today has been the best day ever.'

'Really?' asked Beth, looking askance. 'Even with the Morris Minor and homemade bunting?'

'Especially with those. I've loved it all. Totally beyond even *my* wildest dreams.'

Beth felt a little teary but kept it in line. 'That's a relief! I'm really pleased for you, Carls.' But Carly was squinting into the darkness, watching a figure stagger out of the gloom.

'I think I might be the only sober person here,' said Carly as they watched Jack scramble over the bunting with a For Sale sign balanced on one shoulder. He threw it at Beth's feet and started jumping up and down on it. Men from the wedding party tumbled out of the tepees and started to join in, which was comical to witness.

'Bonkers, completely bonkers,' laughed Beth. While the others continued demolishing the sign, Jack slipped away from the crowd. 'Should I say thank you?' she asked through her giggles.

'Just say you'll stay,' said Jack as he tentatively leaned forward and this time he kissed her properly.

The next morning Beth was woken by the sound of Leo and Denis giggling at the television and the gentle thrum of her hangover. Denis had stayed for a sleepover to give Petra some time to digest what had happened. It was going to be a long journey for Petra but she had good friends to support her.

Beth had vague recollections of a taxi arriving and whisking Carly and Fergus away. She checked the clock – they'd be getting on a plane to the Caribbean in a few hours. Surprisingly she didn't envy them. She lay there smiling to herself and remembering Jack's kiss; that part of the evening was clear and she could recall every blissful moment. She closed her eyes and hummed happily to herself.

There were voices outside and with a reluctant stretch Beth peered out of the window. She could just see the green when the willow tree wasn't blowing across the cottage and the big vans were back and the tepees were being dismantled. It was breezier today but Dumbleford had never looked so enchanting. Beth decided she should probably get the boys some breakfast and go and lend a hand.

As they crossed the green the boys scurried off after the football and were quickly joined by Doris. Beth looked around for Jack and saw him inside the large tepee watching her, as something like happiness bounced around inside her stomach. That or she'd overdone the coffee. When she reached Jack he drew her into a tight hug and for the first time in a very long while she relaxed at being held tightly in someone's arms.

'Good morning,' said Jack, giving her a brief kiss. He paused to study her face before going back for another much longer one.

'Break it up! Cake coming through!' yelled Shirley, as Maureen pitched ominously from side to side and meandered out of the tent carrying the remaining two tiers of cake.

'The cake was amazing, Maureen,' said Beth and Maureen stopped dead. For a second Beth feared the cake was going to keep going but luckily Maureen had a tight hold on it. Maureen turned her head slowly in Beth's direction and Beth held her breath.

Maureen bared her teeth and almost smiled. 'Thank you,' she said. Beth breathed out her relief and Maureen waddled away with the cake. She had got used to the odd ways of most of the people in Dumbleford but Maureen was still something of an enigma.

Jack took her hand and guided her inside the empty tent. 'Everything okay?'

Beth couldn't stop the grin that spread across her face. 'Yes, everything is very okay.'

'And you're definitely staying in Dumbleford? No change of heart?' He looked anxious and it made Beth adore him a little bit more.

'I'm definitely staying in Dumbleford.' It felt good to say it out loud.

Jack held both her hands in his. 'Great. Because I'm thinking about embarking on a serious relationship with someone not a million miles from here.' His eyes twinkled.

'Really? Who with? Is it Shirley?' Beth gave him her best serious face.

Jack played along. 'Yes, yes, it is. I hope you understand.'

'Shirley!' yelled Beth. 'Jack's thinking about embarking ...' but she didn't get to finish the sentence because Jack began kissing her.

'Crazy lady!' said Shirley, shaking her head as she went past, rolling up streams of bunting.

Beth and Jack started to laugh but it dwindled and they stared at each other. Beth was wondering how she got this lucky when the whirlwind that was Doris came charging at them. They both bent down and patted her while she bounced about them, sharing her joy and frantically trying to lick Beth's face.

'I love you,' said Beth to Doris.

'I love you too,' replied Jack but he looked suddenly unsure as realization dawned. A football flew past the entrance to the tent and Doris ran off at top speed, leaving Beth and Jack looking at each other as if someone had put them on pause.

It was Jack's turn to colour up.

'I love you too … too,' said Beth and she took his hand, pulled him to her and kissed him tenderly.

Beth asked Shirley to keep an eye on the boys while she and Jack went to check on Petra.

Petra was getting ready to open up the pub. 'Are you sure you're okay?' asked Beth, her expression one of concern.

'I am, honestly. This is what I have wanted for a long time, for Nicholas to be found and arrested. I didn't know his full name, which made it easy for him to disappear. I thought he had got away with what he did. Seeing him yesterday was a shock after all these years but now I feel like a weight has lifted from me,' said Petra with a brief smile.

'You know you don't have to be quite this brave,' said Beth, taking in Petra's cheery expression and giving her arm a gentle squeeze.

'I was not brave last night. To be honest, I was a bit of a mess and I called my mother. It was a difficult conversation; she never understood why I decided to have the baby. She saw it as *his* baby, but it was my baby too. Last night we talked without shouting which is a start and, you never know, perhaps good things can come from this.'

'I'm sure you're right,' said Beth, feeling genuinely hopeful on Petra's behalf.

'And I have learned a new word. I believe Nicholas is what you call a shit-weasel?'

Beth spluttered her surprise. 'That's a new one on me too but it sums him up perfectly!'

The smiles quickly faded. 'Denis doesn't know.' Petra looked suddenly very sad.

'Of course.' Beth couldn't begin to imagine what Petra had been through but now at least she didn't have to go through it alone. 'I'm here if you need to talk any time, day or night,' said

Beth, giving her a hug. They held each other for a moment.

'Thank you. That's lovely of you. And the police, they have been very good.'

'And Tollek is only a couple of miles away if you need anything else,' said Jack, helping himself to a chocolate.

'Hey, cheeky boy, don't eat my present!' said Petra, playfully swiping away the chocolates Beth had bought her. 'I hear your For Sale sign has gone?' she went on, turning back to Beth and looking instantly brighter with the change of subject.

'Yeah,' said Beth, 'someone took it last night. The crime rate has rocketed around here so I'm not sure I want to stay now.'

'Don't even joke about leaving, that's mean,' said Jack, trying to tickle Beth's ribs. They giggled and chased each other round the bar.

Petra watched them proudly like a mother hen. 'Children, go and leave me in peace,' she said, throwing a packet of crisps at Jack, which he deftly caught. 'Shoo!'

'Take care, Petra,' he called and he ushered Beth out of the pub.

'I will,' said Petra with a wink.

Beth and Jack tumbled out of the pub and they watched Ernie disappear into the willow tree next door. Beth wandered over to take a closer look at Willow Cottage. The willow tree was still huge despite Jack's best attempts at trimming it but the rest of the picture had changed so much from that first encounter all those months ago. As she surveyed all the changes and thought of all the hard work that had gone in to making it a home she realized how much she loved it, even with its awful bathroom.

Jack stood behind Beth, put his arms around her waist and nuzzled affectionately at her neck. 'You going home?' he asked.

'Yes,' said Beth with a smile, 'I think I am.'

Epilogue

Six weeks later

'Mum, wake up, wake up! It's my birthday!' shouted Leo as he bounced up and down on Beth's bed.

'Urgh,' she groaned. Blinking at the clock. 'It's twenty past six!'

'I know, we've got time to open my presents before school!' He stopped bouncing and held out his hands expectantly.

It was hard to stay grumpy very long when his angelic face was beaming at her, even if she was still half asleep. 'Coffee first, then presents. Okay?'

'Okay,' said Leo, hopping off the duvet and heading downstairs.

Beth dragged herself out of bed and her reluctant body followed him. The sun was streaming in through the kitchen windows – it was going to be another glorious July day.

Beth sent a text to Jack. He was usually up by 6.30 for his run so if she was lucky he might join them for breakfast. A few minutes later, large paws scrabbling on the door announced Doris's and Jack's arrival. Beth knew she was smiling even before she'd opened the front door. Jack was wearing running shorts and a tight-fitting top which she would have quite liked to have been able to rip off him but being a parent often interrupted their spontaneity.

'Morning you, did you fancy joining us for a run?'

'Ha, ha!' Beth stood back and let them in.

'Jack!' yelled Leo as he threw himself into his arms. They had become very close lightning fast and it never failed to warm Beth's heart to see them together.

'Happy birthday, mate. Here you go.' Jack handed Leo a squishy parcel.

'Clothes?' asked Leo, his thoughts on this quickly revealed by his expression.

'You'll see,' said Jack, snaking an arm around Beth's waist and pulling her close.

'Thanks, Jack,' Leo added belatedly as he ripped off the paper. 'Oh, wow! It's the latest England football kit!' Leo looked like he was going to explode with excitement and immediately ran out of the room tearing off his pyjamas as he went.

'Coffee?' said Beth with a big yawn, heading for the kettle.

'No, just water, thanks. We're off for a run in a minute.' He rubbed Doris's head and she leaned into his leg for a fuss. 'Beth, I wanted to talk to you about something.' His voice appeared rehearsed and Beth didn't like the way it sounded. She turned slowly and handed him his water.

'Sounds serious,' she said, trying but failing to find a smile. Everything had been going so well. They had been seeing each other daily since Carly's wedding and right up until this moment she had thought they had a relationship that was going somewhere.

'It is kind of serious.' He rubbed his chin. 'I think we need to talk about Doris.'

Beth raised her eyebrows; she had no idea where this was going. 'Is there something wrong?'

Jack patted Doris's flank and she slumped onto her back with her legs in the air, awaiting a tummy rub. 'You see, I think she gets confused moving between my house and yours. I think it would be better for her if she knew where she was going to be from one day to the next but on the other hand I worry that she might think things were moving too fast.'

Beth spotted the twitch of a smile on his lips and instantly relaxed. 'I wouldn't want Doris to worry.'

'No, nor would I.' He reached out and took Beth's hand. 'When it's not just you that you have to think about it's a big decision. I don't want to confuse her or rush into something and …' He paused and did look genuinely serious this time. 'I'd hate her to think this was for ever and then find out that it's not.' He swallowed and his Adam's apple bobbed.

'So just to be sure, are you saying that you think we should move in together?'

Jack nodded. 'You're smart, one of the many reasons why I … Actually, *we*, love you.'

'It feels like a big step,' said Beth, feeling excitement bubble inside her.

'It is. But are we ready?' His eyes didn't leave hers.

She didn't have to think too hard; nothing had ever felt so right as being with Jack. 'I think we're ready.'

Jack hugged Beth tight and kissed her longingly on the lips. 'She said yes!' he called over his shoulder and Leo ran in punching the air.

'See, I told you she would,' said Leo, high-fiving Jack before he dropped to his knees and started to rub Doris's tummy and explain things to her. 'You see, Doris, we're going to be a proper family and that means you don't have to worry about moving ever again.'

Beth wiped away the tears that were pooling.

'It's what he told me he wanted most for his birthday,' said Jack with a shrug. 'And I couldn't think of anything else I would want more.' Beth wrapped her arms around his neck and kissed him.

'Yuck! If you are going to keep kissing perhaps me and Doris will need a place of our own!' said Leo with a smirk before he got pulled into a group hug.

Turn over for an exclusive short story
from the world of Willow Cottage …

'On three you shove and I'll pull!' called Jack through the open doorway of Willow Cottage.

Another icy blast of January wind whipped around Beth as she gripped the Victorian bath and wished she'd opted for just a shower. It would have been so much easier and they wouldn't be here now with the new bath rammed in the doorway.

'One … two … three!' said Jack and Beth put all her weight behind the wedged object and pushed as hard as she could. She could see from the contortions on Jack's face he was doing the same but to no avail – the bath was well and truly stuck.

Beth stopped pushing and threw her hands up in defeat. 'Bugger it!'

'Don't give up,' said Jack, looking disgruntled.

'I'm cold and more than a bit fed up,' said Beth, slumping against the rim of the bath. 'You said it would fit.' It probably wasn't the time for laying blame, but Jack had done the measurements when they had agreed it was time to replace the hideous bathroom at Willow Cottage.

'I think the doorframe has swelled up in the cold and damp,' said Jack, rubbing his stubbly chin and eyeing the doorframe.

'I need coffee,' said Beth, deciding a caffeine jolt and a bit of a break would make all the difference and may even summon up some much-needed ideas for how to move the bath. 'Takeaway from the tearoom?'

'Yeah, go on then,' said Jack with a smile. 'While you do that I'll ring and get them to shift the skip.' He nodded at the over-flowing skip that was taking up part of the front garden. What was left of the rotten picket fence and the disintegrated gate were long gone from when they had tidied up the gardens in the summer. They'd needed the skip for the old bathroom and once that had gone they were going to have a low-level fence and a brand-new gate put up – Beth couldn't wait. They were the last things to be done and Willow Cottage would be officially finished after seventeen months of hard work. Granted, she hadn't done a lot over Christmas as it had been important to all of them to have a proper family time but now she had renewed enthusiasm to get the last few jobs done, with the bathroom being the biggest, and as it was turning out the trickiest.

Beth was making her way back from the tearoom, pondering when she would be able to have a bath in her new tub, when her phone sprang to life in her pocket; she juggled the coffees precariously to answer it. It was FaceTime from Fergus.

'Hi Fergus,' she said, trying to speak clearly to aid Fergus with lip-reading as she was very aware that she couldn't sign whilst holding a phone and two teetering coffees.

'It's happening now!' he said, looking terrified.

There was a momentary pause on Beth's end as she caught up. 'The baby?'

'I can't read what you're saying. Here's Carly,' said Fergus and the picture went fuzzy while the phone was passed on.

Carly's face loomed into view; she was in full make-up and her hair looked perfect. 'We've just got to the hospital. Contractions are about three minutes apart.'

'How are you so calm?' Beth was amazed, she remembered when it was her she'd been a mess.

'I've read loads of books about the birth. There's ages to wait yet. So there's no reason to panic. Fergus has been dancing about me like a *Strictly* finalist for the last hour while I did my make-up,' said Carly with an eye roll.

Beth felt tears appear and she blinked them away. 'In a few hours, you'll be a mum.'

'Don't, you'll set me off,' said Carly as her voice went all wobbly. 'Look we'd better go, the nurse will be getting a bit stroppy. And ooh ouch, here comes another contraction. We'll call you later. Love you loads!'

'Love you too,' said Beth, but the screen had already gone black. Beth knew she had a ridiculous grin on her face, but she was so happy for Carly and Fergus. The next few hours were going to be a tense waiting game.

As she speed-walked up the path, excited to share the news, she could see the bath was still stuck in the doorway and Jack was climbing out of it, to get out of the house and into the garden.

'Guess what?' they both said together, eyes wide as they mirrored each other.

'She's gone into labour!' said Jack – a smile appeared and then quickly disappeared.

'I know!' said Beth wondering how he knew already – Fergus must have texted or something.

Jack was giving Beth an odd look. 'How can you know? Petra just this second called me.'

'Oh, no. I meant Carly. Carly's in labour too!' Beth had to concentrate hard not to wave the coffees about in her excitement, she was so pleased for her best friend.

Jack looked stunned. 'What are the odds?' A huge grin spread across his face. She knew he was just as thrilled for Carly and Fergus as she was.

'Here,' said Beth, handing him his coffee. 'You should go.' She nodded towards the pub.

'I don't know, I'm not good with stuff like that.' He looked momentarily unsure.

'Jack,' said Beth forcefully. 'This is your responsibility. Go!'

'You promise you'll let me know about Carly?' She nodded and he gave her his lop-sided smile and kissed her briefly on the cheek. 'I love you.'

'I love you too, now go. And keep me posted.' Jack gave her a brief squeeze and jogged away.

She studied the bath and decided she'd be better going round the back of the cottage, then her thoughts drifted off to Carly. She had been so calm on the phone and Beth had to admit she'd thought Carly would be screaming for drugs already, but it was all credit to her that she wasn't. Selfishly, Beth hoped it wouldn't be a long drawn-out affair because she was longing to see the first pictures of the baby; she was hoping for a boy. Mainly for Leo's sake as he had his heart set on a boy to play football with and partly because she had a fiver on it with Jack. She was surprised too at how calm Jack was. He had been worrying himself for weeks and now he seemed all laid back – and what were the odds of them both giving birth on the same day? She wished she'd had a fiver on that too.

After her coffee Beth tried in vain to shift the bath alone, but eventually gave up and started unpacking the shower Jack would be fitting later if he could drag himself away. Beth's phone buzzed in her pocket and she fished it out, trying to ignore her stomach flipping over as all the possibilities of who it could be and why flooded her mind.

'I want you here!' yelled Carly down the phone and Beth held it away from her instantly throbbing eardrum.

'Oh, sweetie. I wish I could be,' said Beth in what she hoped were soothing tones. And she meant it, but it wasn't a case of just popping round the corner – Carly was a hundred miles away. Things had apparently changed as Carly's labour pains had ramped up.

'You can! Get on a sodding train now!' bellowed Carly.

440

Beth checked her watch. She knew if train times were in her favour she could be there in a couple of hours. 'Well, I could try,' she said. She wasn't the best choice in medical emergencies but she was a good friend and if Carly needed her at her side then that's where she would be. Looking around at the mess, she just wished Carly had decided this a bit earlier. 'Can you tell Fergus I'll text him?'

'Grrrrr YEEEEEEEEES,' hollered Carly and Beth guessed another contraction had started.

'Okay, hang in there and keep your legs together!' The last thing Beth wanted was a mad dash to London only to miss all the action. Beth got off the phone and mentally ran through things; Leo was on a play date and sleepover, so he would be fine. She didn't have a shift at the pub and Jack had his own situation to take care of. Basically there was nothing to stop her going.

She threw a few things into a bag in case she didn't make it back until tomorrow, flew downstairs, then spotted the bath tub.

'Bugger!' She couldn't really leave the cottage for the rest of the day and possibly the night with the door wide open, the cottage was already freezing and in the middle of a British winter it could snow at any moment. While her brain was going into full-on panic mode a figure appeared on the other side of the doorway and waved happily.

'Oh, Ernie! Am I pleased to see you! I need a huge favour,' said Beth at speed. Ernie nodded and grinned at the same time. 'Can you house sit for me?'

'Here?' asked Ernie, pointing at the bathtub.

'Yes. You just need to make sure nobody comes in, well, no strangers. Okay?' Beth could already see this was causing Ernie a lot of confusion by his puzzled expression, but with Jack off on his own birthing emergency what choice did she have?

Ernie was frowning deeply. 'Okay!' he said and climbed into the bath, sat down and folded his arms. Beth rubbed her eyes, this was going to be a difficult one to explain.

After twenty minutes of stretching her patience to the limit, Ernie was now sitting on a chair in the hallway with a large mug of tea staring hard at the open door. It was the best she could hope for. He had his coat on and she had texted Rhonda asking her to keep an eye on him. Now she had to focus on getting to London as fast as she could and as the taxi swung up the driveway she felt it was a good start.

That classic moment when you run for the train only to see it sail serenely away from the platform … it's always emotional on the big screen. In real life, however, Beth was just pleased that the sound of the train was loud enough to shield the waiting passengers from her torrent of swear words. Some she hadn't ever used before. She finished with a final loud 'Buggeration!' as the end of the train disappeared from sight. She spun round and, seeing a member of railway staff, sprinted towards them.

'Next train to London?' she asked, belatedly adding, 'Please.'

'That one,' he said, pointing to the train waiting patiently on the other side of the tracks.

Beth pointed to the other platform, she couldn't find the words. The railway guard spoke slowly, 'This platform for trains to Hereford and Worcester. That platform trains to London.'

'Thanks!' yelled Beth as she sprinted off again to get to the other platform in time.

Beth heard the doors beeping as she jumped on the train, her stomach awash with wasted emotions. She slumped into a spare seat and waited for her racing heart to find its rightful rhythm as the train slowly pulled away.

By the time they pulled into Paddington station her heart rate was back up to bonkers again. The taxi ride was short in distance but, being London, it took long enough for her to wonder if she could have walked it quicker. She fled the taxi, barrelled into the private hospital and was immediately hit by how un-hospitally it was. It looked more like a hotel reception area and to her surprise she was greeted warmly and quickly ushered to a lift. As the doors closed she caught sight of herself in a mirror and for the first time realized she was still wearing her decorating dungarees. There was a millisecond where she froze but then she shrugged and laughed at herself. Sod it, she thought, the most important thing is that I'm here, not whether I'm wearing the latest London fashions.

Her phone pinged with a message: it was Jack. 'Looks like this will take a while. You okay?'

In all the panic Beth hadn't updated him. 'Now in London. Carly needed me. Ernie on cottage watch. Bath still stuck.'

That appeared to cover everything so she pressed send and as the lift opened she shoved the phone into her bag. Carly was easy to locate thanks to her distinctive mix of screaming and swearing which could be easily heard through the lovely solid wood doors. But before she could go in, Beth was intercepted by a member of staff who got her to wash her hands and pop on a fetching blue gown and silly foot covers. So, looking like someone in a cheap Smurf costume, she knocked on the door and went in.

Carly was mid holler with her eyes tightly shut. Her hair was tied back and her face was a sheen of sweat. Beth remembered this stage of labour vividly, the point where she was sure she couldn't go on. Fergus stood next to Carly whilst she dug her manicured fingernails into his arm and for once he didn't look his usual picture of chilled-out calmness.

Two medical staff, one of whom Beth guessed was the midwife, were at the action end of things and giving Carly stage direction in very calm voices. 'That's right, Carly, keep that breathing steady and hold tight.'

Beth went to the other side of the bed and gripped Carly's hand. As the contraction loosened its hold Carly gasped for breath and opened her eyes. 'You came!' she said as tears spilled down her cheeks.

'Of course I did,' said Beth, feeling her eyes brim with tears. 'It's how you and I work. If we need each other we're there. Whenever, wherever. Trains allowing, obviously,' she said with a smile. Carly pulled Beth into a clumsy hug and had a good cry. Carly pulled away and her eyes widened as she took in Beth's outfit. 'What the hell are you wearing?'

'Surgical gown over decorating dungarees. It'll be on the catwalk this spring, you watch,' she said with a grin, loving the fact that she really didn't care.

Fergus patted Beth's shoulder. 'It's lovely to see you, Beth. Thanks so much for coming. This is a fecking nightmare!'

Beth laughed and pulled away from Carly so she could sign to Fergus. 'She's okay, Fergus, really, this is what labour is like.' She reached across the bed and took his hand.

'There's no translator available and she,' he pointed at the midwife, 'has her head up Carly's bajingo half the time so I don't know what's going on. All I know is she's in pain and I can't help her.' Beth held his hand whilst Carly held tight to the other and then a sudden increased pressure from Carly told Beth another contraction was on the way. Fergus gave a short smile and she hoped he was a little reassured.

'Now then, Carly,' said the midwife. 'This time I need you to push. Slow and steady, okay?'

'If it gets this giant melon out of me I'll do anything!'

'Start pushing, Carly,' said the midwife from between her legs.

'This is it,' said Beth, squeezing both hands. Fergus nodded his understanding.

Carly screamed her way through the next couple of minutes while Beth and Fergus shouted encouragement until a new voice joined in the chorus. The baby was born and it instantly started to wail. The sound that clutches at every parent's heart. Beth tugged at Fergus's hand as he was still focused on Carly. He turned and saw his baby for the first time and burst into tears.

'What is it?' Carly asked between deep breaths.

'It's a girl,' announced the midwife. The baby was small but perfect with a neat swirl of dark Dooley hair. Beth caught a glimpse of her miniature fingers and toes and was instantly filled with love for the tiny infant, the fact that she'd just lost the bet with Jack was completely irrelevant. Carly and Fergus hugged each other and sobbed happily.

A flurry of activity had the cord detached, the baby weighed and wrapped up within moments. The midwife held her out like an offering to the gods. 'So who wants first cuddle?' she asked. Carly nodded at Fergus and he very gingerly took the tiny bundle into his arms.

'You did it, Carls. You're amazing,' said Fergus, as he gently laid the baby on Carly's chest.

'You are both amazing,' said Beth, wiping away a tear. 'The perfect little family.'

Fergus wasted no time getting a FaceTime link with his family in Ireland where it looked to Beth like the party had already been in full swing for some time.

Beth helped Carly wash her face, brush her hair and apply a smear of lippy before any photographs were taken, which was tricky as Carly wasn't keen to let go of the baby. When she did eventually concede that she couldn't brush her hair properly she passed her to Beth. The baby was asleep and didn't even register the change of arms. Beth cuddled her tightly – perhaps she wouldn't be averse to one of these herself, she mused.

Beth's phone buzzed in her pocket. She handed the baby back to Carly and taking out her phone she realized it was Jack with FaceTime news of his own.

'Hiya!' chorused Jack and Petra together.

'Hi!' replied Beth as she squeezed onto the bed next to Carly so that everyone was in the shot. 'We have a baby girl here, what have you got?'

'Er, yuk!' said Leo as his head popped into view and Beth felt a surge of love for him.

'Wow! Congratulations, guys!' said Jack. 'We've got a girl too!'

'Really?' asked Carly, tearing her eyes away from her own infant for a moment.

'Yep!' said Jack, looking every inch the proud father. 'And four boys!' he added as he held up a couple of wriggling puppies.

'How's Doris?' asked Beth.

'She's been a complete star!' said Jack, moving the phone so that a flopped out Doris came into view, as did the other puppies who were happily suckling away. Doris lifted her head briefly.

'She looks as knackered as I feel,' said Carly with feeling.

'Can we keep one, Mum? Please!' pleaded Leo popping up on the screen again with a small puppy held at his cheek.

'Can we also have one, please?' came Petra's voice and Jack turned the camera to show her and Tollek looking very cosy together.

'We'll see,' said Beth. 'We've got a bath to move first!'

'All sorted,' said Tollek, giving a little wave with his large hand. 'I took the front door off to get it in and it didn't take Jack and I long to install.' He added as Beth's face flicked through a number of expressions. At least that was a big problem solved.

'When are you coming home?' asked Jack, turning the camera back on himself and making Beth let out a small sigh of happiness that it was Jack and Leo she was going home to.

Beth looked at Carly and Fergus who had lost interest in the FaceTime and were staring besottedly at their new daughter. 'I'll be on the next train,' she said with a smile.

'Great, I can't wait.'

'Oh, and after the day I've had I'll be needing a very long bath!'

ABOUT THE AUTHOR

Bella Osborne has been jotting down stories as far back as she can remember but decided that 2013 would be the year that she finished a full-length novel.

In 2016, her debut novel, *It Started at Sunset Cottage*, was short-listed for the Contemporary Romantic Novel of the Year and RNA Joan Hessayon New Writers Award.

Bella's stories are about friendship, love and coping with what life throws at you. She likes to find the humour in the darker moments of life and weaves these into her stories. Bella believes that writing your own story really is the best fun ever, closely followed by talking, eating chocolate, drinking fizz and planning holidays.

She lives in the Midlands, UK, with her lovely husband and wonderful daughter, who, thankfully, both accept her as she is (with mad morning hair and a penchant for skipping).